WHITE K...

The Rise and ...

Bill Power is an historian, actively involved
in a wide range of research and heritage issues.
He has worked for several newspapers
and RTE radio.

*For Gerry & Carmel

kindest regards
& good memories

Bill Power
18 V 2000*

Coat of arms of
Edward, 1st Earl of Kingston, 1769.

Great people lived and died in this house;
Magistrates, colonels, Members of Parliament,
Captains and Governors, and long ago
Men that had fought at Aughrim and the Boyne.
Some that had gone on Government work
To London or to India came home to die,
Or came from London every spring
To look at the May-blossom in the park ...
But he killed the house; to kill a house
Where great men grew up, married, died,
I here declare a capital offence.

Purgatory
William Butler Yeats

WHITE KNIGHTS
DARK EARLS

*The Rise and Fall of an
Anglo-Irish Dynasty*

Bill Power

The Collins Press

Published in 2000 by
The Collins Press
West Link Park
Doughcloyne
Wilton
Cork

© 2000 Bill Power

All rights reserved. No part of this publication may be reproduced or transmitted in any form or by any means electronic, mechanical, photocopying, recording or otherwise, without written permission of the publishers, or else under the terms of any licence permitting limited copying issued by The Irish Writers' Centre, 19 Parnell Square, Dublin 1.

British Library Cataloguing in Publication data.

Typesetting by The Collins Press Ltd.

Printed in Ireland by Colour Books Ltd.

ISBN: 1-898256-94-2

Supported by the Ballyhoura Leader Programme.

Cover pictures:
Front cover – In the background lies the coffin and coronet of George, 3rd Earl of Kingston, with, to the front, the coffin and coronet of his wife Helena, in the vault at Mitchelstown Castle.
Back cover – From the top: James, 5th Earl of Kingston; James, 4th Baron Kingston; George, Robert and James King, sons of the 2nd Earl of Kingston; Mitchelstown Castle, *c.* 1920.

Contents

Foreword i
Acknowledgements iii
Picture Credits v
Family Tree of the Kings, Earls of Kingston vi

Chapter 1: Knights and Barons 1
Chapter 2: Empire Builders 10
Chapter 3: In a Strange Land 28
Chapter 4: Rebellion 51
Chapter 5: Georgian Madness 72
Chapter 6: Decline and Famine 95
Chapter 7: End of the Line 113
Chapter 8: Mountain of Misery 135
Chapter 9: The Queen's Cattle Drivers 150
Chapter 10: 'Remember Mitchelstown!' 164
Chapter 11: Feeling the Pinch 189
Chapter 12: Vous-Avez Raisong! 201
Chapter 13: History Gone to Blazes 214
Chapter 14: Doomed Inheritance 233

Appendices 253
Endnotes 261
Bibliography 283
Index 295

Foreword

On an August night in 1922 a great blaze lit the sky above the southern slopes of the Galtees. The Republican forces which had held Mitchelstown Castle for most of the summer had destroyed what might have been of use to the advancing Free State army.

For days Ireland's grandest castle smouldered, the air in the streets of Mitchelstown bitter with the stench of burning. If ever an era had come to an end it was then. The gaunt ruins were later demolished; later still, the past evoked by the place seemed like a dream to Elizabeth Bowen, the castle by now 'a few bleached stumps on the plateau'.

The Gothic extravagance that had gone was, in its heyday, the outward and visible sign of a dynasty's power. The White Knights who lorded it over vast Geraldine estates ended their long reign in the early seventeenth century, their land passing through marriage to the descendants of Sir John King, an Elizabethan adventurer.

Two hundred years later the Kings were still there. In 1823 Big George, third Earl of Kingston, razed the house that had brought another touch of style to a town which had benefited from the architectural splendour of the eighteenth century. In its place, at huge expense, he built a castle that echoed the ambitions and pretensions of the Geraldines.

But a great renaissance was not to be. Trouble followed trouble for the family, until the real Troubles came, banishing even the ghosts of the White Knights and their successors. What survives is the story of the generations, rich and endlessly extraordinary, a thread of history that is Ireland's story also.

WILLIAM TREVOR

ACKNOWLEDGEMENTS

This book began as a quest to discover how and why Mitchelstown Castle was burned in 1922. I soon learned that it would be impossible to write a book about those events without also exploring the world in which its owners lived. With it came the realisation that there was more to the castle than bricks and stone, and that it was the seat of a family who deserved to be regarded as one of the great Anglo-Irish dynasties.

I was helped by many kind and generous people during the time I worked on *White Knights, Dark Earls*. Foremost among these was Colonel Anthony Lawrence King-Harman, and his wife Jeanette. Anthony's support and a gentle stream of letters over the past twelve years have been the foundation of my endeavours.

The corner stones of this book have been generously provided by the good advice and clear vision of Liam Moher. His friendship and peerless editing of my wayward prose deserves far greater reward than these few words of thanks can bestow. I am likewise appreciative of advice given on the text and pedigree by Gerard Crotty and also to John Mullins, Bunty Flynn and Marie Sheehy for reading the manuscript. Their comments on the book and generous friendship are deeply appreciated.

I owe a special debt to Priscilla Congreve and Barclay, Earl of Kingston, for their friendship and assistance. Con Webber very kindly allowed me copy material from his collection.

I wish to posthumously thank CJF MacCarthy, one of Cork's greatest antiquarians, who I know would have been thrilled to see this book in print. Walter McGrath and Rev Br Diarmaid O'Briain have always given me friendship, wisdom and

Acknowledgements

encouragement in this as in my other endeavours. Thanks also to Michael Casey, Anne Doyle, Jim Condon (RIP), Rev. Fr Edward J Kilbride, SJ, Denis J Murphy (RIP) and Rev. Fr Colman Foley, O.Cist, (RIP), who shared their memories with me.

For their efficient service I am indebted to the staffs of Cork County Library (especially Tim Cadogan), Cork City Library, National Library of Ireland, National Archives of Ireland, British Library, Boole Library at University College, Cork, Cloyne Diocesan Archive, and National Army Museum, London.

I am also obliged for the assistance given by Dr Laurence M Geary, the committee of Mitchelstown Heritage Society, Brendan Ryan, Peggy Barry, Vera Jones, the late Niall Brunicardi, Ceall P Hyland, Desmond Fitzgerald the Knight of Glin, Conor O'Callaghan, Rev. Alan Marley, Donal Burke, Rev Fr Tom Murphy, Mark Bence-Jones, Rev Fr Alphonsus O'Connell, and the Cistercian community at Mount Melleray Abbey, Saint Colman's College (Fermoy), Seamus Crowley, Charles and Rosemary Tindal, Declan Hassett, the late Seán Dunne, the late Ven. Archdeacon Albert Frazer, the trustees of Kingston College, Mary Kearney, Seán and Síle Murphy.

I wish to remember Rev Canon Courtenay Moore, MA, (1842-1922) whose writings inspired my interest in history.

Finally, it would be reprehensible of me not to thank my parents, Seán and Bridget Power. When all is said and done I depend on my wife, Kathryn, whose infinite patience and understanding make her 'a woman, the wonder of her kind'. To Kathryn and my parents I dedicate this book.

B.P.

Picture Credits

The publishers and author would like to thank all those who have supplied photographs and illustrations for this book.

Courtesy Author's collection: Mitchelstown Castle; the coffin and coronet of George, 3rd Earl of Kingston and the coffin and coronet of his wife Helena, in the vault at Kingston College, Mitchelstown; South wing, Mitchelstown Castle after the fire, August 1922; Galtee Castle in the Galtee mountains; Kingston College, circa 1889; Mitchelstown Castle, south wing and entrance front; Tennis party at Mitchelstown Castle; Wentworth Alexander King-Harman; Colonel A.L. King-Harman in 1997.
Courtesy A.L. King-Harman: James, 5th Earl of Kingston; James, 4th Baron Kingston; Caroline, Lady Kingsborough; James, 5th Earl of Kingston; Margaret, Countess of Mount Cashell.
Courtesy Webber Collection: George, 3rd Earl of Kingston.
Courtesy of Priscilla Congreve: Mitchelstown Castle, the last summer, 1922; Anna, Dowager Countess of Kingston, in 1885; William Downes Webber in 1885; Rockingham, County Roscommon.
Courtesy of National Library of Ireland: The hall, Mitchelstown Castle; The gallery, Mitchelstown Castle; A drawing room, Mitchelstown Castle; New Market Square in 1887.
Courtesy of Barclay, Earl of Kingston: Henry Ernest, 8th Earl of Kingston, who died in 1896.

Family Tree of the Kings, Earls of Kingston

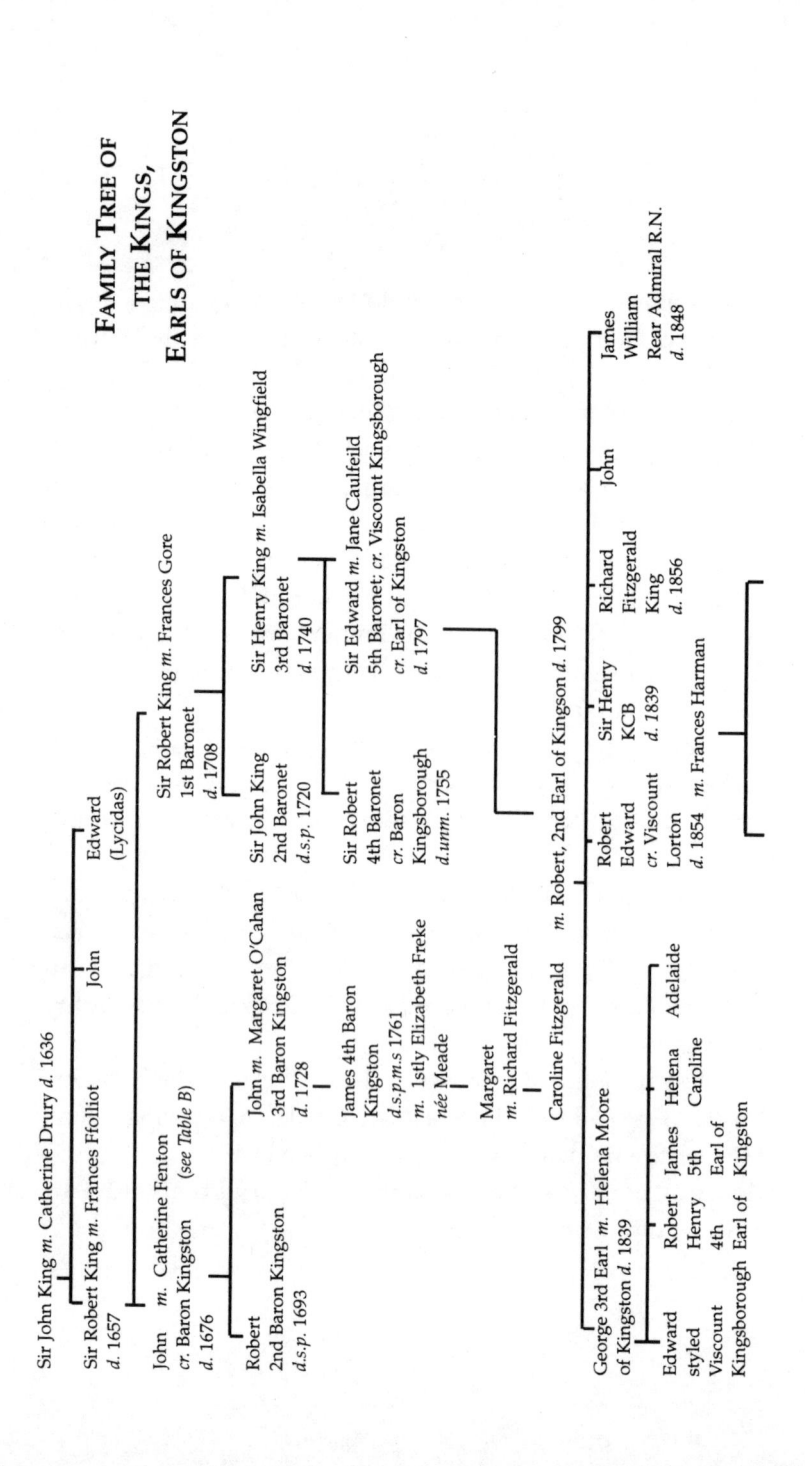

Sir John King *m.* Catherine Drury *d.* 1636

- Sir Robert King *m.* Frances Ffolliot *d.* 1657
  - John *m.* Catherine Fenton *cr.* Baron Kingston *d.* 1676 (*see Table B*)
    - Robert 2nd Baron Kingston *d.s.p.* 1693
    - John *m.* Margaret O'Cahan 3rd Baron Kingston *d.* 1728
      - James 4th Baron Kingston *d.s.p.m.s* 1761 *m.* 1stly Elizabeth Freke *née* Meade
      - Margaret *m.* Richard Fitzgerald
        - Caroline Fitzgerald *m.* Robert, 2nd Earl of Kingson *d.* 1799
  - Sir Robert King *m.* Frances Gore 1st Baronet *d.* 1708
    - Sir John King 2nd Baronet *d.s.p.* 1720
    - Sir Henry King *m.* Isabella Wingfield 3rd Baronet *d.* 1740
      - Sir Robert 4th Baronet *cr.* Baron Kingsborough *d.unm.* 1755
      - Sir Edward *m.* Jane Caulfeild 5th Baronet; *cr.* Viscount Kingsborough *cr.* Earl of Kingston *d.* 1797
        - Robert Edward *cr.* Viscount Lorton *d.* 1854 *m.* Frances Harman
        - Sir Henry KCB *d.* 1839
        - Richard Fitzgerald King *d.* 1856
        - John
        - James William Rear Admiral R.N. *d.* 1848
- Edward (Lycidas)
- John

George 3rd Earl *m.* Helena Moore of Kingston *d.* 1839

- Edward styled Viscount Kingsborough
- Robert Henry 4th Earl of Kingston
- James 5th Earl of Kingston
- Helena Caroline
- Adelaide

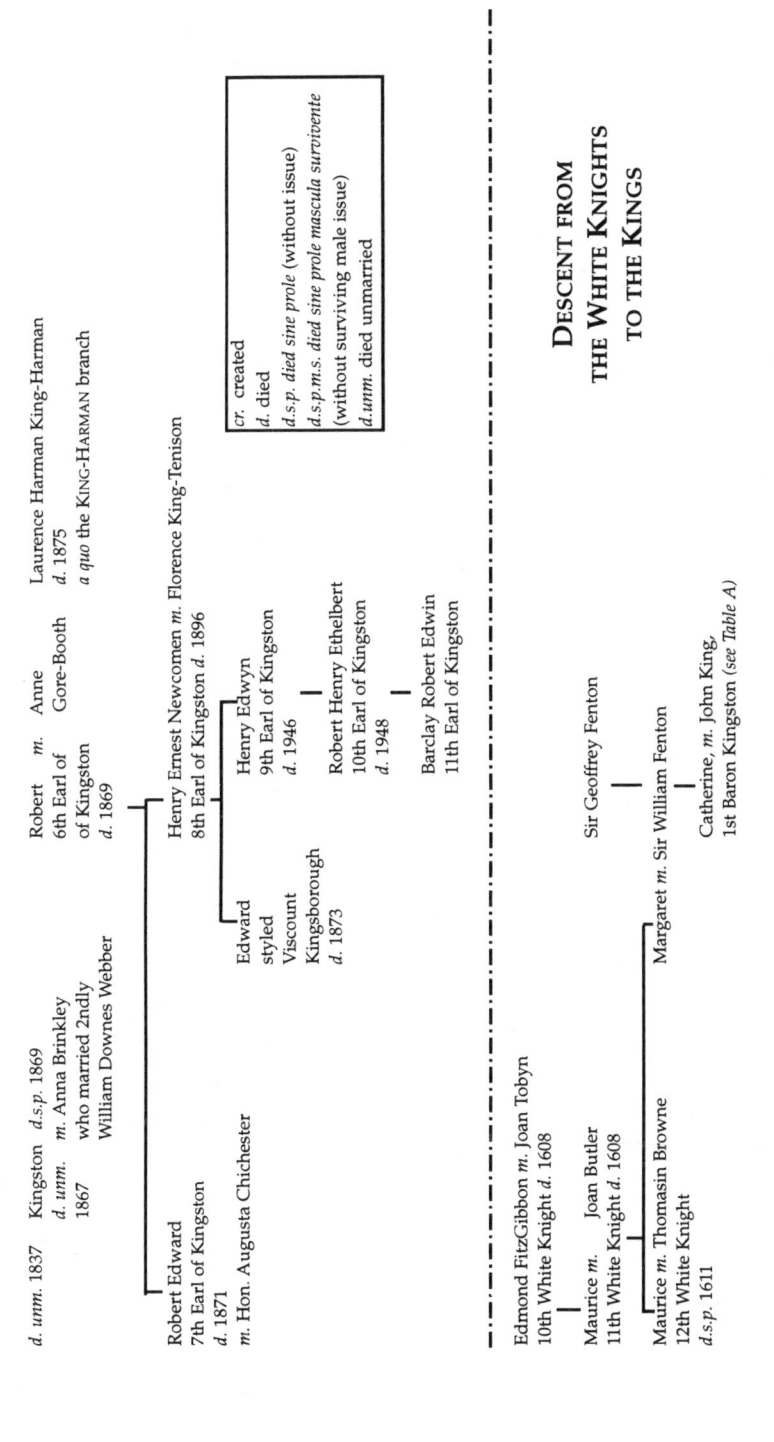

d. unm. 1837 Kingston *d.s.p.* 1869
                 d. unm. *m.* Anna Brinkley
                 1867 who married 2ndly
                        William Downes Webber

Robert *m.* Anne Gore-Booth   Laurence Harman King-Harman
6th Earl of Kingston   *d.* 1875
d. 1869   *a quo* the KING-HARMAN branch

Robert Edward
7th Earl of Kingston
d. 1871
m. Hon. Augusta Chichester

Henry Ernest Newcomen *m.* Florence King-Tenison
8th Earl of Kingston *d.* 1896

Edward   Henry Edwyn
styled   9th Earl of Kingston
Viscount   *d.* 1946
Kingsborough
d. 1873   Robert Henry Ethelbert
                10th Earl of Kingston
                d. 1948

                Barclay Robert Edwin
                11th Earl of Kingston

> *cr.* created
> *d.* died
> *d.s.p.* *died sine prole* (without issue)
> *d.s.p.m.s.* *died sine prole mascula survivente*
> (without surviving male issue)
> *d. unm.* died unmarried

- -

Edmond FitzGibbon *m.* Joan Tobyn
10th White Knight *d.* 1608

Maurice *m.* Joan Butler   Sir Geoffrey Fenton
11th White Knight *d.* 1608

Maurice *m.* Thomasin Browne   Margaret *m.* Sir William Fenton
12th White Knight
d.s.p. 1611   Catherine, *m.* John King,
                                                      1st Baron Kingston (*see Table A*)

DESCENT FROM
THE WHITE KNIGHTS
TO THE KINGS

1

KNIGHTS AND BARONS

When Sir John King arrived in Ireland in the reign of Elizabeth I, the White Knights ruled mid-Munster with ruthless authority. To enforce their supremacy these Norman lords had built strong castles and commanded personal armies with hundreds of foot soldiers and scores of horse. The White Knight was chief of the ClanGibbon, or FitzGibbons, the senior line of the cadet branch of the great Geraldine house which included the Earls of Desmond and Kildare. The FitzGibbon territory, called the White Knight's Country, included some of the most fertile lands of southern Ireland extending from Mitchelstown in the east to Kilmallock in the west.[1]

The White Knights took possession of Mitchelstown after 1340 when the original Norman owners, the FitzDavids de St Michel, petered out.[2] Soon afterwards, a strong castle was built there. John Oge, the tenth White Knight, died in 1569. This did not save him from a posthumous conviction for high treason two years later when his lands were forfeited to the Crown. However, his son, Edmund FitzJohn FitzGibbon, conspired to regain them and, in 1576, his tactical loyalty to the English was repaid when most of his father's domain was restored to him on a 21-year lease. Like many feudal lords, Edmund was frequently at war with his neighbours or relatives and it was in this way that he took possession of

Ardskeagh, Kilquane and Ballylanders.[3]

Within a few years, however, Edmund was again out of favour and out of home. On 1 March 1583, a powerful force led by Sir Henry Walsingham arrived in Mitchelstown and laid siege to the castle. After an obstinate resistance, Walsingham took Mitchelstown and placed it in the charge of James Roche, the son of Viscount Roche, who was an arch-enemy of the White Knight.[4]

'The stout and stately bastard of the Lord Roche' also took ClanGibbon castles at Oldcastletown and Kilbehenny before he was hunted down and killed by the redoubtable knight.[5] Edmond changed sides whenever he felt it was to his advantage and was in trouble with the authorities again in 1587. He was arrested, but extricated himself by swearing loyalty once more and, in 1590, he was rewarded finally with the return of his estates for 'faithful, painful and dangerous services.'[6]

In 1600, during the Nine Years War, Sir George Carew arrived as Lord President of Munster. At first he distrusted the White Knight, who could field an army of 400 foot and 30 horse, but his opinion soon changed when he realised that the Galtee warlord's loyalties were based entirely on self-interest.[7] The Lord President was a shrewd judge of character and, sure enough, he had Edmund on his side when word reached them that the garrison at Mallow had taken Mitchelstown Castle in the outdated belief that it was still owned by a rebel lord. One hundred pikemen, 160 foot and eighteen horse fought the English force. On hearing that the Irish had suffered 60 deaths and countless injuries, the White Knight, 'upon knowledge of the truth of this incident, condemned the people for their folly to enforce a fight'.[8]

The most wanted man in Munster at this time was James, Earl of Desmond, also known as the Sugán Earl or 'earl of straw', who was the leader of the Munster rebels and a kinsman of the White Knight. On 29 May 1601, word reached Edmund that the earl had taken refuge in a cave at Slieve Grot, about nine miles north of Mitchelstown, in the heart of the White Knight's country. One Redmond Bourke led the knight and his followers there. They took the earl prisoner and handed him over to the English, who sent him to perish in the Tower of London. The Queen pledged the White Knight £1,000 in reward and the restoration of his ancient honours and privileges – but this was an empty promise. His reward from the people whom he had betrayed was the wrath of the Gaelic bards. Aonghus Mór Ó Dálaigh, the Bard of Desmond, wrote:

> The sternest pulse that leaves the heart to hate
> Will sink o'erlaboured or with time abate,
> But on the Clan FitzGibbon Christ looks down
> Forever with unmitigated frown.[9]

On 23 April 1608, Edmund, the eleventh and last effective White Knight, died at Kilbehenny Castle, his son and heir having expired the day before at Oldcastletown, a few miles away. Legend has it that both were poisoned by a member of the family. Three years later, on 30 May 1611, Edmund's grandson, Maurice Oge, the last White Knight, died when he was only fourteen. The White Knight's Country passed to Margaret FitzGibbon, a niece of the renegade Edmund by his sister, Margery. She was the ward of Sir Geoffrey Fenton, Secretary of State for Ireland. When it came to marriage, the eleven-year-old had no option but to accept Sir Geoffrey's son, William, whose brother-in-law, the Earl of Cork, wrote in his diary on 29 December 1614:

> William Fenton, was married, in my house of Youghal, by Mr Sneswell, the preacher, to Margaret Neen Morrish Gibbon, heir-general of the White Knight, which young couple I beseech God to bless and prosper.[10]

Sir William and Dame Margaret established the foundations of modern Mitchelstown. Under a Royal Charter dated 23 April 1618, they were granted 'a Thursday market and two Fairs on the feasts of Saint Margaret and All Saints and the day after each'. This charter confirmed the market rights that had originated in the thirteenth century in Villa Michel, alias Mitchelstown. At that period, Mitchelstown was one of at least 37 market towns in County Cork. In later years the weekly markets attracted large numbers who came to sell agricultural produce, while the tolls gave the Fentons and their heirs a valuable source of income. Under a grant of property of the same date the Fentons acquired vast tracts – more than 100,000 acres – in counties Cork, Limerick, Tipperary and Dublin. They were allowed to create a demesne of 500 acres at Mitchelstown, 400 acres at Derronstown, County Limerick, and 400 more at Newcastle, County Tipperary. They were also empowered to close off an additional 2,000 acres with 'free warren, park and chase' at Mitchelstown.[11]

Sir William Fenton was the first lord of Mitchelstown in the post-Elizabethan era, but he apparently spent little time there. He was an adventurer who devoted much of his life to service as an officer in the English army. Most of his Mitchelstown estate was leased to tenants and some portions were sold to new English settlers. He also owned valuable iron deposits at Araglin.[12] During the 1641 rebellion, Sir William's military expertise was badly needed at Mitchelstown where his castle was captured for the Confederacy by the English-born Catholic general, James Tuchet, Earl of Castlehaven. A deposition taken from a witness to these events stated that on 20 June of that year, the Earl of Castlehaven did 'forcibly surprise, subdue pillage and take ... the dwelling house and towne of Mitchelstowne belonging to Sir William ffenton, whereas they have quite demolished and burned; together with the church thereof'.[13]

When Sir William died he was without a male heir as his eldest son, Sir Maurice, had predeceased him. Maurice had been a member of Richard Cromwell's House of Commons and the only baron created in Ireland during the Cromwellian period. The Fentons' second son was drowned off Bristol in 1643.[14] The family's sole survivor was Catherine, who inherited the estates. In the late 1650s, she married Sir John King, a military captain who had distinguished himself on the Cromwellian side in the English Civil War. He was owner of several properties in Ireland including the abbey lands of Boyle, County Roscommon, which had been granted to his grandfather, another Sir John, by Queen Elizabeth. His later zeal for the restoration of the monarchy led to his elevation to the peerage as Baron Kingston in 1660.

Catherine died in 1669 and her husband in 1676.[15] Their two sons, Robert and John, were left in the care of their uncle, Sir Robert King, then living in Boyle. He hired Rev Dr Francis Quayle as their tutor. Quayle accompanied the young Robert, second Baron Kingston, to France in 1677. John was sent to school in Charleville, County Cork, but soon afterwards went to live in the family's new house, Rockingham, near Boyle. John was accused of misspending his time there and keeping 'idle company' with a woman who was one of the Catholic servants. John developed 'a more than ordinary and suspicious familiarity' with Margaret (Peggy) O'Cahan. By the time Robert got to hear about it the 'amour was well advanced' and, within a short time, the couple had married. The King family bitterly opposed the liaison, John's uncle, Sir Robert King, remarking bluntly that

> Few of the nobility of English extraction have ever contracted marriages with Irish papists, but none (up to this case) have married

one who was at once an ordinary Servant Maid and an Irish Papist Bitch who had neither Charms of Beauty nor genteel behaviour nor agreeableness of conversation.[16]

On the accession of the Catholic James II to the throne, John converted to the old Faith and, taking advantage of the new political situation, was appointed a Gentleman of the Privy Chamber. But his luck ran out when King James was deposed and replaced by the Protestant, William III. He succeeded as third Baron Kingston when his brother, Robert, died in 1693. For the next fifteen years his right to the title and estate was the subject of a series of court battles with other family members.[17] Finally, however, he won outright ownership of Mitchelstown and Boyle by conforming to Protestantism and promising that his children would be brought up as Protestants.

Despite their public conversion, John's family practised Catholicism in private, much to the annoyance of his namesake, Archbishop King of Dublin, who protested in a letter to him in 1611 that 'I ought not to conceal from your lordship that it is much observed that your family is altogether Papist, and that you live in much the old Irish style as the merest Irishman in the kingdom.'[18]

While John, in the fashion of the time, regarded religion as an extension of politics, his wife, Margaret, remained true to her Catholic and Gaelic ancestry and eventually was buried alone in the ancient church ruin of Brigown.[19]

John's eldest son, James, who was sworn a Privy Councillor in 1727, succeeded his father as fourth baron in 1728.[20] James was the first of the family to devote some effort to improving Mitchelstown and his family home. He was Grand Master of the Freemasons in England in 1729, before setting up the first warranted Irish lodge at Mitchelstown a few years later. The warrant issued to the Mitchelstown

Lodge on 1 February 1731 is said to be the oldest Grand Lodge warrant in Ireland, and has formed the basis of all such warrants issued since. Similarly, the 'Mitchelstown Oath' is the basis of freemasonry oaths used today. James served as Grand Master of the United Grand Lodge of Ireland in 1731, 1735, 1745 and 1746. For the next two centuries, several members of the family were prominent Freemasons.[21]

Baron Kingston's personal chaplain from 1730 to 1754 was Rev Dr John K'Eogh, a distinguished botanist whose *Botanologia Universalis Hibernica* was published in 1735. In this work he referred to the oranges and liquorice grown in the Mitchelstown demesne gardens, which already had an extensive collection of over 200 species of plants. K'Eogh's book was the first on the botany of Ireland. He listed 500 plants, trees and herbs, which might be used for medicinal purposes, with their Irish, English and Latin names.[22]

James, fourth Baron Kingston, died on 28 December 1761 – his second wife, Isabella, having died the previous month. For the third time in five generations there was no male heir to inherit as his only son had died before him.

In his will James provided for an asylum for elderly Protestants who had fallen on hard times. The endowment of Kingston College, as it was to be known, amounted to £25,000, in addition to funds for its erection. The Protestant Archbishop of Cashel and the Bishops of Cloyne, Limerick and Waterford were appointed trustees. They were to raise the funds from the estate and purchase land to build two houses or colleges – 'one for poor decayed gentlemen and the other for poor decayed gentlewomen.' Under the terms of Baron Kingston's will, the trustees were to apply the rents and profits to 'the maintenance & support of a Chaplain ... and so many poor Gentlemen & Gentlewomen members of the Church of Ireland as by law established with preference forever hereafter of such persons as have been or shall be tenants upon my sd. estate in Ireland'.

James stipulated that the chaplain would perform morning and evening services in the College chapel. He was obliged also to preach a sermon every Sunday and administer Holy Communion at Christmas, Easter and Whit Sunday.[23]

The construction of Kingston College had begun by 1764. For a long time afterwards, the trustees found it virtually impossible to obtain the money from the Kingston estate. This did not help the progress of the work, which cost about £12,000 to complete over fifteen years. A chapel was erected at the centre of the College, beneath which was the Kingston burial vault. To the left of the chapel were the chaplaincy and ladies' houses. To the right were the doctor's residence and houses for the gentlemen. All these fine Georgian buildings, forming half of King Square, were designed by the Midleton architect, John Morrison, father of the great neo-classical architect, Sir Richard Morrison.[24]

However, the trustees were dissatisfied with Morrison's management of the project and forced him to resign as contractor and architect. He was replaced by Oliver Grace of Dublin who, in 1786, added two houses to the original plan. Also involved was Richard Hartland, who was contracted to level and gravel the courtyards and lay out the sewers. At many stages during the construction there were huge interest payments outstanding on the £25,000 endowment, which the family claimed it was unable to pay. Threats of legal action against them did not have much impact on interest payments which had risen to £6,200 by 1780.[25]

The first residents moved into the houses in 1777, thirteen years before the project was finished. The first chaplain was Rev Thomas Bushe whose son, Charles Kendal Bushe, became Lord Chief Justice of the King's Bench in Ireland.

Rev Bushe was paid an annual salary of £80 and accepted the appointment only because he bankrupted his own estate at Kilmurry, County Kilkenny.[26]

Lord Kingston's will also established a library at Mitchelstown – one of the first public libraries in Ireland. He instructed that his book collection, then in England, be deposited in the library which was near the castle.[27]

James provided for a person, 'properly qualified as a Librarian', who would be appointed by the Bishop of Cloyne and paid £30 a year out of two mills in the town. The librarian was

> to take care of and preserve from injury my sd. Library and collection of books. To order & arrange the same and to make & keep exact lists or Catalogues thereof ... Lastly, I will & order, That my two large Bibles shall on my death be sent to Ireland and placed in The Chapel of the alms house ... & shall remain for perpetual use in the said Chapel.

After the first librarian was some years in office 'the mills were thrown down, and the ground on which they stood annexed to the demesne'. The books were removed and deposited in the castle library.[28]

Baron Kingston left his lands in counties Cork, Limerick and Tipperary in trust to his daughter, Margaret, wife of Colonel Richard Fitzgerald of Mount Ophaly. She died soon after her father and her four-year-old daughter, Caroline, became sole owner of the Mitchelstown estate. As she was a minor, her father obtained temporary guardianship of her estate and was very keen to find a suitable match for her. Caroline, with the blessing of her trustees, married her cousin from Boyle, Robert King, Viscount Kingsborough. Once she reached her majority, the couple would have unrestricted ownership of Mitchelstown and the opportunity to realise its vast potential.[29]

2

Empire Builders

Caroline Fitzgerald was only fourteen when she married Robert King, Viscount Kingsborough, who was one year older. This was a marriage of cousins arranged to unite the Mitchelstown and Rockingham estates and to consolidate the Kings' power and wealth. During the couple's lifetime, the family reached its zenith in terms of wealth and prestige. Robert's father, Edward, had been created Earl of Kingston on 25 August 1768.

When Robert married Caroline in Saint Michan's Church, Dublin, on 5 December 1769, it was clear that he would some day succeed to his father's title and lands. In that event, the family's Connacht estates (over 70,000 acres) and most of the old White Knight's Country (at least 100,000 acres) would be brought together under single ownership. The cost of the marriage settlement was put at £12,000 by the earl who, four years later, sought to recoup the money from his son.[1] Nonetheless, the Earl of Kingston was especially pleased that his son had been accepted as Caroline's husband.[2]

After their wedding, the original family mansion at King House in Boyle and a town house at 15/16 Henrietta Street, Dublin, were put at the disposal of the young couple.[3] They had a yearly allowance of £6,000 – an enormous sum in those days – from the Mitchelstown estate. As soon as she was 21, Mitchelstown would become Caroline's property for her lifetime, to be inherited by her eldest surviving son. Meanwhile, Robert's father had hired a Mr Tickell, who was a former master at Eton, as the boy's tutor. He remained with Robert for many years, acting as his secretary and as tutor to the Kingsborough children.[4] Robert and Caroline's eldest son, George, was born on 8 April 1771, at which date the combined ages of mother, father and son were only 32 years.[5]

Meanwhile, the Earl of Kingston was building another new house at Boyle to replace one that had burnt down in the 1760s. The Kingsboroughs lived with Robert's parents, and also from time to time in Dublin. Their first visit to the Mitchelstown estate was a brief one shortly after their wedding. Robert was unusual in that he chose not to involve himself in Dublin society at a time when the Irish capital flourished as the second city of King George's dominions.[6] He was presented to the Lord Lieutenant in November 1771 – an event of great importance for any young gentleman. However, Robert admitted to his father: 'I told you ... that I was to be introduced at the Castle; that operation is now over, which I am very glad of ...'[7]

Endless quarrels between Caroline and her in-laws made it necessary to keep her apart from them. Robert, with his wife and children, departed for London in December 1772, and for some time they rarely visited his parents. In London, the couple were frequently seen at Court. Soon, Caroline became pregnant with her third child – their first daughter, Margaret, had been born the previous year.

The family's departure for London marked the beginning of a remarkable Grand Tour of the Continent. Robert left behind a growing mountain of debt, caused by overspending on his allowance of £500 a month. But he had little reason to worry because Caroline would soon reach her majority, at which time the full financial benefits of Mitchelstown would be at their disposal. The young couple visited all the popular places on their Grand Tour. Within weeks, Robert had been presented to King Louis XVI at Versailles, where he was to visit on four other occasions. He also dined with the Duc d'Aiguillon, who was French Minister of Foreign Affairs, with the English ambassador and with other members of the aristocracy.

In July 1773, Kingsborough was in Bordeaux. At Toulouse he visited the house where he was born. The remainder of the exhaustive tour took them to Switzerland, Tyrol, Venice, Turin, Nuremberg, Munich and Frankfurt, before returning to England from Augsburg, via Brussels. Their travels would have taken them further had it not been for the fact that Caroline was 'breeding again'. They arrived back in Ireland in September 1775, after an absence of almost three years.[8]

With the revenue now available to them from Caroline's inheritance, Robert began building a new family home on the site of the White Knight's castle, beside the medieval town of Mitchelstown. He had seen charming towns and grand houses in Europe, and these had inspired him to devise ambitious plans for improving his estate. However, he realised that, because of his lack of knowledge and expertise in the development and management of estates, nothing could be achieved without professional help. Robert complained that the estate was run by an Irish agent who rarely saw the property except perhaps twice a year when collecting rents. A clerk lived in a summer house at the castle gardens where the tenants went to pay their rent in dribs and drabs. Robert wanted to replace his agent with a diligent resident manager who understood agriculture and would take an active role in developing the estate.

While in London, Kingsborough told a friend, Mr Danby, of his problems with his agent and the difficulty of finding a good replacement. Danby agreed with Robert's assessment of the situation and told him that he knew a young gentleman named Arthur Young who might be the answer. In Danby's view Young was a man who had 'unquestionable knowledge in the management of estates'. Indeed, Young was already on his way to becoming the greatest English agriculturalist of the age. He had spent part of 1776 touring Ireland while writing a book about the state of the country. Danby suggested that Young would be the ideal man to advance Kingsborough's improvements at Mitchelstown.

The Kingsboroughs invited Young to dinner and struck up a good relationship with him. The next day, Danby drew up a contract which made Arthur Young land agent at Mitchelstown on a salary of £500 a year. He would be given a suitable residence rent free and, in addition, a retaining fee of £500 to be paid immediately. Such a large payment befitted the talents and reputation of Young, who sold his farm in Hertfordshire and sent his books and other effects to Cork. Meanwhile, he sailed to Dublin where he waited until a temporary residence was made ready for him in Mitchelstown. His new house would be built to a plan and in a situation chosen by himself.[9]

In September 1777, Young arrived in Mitchelstown where he found Kingsborough's estate in a depressed condition. His *Tour of Ireland* described a property that was very badly managed and tenants who knew nothing of modern agricultural techniques. His description of the state of Mitchelstown and Ireland generally showed a remarkable knowledge of the country and its problems.

The agriculturalist loved the Galtee Mountains, noting that eagles were to be seen in numbers on its cliffs and rocks. Looking down on Mitchelstown, he declared that 'it has at least a situation worthy of the proudest capital'.[10] He was lyrical about the beauty of the Galtees which seemed to him more suited to the boundary between two empires than private properties. Every river, he wrote, was 'alive with trout and eels, that play and dash among the rocks, as if endowed with that native vigour which animates, in a superior degree, every inhabitant of the mountains, from the bounding red deer, and the soaring eagle, down even to the fishes of the brook'.[11]

His writings about Mitchelstown were primarily concerned with the management of the estate and the conditions of the tenantry. He observed that the population was large and that few estates in the north of the country held the same proportion of small farms as Lord Kingsborough's property. 'The cabins are innumerable, and, like most Irish cabins, swarm with children. Wherever there are many people, and little employment, idleness and its attendants must abound.'

The rents on profitable land varied from eight to 25 shillings an acre. However, the average yield per acre did not exceed 2s-6d and the size of farms held by occupying tenants was generally very small. Kingsborough released the farms from the bondage of middlemen who were destroying the prosperity of the tenants. Great tracts were held in partnership; the amount held by single farmers rose from a yearly rent of £5 to £20. Inefficient farming practices left the estate with 'a face of desolation'. On seven-eighths of it the soil was exhausted through overuse and lack of fertilisation:

> The melancholy appearance of the lands arising from this, which, with miserable and unplanted mounds for fences, with no gate but a furze bush stuck in a gap, or some stones piled on each other, altogether form a scene the more dreary, as an oak, an ash or an elm, are almost as great a rarity (save in the plantations of the present Lord) as an olive, an orange or a mulberry. There is no wheat, and very little barley. Clover and turnips, rape, beans, and peas, unknown.[12]

Young said that the absence of trees was such that one had to 'take a breathing gallop to find a stick large enough to beat a dog'. All the oak, ash, whitethorn and birch had gone to England, at six pence a tree, to build ships and fuel the industrial revolution.[13]

A skilled nurseryman, Richard Hartland, was brought from England to manage Kingsborough's twelve-acre nursery and to advise on the ongoing building of Kingston College. Hartland enjoyed George III's patronage and, on the advice of both Kingsborough and the Marquis of Bute, he established a nursery at Mitchelstown – one of several that he set up in Munster.[14]

Hartland persuaded Kingsborough to provide trees free of charge to his tenants as part of a massive effort to replant the estate. Kingsborough paid premiums to those who planted most trees and looked after them with the greatest care. Rewards totalling £80 a year were paid to tenants who carried out desirable improvements in agriculture. Over 10,000 perches of hedging was planted.

Young was surprised by the number of pigs in Lord Kingsborough's towns and villages. 'Pigs and children bask and roll about, and often resemble one another so much, that it is necessary to look twice before the human face divine is confessed. I believe there are more pigs in Mitchelstown than human beings; and yet propagation is the only trade that flourished here for ages.' Labour, he said, was carried out mainly on the cottier system:

> There are here every gradation of the lower classes, from the spalpeens, many among them strangers, who build themselves a wretched cabin in the road, and have neither land, cattle, nor turf, rising to the regular cottier, and from him to the little joint-tenant, who, united with many others, take some large farm in partnership; still rising to the greater farmer.[15]

Young was highly impressed by the work undertaken in

Mitchelstown under Kingsborough's direction. A new mansion, which incorporated the old castle of the White Knights, was under construction. The town was being rebuilt in a new location and a demesne park laid out in lands around the castle. More significantly, Robert was taking important steps to improve the lot of his tenants and, for that, Young could claim a share of the credit.

He encouraged Robert to dispense with the middlemen who were the greatest single curse on the estate. The middleman's 'business and ... industry consists in hiring great tracts of lands as cheap as he can, and re-letting them to others as dear as he can.' This situation prevailed on 90 per cent of the estate and served only to increase the hardship of the poorest tenants. As the middlemen's leases expired, Kingsborough refused to renew their contracts and the lands were leased directly to the tenants. As Kingsborough received the same income the tenants ended up paying considerably less in rent.

Kingsborough transformed Mitchelstown from a 'den of vagabonds, thieves, rioters and Whiteboys' into a place 'as orderly and peaceable as any other Irish town'.[16] Young encouraged his employer to persevere in his plans. 'He will never quit it without having reason afterwards for regret,' said Young, who had already noted some serious defects in Robert's character:

> At many different periods of his life he seemed to possess qualities very much in contradiction to each other. His manner and carriage were remarkably easy, agreeable and polite, having the finish of a perfect gentleman; he wanted, however, steadiness and perseverance even in his best designs, and was easily wrought upon by persons of inferior abilities.

This latter weakness was exploited by one dismissed middleman, Major James Badham Thornhill, a cousin of Lady Kingsborough. He had a large farm at Thornhill Lawn on the estate. In his autobiography, Young said that the Major, 'feeling the sweets of a profit rent upon that one farm, was exceedingly anxious to procure from Lord Kingsborough the profits of others upon the same terms, and in this respect I was placed in an awkward situation.'

Thornhill had his eye 'upon several of the most considerable farms.' Caroline had a high opinion of the Major who was, in Young's view, 'a lively, pleasant, handsome man, and an ignorant open-hearted duelist'(*sic*). Caroline favoured the Major's plans, but Young was carefully non-committal. He often dined at the castle and afterwards played chess for an hour or more with Caroline. She was well pleased with Young saying that he was 'one of the most lively, agreeable fellows'. These chess games gave the Thornhills an opportunity to plot Young's downfall and to bring an untimely end to his career in Mitchelstown. Had Young been as astute in human intrigue as he was in agricultural affairs, he might have seen what was coming. Mrs Thornhill, he admitted, was 'an artful designing woman, ever on the watch to injure those who stood in her husband's way, and never forgetting her private interest for the moment'.

Mrs Thornhill convinced Caroline that Miss Crosby, the Catholic governess, was having an affair with Robert. Miss Crosby was sacked and Young was instructed to draw up a contract to grant her an annuity of £50 a year. This matter, and other business, frequently brought Young to the castle to meet one or other of his employers. Mrs Thornhill planted the notion in Robert's mind that Young, in turn, was having an affair with Robert's wife. Meanwhile, Caroline was led to believe that Young somehow was helping Miss Crosby to secure the affections of Lord Kingsborough.

Though none of the accusations were true, the result was that Robert dismissed his land agent. Young refused to leave

Mitchelstown unless a sum of £600 owed to him by Kingsborough was paid. Thornhill went to Young to say that Robert did not have the money. This was true as Kingsborough was already having difficulties paying what he owed to the trustees of Kingston College. Young then proposed a settlement which Robert accepted. In lieu of the amount owed to him, Young would receive £72 a year out of the Kingsboroughs' estate for the rest of his life. He was satisfied and thus ended, in his own words, 'one of the greatest speculations of my life'. It was no surprise that Major Thornhill succeeded him as land agent.[17]

For all of that, the changes already made on Kingsborough's estate were impressive. Young observed:

> It is not to be expected that so young a man as Lord Kingsborough, just come from the various gaiety of Italy, Paris, and London, should, in so short a space as two years, do so much in a region so wild as Mitchelstown; Men, who from long possession of landed property, become gradually convinced of the importance of attending to it, may at last work some improvements without meriting any considerable portion of praise; but that a young man, warm from pleasure, should do it, has a much superior claim. Lord Kingsborough has, in this respect, a great deal of merit; and for the sake of both himself and his country, I heartily wish he may steadily persevere in that line of conduct which his understanding has once told him, and must continue to tell him, is so greatly for the advantage of himself, his family, and the public.[18]

Robert's interests, however, were not confined to his estates. Early in life he became involved in politics and staunchly supported the independence of the Irish parliament. He clearly saw his own power in terms of a Dublin assembly run by the Ascendancy, with the Sovereign as its constitutional head. In 1783 and 1790, he was elected to the Irish House of Commons as member for Cork and in 1789 he was Governor of Cork.[19] Kingsborough was a prominent figure in the

Protestant-led volunteer force, formed in 1780 in reaction to the perceived threat of an American or French invasion during the American Revolution.

Splendidly uniformed and well armed, the Volunteers paraded and drilled in every town and most villages of the country. Lord Doneraile, for example, had his 'Doneraile Rangers Light Dragoons,' and the Earl of Mount Cashell had his 'Kilworth Volunteers'.[20]

The Mitchelstown Independent Light Dragoons had Viscount Kingsborough as their commanding colonel. He was out of the country when they were established in 1774, but that did not deter the local Protestants from organising their defences. The Mitchelstown Dragoons were the first of the 54 companies founded in Munster. They had a colourful scarlet uniform, with black facings, silver epaulettes, yellow helmets and white buttons, and lining of goatskin, edged black. The names of the officers reflected the pecking order among the local Ascendancy. The Mitchelstown officers in 1782 included Lieutenant-Colonel Henry Cole Bowen (of Bowen's Court), Major James Thornhill and Rev Thomas Bushe.[21]

Following the Dungannon Convention of 1780, provincial conventions were organised around the country. Robert's activities within the Volunteers and in parliament brought him much prominence among the nobility. He was chairman of the Munster Convention, held at Cork; he reviewed Volunteer parades as far afield as Wicklow, Limerick and Clare;[22] he chaired meetings on legislative independence, including a gathering of the Tipperary Freeholders in 1780, called to stress the dire economic consequences of remaining in the Union with England.[23] He represented Munster's 54 Volunteer Corps at the Grand National Convention in Dublin in May 1783. The convention was a turning point for the

Volunteers who were impotent in the face of a parliament which refused to give in to their demands. It seems that, despite all their bravado, the Ascendancy was finally unwilling to take the law into its own hands.

However, it was mainly because of the Volunteers that Henry Grattan was able to secure his Constitution for Ireland in 1782, when the country acquired a modicum of independence from English rule. Such moves inspired a great sense of self-confidence and pride among the Ascendancy, though the system was far from democratic or egalitarian, as it was operated by, and largely for the benefit of, the wealthy and privileged classes.[24]

Locally, during the 1780s, Kingsborough was busily demolishing the towns and villages of his estate in the most remarkable adventure of his life. In their place rose orderly townscapes and wide streets, churches, squares and well-built urban and two-storey rural houses for his tenants. In this manner, Kildorrery was laid out on a crossroads. Likewise, Ballyporeen and Ballylanders were built with wide, imposing streets.[25]

This was a time of prosperity in Ireland. While the English aristocracy was erecting fine civic and public buildings, their Irish counterparts tended to town building and erecting mansions for themselves. The Ascendancy flourished and imagined that things could only get better. In few places was this construction boom more evident than at Mitchelstown. In Robert's grand plan, the town took on a decidedly European character, reflecting his enthusiasm for what he had seen on his Grand Tour. In pursuit of his dream estate, Robert spent the rest of his life pulling down the old and replacing it with the new.[26]

Not satisfied with the old White Knight's castle, which had been remodelled probably in the 1740s, Robert pulled down its handsome corridors which had so impressed Smith, the Cork historian, 30 years earlier. Smith had described a gallery 70 feet long and 20 feet wide above the hall, from which there were fine views of the Galtee and Knockmealdown mountains. 'Several of the chambers are furnished with a variety of coloured marbles, found on the adjacent grounds,' he said. A tower, on the eastern side of the house, contained an elegant study, furnished with books and 'beautiful busts and paintings'.[27] Robert raised the old house by two storeys, made additions to it, and had the whole structure re-roofed. He also built coach houses, a gardener's house, steward's house, storehouse, a laundry and some other offices.

The house was built in the Palladian style then fashionable. The structure was described as 'a large square house with wings in the style of the eighteenth century, not unlike the house at Moorepark [Kilworth].' It was exquisitely decorated with a large ceiling elaborately painted with frescoes by an Italian artist. The principal reception rooms were on the first floor. The new mansion cost at least £36,000. A further £8,000 to £9,000 was spent on the stables and its adjoining facilities.

An ancient tower or turret, part of the outworks of the old castle, was turned into a library and placed in the charge of a salaried librarian, as stipulated in the fourth baron's will.[28] This tower was round and stood opposite the hall-door of the new house, some 50 or 60 yards away, with canons displayed on its outworks. In 1818, Viscount Lorton, Robert's second eldest son, said that it was a 'very ugly object'. He recalled that it was known as the library and had been used by the agents to collect rents.[29] Nearby was an old graveyard that remained in use until the 1870s, and a ruined church (used by the protestant parishioners) that was demolished when the new demesne was developed.[30]

Robert's crowning achievement was the reconstruction of Mitchelstown to a plan that remains largely unaltered 200 years later, which, even for a man of his wealth, was an enormous undertaking. The old town was located about 150 yards from the castle, near King Square, and had evolved over five centuries. King Square was retained as a feature of the new town, which was relocated south and east of the square, and laid out on a simple, but highly efficient, grid pattern. The square, known as the Old Square, became the focal point of the new entrance to the castle.

New Mitchelstown was the supreme example of a well-planned Irish Georgian town. Two parallel streets were intersected by a number of smaller ones. The main thoroughfare ran from Clonmel Street through Baldwin Street, King Square, George Street and Barrack Road. George Street was planned as the town's main avenue but was soon surpassed by Cork Street which became the main thoroughfare.

The Catholic merchants were allocated properties on either side of a muddy roadway built over a riverbed, where they were expected to earn a living. This became Upper and Lower Cork Street, once the river that flowed down Church Street and Cork Street had been diverted into culverts beneath the roadway to Bank Place and the Gradoge River. A curve in the lower end of the street was designed to create the illusion of Cork Street being longer than it was in reality.

George Street was defined by the Protestant Saint George's Church at the southern end and King Square to the north, while all the streets were named by Lord Kingsborough.[31] However, the local people had other names for them. For example, Robert Street was called Butchers' Lane; Edward Street was known as Chapel Lane; Coach Lane, where the coachmakers lived, became Arch Avenue;

James' Street was Coopers' Lane, because it was the location of that trade; Baldwin Street was unique in commemorating a person other than one of Robert's sons.[32] Among the many buildings erected in the town was a new inn, known as the Kingston Arms Hotel, built in King Square at a cost of £1,500. In the townland of Kilshanny, on the Clonmel Road, a cotton mill with a dwelling house attached was built at a cost of £2,000.[33]

In Thomas Street, the barn-like Saint Fanahan's Catholic chapel was built at the behest of Lord Kingsborough who met most of the cost and provided the site. In the light of this one must assume that Robert felt little or no threat from his Catholic tenants. Certainly, he ignored the Penal Laws which prohibited the building of a Catholic place of worship. For this project, Robert was praised by the eminent Catholic Bishop of Cloyne, Dr William Coppinger. In or about 1810, he said:

> Robert, I believe, was the first Nobleman of this Country to distinguish himself in the career of liberality! He took an early lead in it. He gave four hundred guineas towards the building of Mitchelstown Chapel, together with a very spacious lot of ground for the chapel yard. He interested himself in the progress of the work; he frequently inspected it. He conducted his guests to the spot, as if to animate them by his own example. He also bestowed a lot of ground with one hundred guineas for the purpose of building another Chapel in the same parish for his Roman Catholic tenantry: acts of kindness, which, I trust, will be gratefully remembered by them and their posterity.[34]

Meanwhile, New Market Square, halfway along Cork Street, became a busy commercial centre. As the name indicates, the medieval town had its own market place, probably in the vicinity of King Square, and a market house built at a cost of £1,200.[35] There were many changes to the local landscape while Robert was building his new house. A demesne of 1,240 acres – there was an earlier enclosure called Stag Park – was enclosed by a ten foot high limestone wall, six and a quarter miles in length. This took sixteen years to build, from 1775 until 1791, at a cost of at least £16,000. Prior to this, the demesne lands were mostly small holdings whose tenants were removed to make way for their landlord's ambitious undertaking.

The demesne was designed by the landscaper John Webb who also laid out several remarkable parks elsewhere in Ireland and England in the style of Capability Brown, who was the architect of some of Britain's most famous parks and gardens. Webb also designed gardens for Shanbally Castle, County Tipperary, and Ballyfin, County Laois. In order to provide the appearance of maturity at Mitchelstown demesne, Webb decided to retain some of the old hedgerows and trees. It is likely that he was the instigator of the work to demolish the old town as it was considered an eyesore and interfered with his plans for Lord Kingsborough's new park.[36]

The demesne was very extensively planted with American white spruce, oak, ash, beech, Scots fir, elm and larch. When some trees were cut early in the twentieth century the growth rings showed an age dating to 1775. The demesne gardens were formalised, improved and enclosed with a twelve-foot high limestone and mortar wall. The new conservatories and vineries were 470 feet long.

A boat lake and fish pond were excavated in the demesne, with a garden pathway – known as 'the Hanging Gardens' – leading from the house.[37] The boat lake was overlooked by a fine gazebo, decorated with wonderfully carved Burmese teak. There was a wooden bridge leading to an island in the lake. It provided fresh fish and game for the castle table and gave the demesne an attractive water-garden feature. The large ice-house, west of the castle, also dated from around this time. Circular, with fine brickwork and limestone, it was mostly underground and visible from a distance as a small mound in the field. A sophisticated technique of ice storage was designed to provide foodstuffs, some of which were unusual and even exotic, for later use by the chefs at the castle.[38]

The demesne was made up of fields and paddocks where sheep, cattle and deer were farmed virtually up to the castle door. Each field had its own name. The Brick Field was where the bricks were manufactured for the building projects undertaken by Lord Kingsborough. Other names included Torpey's (Troopers) Lough, Parkaphuca (Ghost's Field), Turnpike Field, New Orchard Grove and the Yeoman's Field.[39]

Kingsborough's absolute authority was demonstrated in the closure to the public of all roads through the demesne. The Mallow road, from King Square along by the castle and out to White Gate, was re-routed. The new road ran through George Street and skirted the south wall of the demesne. Road transportation was seen as a vital aspect of economic development at the time and this was reflected in the number built in the Mitchelstown area between 1770 and 1840. The cost was borne largely by the local landlord and merchants.

Elsewhere in the demesne, a few private bridge crossings were built over the Funcheon and Gradoge rivers. Modest gate lodges were erected beside the four main entrances at King Square, White Gate, Limerick Gate and Killaclug Gate.[40] Rev Horatio Townsend described the mansion as 'a large and magnificent building, worthy of its noble possessor'. He added: 'The pleasure ground and gardens are beautiful and extensive. This fine and highly improved demesne contains no less than thirteen hundred acres, English measure, enclosed with a capital wall ten feet high.'[41]

By 1785 Robert had also built a fishing lodge on the estate as well as hunting lodges in the townlands of

Glennacunna and Glennahulla. At the same time he spent £2,000 on the building of a hunting lodge, later known as Galtee Castle, on the Galtee mountains. A local gentleman, James O'Brien, said that from the time of his arrival in Mitchelstown until his death, Viscount Kingsborough was 'constantly employed in the making of plantations and improvements' throughout the estate.[42]

The building boom in and around Mitchelstown had an enormous impact on the local economy. The development of the town, demesne and mansion created desperately-needed work for local labourers at a time when landlords were the only significant employers in rural Ireland. Local folklore has it that the stonemasons building the demesne wall were paid one penny a day, regarded as a reasonable rate at the time. Tenants looked to Kingsborough as their ancestors had to the chieftains of old. He arbitrated in disputes and, as Mitchelstown had a Manor Court, his legal rulings were binding. People went to him to arrange work for their sons or to seek his influence in securing appointments to the Church, the military and civil service.

Like most great landlords, the Kings were a political dynasty supported by the local elite. The first Earl of Kingston was an Irish peer. His eldest son, Robert, Viscount Kingsborough, was elected by the freeholders of County Cork to the Dublin Parliament on three occasions in the 1780s and 1790s, and Kingsborough's sons, George and Robert, also served as MPs.

Kingsborough went to considerable lengths to win the 1790 election. The Earl of Shannon, who backed Robert's opponent, said he had been able to send some of Kingsborough's freeholders to jail for perjury. Writing on 9 June 1790, Shannon said that the county election was still going on 'to the disgrace of the H[igh] Sheriff, Ld. Kings[boroug]h & all his party &

there is no saying where it will end.' Kingsborough was attempting to rig the result by getting support from 'the most infamous perjured, (treacherous) set of villains that can be conceived; fellows so low as labourers ... [wanderers] in rags & lice, polled against gentlemen of property & character ... we have got some of K[ingsborough]'s bucks in jail for perjury – he is distress'd & distracted, his looks & conduct shew it & he has lost his temper.'[43]

In almost every sense, confrontation between Lord Kingsborough and his opponents was nothing new. In the election of 1783, no fewer than 22 duelling incidents took place between his supporters and those of Richard Townsend. However, fifteen apologies were forthcoming from members of Townsend's party; shots were fired in only four duels and in the course of the election, nine Shannonites were horsewhipped by Robert's men. In the election of 1790, relations between Shannon and Kingsborough were no better. But on that occasion, the only recorded duel involving Kingsborough was an exchange with another candidate, Abraham Morris, in which shots were fired but no-one was injured. Such 'macho shows of bravado' were quite common in late eighteenth-century Ireland.[44]

By the beginning of the nineteenth century, Mitchelstown was experiencing great industrial and agricultural activity. Apart from building projects, employment was created through a range of enterprises sponsored by Lord Kingsborough. These included linen, cotton and woollen mills, a brewery and a tan yard. As Arthur Young suggested, Robert, Lord Kingsborough, had his faults, but there is no doubt that he was the most outstanding and reforming aristocrat in the history of the three-county Galtee region and, through his political activities, a landlord of considerable influence much further afield.

3

IN A STRANGE LAND

Life in the Kingsborough household in the later years of the eighteenth century was vividly recorded in the writings of Mary Wollstonecraft, the family's governess from 1786 to 1788. Her affection for the children contrasted sharply with her response to their parents. Mary was generations ahead of her time in her views on the equality of the sexes. Her strongly-held beliefs on such issues led to conflict with her employers, who could never have imagined the trouble they would bring on themselves by employing her.

After the Kingsborough's marriage in 1769, life at Henrietta Street in Dublin was exciting. The capital had acquired a new sense of importance with the evolution of a stronger Irish parliament. There was a constant round of balls and parties at which the Kingsboroughs mixed with Ireland's leading citizens. However, Caroline and Robert rarely had their house to themselves. Relatives, mostly Caroline's, were almost always in residence or passing through, much to the resentment of the young bride. Comments in letters between Robert and his father frequently referred to bickering between Caroline and her father and stepmother. Peace was restored only when the Kingsboroughs left it all behind and went to London in December 1771.[1]

Robert spent his first three weeks there arranging a

house near Berkeley Square at a cost of £360 a year. His letters indicated that matters were far from rosy between him and his wife – but now they had only themselves to blame. His father had realised from an early stage that Robert and Caroline were not well suited and revealed this in a letter to his son:

> I am in truth very sensible of the unhappiness you mention between you & Caroline, & was so much shock'd at it that I have often wished the match had never taken place, but it was then too late & I kept my mind to myself; I am glad at any rate, that mutual dislike has ceas'd, & I hope it may continue so ... My wish is to have you good & happy.[2]

As time passed, the marriage grew increasingly unhappy and ended in separation. Despite his domestic problems Robert kept his head – 'As to Drinking Porter or any other Liquor, I never do but when I am dry,' he told his father in January 1773. 'My Morning & Evening prayers I neither do nor shall omit.'[3]

By the start of their Grand Tour, Caroline and Robert already had three children. The eldest, George (born in Chelsea on 8 April 1771) was taken with them on their travels. The two babies, Margaret and Caroline, were left behind in London in the care of four maids.[4] In all, the Kingsboroughs had twelve children – seven boys and five girls. The boys, George, Robert, Thomas (who died as a child), Henry, Richard Fitzgerald, John and James William, were educated by tutors in Mitchelstown or Dublin until about the age of ten. They were then shipped off to an English college, usually Eton, where their education was advanced and useful personal contacts made with influential figures of the future. The girls – Margaret Jane, Caroline, Mary Elizabeth, Jane Diana and Louisa Eleanor – were educated in Mitchelstown by a governess. They would, in time, become the Kingsboroughs' key to alliances with other families of similar, or even greater, standing.

It was the education of these girls that brought Mary Wollstonecraft to Mitchelstown as governess on a salary of £40 a year. The job was a godsend as she had 'debts haunting her like furies'. Her introduction to her new employers came about while she was staying in the master's house at Eton, where she heard that the position in Mitchelstown was vacant. After her appointment as governess there were several delays before she made her way to Ireland in October 1786. She was met in Dublin by the family butler who escorted her to Mitchelstown Castle. Mary's letters have left us the best account of life within the family and their castle.[5] 'I entered the great gates with the same kind of feeling I should have if I was going into the Bastille,' she told her sister, Everina, in a letter dated 30 October 1786.

When Mary arrived, Lady Kingsborough was confined to her room with a sore throat. She was greeted by members of the extended family: 'a host of females – My Lady, her step mother, and three sisters, and Mrsus and Misses without number – who of course would examine me with the most minute attention.'[6] She was dismissive of Lord Kingsborough – 'his countenance does not promise much more than good humour, and a little fun not refined.' She was much less tolerant of Caroline whom she disliked from the start. Their first encounter took place when she was summoned to Caroline's bedroom where she found her mistress in bed, surrounded by Irish wolfhounds:

> I have seen half a dozen of her companions – I mean not her children, but her dogs – To see a woman without any softness in her manners caressing animals, and using infantile expressions – is you may conceive, very absurd and ludicrous but a fine Lady is a new species to me of animals ... I am in a land of strangers.[7]

As she got to know her mistress, Mary's attitude was little changed:

> Now and then I have seen a momentary start of tenderness – sufficient to convince me she might have been a more tolerable companion, had her temper been properly managed; as to her understanding, it could never have been made to rise from mediocrity. I pity her, but I am deprived of all society, and when I do sit with her, she worries me with prejudices, and complaints. Her conversation is ever irksome to me as she has neither sense nor feeling; besides she torments the children.[8]

Mary found her position difficult and very lonely. She was superior in status to the domestic servants but very much a subordinate to her employers' family. Therefore, she lived virtually in social isolation. In the remoteness of eighteenth-century Ireland this made her position unbearable. She spent her first evening alone beside the fire in her comfortable bedroom which looked out onto the Galtees. Her illusions of a romantic Ireland and its happy people had already been shattered as she faced up to the reality of a dreary October evening in Mitchelstown Castle. There was, she said, 'such a solemn kind of stupidity about this place as froze my very blood ... I hear a fiddle below – the servants are dancing and the rest of the family diverting themselves – I only am melancholy and alone.'[9]

As for Caroline's stepmother and her three stepsisters, all Mary could say of them was that they were 'fine girls, just going out to market, as their brother would say'. On the day after her arrival, the children hardly gave her a moment to herself. They were, she wrote, 'literally speaking, wild Irish, unformed and not very pleasing'. They told Mary that they planned to 'plague and tease' her and would be perfectly happy if she left. But Mary was not going to be put off so easily, and with charm and tenderness of a kind they had not previously experienced she quickly won them over.

Mary observed that the eldest, Margaret, aged fourteen, was 'by no means handsome – yet a sweet girl'. She greatly feared that 'such a creature should be ruled by a rod of iron [her mother], when tenderness would lead her any where'. Margaret became Mary's favourite. 'My little sweet girl,' she called her. She had very special qualities which Mary recognised and nurtured: 'She has a wonderful capacity but she had such a multiplicity of employments it has not room to expand itself – and in all probability will be lost in a heap of rubbish miscalled accomplishments. I am grieved at being obliged to continue so wrong a system.'[10]

But the cold-hearted treatment of the children was a matter of concern for their governess, who became increasingly critical of Lady Kingsborough:

> I go to the nursery – something like maternal fondness fills my bosom – The children cluster around me – one catches a kiss, another lisps my long name – while a sweet little boy, who is conscious that he is a favourite, calls himself my son – At the sight of their mother they tremble and run to me for protection – this renders them dear to me – and I discover the kind of happiness I was formed to enjoy. I am harassed with company – and conversations which have nothing in them.[11]

Throughout her time with the Kingsboroughs, Mary was very concerned that the children were not getting the kind of education that would make them more rounded, caring individuals. She often complained about this in correspondence with friends, but would appear to have had the sense to guard her tongue in front of Caroline. Mary's opinion of her mistress was not enhanced by her obvious preference for animals to her children. 'Lady K's animal passion fills hours which are not spent in dressing,' she complained.

> I think now I hear her infantile lisp – She rouges – and in short is a fine Lady without fancy or sensibility. I am almost tormented to death by dogs ... I make allowance and adapt myself – talk of getting husbands for the ladies – and the dogs ... then I retire to my room, form figures in the fire, listen to the wind or view the Galtees ...[12]

Margaret fell seriously ill shortly after Mary's arrival in Mitchelstown. The only attention she received was from the governess, who found it difficult to understand Caroline's attitude. But the health crisis also improved the atmosphere within the family, and Mary's relationship with Robert and Caroline: 'My poor little favourite has had a very violent fever – and can scarcely bear to have me a moment out of her sight – her life was despaired of – and this illness has produced an intimacy in the family which a course of years might not have brought about.'[13] The girl recovered and Mary's concern so impressed the Kingsboroughs that they rewarded her with privileges not normally permitted to a governess. The most unusual, perhaps, was to be treated more or less as a member of the family and being invited to attend family functions.

For a time Mary was content, and she told a friend that the whole family made the point of paying her 'the greatest attention and some part of it treated me with a degree of tenderness which I have seldom met with from strangers'. Indeed, Mary was able now to confide in the Kingsboroughs, who appeared to appreciate her trust. On the other hand, she critically observed the ladies of the house who

> labour to be civil to me; but we move in so different a sphere, I feel grateful for their attention; but not amused ... I am treated like a gentlewoman – but I cannot easily forget my inferior station – and this something betwixt and between is rather awkward.

Mary remained ill at ease with the nobility:

> Shall I try to remember the titles of all the Lords and Viscounts I am in company with, not forgetting the clever things they say – I would sooner tell you the tale of the humbler creatures. I intend visiting the poor cabbins as Miss [Margaret] K. is allowed to assist the poor I shall make a point of finding them out.[14]

The plight of the Kingsborough tenants shocked Mary. Some years earlier she had seen awful poverty in Lisbon, but the condition of the poor in Ireland was exacerbated by the cold and wet weather. Like Arthur Young ten years previously, Mary had never before witnessed the squalor to be found in Ireland. For most of the Kingsborough tenants, life was concentrated on a struggle for survival and Mary felt like 'a sojourner in a strange land.' The experience made her realise that her own troubles were very small and that there was very little she could do to help. She resolved, instead, to devote more time to study and to writing her first novel.

True happiness eluded Mary Wollstonecraft throughout her life, and this tended to colour her feelings while staying with the Kingsboroughs. In Mitchelstown, she resented being 'confined to the society of a set of silly females' who had 'hourly domestic bickerings', and were only concerned with the topics of marriage and clothing: 'I almost wish the girls were novel readers and romantic, I declare false refinement is better than none at all; but these girls understand several languages, and have read cart-loads of history, for their mother was a prudent woman.'[15]

Mary's unhappy situation was alleviated when she met George Ogle, a relative and close friend of the Kingsboroughs, who was an MP, a privy counsellor, a mediocre poet – and a married man. Ogle made a great impression on her. He was 'a genius and unhappy', she said in a letter to Everina. 'Such a man, you may suppose, would catch your sister's eye.' Unfortunately, Ogle was Caroline's flirt and the attentions he paid to Mary were resented by Lady Kingsborough.[16]

After a short stay with friends in Tipperary, Mary returned to Mitchelstown where the family was preparing to go to their new town house at 15 Merrion Square in Dublin. There she was given a suite of rooms which included a drawing room furnished with a harpsichord (which she could not play) and a parlour for receiving male visitors. She remarked that, by contrast, the Kingsboroughs' last governess had been treated like a servant. Mary referred to being in love but she did not reveal with whom. One of her possible lovers was Ogle; another was Lord Kingsborough himself. Ogle certainly visited her in Dublin and greatly impressed her when he presented her with a poem of his own composition. 'Poor half-mad Mr Ogle was the only Right Honourable I was ever pleased with, and I pity him,' she said.[17]

But Caroline's patience with Mary was running out. She had every right to feel that everything had been done to make Mary happy, but it had rebounded on her. The governess had won the affections of the children, who preferred her to their temperamental mother. Worse still, Mary was getting too much attention from Ogle and that went down badly with a woman who expected to get her way in all matters. Nevertheless, Caroline did her best to get on with Mary. She took her to the Dublin Handel Festival and even coaxed her into going to a masquerade, where Mary wore a black mask and indulged in satirical talk with several ladies.

When the governess fell ill in March 1787, Caroline brought in her personal physician who charged an 'aristocratic fee' which Mary had to pay out of her own purse. Margaret fell ill again and her mother's handling of the sick girl prompted further vexed criticism from Mary. Privately, she accused Lady Kingsborough of tormenting the children. Once, in frustration, she blurted out to Caroline: 'Thank heaven I am not a Lady of Quality.' Whenever Mary thought Caroline had shown disregard towards her, she would go off to sulk in her room. On one occasion Mary refused to go downstairs to meet the Earl of Kingston until persuaded to do so by a three-strong deputation: Mrs Ogle, her sister and Caroline.[18]

Preparations for a great ball at Mitchelstown kept Caroline occupied for some time. Her dress was prepared with artificial flowers and the whole household – 'from kitchen maid to Governess' – had to make artificial roses for it. When Caroline's stepmother, Mrs Fitzgerald, left the house for a while, relations between Lady Kingsborough and her governess deteriorated even further: 'You know, I never liked Lady K, but I find her still more haughty and disagreeable now she is not under Mrs Fitzgerald's eye. Indeed, she behaved so improperly to me once or twice, in the Drawing Room, I determined never to go into it again.'[19]

Of course, Mary eventually returned to the drawing room, mainly because George Ogle was there and she yearned for his company. Ogle sat beside her in a corner of the room, paid 'attentions to a poor forlorn stranger' and gave her 'some fanciful compliments'. Then something happened which embarrassed her greatly: 'Lord K came up – and was surprised at seeing me there – he bowed respectfully – a constellation of thoughts made me out blush her ladyship's rouge. Did I ever tell you she is very pretty – and always pretty.'[20]

A few years later, when Lord and Lady Kingsborough separated, Mary was accused of having wanted 'to Discharge the Marriage Duties' with Robert. Suspicion of a relationship between them was also fuelled by revelations in Mary's letters that she had become close to someone in the Kingsborough home. However, the dreadful lives of society couples, of which the Kingsboroughs were a typical example, drew scorn from Mary. She was well aware of Robert's reputation for making advances toward his governesses. As far as she could see, aristocratic couples were 'seldom alone together but in bed – the husband perhaps drunk, and the wife's head full of pretty compliments that some creature that nature designed for a man paid her at the card table.'[21]

Financial problems continued to trouble Mary. She worried about the expense of hairdressing and the cost of hats and clothing, but when Caroline offered her a poplin gown and petticoat, she refused them, causing an explosion of anger from her employer. Very often, as on this occasion, the intervention of Mrs Fitzgerald calmed things down but tensions between the governess and her Lady remained beneath the surface.[22]

In June 1787, the whole family crossed to Bristol to take the medicinal waters at the hot wells and mingle in other social circles. It was there, in August, that the Kingsboroughs prepared for another tour of the continent. As Mary was about to take a few days leave from the family before the tour, the children, and Margaret in particular, kicked up a great fuss – they did not want her away from them, not even for a few days. In a fit of temper and jealousy, Caroline sacked the governess. In letters written after this sudden departure, Mary mentions that she received money which 'a friend whose name I am not permitted to mention has lent me'. Mary made no secret about having previously received loans from Mrs Fitzgerald. However, her biographers have speculated that the mysterious patron on this occasion was Robert himself.

Undoubtedly, her dismissal caused great inconvenience within the Kingsborough household, which urgently required a new governess so that the tour could go ahead. But it was not the end of Mary's links with the family and Caroline would rue the day when she first took her on. Mary's first book, *Mary, A Fiction*, published in 1788, was primarily an attempt at self-analysis. Curiously, she merged Kingsborough and Wollstonecraft characters to tell her story. One character (the heroine's mother) is clearly a hostile sketch of Caroline. Her attractive daughter, Mary, was married off to unite the relationship between two important families, just as the young Margaret was married into the Mount Cashells of Moorepark.[23]

Controversy surrounded Mary's most famous work, *A Vindication of the Rights of Woman*, which was partly prepared while she was in Mitchelstown. Her *Vindication* was a criticism of Caroline and ladies like her and it established Mary as the first English feminist of historical importance. In 1792, she went to Paris, where she observed the progress of the French Revolution, lived through the Reign of Terror and acquired an American lover, Gilbert Imlay, by whom she had a daughter, Fanny. Back in London, she experienced a personal terror when she attempted suicide at Putney Bridge after Imlay had shunned her. Soon afterwards, she fell in love again, this time with the philosopher William Godwin, whom she married in 1796. But Mary died tragically after giving birth to their only daughter, also Mary, who grew up to marry the poet Percy Bysshe Shelley. As Mary Shelley, she achieved fame as the author of *Frankenstein*.[24]

In Mitchelstown, meanwhile, the Kingsboroughs were exercising the feudal rights of the nobility. If folklore is to be believed, one of Robert's dubious privileges was the *jus primae noctis*, the so called 'gentleman's right' – the bedding of any young maiden of his choosing on the estate. Loss of virginity was considered much less important than the loss of his Lordship's favour, or indeed, eviction of the maiden's family from their holding.

This kind of thing seemed to run in the family. During the rebellion of 1798 Kingsborough's eldest son, George, was colonel commanding the North Cork Militia and governor of Carrick-on-Suir, when several 'pretty women' came before him to beg mercy for their husbands, brothers and fathers. George boasted afterwards that he told them, 'if you'll grant me one favour, I'll grant you another'. Very few refused those terms, and he added: 'I have hitherto only had two Maidenheads.' An English officer, who strongly disapproved of what had transpired, said: 'This peer was afterwards asked by a soldier for a Pass, which he refused to give unless (in his own words) you send me your sister and I'll make you a corporal into the Bargain.'[25]

George's lust for women knew no bounds. One moonlit evening years earlier, he was walking through St Stephen's Green in Dublin with a Miss Johnstone. In a moment of passion, he remarked: 'What a fine night to run away with another man's wife.' She replied: 'And why not with another man's daughter?' 'Done,' said George, taking hold of her hand. He sailed her off to the British West Indies, where she bore him three children, all outside marriage. Eventually, George was made to realise the folly of having had his way with Miss Johnstone.[26] In 1794, he came home to marry Lady Helena Moore, sister of the Earl of Mount Cashell, who was said to be 'a pretty, pleasing little woman'. They had three sons (Edward, Robert Henry and James) and two daughters (Adelaide and Helena Caroline).[27]

Five years before George's marriage, his mother, Caroline, had walked out on his father, accusing him of persistent ill-treatment. By the time of their formal separation, Robert had already replaced her with a mistress named Eliner Hallenan. Eliner lived with him at the time of his travels between Mitchelstown, Dublin and London, and bore him two children.[28] Caroline's separation did not curtail her social life. A year later, in April 1790, she

> gave a superb rout, ball, and supper at her house in Henrietta Street, to a very numerous party of the nobility and gentry. The entertainment was perfectly magnificent, taste being in it united with expense. At this splendid party the Countess of Westmoreland [wife of the Lord Lieutenant of Ireland] appeared in an entire dress of Brussels lace laid over a pink Irish satin, the estimated expense of which exceeded 500 [pounds].[29]

A 'cottage' at Windsor became Caroline's home during the 1790s. There she often met George III and members of the Royal family during walks in the neighbourhood.[30] In 1797, while in the company of the famous Irish beauty, the Honourable Mrs Francis Calvert, they met the Royal family with some important guests on Windsor Terrace. Mrs Calvert said:

> The Duchess of Wurttemberg looked very happy, leaning on her husband. I never saw such a large man [the Duke and subsequently King of Wurttemberg]. You could have sat upon the projection of his lower Stomach with as much ease as an arm-chair.[31]

When the Kingsboroughs' second daughter, Mary Elizabeth, eloped in London in 1797, the scandal caused a sensation in polite society and was the topic of gossip at dinner tables all over the capital. At seventeen, Mary Elizabeth King was, by all accounts, very attractive. On Sunday, 3 September 1797, there was consternation when she left a note in her room stating that she had gone to commit suicide in the Thames. Lady Kingsborough's servants dragged the river near the family home but her body was not found. Three days later, however, a note arrived from Mary Elizabeth to assure her mother that she was alive and well.[32]

Lord Kingsborough arrived in London with his son, Colonel Robert King, who had recently returned from the wars in North America. From the outset, Kingsborough had been suspicious about the circumstances of his daughter's disappearance. His feelings were confirmed when a post boy, responding to appeals for assistance, called to his house and said that, while taking a gentleman in a postchaise to London, he had been ordered to stop to pick up a young lady. When the postchaise arrived in the city, the lady and gentleman walked off together.[33]

Kingsborough placed advertisements and posters all over London, and offered a 100-guinea reward for information about his daughter's whereabouts. One of those offering support was Colonel Henry Fitzgerald, who was an illegitimate son of Lady Kingston's half-brother. Some family friends suggested that the Colonel was intimate with Mary Elizabeth, but it was an accusation that he vehemently denied when it was put to him by Robert.[34]

On Wednesday, 27 September, a servant girl called to the Kingsboroughs to tell of a young lady who had been brought by a gentleman to her employer's lodging house in Clayton Street, near the Kennington Turnpike. The gentleman had visited the young lady constantly. One day, the girl walked into the lodger's room to find the lady cutting her long hair. Having seen the advertisements and heard the story, the girl's suspicions were aroused. As the woman was telling her story, Colonel Fitzgerald walked into Kingsborough's house. 'Why, there's the very gentleman who visits the young lady,' exclaimed the girl. Fitzgerald turned and fled, thus betraying his involvement in the sordid affair. Mary Elizabeth was found and brought back to her father's house at Great George Street, Hanover Square, where she was kept out of sight until she could be sent to Mitchelstown.

The King family honour had to be vindicated. The Kingsboroughs had shown the Colonel every courtesy and had helped him to purchase his commission in the army. Kingsborough's military son, Robert, challenged Fitzgerald to a duel in Hyde Park. The codes of duelling demanded that each combatant should have a second. Fitzgerald, however, failed to find one, presumably because his behaviour was considered particularly disgraceful. King was determined to go ahead, regardless; so on 1 October 1797, the two men paced the customary ten steps. Accidentally or otherwise, each missed with three shots. After the third round, Fitzgerald, 'who seemed bent on blood', admitted that he had acted wrongly but refused to acknowledge that he was 'the vilest of human beings'. King called him 'a damned villain', and they each got off three more shots, again missing each time. Fitzgerald ran out of ball and powder. They arranged to meet again next morning but, in the meantime, both were arrested for duelling.[35]

Four days later, Kingsborough sent Fitzgerald a note warning him that, 'If you ever presume to appear where I or any part of my family may happen to be, depend upon it the consequences will be fatal'. Mary Elizabeth was brought back to Mitchelstown Castle. The threat against Fitzgerald did not prevent him from travelling to Mitchelstown, where he stayed at the new hotel in King Square. He remained indoors during the day and only moved out after dark. Kingsborough was in Fermoy at a review of the militia and yeomanry when word reached him of Fitzgerald's presence in Mitchelstown. Kingsborough raced to the hotel to find that his quarry had left the town in the direction of Kilworth.

Accompanied by his son, Robert, and a former militia private named John Hartney, Kingsborough followed Fitzgerald to a hotel in Kilworth where he had taken lodgings. A waiter was sent up to his room with a message requesting him to come downstairs to discuss business. When Fitzgerald refused, Kingsborough and his allies charged up the stairs and broke open the bedroom door. During a scuffle between him and Colonel King, Lord Kingsborough shot Fitzgerald dead. Describing what happened to his family later that night, Kingsborough is supposed to have said; 'God, I don't know how I did it; but I most sincerely wish it had been by some other hand than mine.'

All three assailants were charged with murder. They were summoned to appear before the County Grand Jury, comprising the first commoners of the county, under the chairmanship of Viscount Boyle (later Earl of Shannon). The first Earl of Kingston died on 13 November 1797, a most timely exit as far as his son was concerned. On succeeding to the peerage, Robert now availed of his right to be tried by his peers in the Irish House of Lords. He was only the third to be tried for murder in the Irish Upper House in the eighteenth century; Lord Santry was tried and convicted in 1739; Lord Netterville was tried and acquitted in 1743. In the Colonel Fitzgerald murder case, no prosecution evidence was offered against the earl's second son, Colonel Robert King or John Hartney at the Assizes of April 1798, so both were acquitted.

The second Earl of Kingston's murder trial opened on 18 May 1798, in the House of Lords in Dublin. All the Lords of the Kingdom were summoned. Few peers were absent for the most spectacular trial in the history of the Irish Parliament. In total, two marquesses, 27 earls, fourteen viscounts, three archbishops, thirteen bishops and fourteen barons assembled in the House. For several it was their first time attending to their public duties in parliament, as many Irish peers were notoriously indifferent to parliamentary affairs.

Sir Charles Fortiscue, Ulster King-at-Arms, called the roll. The gathering then adjourned to the House of Commons which had more space to accommodate the proceedings. The procession was one of the last occasions of pageantry in the Irish House of Lords which, less than three years later, was abolished under the Act of Union. The peers walked two by two into the House of Commons, the Masters in Chancery and the robed judges of the courts of law led the way. Immediately before the Lords, walking in procession, were the minors of their order, not entitled to vote, and the eldest sons of the peers. The Lord Chancellor, bearing a white wand, sat in the speaker's chair. The temporal peers were ranged on his left and the spiritual peers on the right. The judges, dressed in their robes, occupied the table in the centre.[36]

The trial, which was described as 'by far the most impressive and majestic spectacle ever exhibited within those walls', got under way in the presence of a 'brilliant audience'. Peeresses and their daughters, Members of Parliament with their families and friends, filled every seat and waited in quiet anticipation of the events about to unfold.[37] After customary salutations and reverences, the King's commission appointing the Earl of Clare Lord High Steward was read aloud. Clare was Lord Chancellor of Ireland and the most powerful man in the land. The Grand Jury's indictment was read. Then the sergeant-at-arms proclaimed: 'Oyez. Oyez. Oyez. Constable of Dublin Castle bring forth Robert Earl of Kingston, your prisoners, to the bar, pursuant to the order of the House of Lords. God save the King.'

Ulster King-at-Arms, carrying the Earl of Kingston's armorial bearings, entered the chamber followed by the accused. Robert was 'clad in deep mourning' and he entered the House with his eyes fixed on the ground. He stood beside the King-at-Arms who held the armorial bearings at shoulder height. The most ominous sight at the trial was the Deputy Constable of Dublin Castle, who held an axe with an immense broad blade painted black to within two inches of its shining edge. He stood at Robert's left side. If the verdict was guilty, the axe would be turned towards Lord Kingston by his executioner, indicating at once his sentence and his fate. Robert knelt before his peers as Lord Clare set the scene:

> Robert Earl of Kingston, you are brought here to answer one of the most serious charges that can be made against any man – the murder of a fellow subject ... You are to be tried by the laws of a free country, framed for the protection, and the punishment of guilt alone; and it must be a great consolation to you, to reflect, that you are to receive a trial before the supreme judicature of the nation ... the benignity of your law has distinguished the crime of homicide into different classes. If it arose from accident, from inevitable necessity, or without malice, it does not fall within the crime of murder ...

Kingston replied 'not guilty' to the charge against him. In answer to the question, 'Culprit, how will your lordship be tried?' he replied, 'by God and my peers'. The sergeant-at-arms then proclaimed:

> Oyez. Oyez. Oyez. All manner of persons who will give evidence upon oath before our Sovereign Lord the King, against Robert Earl of Kingston, the prisoner at the bar, let them come forth, and they shall be heard, for he now stands at the bar upon his deliverance.[38]

No witnesses appeared for the prosecution. The defending counsel was the celebrated John Philpot Curran, who later defended prominent United Irishmen, including Theobald Wolfe Tone and Napper Tandy. His daughter, Sarah Curran, was the fiancée of the republican Robert Emmett (whom he refused to defend at his trial for high treason). Curran called witnesses on behalf of the Earl of Kingston. Finally, Lord Clare called every peer by name, beginning with the most junior baron, and asked him, 'Is Robert Earl of Kingston, guilty of the murder and felony whereof he stands indicted, or not guilty?' Each, in turn, stood, laid his hand upon his heart, and declared: 'Not guilty, upon my honour.' Having announced the judgment of innocence, Clare took the white staff in his hand. Breaking it in two, he declared that the commission was dissolved.[39]

How the unfortunate Mary Elizabeth felt about all this is unknown, but, conveniently, her family found a scapegoat in Mary Wollstonecraft, whom they criticised for having given her pupil such independence of mind. According to the popular version of her story, Mary Elizabeth spent the rest of her days married to a clergyman in Wales. It was even claimed that he knew nothing of her background. In fact, she married George Meares of Meares Court, an estate close to Lord Kingston's property in County Westmeath in the midlands, and by him she had four children.[40]

Mary's eldest sister, Margaret, was already the victim of an arranged, loveless marriage to Stephen, second Earl of Mount Cashell, of Moorepark, Kilworth, who owned 48,600 acres in County Antrim and another 12,300 acres in counties Cork and Tipperary. Margaret's parents had benefited from an Act of the Irish Parliament in 1777-'78, which allowed them exact a levy of £23,000 from their estates in Ireland. They now chose to apply £6,000 of that sum to 'the advancement and for the portion' of their daughter, Margaret.[41] Some years after her marriage at Mitchelstown in September 1791, she admitted that she was

> Guilty of numerous errors & none greater than that of marrying at

nineteen a man whose character was perfectly opposite to mine. Stephen Moore Earl of Mount Cashell was about one & twenty, a handsome man with gentle manners and the appearance of an easy temper. His education had been of the meanest sort: his understanding was uncultivated and his mind contracted ... To my shame I confess that I married him with the idea of governing him, the silliest project that ever entered a woman's mind.[42]

The Mount Cashells and a friend, Katherine Wilmot, toured the continent between 1801 and 1803. It was a tour made memorable because of encounters with an astonishing number of celebrated aristocrats, politicians, diplomats, scientists, actors and churchmen. In France, the ladies secured a rare invitation to a banquet in the Tuilleries as guests of the First Consul, Napoleon Bonaparte, and his wife Josephine. Katherine described how:

> After passing through various ante-chambers where there were bands of military music, we at length reach'd the room where Madame Bonaparte sat under a canopy blazing in Purple and diamonds. More than two hundred persons were assembled and Bonaparte walk'd about the room speaking politely to everybody. His countenance is delightful when animated by conversation, and the expression in the lower part of his Face pleasing to the greatest degree ... so charming a smile as his, I never scarcely beheld ... Lady Mount Cashell looking beautiful and dress'd in black crape and diamonds was handed in to dinner by the English Minister.[43]

This remarkable hospitality towards the Irish aristocracy was in marked contrast to the treatment of their English counterparts in France. After the Revolution, the Irish aristocracy was treated differently because it was considered to be in some way sympathetic towards the new French republic. This also indicates the extraordinary perception of the Ascendancy in mainland Europe and England where members were always regarded as Irish, and in Ireland where they were always seen as English Protestants. The Mount Cashells took every advantage of this and found themselves in the best of company while in Paris.[44]

From Paris they went to Rome where, on one of their first expeditions, they went to Frascati, the residence of Henry, Cardinal Duke of York, Pretender to the throne of England. They were presented to the Cardinal, who insisted on being called 'Your Royal Highness' and conducted his court with as much regal etiquette as possible. At dinner they were the only women present – Lady Mount Cashell being seated to one side of the cardinal and Katherine Wilmot on the other. Afterwards, Margaret was presented with a medal bearing a likeness of the cardinal on one side and 'Henry IX' engraved on the other.[45]

During their stay in Rome the Mount Cashells attended Holy Week ceremonies in the Vatican, where the audience included the two Kings of Sardinia. One of these, Charles Emanuel IV, had abdicated from the throne in 1802 so that he could become a Jesuit priest. His brother, Victor Emanuel I, then ruled Sardinia until 1821 when he also abdicated in favour of another brother.[46] But the highlight of the visit to Rome took place when, in the company of Princess Borghese, Margaret and Katherine met Pope Pius VII and his entourage in the Vatican Gardens, on Good Friday, 1803.

> The Princess, as we approach'd his holiness, stepp'd forward and throwing herself on her knees, kiss'd his toe, Lady Mount Cashell and I advanced and were half bent to perform the like operation, when, I am grieved to say, the Pope by a motion of his hand dispensed us from this tribute, which we would most gladly have paid, and sincerely disappointed at the compliment, we walk'd with him towards a Pavilion into which he walk'd first, tho' this prerogative he made appear as much the effect of accident as possible.

In the course of an hour-long conversation in Italian, Margaret mentioned to the Pope that she would like to visit a Capuchin convent. Much to her delight, a letter granting such permission from the Pope arrived the next morning. This was a very unusual honour for a woman, especially a Protestant, and it suggests that Margaret had made a strong impression on His Holiness. Before parting, said Katherine, 'the Pope very gallantly pull'd a hyacinth and gave it to Lady Mount Cashell, and desired one of the cardinals to follow his example, which he did by gathering me a bouquet and presenting it likewise in a very gallant manner'.[47]

On revisiting Rome with her husband early in 1804, Margaret fell in love with George William Tighe, a barrister and the owner of a small estate in County Westmeath. In 1805 she travelled with Lord Mount Cashell and their children to Germany. There they parted company never to meet again. Margaret went back to Tighe at Pisa in Italy and eventually divorced Mount Cashell. Her annuity of £360 from the Mitchelstown estate, together with an allowance of £1,000 a year from her former husband and Tighe's annual income of £482 from his Irish lands gave them a comfortable standard of living. It was with Tighe that Margaret found the happiness which had eluded her for so long. By this second marriage she had two daughters, Nerina and Laurette, whose descendants still live today at San Marcello.[48]

Percy Bysshe Shelley and his wife, Mary – the daughter of Mary Wollstonecraft – were among Margaret's closest friends in Italy, where she also knew Lord Byron. Shelley and Margaret enjoyed each other's company, talking of politics and literature. It was Margaret who had to cope with the immediate aftermath of Shelley's drowning off Leghorn and help his widow get over her great loss.

By this time, Margaret had become a writer of popular

childrens books. She chose the pseudonym Mrs Mason – 'a woman of tenderness and discernment' – from one of Mary Wollstonecraft's novels. Her *Advice to Young Mothers on the Physical Education of Children* and *Stories of Old Daniel* each ran to over fifteen editions. Her other publications, particularly stories for children, were popular in several countries. Many of her writings, like those of her governess, were ahead of their time because of her views on education and women's rights. Her treatises on post-natal care are also considered far-sighted.

Shelley was greatly impressed by Margaret's beauty and intelligence. She was, he said, 'a superior and accomplished woman, and a great resource to me'. In March 1820, Margaret was the inspiration for his acclaimed poem, *The Sensitive Plant*, which was set in her garden, and in which she was 'A Lady, the wonder of her kind, whose form was upborne by a lovely mind'. She died at Pisa and was buried in the Protestant cemetery at Leghorn. The monument over her last resting place reads, 'Here lie the remains of Margaret Jane Countess of Mount Cashell – born AD 1773 – died 29 January AD 1835'.

But it is in Shelley's lengthy poem featuring a garden in bloom, tended by a beautiful Lady, that we find Margaret's true epitaph.

> That garden sweet, that lady fair,
> And all sweet shapes and odours there,
> In truth have never passed away:
> 'Tis we, 'tis ours, are changed! not they.
> For love, and beauty, and delight,
> There is no death nor change; their might
> Exceeds our organs, which endure.[49]

4

Rebellion

During the trial of Robert, second Earl of Kingston in May 1798, the United Irishmen planned a spectacular coup d'etat that would have removed virtually the entire ruling class in one master stroke. On the day before the trial, the National Directory of the United Irishmen met in secret to reconsider their plans for the rebellion that was about to break out around the country.

The original objective was to take Dublin Castle and military barracks in the capital in a series of surprise attacks. But the Kingston trial prompted the rebel leaders to consider an assault on the House of Lords while the high and mighty of the land were in solemn assembly. The plan was breathtakingly daring and, were it to be attempted, there was every chance of capturing most of the government, including the Viceroy, the Lord Chancellor and the Chief Secretary of Ireland. Numerous leading peers, members of parliament and their families, all in their best finery, could also be taken hostage and thus the whole Irish administration would be thrown into chaos.

Advocates of the plan were convinced that the government could be seized almost without a shot being fired. Its opponents warned that failure would cause thousands of casualties or, at best, end in disaster. The scheme was rejected by just one vote in a secret ballot of the Directory.[1]

Remarkably, Kingston's eldest daughter, Margaret, openly

described herself as a 'United Irishwoman and a Republican', who sympathised with the aims of the rebellion, thus becoming an enemy of the very class upon whom her father's fate depended. She was a friend of Lord Edward FitzGerald, military chief of the United Irishmen, who had occasionally stayed with the Mount Cashells at Moorepark. Lord Edward was arrested in May just as the rebellion was about to begin and was imprisoned in London. He died on 4 June from wounds sustained during his arrest. Lady Mount Cashell was one of the first to be informed that he was mortally wounded. She at once dispatched a servant to order his staff to wait until the following morning to tell his wife the tragic news.[2]

The rebellion, which began on 23 May, was one of the bloodiest and most sectarian episodes in Irish history. The rebels regarded all Protestants as Orangemen, unless they could prove otherwise. The loyalists labelled all Catholics as rebels. In many parts of the country, innocent and guilty alike were raped, tortured and killed. Frequently, the yeomanry (four-fifths of them Irish) flogged people until organs and bones were exposed. Both loyalists and republicans became victims of the unparalleled horrors inflicted on the population. At Clogheen, County Tipperary, ten miles from Mitchelstown, General Sir John Moore, who was remembered as one of the more honourable and humane military commanders, arrived there one morning at about ten o'clock to observe a routine flogging session. It was a hot day and savage floggings were being carried out on the orders of the County High Sheriff:

> The rule was to flog each person 'til he told the truth and gave the names of other rebels. These were then sent for and underwent a similar operation ... The number flogged was considerable. It lasted all afternoon. That some were innocent is I fear equally certain.[3]

Evidence of guilt was not an issue for the North Cork Militia, under the command of Colonel George King, Viscount Kingsborough. The North Corks were founded in Mitchelstown in 1793 by his father, who had offered each of the first 244 volunteers a small farm in Munster at a reasonable rent provided that they continued to reside there after service in the militia had ended. By 1798, George had 25 officers, sixteen drummers, twelve fifers and 546 rank-and-file militiamen in his command. Their barbarism in 1798 made the North Corks one of the most notorious units ever to terrorise Ireland.

The militia's special brand of punishment was the pitch-cap. This dreadful form of torture was devised in response to the United Irishmen's fashion of cropping their hair short like the French republicans. The North Corks' victims had molten caps of tar jammed onto their heads. As the frantic victim tried to tear it off, burning tar fell into his eyes and onto his face. It could be removed only with the loss of a considerable amount of hair and scalp. Not surprisingly, many died in the process. The pitch-cap was promoted by George, an accomplished torturer who seemed to derive perverse pleasure from its horrific effects. The English historian, Francis Plowden, said:

> As a gentleman of respectability was passing near the old Custom House [Dublin], in the afternoon of Whit-Sunday, 1798, two spectacles of horror covered with pitch and gore, running as if they were blind through the streets arrested his attention. They were closely followed out of the old Custom House by Lord Kingsborough, Mr John Beresford and an officer in uniform. They were pointing and laughing immoderately at these tortured fugitives, one of them John Flemming, a ferry-boatman, and the other Francis Gough, a coachman. They had been unmercifully flogged to extract confession, but, having none to make, melted pitch was poured over their heads and then feathered. Flemming's right ear was cut off, both were sent off without clothes. Lord

> Kingsborough superintended the flogging, and almost at every lash asked them how they liked it.[4]

The North Corks' colonel-commandant has been described as a flamboyant, tall, strongly-built man of imperious and insanely cruel temper who cut a striking military appearance. At least some of what emerged about him after the rebellion suggests that he favoured conciliation towards Catholics but not towards anyone who took arms against the King.

George was still in Dublin after attending his father's trial when the rebellion broke out. Not realising that Wexford town had fallen to the rebels, he hired a small boat at Arklow and sailed down the coast with the intention of rejoining his regiment there. Unwittingly, on 3 June 1798, he sailed right into the hands of the rebels, thus presenting them with their most important prisoner of the rebellion. They had in their hands a man whose reputation for brutality was more than sufficient to warrant his execution. But the rebel leaders chose instead to keep him under tight protection in an inn called 'The Cape of Good Hope' as a bargaining tool. He was held there with an old family friend and relative, Mrs Ogle, the wife of George Ogle. Viscount Kingsborough greatly feared for his life and was convinced that the rebels would murder him.[5]

On three occasions a mob gathered outside George's place of confinement looking to have him strung up. In one incident, Captain Thomas Dixon and his wife led the mob who waved a pitch-cap on a pike and shouted for vengeance. There was a distraction which gave some of the rebels the chance to whisk George off to the safety of a prison hulk in the harbour where he remained until the situation calmed.

All prisoners were, in effect, hostages. In an attempt to save himself and his compatriots, George convinced the rebel leaders that the people should again take the United Irishmen's oath. This, he hoped, would ensure that they would obey their leaders' orders not to harm their captives. As part of the negotiations, George signed a letter addressed to the Viceroy in the name of the captives. It stated that they had been properly treated as prisoners of war. They hoped that the government's prisoners had been treated similarly; otherwise they faced 'inevitable destruction'. Lieutenant Bourke of the North Corks was dispatched with the letter for delivery to the Government, but Captain Dixon had him intercepted and forced to return, thus heightening the danger facing the hostages.

The strain on the prisoners in Wexford was unbearable. Hysteria mounted as the rebel cause waned. Despair spread among the captives when another mob assembled to kill them, but they were saved by the timely arrival of two priests. By 19 June, waves of refugees were descending on Wexford with accounts of defeat by the government forces. Puppet courts were organised by Dixon who appointed himself as prosecutor. These proceeded to sentence to death anyone thought to be a loyalist. Within hours, 97 prisoners lay dead on the wooden bridge across Wexford estuary. Only the intervention of a priest, just returned from the countryside, prevented many more from being slaughtered.[6]

With cannon fire thundering in the distance, the rebels in charge of the town were as fearful as their prisoners. A plan was worked out whereby George would accept the surrender of Wexford in the name of the King. Without authority from the government he agreed that the town and its inhabitants, except murderers, would be protected. George put on his militia uniform and went out to accept Captain Keogh's sword of surrender. Word had to be sent to the English forces that Kingsborough had accepted Wexford's conditional surrender. In his urgent dispatch, George stated that 'the people here have treated their prisoners with great humanity and I believe will return to their allegiance with great satisfaction'.[7] Lieutenant-General Lake refused to accept the terms of surrender. The government, he declared, 'cannot attend to any terms offered by rebels in arms against their sovereign'. Lake's response was not broadcast in Wexford until after the surrender. Had it been known earlier, it is doubtful that the hostages' lives would have been spared or that the rebels would have surrendered without fierce resistance.

The prisoners again feared for their lives pending the arrival of government forces. The rebels who were still retreating towards Wexford vowed vengeance on all Protestants. Kingsborough and Keogh went to the Catholic Bishop Caulfeild and persuaded him to convince the rebels that their best course of action would be to flee the town. Another mob surrounded George's house, but the yeomanry and militia arrived to save the loyalists from a massacre. Wild scenes of jubilation followed as the prisoners were released.

Dressed in his scarlet regimentals and wearing Keogh's sword, George emerged to welcome the English, under General Moore, who described his work that day as 'one of the most pleasing services that could fall to the lot of an officer'. However, General Lake was furious that there had even been a hint of conditional surrender and refused to accept its terms on the grounds that the Colonel of the North Cork Militia had no authority to sign such an agreement.[8] In London, news of Wexford's surrender was received with tremendous relief. Queen Charlotte went to Helena, Lady Kingsborough: 'I have ventured to call upon your ladyship to tell you that Lord Kingsborough is safe. I think the news we have had at the castle [Windsor] may be earlier than what your ladyship may have received.'[9]

The Militia, still under Kingsborough's command, participated in many atrocities during the post-rebellion period.

At Carrick-on-Suir in July, he 'flogged a man and during the punishment threw salt on his back'. An English officer who witnessed the flogging described the conduct of the Militia as disgraceful. George's savage behaviour made him notorious in his lifetime and, two centuries later, his memory was more reviled in Mitchelstown than that of any other figure in its long history.[10] George was incensed at General Lake's rejection of his surrender terms for Wexford. He took a staunch anti-government line over the affair and resigned from the North Cork Militia in November 1798.

For reasons polite or political, this horrifying chapter in George's life story has been glossed over by most of his biographers. There has been a tendency instead to concentrate on his activities after his father died, aged 45, on 17 April 1799. Robert was buried in the family vault beneath the chapel in Kingston College. Many of his achievements endured long after him, but some were obliterated by his eldest son who quickly strove to enhance his own wealth and prestige. In his lifetime, Robert had added £19,000 in debts to the estate, and left another £8,000 chargeable in legacies, mostly in favour of his younger children. These were added to the first earl's enormous debts of £71,981 and £20,000 in legacies charged against the Rockingham estates.

To complicate matters for George, his mother held absolute ownership of Mitchelstown during her lifetime. Therefore, he could get an income only from his Sligo estates, which were a small part of the family's properties. By his father's will, Rockingham passed to George's brother, Robert, and this left the new earl with a mere fraction of what it would have taken to live up to his self-proclaimed status as 'the principal man of County Cork'. George and his mother had a very strained relationship. He was frustrated at having to wait for his inheritance, while she had good reason to keep him at arm's length. He lived away from Mitchelstown until her death which, as far as he was concerned, could not come soon enough.[11]

Another great battle for George was the Act of Union, which abolished the Irish parliament and transferred control of the island to London. It was a disastrous decision for many Irish peers who had enjoyed the life and privilege of the College Green assembly, and especially the gaiety of Dublin whenever parliament was in session. After failing to get an Act of Union through in 1799, the government spent £1.25 million buying borough seats to ensure that when the Act went before parliament for the second time, it would not fail. Those who voted for it were promised generous rewards in money, patronage and titles. However, George would not be bribed, fearing that the abolition of the Irish Parliament would have serious consequences, not least for himself as a peer. Like his father before him, George became a vociferous opponent of the Act, especially after the newly-appointed Lord Lieutenant alienated several peers by failing to communicate with them, even on convivial business. This failure to keep influential gentlemen on side cost the government valuable votes in the Lords and Commons.

In the final vote in the House of Lords, only nineteen Irish peers voted against 'The Act for the Union of Great Britain and Ireland'. Among them was George, third Earl of Kingston, and his brother-in-law Stephen, second Earl of Mount Cashell. Their 12,750-word protest, signed by two fellow peers, was entered in the Lords' Journal. It foretold much of what would come to pass in Ireland during the next century:

> We have endeavoured to interpose our votes and, failing, we transmit our names to after times in solemn protest on behalf of the Parliamentary Constitution of this realm, the liberty it secured, the

trade which it protects, the Connection which it preserved, and the Constitution which it supplied and fortified. This we feel ourselves called upon to do in support of our Characters, our honour, and whatsoever is left to us worthy to be transmitted to posterity.[12]

The Act of Union came into law on 1 January 1801, marking a major watershed in Irish history. George was angry over the resultant loss of his parliamentary seat and, for the next twenty years, canvassed for a United Kingdom peerage, and thereby a seat in the House of Lords. He also went to considerable effort to obtain a royal recognition of the title of White Knight for himself. Favours were called in and friends of high rank were petitioned. His godfather, George III, had become insane in 1811. Kingston's close friend, the Prince Regent, who became George IV on his father's death in 1820, was also unable to help because, as the Prime Minister, Sir Robert Peel, explained, the King could not allow the title to descend through the female line. 'One of the difficulties in the way is the formal recognition by the Crown of a new species of Distinction, which it appears to me can neither be considered as a surname, or known name or Title of Dignity, nor a name of Office,' he said.

Kingston had to accept defeat. He told Sir Robert Peel that the titles of White Knight, Knight of Kerry and Knight of Glin would remain attached to their respective families 'as long as tradition exists in Ireland'. He advised the Prime Minister on 12 May 1823 that if the only objection to giving those titles hereditary status was his own claim, then he withdrew it so that the the Knight of Glin and the Knight of Kerry might obtain recognition. 'I shall be satisfied with the recognition of the people, & that nothing can deprive me of,' he said defiantly. 'I am proud of the title & of the affection of the lower classes of the people to it.'[13]

George made powerful enemies because of his stance

against the Union. He must have known that it would cost him dearly in terms of advancement and political support. Finally, after more letters and petitions, he was created Baron Kingston of Mitchelstown, County Cork, in the Peerage of the United Kingdom, on 17 July 1821. This title at least gave George and his successors the right to sit in the House of Lords. Meanwhile, his younger brother, Robert, had been more successful in obtaining titles. He was created Baron Erris of Boyle, in the Peerage of Ireland, on 29 December 1800, as reward for his vote in support of the Union. On 22 May 1806, he was further elevated as Viscount Lorton of Boyle. Robert joined his older brother in the House of Lords when he became a representative peer for Ireland in 1822.[14]

In the years after the Union, George spent much time between 35 Alpha Road in London, his estate at Myross Wood in Leap, west Cork, and at his brother-in-law's Moorepark.[15] Denied ownership of Mitchelstown, he unsuccessfully pursued the matter in the courts in 1818 when he accused his mother of wrecking his inheritance through mismanagement of the estate. She, on the other hand, was determined to prevent him from getting hold of Mitchelstown for as long as possible. The legal costs of all this bickering aggravated the estate's debt. Among those hired by George to prove his case was Richard Hartland, who had been involved in the original planting of the demesne. He alleged that 'many acres of the plantation had been destroyed'. Depositions were also sworn alleging that two brothers, William and Thomas Disney, had failed to collect rents after being employed to do so in March 1802.

But the matter was not as clear-cut as George had led himself to believe. Ireland was experiencing an economic depression resulting from the Napoleonic Wars and the income of the estate had suffered as a consequence. Thomas

Disney, the estate agent, said that in the year ended September 1816, he had received £22,461-11s-8d in rents and the income for the following year came to £23,594-8s-1d. From this he had had to deduct enormous charges and encumbrances. These included £4,000 a year for the Earl of Kingston, £1,200 for his brother, Robert, and £600 each for Henry, John, Richard and James King, Lady Caroline Morrison and Lady Jane de Ricci. When all the charges payable to Lady Kingston's children and relatives, and £1,250 per annum payable to the trustees of Kingston College were added up, the outgoings of the estate came to £12,625-1s-8d. This did not include Lady Kingston's annual expenditure of £4,000, or other costs such as agents' fees which amounted to £1,000 and annual legal expenses of £500. The total expenditure came to £18,125-1s-8d a year.

Disney estimated that the annual income of the estate should have been about £27,000, but as a result of the inability of many tenants to pay rents, the actual income was only £23,594 in 1815, £22,461-11s-8d in 1816 and £23,594-8s-1d in 1817. He found that the rental was decreasing. He advised Lady Kingston to reduce the payments to herself and her children. Caroline, he said, 'readily consented to the reduction of her own income, sooner than reducing the interest payable to her younger children, which she had the power to decrease from six to five per cent'.[16]

Despite her son's antagonism, for which the dowager countess was partly to blame, she was known as 'The Good Countess' among her tenants because of her charitable works. This contrasts with the image of her presented in Mary Wollstonecraft's letters.[17] She was also a good employer. The number working inside the demesne walls is indicated by the garden accounts book from this period. In October 1809, there were 99 men and boys employed in the gardens and nursery. By the following April, seasonal factors had pushed the number up to 154. As many as ten boys at a time brought food from the gardens to the kitchens.[18] Outside the walls, 400,000 mulberry trees were planted at Brigown, for a silk industry run by the British, Irish and Colonial Silk Company, in which Caroline held an interest. The venture was intended to capitalise on the absence of silk imports from France (caused by the war) which had caused a considerable increase in the price of the material. Nurserymen were brought from England to manage the plantation – the biggest of its kind in these islands. Some time after 1827, the enterprise became unprofitable and was abandoned. Mulberry Lane, on the eastern side of town, was laid out in a row of cottages for the nurserymen and labourers of the plantation.[19]

Generally, tenants occupied their houses from year to year and had no security of tenure. However, tenants with life-leases were in a different situation. Indentures between the Kingstons and their tenants were very detailed and complicated documents of about 4,000 words. It is not known how many held this valuable form of tenancy, but most tenants occupied their holdings from year to year. A few indentures bearing Caroline's signature have survived. These set out what was expected of a tenant and the penalties to be imposed for a breach of the agreement.

Typical of most indentures was that issued to John Power, a farmer at Glenatlucky, on 4 April 1818. Power held 7 acres, 3 roods and 19 perches on a lease of 21 years, or for the lives of Robert Hoops, aged 13, or Darby Sullivan, aged about ten years; whichever was the longest. His annual rent was fixed at £1 per acre, or £7-17s-4d. Power could not sub-let any land without permission from the dowager countess, subject to a penalty of £15-14s, payable annually. However, he was permitted under the indenture to sub-let

Rebellion

up to two acres to his labourers.

Caroline retained all manorial rights, including 'all manner of Wild Fowl, and every sort of game, and other Royalties ...' Power had to do suit and service to the Courts Leet and Courts Baron of the Manor of Mitchelstown and had to pay the Seneschal of the Manor 'his usual and accustomed Fees and Perquisites'. She had exclusive hawking, fishing, hunting and mining rights over the property. Power had to have all his wheat, barley, oats, peas, malt and other grains ground in the Manor Mill, under penalty of ten shillings for every barrel ground elsewhere.

Special emphasis was placed on trees. The Kingstons reserved ownership of 'every sort of Tree, now standing and growing, or hereafter to stand or grow'. While the dowager countess could have a tree cut at will, tenants would be fined £5 for each one damaged, cut or felled on their holdings. All buildings, fences, hedges, drains, etc, were to be kept in good repair. Tenants were obliged to build specified lengths of ditches and fences, subject to penalties. Both landlord and tenant undertook to plant and sow their proportion of fences and ditches 'with White Thorn or Crab Quicks, at the usual Distance, as also with Oak, Ash or Elm, Layers or Plants, at ten feet Distance one from the other, and also with Furze at the back of such Ditches'.

Finally, the Kingstons and their agents had the right to walk the farm to ensure that Power kept his part of the agreement. They could also take whatever measures were necessary to collect the fines or rents. But if he proved to be a diligent tenant who paid his rent on time, she guaranteed that he 'shall and may peaceably and quietly live, hold, occupy, possess and enjoy all and singular the Premises hereby demised ...'[20]

Mitchelstown was 'a very wretched village' until it was

greatly improved and enlarged by the second Earl of Kingston, said Rev Horatio Townsend, who visited the locality in or about 1809. It was now, he remarked,

> a handsome and populous town ... Everything, however, has been done by its present possessor, the Dowager Lady Kingston, which the happy union of charity and affluence could suggest, to enlighten the minds of the rising generation, and ameliorate the condition of the people.

'Liberal and munificent expenditures' by Caroline included the building of an orphan school where twelve girls were lodged and taught reading, writing, arithmetic and Christian instruction. 'They make their own clothes, spin flax and wool, knit stockings, work muslin, and keep the house clean,' he said. Poor girls went to a spinning school, also established by Caroline, where they learned to make shoes and spin flax. Another school in the town taught between twelve and fourteen girls how to weave linen. A Sunday school, which was extended to Wednesdays and Fridays, had 200 pupils. Townsend stated:

> Establishments of this kind evince a degree of discernment as well as liberality above all praise. They are happily calculated to produce, what is so much wanted by the lower orders in this country ... They exhibit an example worthy the imitation of the great, and of more real value and importance than the expenditure of thousands in works of show and splendour.

The Good Countess paid a doctor £60 a year to visit the sick poor. On her authority, he could order medicines from local apothecaries, and oatmeal and wine from the castle's housekeeper. One shop offered basic provisions such as tea, soap, candles, salt, oatmeal and sugar at wholesale prices and the needy were given purchase coupons. Another shop sold blankets, sheets and clothes for men, women and children, also at wholesale prices.[21]

Caroline funded the town library, which was 'well stocked with select books, religious and entertaining.' These included the poetical works of John Milton whose *Lycidas* was composed as a lament for his friend, Edward King, who was drowned on a voyage between England and Ireland in 1638, at the age of 25. Library membership cost one shilling a quarter, which was not cheap and certainly beyond the reach of the very poor, most of whom could not read anyway.[22]

Caroline financed the building of a new parish church, Saint George's, at the southern end of George Street. In its year of consecration, 1805, Mitchelstown had 71 Protestant families.[23] Townsend described their church as 'a new, elegant and expensive building' which owed everything to Lady Kingston's charity, except for £400 donated by the yeomanry, parishioners, the rector and the Kingston estate agent. Caroline donated a service of silver plate for the communion table.[24] She also provided twelve acres and a donation for a new rectory at Brigown, which was completed in 1807.[25]

In his *Statistical Survey*, Townsend noted religious tension as a result of these developments. The parish priest, Fr John Nugent, ordered the Catholic children out of the Sunday School when it was moved from the market house to Saint George's Church. Catholic doctrine prevented them from entering a Protestant church under pain of excommunication. The school was returned to the old market house, but the ban on Catholic children attending it was maintained. A similar boycott was placed on the weaving and spinning school because the Protestant mistress read prayers to the children. An offer from the rector to the parish priest to compose prayers acceptable to both faiths was rejected.[26]

Such religious bigotry is understandable in the context of

the times. In this instance, however, it is difficult not to conclude that the hand of the Good Countess was being bitten by those she fed. After all, her late husband had permitted the erection of 'a handsome Roman Catholic chapel' at Thomas Street and several other chapels on the estate. He had donated land and generous sums to build Catholic churches. The boycott sparked a major controversy after Townsend published the details in the *Statistical Survey*, and the Catholic Bishop of Cork, Cloyne and Ross, Dr William Coppinger, took exception to many of Townend's comments.[27]

The Catholic clergy claimed that agents of Lady Kingston were trying to convert the children attending the spinning and weaving schools, but she vehemently denied this in a declaration issued on Monday, 13 November 1809:

> Finding that all her endeavours to give the people habits of INDUSTRY, and consequently to promote their comforts and happiness, are thus rendered fruitless; and being convinced, that mere ALMS-GIVING tends only to promote Idleness and Sloth; she feels herself under the painful necessity of taking this method to inform the People, that it is now her absolute determination immediately to withdraw all Pecuniary DONATIONS from the Roman Catholics of this Parish.

Caroline declared that she had no intention of 'making the least attempt to alter their Religious Opinions'. Neither was she trying to undermine the Catholics' respect for their clergy. But in her final salvo, the dowager countess warned that she was 'determined to Prosecute according to Law, any person who attempts to withdraw any of the Apprentices from her Schools'.[28] Caroline was closely related to Dr James Butler, Catholic Archbishop of Cashel, who had been embroiled in previous controversies in Mitchelstown. Butler regularly visited the castle, where he openly remonstrated with her about all

Rebellion

that was going on with the Catholic children. Coppinger regarded her endeavours as 'wholesale aggression', and believed that 'assaults made upon the religion of our poor children in Mitchelstown' went back to 1789. He alleged that up to 500 children at a time had been lured 'to receive instructions from anti-Catholic teachers in the Protestant church, while at the same time, they were supplied with religious tracts in direct hostility to their own Catechism'.

A child sent to Mitchelstown on an errand was picked up and taken to a house where her hair was cut, new clothes put on her, and she was placed in Lady Kingston's orphanage. Her mother's protests brought about the child's return. Coppinger said that the circumstances of her case were communicated to Robert, Earl of Kingston, who 'sent for the parish priest; interrogated him minutely; and when he ascertained the particulars, expressed his dissatisfaction in the warmest language at the aggressive process, in presence of Mr G. Ogle'. Coppinger said that these conflicts declined during Lady Kingston's absences in England, but problems intensified whenever she was due to return. He added: 'the late Earl of Kingston reprobated aloud this degrading fellowship ... I now most gratefully acknowledge the princely largesses of her deceased Lord.'[29]

Arrogance was Caroline's greatest character flaw. She felt no obligation to consider those around her, regardless of the consequences. She was involved in another confrontation, also in November 1809, with Emily, Lady Cahir, to whom she refused admission, with a party of guests, to the Kingston's picturesque hunting retreat known as 'Mountain Lodge' on the Galtees. Lord and Lady Cahir had invited the Duke of Leinster and his party, then on a Vice Regal tour of Ireland, to a fete at Lady Kingston's hunting lodge apparently without first obtaining her permission. Caroline took exception to her property being used to entertain the Viceroy, especially as she was not hosting the event. When Lady Cahir's party arrived in grand procession at the lodge, they found its gates locked before them. The walls were lined with a strong guard ready to repel any trespassers. 'Lady Cahir demands admittance and is refused,' said an observer. 'She supplicates in vain and then resorts to that elegant style of language which she displayed some years ago at a Parisian theatre – the party stood aghast!'

A drizzle fell so the Viceroy and his companions retreated to 'the humble cabin of an emaciated peasant', and there, to amuse themselves, they shared their rich food and silver cutlery with the poor man's family. The gentlemen and their ladies were tired, wet, disappointed and humbled on their return to Cahir. They did not get over their embarrassment easily. Emily resolved never again to be outdone by the Kingstons and the rebuff inspired her to build a beautiful Swiss cottage in Cahir Park. Thanks to Lady Kingston, the Cahirs created one of the finest houses of its kind in Ireland. In later years, Lord Cahir used the 'cottage ornée' as a *boite d'amour*, while his wife turned it into a retreat for entertaining her guests.[30]

Rivalry and confrontation were nothing new to the Kingstons. Caroline's sons, George and Robert Edward, were bitter rivals and competition between them was intense. This may explain, in part, why they spent such vast sums on their parks and houses. Robert Edward, who became first Viscount Lorton, spent £400,000 developing those parts of the Rockingham estates which his father had left him. He commissioned John Nash to build a splendid mansion, Rockingham, overlooking Lough Key. In the early 1820s, a third storey was added when Lorton tried to compete with his brother's new mansion at Mitchelstown. Robert Edward sold the family's town house in Dublin in 1829. During the Great Famine of the 1840s, he spent, according to himself, £20,000 on relief measures. He also had to pay several charges on the estate, including the £80 annuity to Arthur Young.[31]

Lorton died at Rockingham on 19 November 1854. 'No man ever possessed in a higher degree the elements of true greatness and elevation than his lordship,' said one obituary. Thousands attended his burial at four o'clock in the morning of 25 November in the family vault at Boyle Abbey – 'it being long the custom of this family to bury at night.' He was probably the last of the Kings buried at such an unearthly hour.[32]

Unlike George, who caused her endless anguish, Caroline had reason to be pleased with the progress of her other sons, all of whom achieved high-ranking positions in the military, navy, and the church. Robert Edward had taken control of the Roscommon Militia and was promoted to the rank of general. But the most distinguished soldier produced by the family was her fourth son, Lieutenant General Sir Henry King, KCB. Born on 4 July 1776, just after his parents had reached their majorities and obtained ownership of Mitchelstown, he entered the army in 1794. In August 1799, during the Napoleonic Wars, he sailed with Abercromby's expedition to Holland and was severely wounded in both legs. In 1806, he was captured by the Dutch. After his release, in a prisoner exchange, he re-entered the battlefields of Holland but ill-health forced him to return to England. In 1814 he was promoted to colonel, becoming a Major-General in 1825 and Lieutenant-General in 1838. He was made a Companion of the Bath in 1815 and advanced to a Knight Commander of the Bath in 1835. He was a Conservative MP for Sligo from 1822 to 1830. In 1817 he was appointed Groom of the Bedchamber to the Prince Regent. He held that office until 1830, when he was dismissed by George IV, who was displeased at certain votes by him in the House of Commons.[33]

The fifth son, Richard Fitzgerald King, fought in the Napoleonic Wars before taking Holy Orders. He was Vicar of Great Chesterford and rector of Little Chesterford in Essex. He died on 22 September 1856, having outlived all his brothers.

The next son, Rear-Admiral James William King, was born in Mitchelstown in 1786. He joined the navy at the age of eleven. As his career progressed, he moved rapidly up the ranks while serving at various locations in the English Channel, the West Indies and the North Sea. As a newly-promoted colonel in 1814, James William was part of the escort for the return of Louis XVIII to France following Napoleon's defeat and abdication. James William served under the Duke of Clarence, afterwards William IV, during the visits of the King of Prussia and the Emperor of Russia to England. Caroline, the Prince Regent's wife and future Queen, presented Admiral King with a silver loving-cup as a token of thanks for having escorted her to England. In 1815, James William married Caroline, daughter of the Most Rev Euseby Cleaver, Archbishop of Dublin.[34]

John King, the sixth son, became famous for his affair with the Duchess of Wurttemberg, in Austria, where he publicly demonstrated the King men's talent for seduction. He was Secretary to the Elector of Wurttemberg, and the Duchess was George IV's sister. The Prussian traveller, Prince Puckler-Muskau, recalled having known John King in Vienna. 'He was a remarkably handsome man, and celebrated for his bonnes fortunes,' said the Prince. King was the 'avowed lover' of the Duchess:

> whom he treated with so little ceremony, that once when he invited me to breakfast at the hotel where they were living, I found the Duchess alone, and he came into the room some time after, in dressing gown and slippers, out of his or their chamber.[35]

Apart from Margaret and Mary Elizabeth, little is known about the daughters of Caroline and Robert. Lady Jane Diana King married General John Robert Augustus de Ricci, and spent most of her married life in Florence. In 1837, she left her husband. Her son, Herman Robert de Ricci, frequently visited Mitchelstown in the 1860s and played a critical role later in the business affairs of the estate.[36]

Caroline, 'The Good Countess', was not Mary Wollstonecraft's ideal woman but her contribution to Mitchelstown was impressive. Much of what she built on the estate is proof of her determination and single-mindedness. But many of her achievements might not have been attained if George had accepted her offer of the castle and demesne after the second earl's death in 1799. His explanation was that Caroline could not afford to part with the place and he could not afford to keep it. He later changed his mind and asked for the property, but was refused it. That, said William Roper, Caroline's agent and rent collector, sparked 'a great deal of harshness and acrimony' between them. Roper stated that her behaviour towards her son was 'calculated to wound feelings and irritate [his] mind'.[37]

Caroline, it seems, was determined after all to ensure that in her lifetime neither the property nor its tenants should fall prey to George's volatile temperament and extravagant spending. On 13 January 1823, she died in London. She was buried in Putney Cemetery. Her death left the way open for George to realise his life-long ambition, though at the age of 52 he had little time to lose if he was to realise his grandiose dreams for the family seat at Mitchelstown. His popular nickname, 'Big George', aptly described both his physical stature and his ambition. As third earl he indulged in the pursuit of folly to a degree unsurpassed even in a class notoriously prone to it.[38]

5

Georgian Madness

Within days of his mother's death, Big George met the architect brothers James and George Richard Pain. 'Build me a castle,' he ordered. 'I am no judge of architecture; but it must be larger than any other house in Ireland, and have an entrance tower to be named the White Knight's Tower. No delay! It is time for me to enjoy.' With enormous funds at their disposal, the brothers set about designing a gigantic pile for Big George, whose father's 50-year-old mansion was torn down to make way for it. The remnants of the old White Knight's Castle were levelled also as part of the site clearance.[1]

The Pain brothers had trained in London under Wyatt, the architect who reconstructed Windsor Castle. Some of their ideas for Mitchelstown came from Windsor. They also studied under the celebrated architect John Nash, who sent them to Ireland to supervise the building of Lough Cutra Castle for Lord Gort. The Pains started their own practice, and soon earned reputations as the leading architects in Ireland. Following Mitchelstown, their works included Dromoland Castle for Sir Edward O'Brien, Elm Park for Lord Clarina, Limerick and Cork prisons, and several churches, Protestant and Catholic. James Pain was also a distinguished Freemason and this is how he may have got to know the Earl of Kingston, who was Grand Master of Ireland.[2]

Brick for Mitchelstown Castle was fired in the demesne

brickfield; limestone was cut from local quarries, some as far away as Grange near Fermoy, and carted to the building. Some of the marble for the mantelpieces came from a quarry at Mulberry Lane. The best timbers from the Baltic and India were imported through Youghal and Dungarvan and transported by road and boat along the Blackwater. The fine set of oak doors for the state apartments cost the then enormous sum of £900.

It took an army of labourers, stonemasons, carpenters, plasterers and other skilled craftsmen to realise Big George's grand designs. Their combined efforts produced a castle of unrivalled neo-Gothic extravagance, rising above the verdant woodlands of the demesne. No expense was spared and, within two years, Big George was ready to move in. The castle cost more than £100,000 to build. A further £100,000 was spent on estate projects, particularly within the town and demesne. The castle dominated the life and landscape of Mitchelstown for the next 100 years. Standing on a cliff edge with gently sloping woodland and lawns on the southern side, it was a castellated, quadrangular mansion with a spacious courtyard in the middle. A spectacular sight, it was visible for miles around.[3] Every structural detail was of the highest quality. One visitor noted:

> The roof is leaded over, so that it will last for centuries ... Every part of the castle is abundantly supplied with water from a lake below. A tower at one angle of the pile is expressly constructed for a reservoir, and into this, by means of force pumps, there is a continual flow.[4]

Visitors entered through the new White Knight's Tower. The entrance door was about fifteen feet high, beneath an archway of about 25 feet. Above the door, a single piece of five-foot-high limestone bore the Earl of Kingston's coat of arms with coronet and supporters, and other large plaques displayed the arms of the White Knights and the Fentons.

The 80 stately rooms were linked by a gallery, which was itself the most splendid room in the house.[5] It was 100 feet long, 22 feet wide and its Gothic ceiling was 33 feet high. One side of the gallery had large windows facing the Galtees, Ireland's highest inland range. On the walls opposite hung the family portraits, including one of Big George by Sir William Beechey, the Portrait Painter to Queen Charlotte (queen consort of George III). The grand stair enclosure was 36 feet long, 25 feet wide and 48 feet high;[6] from here one could approach the numerous stately bedrooms, which were over the main function rooms: 'Sixty principal and twenty inferior bedrooms are in these compartments; and on an emergency, as many as a hundred persons have, without difficulty, been accommodated with chambers in the mansion.'

Along the ground floor were a gentlemen's drawing room and a smaller one for the ladies. There were four libraries – two of them adjoining the gallery, which was also linked to a morning room, a large dining-room on the west end and a billiard room.[7] There was a great range of offices – a broad term that could also cover cellars and out-buildings. There were at least twelve of them – the four longer ones ranging from 105 feet to 150 feet. The kitchen, bakehouse, wine cellars, a 100-feet-long food store, a larder, twelve large servants' quarters and several smaller 'dwelling rooms' for staff (some with ceilings as high as 30 feet) were along the back of the castle, or in the basement. Here, too, were rooms for senior staff such as the governess, butler and housekeeper.[8]

The most important bedroom, however, was to be found in the Royal Tower. The construction of the King's Room – indeed the whole castle – anticipated a promise from his

Georgian Madness

friend King George IV, on a visit to Howth in 1821, that he would stay with his friend in Mitchelstown on his next Irish trip. This second trip to Ireland never materialised.[9] Forty-one steps led to the King's bedroom which, according to the Hon Mrs Nora Robertson, was

> of such a size that on a misty night it was difficult to see across it. I have a recollection of a deep crimson flock wall paper with a velvety pile that had resisted deterioration for upwards of a century. The immense canopied four-poster was like a fortress, only gained by assault, crowning, as it did, the summit of a raised platform.[10]

The building was so big that sections of it were never furnished. One visitor felt that, 'as many of the fittings belonged to an old residence, they appear ill-adapted for the present structure'. Nonetheless, Mitchelstown 'may well be envied'. To the south of the castle, concealed by a shrubbery, were the stables and out-offices: 'The stables of the Douglas, made famous by Sir Walter Scott, did not boast more ample accommodation. Four-and-twenty steeds may here be kept ready for war or chase. The stables are of stone, even to the very stair-cases.'[11] Big George bought a magnificent carriage in London for 250 guineas. As a nobleman immensely conscious of his lineage and position in life he had his coat of arms emblazoned on it and this was his 'state carriage' in Mitchelstown.[12]

However, not everyone was impressed by his new edifice. One of the earlier visitors was Prince Puckler-Muskau who condemned the building and its demesne. He arrived in Mitchelstown on 9 October 1828, in the company of a lady who was 'seventy, and a puritan'. He declared that her 'disagreeable company' only made him feel the worse for wear by the time he reached Mitchelstown. The castle, he remarked, was too high for its extent; the style was confused with variety and the outline was too heavy: 'It stands, too, on the bare turf, without the slightest picturesque break, which castles in the Gothic or kindred styles peculiarly need, and the inconsiderable park possessed neither a handsome group of trees nor a prospect worth describing.' The interior decorations also failed to impress the Prince: 'In five minutes we had quite enough of them,' he said, 'as we heard of a fine prospect from the top of the tower, but the key was nowhere to be found, we all returned in no very good humour to our inn.'[13]

He added that Kingston and his family had been remarkable for their 'very extraordinary adventures'. Big George, he said, 'is now one of the most zealous Orangemen, and is rather feared than loved'. Later in the day, at Cashel, the Prince spoke of arrests at a review of 'O'Connell's Militia'. This unarmed, but uniformed, body had been formed on behalf of the new Catholic Association, through which Daniel O'Connell strove to obtain Catholic Emancipation and repeal of the Union. The Prince added:

> My promising citizen-soldier was furious against Lord Kingston, who has arrested all his tenants (little farmers who are dependent on their lords as serfs) who were present at the review. 'But,' he added, 'every hour that they sit in prison shall be paid by their tyrants, whom we had rather see dead than alive ... O'Connell never comes here, even when it's his nearest way, for he cannot endure the sight of Kingston.'[14]

Scathing criticism of Mitchelstown Castle was rare, although criticism of its master was common and usually justified. Later visitors were full of praise and impressed by the edifice and its setting. Lady Chatterton said in her *Rambles in the South of Ireland*, published in 1839, that she left Cork for Mitchelstown:

> We went through Fermoy, and turned off the Dublin Road, near

> Lord Mount Cashell's place. A pleasant drive of about five hours brought us to Mitchelstown Castle. It is a noble pile of building, surrounded by fine woods, and commanding extensive views over a broad and fertile plain of the splendid range of the Galtee Mountains.[15]

Lady Chatterton's party arrived for a pre-dinner walk in the demesne gardens where they 'enjoyed the sight and perfume of the flowers in the magnificent conservatory'. Another visitor said that in Big George's time, 'at every show of fruit for miles round, the grapes, the peaches, the apricots of Lord Kingston's gardeners have carried off the prize, without leaving a chance for any other exhibitor.'

This was one of Big George's interests. His gardens had a botanical library containing rare works kept for the benefit of the gardeners. Lady Chatterton added: 'There is also a lodge expressly devoted for the reception of picnic parties, who from time immemorial have been permitted free range of all the grounds and gardens, and inspection of the castle upon application at the door.' [16]

Castle dinners were fabulous affairs. The last master of the castle, Willie Webber, recalled stories of the formalities in Big George's time:

> The long suite of rooms were lighted brilliantly by large chandeliers, and when the guests had assembled in the morning room at one end, the folding doors were thrown open by three pairs of liveried footmen, between whom the procession passed to the dining room at the other end.

The silver plate was magnificent. The chef, a Mr Moore, had William Claridge as one of his young under-cooks. The apprentice chef learned quickly and well before leaving for London to found one of the world's most renowned hotels.[17] A large party was staying during Lady Chatterton's visit:

> The evening was enlightened by the exertions of the family piper; he was an excellent musician, and played Irish airs with a degree of taste and execution which I hardly imagined the instrument would allow him display. An expedition to the mountain lodge, and the curious caves about six miles off, was arranged for the morrow.

Lady Chatterton and her 'most merry, scrambling party' set off in carriages and on horseback for Galtee Castle. The Kingstons' prestige was never greater and this was reflected in the finest detail, even of their hunting lodges.[18] Big George had just spent over £3,000 remodelling his father's Galtee retreat and laying out its pleasure grounds.[19] Fishing, hunting and shooting were the sports of the gentry and on the Galtees wild game was varied and plentiful. Of Galtee Castle, the visiting Lady said:

> It is a most comfortable abode, in the midst of wild mountain scenery, rushing streams and rocky glens, adorned with heath of the brightest hues. The views from the sweet jessamine-curtained windows of the drawing room put me in mind of some of the smaller Swiss valleys but with an impression of greater solitude and seclusion.

The spacious lodge was well furnished and the rooms were always ready for guests. Lady Chatterton noted that 'books laid out on the tables, and luxurious chairs, give the rooms a most comfortable appearance'. A flower garden, farm, stables and a pretty cottage nearby reminded her of the 'residences of German Princes'. The touring party also went to the recently-discovered Mitchelstown Caves. Though closer to Ballyporeen in County Tipperary, these natural wonders were named for their location on the Mitchelstown estate. One of the large caverns was called the Kingston's Gallery. Lady Chatterton declared: 'I do not know when I have been so impressed with a feeling of awe, as while clambering down the ladder, which leads to the steep and narrow passage to the caves.' Fatigued, she waited in another cavern called the 'House of Commons', while her companions continued their exploration: 'There was something peculiarly awful in the dead, still darkness of the place ... I almost felt as if I had been transported to some other planet and condemned to eternal loneliness.'[20]

Work on the castle was still in progress when a manufacturer began to build a chimney for a new factory in the town. Big George told him to leave, but he refused. The earl drove his carriage into town and told the crowd who gathered around him: 'I am come to wish you goodbye, boys. This place is but a small place, and there is not enough room for me and that man (pointing at the chimney). He says he has the law on his side, and I daresay it is. Consequently, I go to England tomorrow morning.' During the night, some loyal tenants visited the manufacturer and the following day, no smoke came from his chimney. By the third day the manufacturer was gone.[21]

The story, true or false, underlines the landlord's influence over his tenants. Big George ruled with godlike sway throughout his estate and he was probably the last Kingston to exercise the *droit de signeur* over the maidens of the property. Although he was subject to the law, he exerted immense personal influence on local society and, through the Manor Court, considerable legal influence as well. The court was established at Mitchelstown in 1638, where the judge – or Seneschal – was the landlord or his appointee. The court had powers to impose fines of up to 40 shillings, but it could not imprison. There was also a Manor Pound for the custody of animals taken in execution of court decrees. Tenants who seriously misbehaved were brought before the court, where they were at the mercy of a hand-picked jury under the earl's direction.[22]

The law-abiding who could find work received wages regulated by the rate paid to Kingston's labourers. 'Lord Kingston generally gave eight pence a day through the year to his labourers,' said Fr John Kiely, parish priest of Mitchelstown, in evidence before a House of Commons inquiry, on 15 April 1825. When Fr Kiely told Big George that the wages were not enough to meet the cost of living, the landlord raised the rate per day to ten pence. The 'very great works' being carried out in Mitchelstown made Kingston its biggest employer. According to Fr Kiely, the only other work available was tending gardens or farm labouring. Although the country was going through a crisis in agriculture, Fr Kiely was able to state that he knew of no other parish as well off as Mitchelstown because of the employment created by its landlord. He added:

> There are a great many dependencies upon the works of Lord Kingston, such a brick-making, lime-burning, plant-ing, making improvements, and building in the town of Mitchelstown, &c. and the labourers are employed as well there, as they are immediately by Lord Kingston.

The inquiry was told that the largest farm in Mitchelstown was less than 100 acres; the average was between 20 and 30 acres and a few were as much as 80 acres. Land was leased directly to the tenants, who were forbidden to sub-divide holdings among family members, although they could assign property to a son or daughter as next of kin.[23]

The earl continued the same type of leases issued by his parents. However, those issued to tenants of properties in the town were different. An example was one granted to James Mahony of Robert Street, on 25 March 1829. He paid an annual rent of two shillings and six pence to the landlord and five shillings and six pence towards the support of the fever hospital at Brigown, which had been built by the second earl. Like most of his lease-holding neighbours, Mahony could not carry out any alterations to his slated house without written permission from the landlord. For fire-safety reasons, he was not allowed to thatch any buildings on his property, subject to a penalty of ten shillings yearly for every yard of thatch. The Mahonys had to paint the woodwork every three years and they also had to

> Dash and Colour their houses in the Spring Season, previous to the First of May in every year, with such colour as the said George, Earl of Kingston ... shall direct or appoint, and shall and will keep the Foot-ways, Passages, and Pavements before their Doors well swept and cleaned ...[24]

As his great castle rose up over Mitchelstown, Big George was faced once again with the spectre of bloody rebellion – this time much nearer home than the United Irish uprising in Wexford 25 years earlier. Now it was the turn of the Whiteboys, an anti-landlord secret society which had been formed in 1761.

Thomas Franks was middleman on part of Big George's estate in the Kildorrery area. He and his family were attacked by the Whiteboys on five occasions in January 1822. Thirteen acres of oats, six acres of wheat and three acres of hay were destroyed in December by tenants whose animals had been seized in lieu of rent. On a September night in 1823, Whiteboys entered a new house built at Lisnagourneen for young Henry Mansfield Franks and his bride-to-be, a Miss Kearney, who had inherited a farm.[25] As they entered the home, a servant named Mary Myers hid under the table in the dimly-lit kitchen. She remained there, unseen, as the men, dressed in white shirts over their clothes, demanded firearms, but there was none. One of the gang smothered Margaret Franks and the others bludgeoned and shot her husband and son.

The rector of Glanworth, Rev Richard Woodward, said the Franks family had been killed because they had dealt harshly with several Kingston tenants who had not paid their rents. Some believed that an O'Keeffe who managed her farm perpetrated the crimes because he was afraid of losing his income from her land.[26] Just days after the murders Lord Kingston wrote to Marquess Wellesley to ask that a reward be offered for information leading to the arrest of the murderers. 'I am sorry to say that the harmful system of the Whiteboys, tho' lately to appearance declining, is by no means so ... assassination is now their object,' he said.[27]

At the Spring Assizes at Cork in April 1824, three Cronin brothers were convicted of the murders. Meanwhile, two of Kingston's under-tenants, named Murphy and Hogan, were detained for five months in Buttevant military bridewell, awaiting trial for their alleged part in the murders. Big George did all in his power to have the two released because, for reasons best known to himself, he was convinced of their innocence. It was only when a witness against them (who was also implicated in the murders) disappeared that the two were freed. When O'Keeffe and a man named Bourke were tried also for the murders, they were defended by Daniel O'Connell. A few years later, O'Connell created a sensation as defence counsel in the Doneraile Conspiracy which also involved Whiteboy activities. In the Franks' murder trial 'respectable gentlemen' were called to give character references for O'Keeffe and Bourke, who were acquitted.[28]

In May 1825, Lord Kingston gave evidence before the House of Lords Select Committee on the State of Ireland. He said it was generally believed that one of the men transported for their part in the Franks' murders was guilty. Young Franks, said the earl, had been 'extremely oppressive' to his tenants and under-tenants. Franks extracted 'the rent from them, as heavy a Rent as he could, when it was due, never by chance, paying his own, I am sorry to say (I was his Landlord).' After the murders, Kingston set about collecting his rents in person and, 'finding that people had already paid their rent (to Franks) and that I must have taken absolutely the clothes of their back to have got anything, I gave up the distress.'

In another area one of Big George's agents drove off cattle in lieu of unpaid rent. Told that the Franks had already collected the rents, but had not handed them over, the earl ordered the return of the animals. He remarked that some of his worst-paying tenants were Protestants. 'One of that family of Franks is Protestant and he does not like to pay at all,' he added.[29]

In the early 1820s, Big George resolved to put an end to one of his most serious problems with tenants. Many small farms on the estate had evolved through the repeated subdivision of holdings between farmers' sons. This created critical social problems, not least the inability of the tiny farms to support a tenant and his usually large family. The solution was to get farmers off the smaller holdings. This was accomplished partly by offering them the fare to Canada in the Robinson Expeditions of 1823 and 1825. Initially, Big George was sceptical about the idea when it was suggested to him by its promoter, Peter Robinson. But once the earl realised the advantages, he became one of its most ardent supporters especially after he had decided to recommend some of his more troublesome tenants for a new life in the virgin forest lands around Ontario.

In April 1824, Robinson reported rapid progress to his superiors in the British government. Several hundred copies of the emigration terms were distributed in Mitchelstown, Fermoy, Mallow, Kanturk, Doneraile, Charleville, Newmarket, and villages across north Cork. The nobility and principal magistrates took the names and particulars of those wishing to go and gave them to Robinson. His exhaustive labours led to the emigration of thousands of people from Ireland to Canada. On arrival, Robinson's priority was to build log houses for the emigrants. Each of the settlers then obtained basic farm implements and seeds, and 30 acres of land. If, after five years, they proved to be industrious and law-abiding, they were granted a further 70 acres. However, bad weather, poor land and an alien environment caused a general failure of the venture.[30]

Kingston, meanwhile, was also endeavouring to erect public buildings on his estate. One undertaking, in 1823, was the replacement of the old market house with another incorporating a courtroom in New Market Square. Despite petitions to the government, he failed to obtain a grant towards the building costs which came to the substantial sum of £3,000.[31]

The architects of the new market house were the Pain brothers. They also designed Saint George's church spire which was erected in 1830 with a donation of £500 from Big George. In the same year he provided £200 for a new Protestant church at Marshalstown.[32] The earl also donated the site and £420 for a new Saint Fanahan's Catholic church of Mitchelstown. It was consecrated in 1834. The site was an old quarry from which stones had been drawn for buildings in the town and demesne. He also gave another £105 for a chapel elsewhere in the parish. If local folklore is to be believed, he was afforded the privilege of laying the foundation stone for the new Gothic-style edifice which complimented his grand castle less than a mile to the west. The plasterers and artisans who built the church did not lack top-class experience – they were, after all, the same men who had built the castle.[33]

These are just a few examples of a wide range of civic projects undertaken by the third earl. He also encouraged road construction and other public building on the estate, such as the erection of a fever hospital in Mitchelstown. He helped to finance new roads from Mitchelstown to Limerick, and others to Lismore, Clogheen, Mallow and Kilworth. An unspecified number of local roads were also built at his behest.

Big George's letters indicate that he was often asked to write references for people seeking positions in the civil service, the military and the police. As a magistrate, he had the power to appoint men to serve with the County Police. Many of his petitions to the Lord Lieutenant and his friends in the Government were on behalf of his relatives or his tenants' sons.[34]

While he used his influence to secure the future of others, he was helpless when faced with the consequences of his own extravagance. He reduced the estate to virtual bankruptcy with his new mansion and a lordly indifference to the cost of his pursuits. There is no knowing what debts he accumulated prior to taking over the estate from his mother. Though he had an estimated annual income of £50,000 in 1825, he had already incurred large debts during the long wait for his Mitchelstown inheritance. Indeed, judging by Thomas Disney's statements in 1818, it is unlikely that the Mitchelstown property yielded Lord Kingston more than £27,000 a year, in the years immediately after its acquisition from his mother.

Soon after inheriting Mitchelstown, he was the defendant in a very expensive and bitter lawsuit with his brother, Viscount Lorton, who claimed that the Sligo estate was rightfully his. That estate had been owned by Henry King, brother of the first earl, who died around 1818. The Sligo property passed under settlement to Big George, but the court upheld Lorton's claim in January 1830. Big George lost almost all of the Sligo estate, worth £7,000 a year, and was ordered to pay his brother seven years' back-rent and heavy legal costs.[35]

This was the first major blow to the Kingstons whose political prestige was facing further decline as a result of changes in the electoral system. Like his father before him, George was the leader of the County Cork Whigs whose liberal aristocrats included the Duke of Devonshire, John Hyde of Castlehyde, and the wealthy Ponsonby family. The Tories were traditionally led by the Earl of Shannon whose followers included the Earls of Bandon and Listowel, Lord Bantry, the Eyres and the Longfields. The Kingstons did not lightly give their political support to anyone. In the early months of 1817, as an election loomed, Big George's power increased spectacularly when Shannon suddenly switched his support from the Tories to the Whigs.

By the time of the election of 1826, Kingston could count on more than 2,000 of the 20,000 votes in County Cork – twice that controlled by the Eyres and Lord Bantry.[36] With such voting power it was quite easy for him to secure a Commons seat for his son, Robert Henry, in the 1826 election.[37] Throughout this period, George could secure the support of a substantial number of MPs not just in Cork, but in other counties including Limerick, Tipperary, Sligo and Roscommon. It was a simple arrangement as far as everyone was concerned, because without the Earl of

Kingston's support many of them would find it almost impossible to be elected.[38]

The first real sign of a crack in Big George's political power appeared in the Limerick by-election of February 1830. The Earls of Kingston, like some other peers, enjoyed strong political influence through their patronage of parliamentary seats. Catholic emancipation had just been granted in 1829 and with it came major electoral reforms. This gave the Catholic tenant freeholders rights that inevitably ended the dominance of Protestant gentlemen in Irish politics.

Mutiny threatened as the Limerick election drew closer. Rumours circulated that the Kingston tenants could not be relied upon to vote for James Hewett Massey Dawson – their landlord's candidate. Massey Dawson had an income of £10,000 a year from his estate and was a typical representative of the Ascendancy. On the question of the tenant vote, Big George was determined that nothing should go wrong. He always had their votes in his pocket and he could see no obstacle, not even emancipation, to his candidate's success. In conversation with a fellow peer a few days before the by-election, Big George expressed disgust that the Kingston political machine had been considerably reduced since the Union. Slamming his hand on the table, he exclaimed:

> Sir, I will tell you the simple truth of the case. The Irish people are gone mad! My father returned fourteen members of [the Irish] Parliament, and it is with difficulty that I return eight! I have just sent orders that the whole of my county of Limerick tenants shall ride into Limerick on the first day of election, and be the first to vote. Once they have set the example, the other fellows of course will follow it. I shall go into Limerick myself.[39]

Two days later, Kingston rode there. He stayed with his friend, Lord Limerick, but he was unaware of a change of mood among the voters. Kingston and his candidate quaffed champagne and joked as they watched proceedings through a window facing onto a wide street. Outside, the crowd cheered Massey Dawson while, inside, Kingston dismissed rumours of his candidate's imminent defeat.

The bells of Saint Mary's Cathedral rang out. In a mile-long cavalcade the Kingston tenantry rode and walked down the city's main street on their way to vote. Within a few hours, however, there was dismay in the Kingston party. People spoke in whispers. Big George guessed that something was amiss. 'You are hiding something from me,' he said. 'Something has gone wrong; what has happened?' One of his supporters moved forward and replied: 'My lord, what has gone wrong is this; the Kingston tenantry have voted ... My lord, they have voted with the enemy to a man! The other tenants are following their example. The election is lost!'

Kingston stormed out. All through the night he rode to Mitchelstown, arriving at his castle at dawn. Defeated and bitterly disappointed, he sat alone all day, refusing to see or speak with anyone. Matters had taken an historically ominous turn and his rage could not be contained.[40] In May, the new Limerick MP, Lieutenant Colonel Standish O'Grady, was removed on petition and Massey Dawson installed in his place, but not even this blatant fraud could save Kingston.[41]

After the initial by-election shock, he calmed down for a while, although it was apparent to everyone that he was ill. Dr Eugene O'Neill was first called to treat him for lunacy on 9 April 1830. O'Neill told the commission set up to investigate the earl's health that Lord Kingston had

> appeared to be labouring under great nervous excitement ... He evinced much alarm, stating that persons were in the house who were about to deprive him of his property and life. He also expressed his suspicions that his nearest and dearest friends

meditated his destruction, as well as his agent's brother, Mr Arthur Montgomery, who, he said, had robbed and plundered him.

O'Neill had known Lord Kingston for at least seventeen years. He told the inquiry – which was held in July 1833 – that he had been a physician to the King family for eleven years. The earl he had frequently attended for 'bodily complaints, principally bilious attacks, but afterwards severe erysipelas' – a most painful skin disorder which, in 1830, was incurable. When the doctor accompanied him from Ireland to Brislington in 1830, 'he became violent.' O'Neill stated that before the attack on 9 April, Big George had been able to attend to his own affairs. He did not believe there was any truth in the accusation against Montgomery. 'His lordship's mental disease had arisen from bodily infirmity,' reported the *Cork Constitution*.

Dr Charles Joseph Fox, of Brislington, said he visited Kingston three times a week since he had been taken to Fox's asylum in July 1830. Big George, he said, was 'labouring under various delusions and erroneous ideas'. He was convinced that Ireland no longer existed, and that he had no property there. 'Daniel O'Connell would be with an army in the neighbourhood of Bristol in a week or two. He was unwilling to conform to any regulations, but displayed sound judgment on some points ... [he knew] the value of cattle.'

In September 1831, the once powerful and tyrannical earl 'experienced an attack of paralysis'. Its consequences were 'impaired memory, an affliction of the speech and bodily powers, and a state of dementia'. He endured another serious attack 'followed by increased impairment of the faculties'. Robert Boyce, Kingston's personal servant for almost three years, said that sometimes the earl was 'very steady', but at other times 'very contradictory'. Boyce could not recollect ever seeing the earl in a sound state of mind. On occasions, the earl said that his son, Lord Kingsborough, would never sit in his house while he could help it. How he proposed to prevent that from happening was anybody's guess, since Big George had gone mad and he would never again rule at Mitchelstown Castle.

When he arrived at the lunatic asylum, his 'excited state of mind' was witnessed by Dr Francis Ker Fox. Big George had suffered two strokes. The first 'weakened his faculties considerably;' the second made him 'still more imbecile'. The earl believed that his property was in America and that he was an officer in the army of Emperor Paul. However, he had 'nothing like a lucid interval to render him capable of managing his own affairs – he would laugh and cry by turns'.

Kingston was literally incapable of adding two and two when it was written down for him. Neither could he state his own name. 'His Lordship's present stage is a want of comprehension and an incapacity for any train of reasoning,' said Dr Prichard. The inquiry, finding that Big George was insane, ordered that 'neither the person nor the property of the earl should be improperly treated'.[42] The management of the estate was placed in the hands of the Lord Chancellor. He decided to give an allowance of £6,000 a year to the earl's son, Edward, Viscount Kingsborough, to run the estate. Kingsborough also had permission to reside in the castle. This would continue until the earl died, at which time Kingsborough would inherit the estate.[43]

The years that followed were dismal ones for the Kingston property. Henry D. Inglis said in 1834 that

> Mitchelstown and its neighbourhood have suffered grievously, by the late affliction which has fallen upon the Kingston family. The deprivation of an expenditure of £40,000 per annum, has been most seriously felt in the country; and the deterioration of Mitchelstown and its neighbourhood, has fast followed the

misfortune to which I have alluded; – if I were to search Ireland throughout, I could not find a better illustration of the difference between residence and non-residence, than in the present situation at Mitchelstown.[44]

If Big George now imagined that Ireland no longer existed, great numbers of his subjects at home had good reason to wish it so. Inglis wrote that 1,800 of the town's 5,000 people were starving. Some 1,200 were unemployed labourers, or their families, and the remaining 600 were elderly, infirm, widows and children. A further 1,200 in the parish were destitute. Yet despite Kingston's huge financial problems there was no rack-renting on the estate:

> The average rent of land to the occupier may be stated at about 25s. The mountain farms are let very low, as low as 5s. an acre: and it was no unusual thing with Lord Kingston, to remit altogether, the rent of a man who was active and of improving habits. Few thatched farm houses are to be seen. They are mostly slated houses, built in the English mode.

Mitchelstown's petty sessions came in for Inglis' scrutiny as he considered court proceedings to be a useful indicator of the state of society. He found that of the 26 cases called, none was for theft, but many were for crimes of violence:

> Five were cases of assault, generally arising out of the merest trifles; and some of these, assaults of the most aggravated character – so much so, that in England they would certainly have been transportation cases: here they were punished summarily, by fine, and by imprisonment at hard labour.[45]

Weapons used in assault cases included staves 'that would have felled an ox', but stones 'that would have shivered a three-inch board' were among the more favoured weapons produced in court as evidence. The remaining cases were made up of summonses against employers for non-payment of wages. The sums claimed were mostly for wages at eight pence a day, without food. One youth sought wages at the low rate of five pence a day. A mason was paid two shillings for a day's labour. Carpenters were paid 2s-6d per day, but constant employment was scarce. With these low wages in such difficult times, it was not surprising that Inglis described Mitchelstown as 'a very cheap place of residence'.[46]

Meanwhile, Big George's income remained at £40,000 a year, even with the loss of the Sligo estate. He lived for six years after he had been declared insane. In that period, as Mitchelstown went into decline, local people considered his madness to have been the inevitable consequence of the demonic temper to which so many of them had been subjected at various times. Of all the Earls of Kingston, Big George was the one who inspired the greatest fear and the most hatred among his tenants. Despite that Mitchelstown in his time briefly glimpsed the peak of its potential, but it all came to nought as a result of one man's megalomania.

Big George died in London on 18 October 1839. Five weeks later, on 26 November, his brother, General Sir Henry King, also died. Big George's body was taken back to Mitchelstown, via Dublin, on the last day of October, to be interred in the family crypt at Kingston College. According to the *Cork Constitution*, the funeral procession formed 'an unbroken mass of noiseless and solemn motion for miles along the road leading from Cahir to Mitchelstown'. The tenantry on the Kingston, Glengall and Lismore estates were issued with long scarves and hatbands to wear to the funeral. 'The remains ... were conveyed in an elegant hearse, drawn by six jetty steeds, and followed by two mourning coaches, each drawn by four black horses.' During the night the earl's body lay in state:

'it was enclosed in three coffins, the exterior covered with scarlet velvet, richly ornamented with the coronet, family arms &c. On the head of the coffin was placed a scarlet velvet cushion, on which rested the coronet.'

The coffin was brought to the castle. The *Cork Constitution* described the scene in the gallery where all were admitted to witness the solemn spectacle. Opposite the coffin was a platform

> covered with a rich pall of black velvet, terminated by a full border of white and satin. On this stood twelve magnificent plumes of black feathers full three feet in height, and from these depended a number of drooping ones which hung more gracefully over the front and sides of the pall, surmounting them and supported by two pillars. Covered with black velvet, were the armorial bearings of the noble house of Kingston ...

On the following day at noon, the procession wound its way back down the castle avenue to the chapel in Kingston College:

> In front came a large body of the tenantry, habited as on the previous day; after them were four clergymen with rich black scarfs and hoods; immediately following were the female domestics of the family with white cloaks and hoods; then was borne the platform of plumes by six bearers; following them rode the land steward uncovered, carrying the coronet on a velvet cushion; then the hearse conveying the body drawn by six horses, covered with black velvet, and carrying plumes on their heads.

The chief mourners included the new Earl of Kingston with his brother, James, their sister Adelaide and her husband, Charles T. Webber. A second mourning carriage contained Big George's nephew, Stephen, the third Earl of Mount Cashell, and other relatives.

Then succeeded a long line of equipages, among which I identified those of the Earls of Kingston, Listowel, and Mount Cashell; Lords Riversdale, and Lismore &c. Sir Denham Norreys, Baronet; Sir John Franks; Captain Collis; Messers Montgomery and Coote; with many others ...

The third earl was interred in the vault with his coronet placed on the head of the coffin which also bore the Kingston coat of arms. The era of Big George, a medieval lord out of his time, was over, and privately his family knew that the cost of his extravagance threatened the existence of all that he had inherited and created. The *Cork Constitution*, for its part, expressed the hope that the tenants and their dependents would find in the new earl a 'kind friend and considerate landlord'.[47]

6

DECLINE AND FAMINE

Big George's eldest son, Edward Viscount Kingsborough, was the outstanding scholar of the King family. In 1818, and again in 1820, he was elected MP for County Cork. He resigned his seat in 1826 in favour of his younger brother, Robert Henry, to spend the rest of his life, and £32,000, researching his celebrated *Antiquities of Mexico*. The young scholar's imagination was fired when he found an important Mexican manuscript in the Bodleian Library at Oxford University while he was a student there. In his work he sought to prove the once widely-held theory that the ancient peoples of Mexico were descended from the Israelites. This we know to be completely unfounded, but at the time it was a popular fancy. While writing the *Antiquities*, Kingsborough worked in seclusion in rooms high in the White Knight's Tower. He stored his valuable collection of manuscripts and pictures in the tower and generally refused to be disturbed by anyone. After years of research, Edward published his gigantic work

> comprising facsimiles of ancient Mexican Paintings and hieroglyphics preserved in the Royal Libraries of Paris, Berlin, and Dresden; in the Imperial Library of Vienna; in the Vatican Library; in the Borghian Museum [Borgesi] at Rome; in the Library of the Institute of Bologna: and in the Bodleian Library at Oxford. Together with the Monuments of New Spain, by M. Dupaix, with their respective scales of measurements and accompanying

descriptions. The whole illustrated by many valuable unedited Manuscripts, by Augustine Aglio.[1]

The first volume appeared in print in 1830. Six more were published in 1831. Priced at the enormous sum of £170 a volume, the work was never destined to become a best seller. Of the nine volumes published, two appeared posthumously in 1848; 60 pages of a tenth were drafted, but never published. Four specially-printed copies, on vellum, were donated to the Bodleian Library, the Imperial Library at St Petersburg, the Louvre in Paris and the Royal Library at Berlin. In appreciation of this gift, King Frederick William IV of Prussia sent Edward a painting of the Royal Palace in Berlin in 1834, by William Conrad. The Emperor of Russia sent him a pair of large malachite vases which were afterwards sold by his executors.[2] The historian, W.H. Prescott, said:

> By his munificent undertaking, which no Government probably would have, and few individuals could have executed, he has entitled himself to the lasting gratitude of every friend of science.[3]

But Prescott pointed out that he considered the presence of Jews in pre-Colomban America to be as fanciful as the stories of Queen Scheherazade in the *Arabian Nights*. For scholars, the value of Kingsborough's research was not his conclusions, but his reproduction of numerous illustrations and manuscripts.

The nine-volume collection was an astonishing piece of research that involved the extensive use of old manuscripts, mostly Spanish. Many have since been lost in wars, fires and through neglect. Edward travelled to Berlin, Paris, Dresden, Bologna and to the Bologna Museum in Italy to copy several collections. He also paid the expenses of explorations in Mexico and the collecting of manuscripts from several major European libraries. One of his work's greatest flaws was that

Decline and Famine

it all but ignored some of the most extensive manuscript collections in the Vatican and in Spain. Remarkably, Edward never went to Central America and, consequently, his work could never be regarded as complete.[4]

Following Big George's descent into madness, the Mitchelstown estate faced critical times. The Court of Chancery gave Viscount Kingsborough a comfortable allowance, but the vast sums spent on researching the *Antiquities* brought him to the brink of bankruptcy. Pleas for an increase in the allowance were ignored and, in 1837, Edward was thrown into the Sheriff's Prison in Dublin for a second time. On this occasion, he was arrested at the suit of a paper manufacturer to whom he owed a small sum. Unfortunately for him, jails then were the source of many incurable diseases. Within days he contracted typhus and was released when his illness became known. Two weeks later, on 27 February 1837, he died at the age of 41. The family was shocked; but even as they buried him in the chapel at Kingston College they could not have imagined that worse would soon befall them.[5]

The famous French traveller, Alexis de Tocqueville, visiting Mitchelstown in the 1830s, said he was told that the earl 'has gone off his head'. He also heard that the estate was burdened with £400,000 in debts 'without hope of ever being able to pay them off'. Kingston had taken loans from Catholic merchants in Cork to whom he had mortgaged the estate. Loan repayments had absorbed almost every penny of the estate's income. De Tocqueville observed:

> It is like that almost everywhere in Ireland. Witness the finger of God. The Irish aristocracy wanted to remain separate from the people and be still English. It has driven itself into imitating the English aristocracy without possessing either its skill or its resources, and its own sin is providing its ruin.

Writing of the Kingston property, de Tocqueville saw 'a huge clearing which he [Big George] has made, and which is covered with fine crops; and a row of clean and convenient cottages which he has built for his tenants.' Kingston, he added, 'has made money out of doing this. The town ... does not look as wretched as the rest of the country.'[6]

As Big George's eldest son – the bankrupt scholar, Edward – was unmarried, the estate and its debt passed to his second and eldest surviving son, Robert Henry, in 1839. The fourth earl's homosexuality was described by another visitor to Mitchelstown, John Kegan, who said that Robert Henry was 'unmarried and will so remain in view of his great repugnance for the ladies'. His favourites 'he generally selects from the most vulgar of the people'. Eccentric, but kind-hearted, Robert Henry had

> large eyes, an inanimate inexpressive countenance, and a restless fidgety manner, always catching the person to whom he speaks by the ear, nose, collar or button-hole, he scarcely ever walks, but goes in a canter or Connaught-man's trot, with all the children and blackguards of the town running and brawling after him.

It was now open house at the castle, where strangers and the poorest tenants were made welcome. Frequently, the earl would drag in a poor tenant, take the food from the gentleman dining with him and bring it to his 'ragged, bare-footed guest who has left his brogues outside the door.'[7] Robert Henry's welcome to all and sundry would have been the envy of an Irish Tourist Board copywriter 150 years later:

> If you are a scholar, you shall be conducted to scenes renowned in history; if you are a lover of the picturesque, you shall have a room commanding a dozen prospects; if you are a sportsman, the horse and hound invite you to follow them; or there are hills abounding with grouse, and streams alive with trout; bring your gun, your

rod, your pencil, or your book, you shall be equally welcome and equally gratified. Come and visit me at Mitchelstown.[8]

Since Edward's time, the demesne had been open to all 'respectable persons'. In the castle, during Robert Henry's ownership, balls and parties were held as never before. Henry Inglis wrote:

> Free admission into Lord Kingston's park, is a great advantage, possessed by all the inhabitants. Lord Kingston's domain ... whether in forest paths, or grassy walks, or wide gravel roads, offers all that can be desired, either for the gay promenade or the solitary ramble. The house – Mitchelstown Castle, is one of the most magnificent in Ireland.[9]

According to another visitor, the drive up to the castle from the main gate was 'short and pleasant'. The avenue was quite unlike the more common long drives of other big houses. 'A lawn and pleasure grounds are passed, and the castle itself stands before you in all its princely grandeur,' the visitor said. 'It consists of a pile of castellated buildings, extensive and elegantly proportioned, and built of stone of the purest white.'

While financial misfortune made it difficult to keep up appearances, 'nevertheless this demesne is in better order than many of the estates to be seen in Ireland'. The demesne was farmed for Kingston. Its farm buildings were 'a perfect model'. One yard had a dairy, cheeseroom, lodgings for dairywomen, stables and cattle sheds. An adjoining yard had open sheds for 100 cattle; a third had more sheds for cattle and sties for pigs, as well as a large barn. The fourth yard connected to a shrubbery which concealed a pheasantry and an aviary. It also had blacksmiths' and carpenters' shops, sawpits and a mill.[10]

Before becoming Viscount Kingsborough, Robert Henry

had pursued follies of his own. One was the building of Mounteagle, 'a beautiful cottage' which was used as a summer residence. Situated on the banks of the Funcheon River, noted for its brown trout and salmon, Mounteagle doubled as a fishing lodge within a short ride of Mitchelstown. However, he felt compelled for financial reasons to lease it to Edward O'Brien, manager of the National Bank, for £50 a year annually in 1844.[11] At Araglin Kingsborough created an architectural gem, in 1838. It was a castellated fishing lodge built in the remote river valley of the same name on the County Waterford border. Beautifully carved oak on the eaves depicted a huntsman and pheasant, as well as a chalice, honeycombs, salmon, oak leaves, trout, eel and other pretty decorations which still survived, though in a poor state of preservation, into the twenty-first century.

Anderson, its architect, had his name (a letter at a time) carved on the eaves of the west gable. The White Knight's coat of arms, with the motto *Shanet Aboo* ('the old [clan] forever') was sculpted on the limestone gable. The southern front gable had a limestone carving of the Kingston crest embellished with their motto, *Spes Tuitissima Coelis* ('The Safest Hope is in Heaven'). In Mitchelstown, two romantic iron and limestone bridges – the White Bridge and Black Bridge – were built over the Funcheon on one of the demesne's winding avenues. The railings incorporated metal representations of the Kingston crest. A plaque on each bridge recorded that Perrots of Cork made the decorative ironwork in 1839.

Because of all the ornamentation, the estate debts remained large and, inevitably, the creditors moved to salvage their interest. In 1844, Robert Henry's uncle, Lord Lorton, successfully took action to safeguard his charges against the property and John Massey was appointed receiver of the

Mitchelstown estate. At this time, the rental was about £35,000 a year. 'The tenantry on the estate varied very much, but those on the part abutting the [Galtee] mountain were very poor – they were wretchedly poor,' Massey said. Indeed, they were so destitute that he felt compelled to give £100 out of his fees to assist those in trouble. He also wiped out arrears amounting to £20,000, and gave security for £140,000 in loans to the estate.[12] A possible saving factor for the King family was that Big George had entailed almost all of the County Cork and part of the County Limerick portions of the estate, including the castle, under a settlement of 7 November 1823. In future, Mitchelstown would pass to the holder of the family titles. The deed made it impossible for any individual to sell the entailed portions of the property.[13]

In Mitchelstown in 1841, the population – reflecting the national trend – had grown rapidly to 4,181, with a further 6,433 in the surrounding civil parish of Brigown and 2,956 in Marshalstown civil parish. Though the population on the entire Kingston estate is difficult to calculate, it was more than 40,000, with many tenants on holdings of less than one acre. Because of Kingston's financial problems, the number of people employed by the estate had fallen and this aggravated the wretched economic situation in the locality.[14] The distressed state of the country in general prompted the government to introduce the Poor Law Act of 1838. Under this act, Boards of Guardians were set up to operate poor relief schemes and encourage subsidised and organised emigration. The country had 130 Poor Law Unions, each centred on a market town, where a workhouse or union was built for the relief of the distressed. However, the system was strongly opposed by all sections, including the landlords.

At first, Mitchelstown was in the same Union as Fermoy where the workhouse was in a disused military barracks. The only way to get relief was to become an inmate of the workhouse, which operated under draconian rules. The level of confinement also made conditions intolerable for people used to the freedom of the countryside. The unions were financed by local rates, paid mostly by landowners and landlords. After 1844, landlords had to pay rates on holdings worth less than £4; over that amount the levy was shared between landlord and tenant. Robert Henry, now confronted by appalling social and financial problems, evicted many tenants from smaller holdings. On the other hand, he made at least some effort to help the poor and sick long before the Great Famine wreaked havoc on his estate.[15]

The Parliamentary Gazetteer of Ireland said in 1846 that Mitchelstown's fever hospital built by Lord Kingston at Brigown was well adapted to hospital purposes. It had 20 beds and could accommodate 30 patients.[16]

The true state of affairs was well known to Dr John O'Neill. He stated in September 1845 that 'upon the Kingston estate the farmers are very much impoverished; on other estates they are improving'. The estate was 'badly managed, involved in a good deal of litigation, with no understanding between landlord and tenant'. A similar view was expressed by Stephen Barry, a local merchant, who said that the rents had been raised considerably before the estate was placed in chancery. The agents were obliged to collect the rents and no allowance was made for individual hardship.[17]

When the potato crop failed in 1845, the tenants sought a reduction in rents; this was refused by John Massey and Kingston refused because the estate was in such serious financial difficulties. Massey followed with a series of evictions that met with little opposition from tenants. The potato failure of 1845-'47 was Ireland's greatest calamity. Partial crop failures between 1848 and 1850 added to the crisis. As the wretched small holders and labourers dug out one rotten potato patch after another, whole families died of starvation or related diseases. Despite his financial woes, Robert Henry eventually reduced his tenants' rents by one-fifth while donating one-fifth of his own income to famine relief. He also initiated work schemes, but as food was so scarce the money earned was of little use to its starving recipients.[18]

The Mitchelstown Poor Relief Committee, comprising the area's influential citizens, informed the authorities that local conditions were disastrous. An area around St Fanahan's chapel in Thomas Street (by then a National School) was the site of an unknown number of burials. The soil level in Brigown's ancient graveyard rose as more and more bodies were piled into it. At least three local priests died from diseases contracted as a result of their trojan work for the poor.[19]

Arriving in Mitchelstown on 1 October 1845 to spend a few days at the castle, James Dillon Croker of Quartertown, Mallow, was appalled at the sight of countless ravaged potato fields along the way. Occasionally, he stopped his carriage to enquire from the tenants about the state of their crops. He was horrified when they dug into the beds to release the putrid mass. A week later, Capt William Cooke-Collis, who lived at Castle Cooke above the Araglin Valley, confirmed that the panic was justified while, in Kilworth, Lord Mount Cashell called for a total ban on potato exports. Priests, meanwhile, advised their flocks to dig up potatoes and separate the good from the bad.

Amid all the distress and death, in March 1846, the third Earl of Mount Cashell found the time and resources to arrange an enormous party for his son's coming of age. Sports were held; there was a fireworks display and a band played to the amusement of thousands who came to drink gallons of porter which he supplied gratis.[20]

Meanwhile, Dr Eugene O'Neill reported that the number of Mitchelstown patients who died in Fermoy workhouse had increased by one-third, mostly as a result of typhus. Relief measures were widespread, but wholly inadequate. One way of creating work was through presentment sessions convened on a baronial basis to 'present' public works for which the cess (county tax) had to be raised. One presentment in 1846, for the 206,000-acre Barony of Condons and Clangibbon approved a new road from Kilworth to Mitchelstown at a cost of £217. Mount Cashell, who expected to benefit commercially from the road, agreed not to charge for the land required to build it. The session sought approval from the Board of Works to build a new line from Mitchelstown to Lismore. Another road was built from Brigown through Glenatlucky Wood to meet the Mitchelstown to Kilworth road. As the famine worsened, meetings of relief committees and presentment sessions were desperately seeking ways to save the dying. The starving people of Mitchelstown poured into the workhouse in Fermoy.[21]

Throughout the summer of 1846, the Mitchelstown Committee laboured to dispense food and as winter approached funds were rapidly running out. One report said: 'Wretched looking objects that throng the roads and highways would be sufficient to convince the most sceptical of the alarming extent to which misery and starvation prevail.'

Of the 15,000 people in Brigown and Marshalstown civil parishes (which together make up Mitchelstown Catholic parish), only 500 had work at the end of October. In Marshalstown, once noted for its lime kilns, only five men out of 400 were working. One harrowing scene at Mitchelstown was typical of the state of the area. When a

Bianconi coach pulled up in the town, a traveller was surrounded by at least twelve starving people pleading for charity. One man, provoked by the sight of a child passenger eating a biscuit, leaned forward and snatched it out of the youngster's mouth. A policeman rushed forward to tear the morsel from between the man's teeth.[22]

The landed gentry of the barony attended the presentment sessions in Fermoy courthouse on 30 September 1846, when the enormity of the distress took up the day's business. The barony's 92,000 people lived in Fermoy, Mitchelstown, Kilworth, Glanworth, Kildorrery and the surrounding rural areas. The presentments approved £16,000 to be spent over three months on public works in the barony. The chairman, Lord Mount Cashell, said that the relief committees should not confine themselves to the making of roads. They wanted to establish food depots and recommended to the government that it ought to provide food as well as employment. 'If the price of food cannot be kept down it would be impossible to carry on the public works at the estimated cost of other periods,' Mount Cashell warned. Amid loud applause, he made a plea for the country:

> The people of Ireland call for support, immediate support and assistance. And they will be greatly disappointed and dissatisfied with the present Government, if they do not adopt speedy measures for affording extensive and general employment, and make immediate arrangements for establishing depots of Indian meal throughout the country.

At the presentments, Richard Rice of Kilworth objected to building a new line of less than one mile from Sullivan's orchard to the factory bridge in Mitchelstown at an estimated cost of £350. Rice felt that this 'was one of the most destructive roads ever contemplated ... it would completely destroy the town of Mitchelstown, inasmuch as it would take out of the town its only valuable traffic – the trade in corn.'[23] Bad weather hindered road works, with the average working week in Mitchelstown reduced to three days. Publicans tried to exploit under-employed workers by erecting shabby drinking dens on the roadsides.

With 1,000 inmates in Fermoy workhouse, five or seven to a bed, disease was rampant. Rate payments that funded the workhouse were slowing down as the landowners could no longer afford to meet them. Consequently, the Board of Guardians was short of money to run its relief programme. The Prime Minister, Lord John Russell, was accused of being unequal to the task of saving Ireland from destruction.

A grant of £1,500 for the area was barely enough to keep half the population in work for a month, according to Michael O'Brien of Mitchelstown Cottage: 'what, then, in the name of God, will become of the thousands without food, clothing or firing?' Road building, in his view, was a waste of time when large tracts of land needed draining and cultivating. It would be easier, he felt, to accommodate the destitute in the workhouse rather than have 'the poor creatures, shivering in the wet and cold, endeavouring to have their names enrolled for the miserable pittance they receive for a day's pay'.

Three times a week, 80 gallons of soup from the Earl of Kingston's kitchens were dished out to Mitchelstown's starving people. The earl funded the cost of the kitchens; he also donated bullocks, deer from the demesne, vegetables and other supplies to feed his tenants and their families.'[24]

In the opinion of a *Cork Examiner* correspondent, the crisis in Mitchelstown was being ignored in comparison to Skibbereen and Bantry. A thriving coffin trade in the town proved that it was as catastrophic as West Cork. As regards the Earl of Kingston, the correspondent said, 'I am perfectly satisfied that the relief committee of this town would be perfectly satisfied not to receive any subscription from him, provided he supported the beggars on his estate and gave employment to those who are able to work'.[25]

In January and February 1847, the Mitchelstown Poor Relief Committee tried desperately to get two 100-gallon soup boilers from Limerick to augment its 75-gallon boiler, which had been in use for only a month. In the previous two months, the committee collected £85-1s-10d to support the soup kitchens. A further £300-10s was collected for the general work of the committee. Kingston gave £130 to the general fund and £40 for the soup kitchens. Other contributors included farmers, shopkeepers, Catholic and Protestant clergy, soldiers and bankers. Rev Henry Disney, secretary of the Mitchelstown Committee and chaplain of Kingston College, stated in his report to Sir Randolph Routh, chairman of the Relief Commission, that the money collected for the soup kitchens would make it possible to sell soup to the poor at cost: 'It is, however, contemplated in cases of extreme destitution in future to give a portion at half price and in some very bad cases to give gratuitously. They [the relief committee members] wish to add that the workhouse for the Electoral Division is full to overflowing.'[26]

When Mitchelstown's profiteering bakers raised prices, Robert Henry built a bakery to provide cut-price bread to the poor. Every day, according to E. O'Meara, bands of starving wretches struggled to the castle seeking assistance and few left empty handed.[27]

In March, the rector, Dr Richard Hastings Graves, and the parish priest, Dean Morgan O'Brien, both wealthy men, donated £10 each to the fund. Contributors also included local businessmen; 'a military friend'; Dr O'Neill who donated three guineas, and sums of between £1 and £4 from other local clergy. The Lord Lieutenant recommended payment of a sum of £246 to match donations received since the previous grant to the committee.[28]

Dr O'Neill complained of being overworked and unable to cope with the demands placed upon him. He pleaded with the Board of Guardians to employ another medical officer, as there was too much for one man to do: 'From the great number of sick I would implore the Board the necessity of procuring further medical assistance as I cannot under the present circumstances have the responsibility for the painful position I fill.'[29]

By the end of May 1847, there was a five-fold increase in the number of Mitchelstown inmates in the workhouse, compared to a doubling of the number from the Fermoy area itself. At the end of that dreadful year – on 9 December – Big George's widow, Helena, who had cared for her husband through his nine years of madness, died at her home in Middlesex. She left three sums of £100 each to be invested by her trustees 'in some Savings Bank or in Government Securities for the benefit of the poor at Mitchelstown, Kilbehenny and Ballyporeen'. They could apply the money 'in such manner as they shall deem most conducive to the advantages of the poor people of the above named places'.[30]

At around the time of Helena's death, another widow passed away in a field near Mitchelstown Castle. She was Ellen Murphy, a mother of three. Once she had land rented from the Kingstons, but the Great Famine forced her to sell her tenancy to a neighbour and, after that, she had to beg for food for herself and the children. Mrs Murphy was turned away by her neighbours after her children caught fever. Such was the fear of the workhouse that she refused to submit herself and her family to its guardians. Instead, she built a roadside shelter and went out each day to scavenge and beg for food. Finally, the ordeal proved too much for the unfortunate woman, who collapsed and died. A relief officer found the three orphans naked and took them to hospital.[31]

In January 1848, the Board increased Mitchelstown's rates from 20 pence in the pound to 10s-6d; while Fermoy was increased to just 5s-10d. Amazingly, the Fermoy Union began 1848 with £7,000 in the bank. With the enormous demand for relief, it seems reasonable to conclude that the guardians wanted to save money as much as life.

The situation in Mitchelstown worsened and crime began to increase in the spring. Sheep stealing, once a capital offence, was common again among people who had nothing to lose, while in the Kilworth area cattle rustling was a growing problem. Rates were almost impossible to collect in the later 1840s. Angry ratepayers at Kildorrery took back cattle seized in lieu of arrears. Notices were hung on the rate collector's house warning him that if he came back there would be a few 'ounces of lead and powder in store'. While there was no blight in 1848, few potatoes were planted and the hunger persisted.

Eventually, in early 1850, steps were taken to establish Mitchelstown as a separate Poor Law Union of parishes, with a total population of 41,500 living on 97,000 acres. The first meeting of the new Mitchelstown Union was held on 21 May. Their workhouse, on the Clonmel Road, opened at the end of 1851. By then, the Great Famine had run its course. Mitchelstown's population fell by over 4,000 to 6,504, and 1,228 were still in the workhouse. Its high boundary walls gave it the appearance of a prison. Hundreds of inmates died there and many were buried in unmarked graves outside its back wall.[32]

Two sisters, Margaret and Ellen Flynn, who lived at Lower Cork Street, had reasons other than hunger to fear Black '47. On 13 March, they had four surprise visitors – their landlord, the fourth Earl of Kingston, and three of his bailiffs, who burst into their home, beat them with a stick and dragged them by the hair across the floor. The earl was angry that the Flynns had not paid their rent for some years. Soon, however, he would get a shock as great as the one he had inflicted on the unfortunate women. The dirty business done, Robert Henry subsequently left for London where he was expected to remain for at least two months. In his absence, the authorities decided it was time to put an end to this kind of feudal tyranny, and a warrant for his arrest was issued by the resident magistrate, Neal Brown. On 9 May, Brown said in a report to the Under Secretary:

> This business has attracted a great deal of notice and as the confidence of the public in the administration of Justice will be much increased or diminished by the course adopted in this case, I beg respectfully to recommend that a proper person be sent to execute this warrant in London where Lord Kingston I understand is now.

One of the bailiffs, Patrick Cullinane, swore that the Flynns were 'very violent' and had assaulted him and his companions. They had gone to the house to take furniture and other articles in lieu of rent due between 1833 and 1839. This statement was corroborated by Kingston, who said that the eviction was carried out to prevent the Flynns from establishing a right of possession. However, his statements did not explain why he became involved in the assaults for which, it appears, he got off scot free.[33]

Kingston was still in London a few months later when he again found himself on the wrong side of the law in an episode which was described as 'one of a very extraordinary and serious nature'. It concerned an allegation that he had indecently assaulted a 21-year-old London painter and glazier, named George Cull, with intent to commit 'an unnatural offence'.

Decline and Famine

On the night of 30 March 1848, Kingston initiated a conversation with Cull in Oxford Street and offered to buy him a cigar. 'We went into Woodstock Street, where he laid hold of my hand and gave me a piece of paper which I lighted at the fish stall at the corner of Oxford Street,' said Cull, in evidence before a police court on the day after the incident. 'He then laid hold of me by the hand and asked me if I'd cross Oxford Street with him.' The invitation was accepted and the two entered Marylebone Lane. It was here, reported *The Times*, at the rear of a police station, that 'acts of a filthy and disgusting nature [took place] to which it is impossible for us, with any regard to decency, further to allude. Suffice to say that complainant swore distinctly to an indecent assault upon his person.'

Cull told the court that he tried to escape from the earl's clutches but for some reason they ended up in an ale house. Kingston ordered a glass of ale, paid for it and left. Cull went after him. He called a policeman and, when arrested, the nobleman denied everything. Lord Kingston's bail was fixed at £5,000, and two sureties of £2,500 each. Kingston tendered £5,000 as his own bond, with sureties of £2,500 each being paid by his brother-in-law, Philip Davies Cooke of Yorkshire, and William Holmes of London. In the end, Kingston went unpunished because the authorities privately felt that the earl was, to put it mildly, not in possession of his full faculties.[34]

However, other ominous forces were about to emerge back home. One Saturday evening in 1849, upwards of 100 guests gathered in the castle after a day of sport and entertainment. As they were about to sit down to dine a Fermoy solicitor, Jonathan Wigmore Sherlock, who was familiar with the affairs of the estate, arrived at the front door. Described by James Kegan as 'a low, upstart, unprincipled attorney', Sherlock nonetheless was a Kingston favourite. On this occasion, as usual, he was made welcome at Kingston's table. The solicitor was graciously invited to stay the night, so he willingly remained to drink toasts to the health and happiness of his host. On Sunday morning, Kingston and his other guests went to Saint George's, but Sherlock stayed behind on the pretence that he was indisposed. When the others had gone, servants noticed him admiring the grandeur of several rooms: 'He examined the furniture, the books, the plate upon the sideboards, the chandeliers pendant from the ceilings. Early in the day he took his departure. Lord Kingston little augured what would follow.'

A few days later, the County Sheriff came to see Kingston 'on a most unpleasant duty'. An order had been received at the suit of Sherlock and he had been told to give it immediate effect. He had details of furniture and other valuable articles that were to be seized for sale to pay debts. The sheriff assured Kingston that he would carry out his duty as delicately as possible, and that his officers could be regarded as servants. He then withdrew to the main gate to summon his men. As soon as he left, Robert Henry called a 'war council' of friends and guests. Convinced that such action could not succeed against an aristocrat as important as himself, he took his guests' advice to bar the doors and prepare for battle.

For nearly a fortnight, Mitchelstown Castle was placed under siege by the sheriff and his bailiffs who were determined to gain entry any way they could. Meanwhile, Kingston held several 'councils of war' until, at last, reason prevailed. Since no relief was at hand and food was running out, Robert Henry now took the contrary advice of his guests to admit the sheriff's men. Late that evening, Kingston left the castle, though probably not, as some have suggested, for the last time. For two sisters in Lower Cork Street, it must have been pleasing to see their master get a taste of his own medicine.[35]

7

END OF THE LINE

Imprudence was the hallmark of the fourth earl's tenure of Mitchelstown. Like many sons of the Ascendancy, Robert Henry was neither trained nor disposed to run his estate efficiently. Since his sexual orientation precluded marriage, there was no question of him producing a male heir to inherit the property and family titles. Throughout his life, Robert Henry surrounded himself with self-serving favourites. Little had changed since John Kegan's unflattering description of them. Each, he said, made

> such good use of his [the earl's] time and advantages, such as obtaining large farms and long leases at low rents, that he becomes comparatively independent. It is humiliating to see the abject and slavish conduct, respect I cannot call it, shown by the tenantry to these mean upstarts. This crawling, fawning conduct is very common among the country people and must lower them in the estimation of every independent and proud mind.

The 'slavish conduct' of the Kingston tenants disgusted Kegan. Not only were they poor; they had among them the worst kind of beggar and vagabond. He described how they ran

> bareheaded after a common fellow who may have a temporary command or power over them, with hat in hand, 'your honour, your honour.' It is absolutely sickening! Charlie Daly, 'the Able Dealer,' was the last favourite, and the present one is a farmer's son named Bryan.[1]

By 1845, the rent arrears on the Kingston estate stood at £17,000. The earl had lost a further £17,000 in various legal actions involving creditors. Mismanagement and debts inherited from his father and grandfather placed him in a precarious position. His downfall, however, was the result of an extraordinary fraud perpetrated by a man who at first appeared on the scene as Robert Henry's friend. A chance encounter between the earl and John Sadleir, a solicitor and a Nationalist MP, led to Sadleir being appointed to manage the earl's financial affairs. Kingston asked the Tipperary Joint Stock Bank through Sadleir, who was its solicitor, for a mortgage of £50,000 on the estate.[2]

The solicitor successfully collected £8,000 of rent arrears before sending Patten Smith Bridge, who had been manager of the Tipperary Bank branch in Thurles, to Mitchelstown. Bridge claimed that he audited the books, which were in 'great confusion'. He further claimed that 'the tenants were all at loggerheads with the rents office and greatly in arrears, and I went down there to settle it'. Against Kingston's wishes, Sadleir evicted numerous tenants who had not paid their arrears. He was able to ignore Kingston's wishes because he had persuaded him to vest the estate in the names of his business associates, Thomas J. Eyre and Vincent Scully.

The £50,000 mortgage was approved by the bank. Kingston had to execute a deed which vested his furniture, plate and goods, in addition to the castle and parts of the estate, to secure the loan. He was only paid £16,700 of the agreed sum. To receive this, he was compelled to take out an insurance policy with the Albion Company, at six per cent interest. In return, he was promised an annuity of £4,000 from the income of the estate until the debt was paid. This annuity was never paid – during the ten years the estate was in receivership he obtained only £8,000 by way of income from the rents and was denied use of the castle.

Unknown to Kingston, the Albion had already paid the £50,000 to the Tipperary Bank, via Sadleir, who issued the insurance company with false receipts for the money. To further complicate matters, Sadleir persuaded Eyre (to whom he was related) to advance £40,000 to Kingston. This was to be payable into Vincent Scully's account in the Tipperary Bank in the months of June and July 1845. Only £7,000 of this was passed on to Kingston.

By July 1846, Eyre had become a trustee of the Kingston estate but he, like everyone else except Sadleir, was entirely unaware of what was going on. Sadleir appointed his cousin, Nicholas Sadleir, as agent over the Cork portions of the Kingston estate. His main task was to collect the rents and to repay Lord Kingston's loan. Nicholas collected the rents, from the County Cork lands, amounting to about £19,000 a year, and lodged them in the Tipperary Bank. He did not know that the receipts sent to him were fraudulent and that the money was being used by John Sadleir for land speculation.

In the spring of 1849, the bank foreclosed on Kingston, claiming that he owed them £82,000. Sadleir, ostensibly acting on behalf of the bank, moved to have the estate sold in the Encumbered Estates Court (renamed the Landed Estates Court in 1852). This court was established under the Encumbered Estates Act to sell properties on the application of the owner or encumbrancer. After a sale, the court distributed the money among the creditors and guaranteed clear title to the new owner. Existing tenants were not protected by the legislation.

Sadleir also endeavoured to sell Kingston's furniture and silver, but was stopped by the earl's new solicitor, John McNamara Cantwell. A member of the Young Ireland movement, Cantwell became Kingstons' right-hand-man. He intensely disliked Sadleir and eventually unseated him as MP for Carlow. However, despite his unscrupulous activities, Cantwell was unable to prevent the sale of substantial portions of the Kingston estate.[3]

The first sale took place in Dublin on 17 June 1851, when 20,985 acres in the parishes of Ballylanders and Kilbehenny went under the hammer. A further 18,181 acres in Ballyporeen, and 3,951 acres in Macroney were sold a few weeks later. Within another four years, on 20 February 1855, the estate shrunk by a further 26,743 acres with sales in the County Cork baronies of Condons and Clangibbon, Fermoy and Duhallow, and the barony of Coshlea in County Limerick. Other sales followed on 5 June 1855 and 19 February 1856. The immensity of the sales was astonishing. By 1856, 70,800 acres in three counties had been sold off. In several instances, sales were postponed as the bids were considered too low by the selling agents.

The Landed Estates Court had some difficulty in selling 7,270 acres of the very worst land, which was considered so barren as to be almost worthless. These lots included Quit Rent Mountain, near Kildorrery, Skeheen Upper, Killickane and Glenatlucky, near Mitchelstown. The Kingston hunting lodge in Araglin was included in the sale of 1 July 1851. It was described as 'a neat and comfortable residence, formerly occupied by the present Earl of Kingston, during his father's lifetime ... with extensive plantations.'[4] But it was withdrawn from auction and sold privately to a John Morland.[5] On the same day, Ballyporeen went out of Kingston hands.

The Landed Estates Court rentals give interesting information on tenancy agreements and the condition of the lands for sale. In the disposal of 9,117 acres along the Blackwater River in Duhallow, Kingston was allowed retain all fishing, hunting, mining and some other rights.

Six horses with carts, tackling and guides had to be supplied annually by Francis Baily of Glennahulla 'for work, guiding, etc, within a 34-mile radius of Mitchelstown, or ten shillings for each horse not supplied.' Similar terms for twelve horses applied to the widow Mary Baily, also of Glennahulla. Other tenants were required also to supply their horses for work on the estate. Such terms reflected practices associated with feudal service and tenure in the Manor of Mitchelstown. Dr Eugene O'Neill, who leased 130 acres at Glennahulla, was required to provide a man, horse and car for twelve days of each year to repair public roads.[6]

As part of his land speculation exploits, Sadleir had established the Irish Land Company, which he used to purchase property under the Encumbered Estates Act. Foremost among these properties were the Kingston estate, the Glengall estate to its north and the Castlehyde estate to its south. He spent £63,000 purchasing Kingston lands. Sadleir became a Lord of the Treasury and also speculated heavily in America. However, when his investments failed, it was found that he had embezzled £1.25 million from the Tipperary Bank, before committing suicide in 1856.

To make matters worse, it transpired that rent arrears on the Kingston estate had increased to £73,000 during Sadleir's receivership. Instead of owing money to the Tipperary Bank, which went bankrupt in 1856, Kingston was owed as much as £250,000 from the rents collected during the ten years the property was run by Sadleir, who operated on the bank's behalf. There was no hope of ever collecting this sum. Sadleir's criminal activities also left numerous friends, relatives and business associates in serious financial difficulties. His greed became the overriding factor in the demise of the Kingstons' great property.[7]

Shortly before his suicide, Sadleir's Irish Land Company had bought the old Galtee estate of 20,800 acres, which stretched from Galtymore almost to Ballyporeen. Galtee Castle was included with this lot. It was described as a

> beautiful and romantic mansion ... the residence of the late Countess of Kingston, with its vast plantations and mountain scenery.... The river Funcheon runs through the demesne, and divides the counties. A sum of £1,780 was borrowed by the present Earl of Kingston under the Land Improvement Act, and was laid out in the improvement of those estates.[8]

Part of the Limerick lands were bought by Wyndham Smith who at once increased the rents to 50s an acre from the old rate of between 15s and 18s an acre. Within a few years rent increases of between 100 and 500 per cent would put the Galtee estate in the international headlines when landlord-tenant conflict there provided the spark that ignited the Land War of the 1880s. Nonetheless, the Kingston rents initially were very low compared to the real values of the holdings. In the years after the Famine, rent collection became relatively easy again, but as rents were extraordinarily low compared to other estates, the income of the Kingston property was well below its potential.

Remarkably, agriculture enjoyed a boom after the Famine. Kingston rents had been reduced by the land agent, John Massey, in 1843, but were not increased subsequently to match the improved incomes of the tenants. Rack-renting was unknown on the property. William Downes Webber, Mitchelstown's last landlord, said that 'while the price of the principal products had nearly doubled in the last forty years, the increase of the rents has scarcely exceeded ten per cent, most of which occurred before 1867, the date the majority of the leases were granted'.[9] Between 1869 and 1875 the rental income increased by £56, a mere 0.3 per cent of the annual total. Webber claimed in 1881 that 'the average rental of the whole estate was 'only 16 per cent above Griffith's Valuation of 1851'. By 1880, Griffith's Valuation was as much as 30 per cent below market rental values.

Butter, pigs, potatoes, oats and cattle were the main products of the estate. These made dramatic price improvements, particularly during the 1870s, but it was not the Kingstons who profited. Publicans gained most from the farmers, whose alcohol consumption went up in proportion to their increased incomes. Some contemporary accounts also suggest that the standard of farming on the estate generally left a lot to be desired. In 1880, Fr David Burdon informed the Bessborough Commission that 'many of the farms could produce, according to competent authority, nearly double what they do. The farming is not of the thriftiest.'[10]

Dean Morgan O'Brien took advantage of the sales of the 1850s to purchase significant amounts of land for the Catholic Church adjacent to the town centre, using some of his personal fortune to do so. By 1855, he had built a new parochial house for himself on lands overlooking the town. In June 1853, he introduced the teaching order of Presentation Sisters to Mitchelstown, followed by the Christian Brothers in February 1857. Both orders were established in buildings and on land provided largely at the personal expense of the Dean. Their presence reflected the increasing influence of Catholic institutions in every town in Ireland.[11]

However, the confused state of affairs on the estate continued after the land sales of the 1850s. Matters were exacerbated by Robert Henry's incompetence and events leading up to 1860, when he was declared insane. Sometime after 1856, he became increasingly unstable. He frequently appeared before the metropolitan police courts in London where he was sued by cabmen for refusing to pay fares. He was placed in private care in Dublin but he remained free to do whatever he wished.[12] At Chester in England, Kingston caused consternation when he went onto the Holyhead railway line and persisted in walking through the railway tunnel. He was arrested by the police, but they released him after a few hours. He then made his way to the cathedral where he refused to take off his hat on entering. He was forcibly removed, and a policeman brought him to the Royal Hotel where he remained for the night. *The Illustrated London News* took up the story: 'The first thing on Monday morning he got out into the streets naked, and was again made captive. About twelve o'clock he went to the Bishop of Chester's palace, and so annoyed his Lordship that he requested the police to take charge of him.'

During the proceedings of Kingston's insanity hearing, the earl went up to the magistrates' bench where he sat with his hat on. He made a long, rambling statement in which he accused the Bishop of Chester of insulting the House of Lords by insulting him. Robert Henry threatened to 'bring his Lordship to justice at the bar of the House at the next session, and deprive him of his living'. He was going to write to his friends to have them bring the matter before the House of Commons. 'Bishops had no right to be seated in the House of Lords,' he said, and he would see to it that this privilege would be abolished. He was also going to write to his lawyer, Lord Chelmsford, to enter an action against the Holyhead Railway Company for £100,000 because he alleged that he had been insulted by them.

The earl went on to state that his brother, James, wanted to marry and had 'perpetrated a fraud upon him to take possession of his estates, worth about £50,000 a year, and settling upon him a miserable pittance.' It was enough, said

Robert Henry, 'to make any man insane'. That, more or less, is what the court thought as well. Having heard the evidence of two doctors the magistrate signed an order to have the fourth Earl of Kingston committed to the County Asylum.[13]

Big George's third son, James, now had the onerous task of looking after his brother's affairs. Born on 8 April 1800, he was not in the unstable Kingston mould. Webber said he was 'sober, quiet and capable. Of a just and kindly disposition, he was well liked by all who had dealings with him and extremely popular both before and after his succession to the title and estates.'

Apparently, James was also well versed in business but encountered occasional problems because of his own financial liabilities. When not practising law in Dublin, he resided at Gardenhurst, a comfortable town house in the south-east corner of King Square, outside the castle gates. Following his brother's committal, James tended to live in seclusion in order to avoid the creditors who were clamouring for repayment of loans for which he had signed as guarantor on behalf of his brother. Indeed, it is said that James left Gardenhurst only on Sundays, when he went to Saint George's Church to attend services. His only architectural legacy was the building of a Protestant church at Ballylanders which had stone carvings of the family crest displayed on several windows.[14]

James befriended the elderly Rev Dr Richard Hastings Graves, who was the controversial rector of Brigown for 46 years and the author of several minor publications. James occasionally dined with the Graves family in the rectory at Brigown and it was there that he met and fell in love with Anna Brinkley. A niece of the rector, she was the fourth daughter of Bishop Matthew Brinkley, of Birr, County Offaly, and a granddaughter of the Astronomer Royal. Anna was a pretty 26-year-old when she married James, who was then aged 60, in Saint George's Church on 25 August 1860. By all accounts she was a devoted and affectionate wife. During the very difficult years before James succeeded to the estate, they lived on a small allowance which deriving from Big George's legacies to his children.

Mainly because of his ill-health, James and Anna spent the early years of their marriage in Italy and France. Aristocratic couples often spent long periods abroad especially when they had little else to do but await their inheritance. It was only after Robert Henry died, on 21 January 1867, that James finally succeeded to the family lands as the fifth Earl of Kingston.[15]

This was the year of the Fenian Rising which threw the country into turmoil for a brief period. The Fenians were led by Colonel John O'Mahony, whose family had been tenants and middlemen on the Kingston estate for upwards of a century. The O'Mahonys had leases of Kingston lands at Loughananna, near Kilbehenny, and almost 200 acres at Clonkilla, just outside the western demesne wall at Mitchelstown. There was fierce animosity between the proud old Gaelic family and their Anglo-Irish neighbours on the other side of the high stone boundary. One possible cause of this bitterness was the ejection of the O'Mahonys from their lucrative position as middlemen by the second Earl of Kingston.

John O'Mahony was born on 12 January 1815, at Clonkilla, on the banks of the Funcheon River, but he probably grew up in Loughananna. It was said that his grandfather had horse-whipped one of the Earls of Kingston (probably Robert) for some insult. Both his uncle and father were involved in the 1798 rebellion.

The lease on the Kilbehenny lands expired in 1840 and

some of the family were forced to move to a farm near Carrick-on-Suir. This eviction was also a factor in O'Mahony's revolutionary outlook. In the futile Young Irelander rising of 1848, he met James Stephens, Michael Doheny and Terence Bellew McManus. For several weeks, O'Mahony held out with 2,000 followers on the Comeragh Mountains, thus earning himself the nickname 'Chief of the Comeraghs'. When the rising failed, he fled to Paris where with Stephens and Doheny he conceived the idea of the Fenians. Meanwhile, he gave his property in Mitchelstown and Carrick-on-Suir to his sister's husband, James Hackett Mandeville.[16]

In New York, in 1858, he became the founder and Head Centre of the new revolutionary movement of the Fenian Brotherhood. The name was chosen by O'Mahony in memory of the ancient Fianna warriors. It came to denote physical force to secure independence and the establishment of an Irish Republic. Their military wing was called the Irish Republican Brotherhood.

Regardless of his personal qualities there was discontent with O'Mahony's autocratic style of leadership which led to a reorganisation of the Fenians in 1865. During the upheaval and subsequent fragmentation of the movement, the powers of the Head Centre were curbed by the creation of a Fenian senate that could exercise a veto over O'Mahony.[17] Stephens said that O'Mahony was 'far and away the first patriot of the Irish race'.

In the 1867 rising, Mitchelstown made its mark when a farmer named Peter O'Neill Crowley, from Ballymacoda in east Cork, was shot at Kilclooney Wood, between the town and Kildorrery. Crowley was in a party of men commanded by Captain McClure, who had successfully raided Knockadoon coastguard station. They fled in the direction of

Mitchelstown and took refuge near Kilclooney Wood on Sunday, 31 March.[18] A detachment of the Warwickshire Regiment, billeted at Mitchelstown military barracks, hunted them down and O'Neill Crowley was mortally wounded. His remains were removed to the workhouse mortuary in Mitchelstown before being taken for burial in Ballymacoda. O'Neill Crowley's gun was said to have been taken to Mitchelstown Castle. The rising also brought tragedy to the King family when Lieutenant General Sir Henry, a son of Lord Lorton, was shot dead while walking through Sligo town.[19]

At the time of O'Neill Crowley's death in 1867, fears for the security of Mitchelstown prompted the army to seek permission from Lord Kingston to use his stables as a temporary military barracks. Both he and J.B. Kennedy, the Dublin solicitor acting for the castle's mortgage-holders, opposed the idea as it might also require the occupation of part of the castle itself. 'All the Furniture, plate, the Library, the wines &c are still in mortgage to my Clients,' said Kennedy. 'Possession of the Castle was given by me to the present earl on his undertaking to preserve it.'

James believed that the military would cause 'extreme anxiety' by sending extra troops to the town. The existing military barracks, enlarged since 1823, were more than adequate for the defence of Mitchelstown. He added:

> I am not disposed to adopt any course of action calculated to increase the Public Panic by making it appear that I considered so much ground existed for alarm about the Mitchelstown District that I deemed it really necessary to have a large addition of Troops there, and even to have my own stables and offices filled with military defenders.

The area was bubbling with rumours which Kingston dismissed on the grounds that they were fuelled by shopkeepers who hoped to benefit financially from having more soldiers in the town. In refusing use of the castle, he offered instead to make the old orphanage and infant school in New Square available as a barracks if the need arose. Assuring the government of his resolute loyalty, he declared:

> I will be ready (DV) to go down to Mitchelstown whenever they may find it necessary for me to do so - and I will do what my ancestors have frequently done ... I am neither afraid of open enemies or pretended friends or of any crafty concealed traitors – and I believe that the People generally know (at least on my estate) that I wish and endeavour to act both justly and considerately towards them, and they will also remember (I expect) that I never evicted any [of them] ... Though I am considerably older now, I am still much younger than my gt. grandfather, Edward Earl of Kingston, was during the disturbed times just previously to the breaking out of the Rebellion of 1798. He would not be induced to leave his property of Boyle, but contributed by his presence and influence to keep that part of the country comparatively quiet.[20]

Kingston's views on additional soldiers in Mitchelstown were fully justified. The rebellion was doomed and served only to split the Fenians. O'Mahony suffered the consequences of failure, and ended his days as a pauper in a New York tenement.

The atmosphere in Mitchelstown was much improved on James' succession to the title and he proved true to his word in his dealings with his tenants. Many of the Kingston leases had been drawn up in the early years of the century. Faced with financial ruin, James authorised his agent and relative, Captain Richard Henry Farrer, to offer 31-year leases at existing rents. In effect, he granted tenants the famously-touted three Fs – fair rent, free sale and fixity of tenure. The only condition was that the tenants would 'loan' him one year's rent in advance so that he could keep the mortgage-holders at bay. Several hundred tenants took up the offer, though many were happy to retain their holdings in the old way.[21]

Within a year of James' succession, 470 leases were granted on the new terms. All except 189 of the 890 agricultural holdings on the estate were held on leases of three lives, or 31 years. The percentage of leaseholders on the Kingston Estate was 'considerably above the average' for County Cork. Relations between landlord and tenant in Mitchelstown were never better. When Fr Burdon went before the Bessborough Commission in 1880, he declared that 'the management of the Kingston estate contrasts most favourably with that of any other in my knowledge'.[22]

There was great expectation in July 1868 when it became known that Lord and Lady Kingston intended to take up residence at the castle. Twenty years had passed since the owner of the estate had lived there. Recent evidence of how well the tenants would be treated by the new earl made his return highly popular. A broadly-based welcoming committee, which included Catholics and Protestants, was formed under the chairmanship of the parish priest, Dean O'Brien. Triumphal arches were erected around the town and many houses were decorated with evergreens. The entrance hall of the castle had a display of flowers, laurels and exotic plants as well as ornate expressions of greeting such as 'Health and Happiness', and 'Home Sweet Home'. An arch bearing the legend *Céad Míle Fáilte* hung over the entrance to King Square.

On their journey from Dublin to Mitchelstown, the Kingstons were greeted by a party of tenants at Knocklong railway station and escorted for the final twelve miles to Mitchelstown. At Ballahaderig Bridge on the Limerick Road, the tenants began to untackle the horses and pull the carriage the rest of the way to the town. 'But this honour the noble lord firmly declined.' Cheers of welcome 'reverberated amongst the neighbouring hills with thrilling cadence. Lord

Kingston bowed repeatedly, and seemed scarcely to have calculated upon such a heart-stirring welcome'.

Thousands on foot, horseback or in vehicles followed the procession into town, led by the band of the 48th Regiment from Fermoy. The *Cork Examiner* stated that the welcome was, 'without exaggeration, immense and enthusiastic, nothing like it had ever been witnessed in Mitchelstown before'. The procession wound into New Market Square and around to the castle via King Street and George Street. In Robert Street a 'great wealth of the national colour, and *Erin go Bragh* decorated the crown of the triumphal arch'. At the avenue of limes leading up to the castle, the band struck up *Home Sweet Home* which was 'echoed a hundred times by the voices and hearts of ten thousand people'. Soon after nightfall, the windows of every house in town were lit and 'an artificial day shone within the town ... Standing out in prominent radiance above the town, were the [Presentation] Convent on one hand, and the [Christian Brothers'] Monastery on the other – both brilliantly lighted.'

Large parties, supplied with gallons of porter, danced around fires in both squares. Festivities centred on King Square, where the army band performed from an extensive repertoire. A 'pyrotechnic display' created further excitement.

> Lit by brilliant coloured fires, the square looked an extract from fairy-land, and the novelty of the many curious effects and explosions greatly amused the people. The exhibition concluded with a large device – a Brunswick star, formed by great jets of fire, displaying in the centre the word 'Welcome' in letters of dazzling brilliancy ...

Next day the committee went to the castle to present an illustrated address to the Kingstons on behalf of their appreciative tenants. They were invited to lunch with the master and his lady. The contents of the address indicated why the return of the earl and his young wife was received with such enthusiasm and excitement. 'On your accession,' said the address, 'there was scarcely a lease on the estates, and you directed leases of long duration to be prepared at the existing rents; and no doubt such wise and unsolicited kindness will rebound to the mutual benefit of landlord and tenant.'

Kingston was visibly moved by the address, which referred to industry and energy being 'manifested in all quarters'. Labourers were finding it easier to get work in the locality. 'Your bounty was extended to the destitute poor last winter, under the direction of your respected agent, Captain R.H. Farrer,' said the address. Farrer's efforts had resulted in a building boom in the district, including town improvements and the building of roads and bridges. James was equally fulsome in his reply, for his treatment of the tenants had elevated him almost to the status of a chieftain of old.

> I considered it was my duty to do to others as I would be done by, and to protect my tenants, as far as I possibly could, against a species of injustice from which I had most severely suffered myself (hear, hear and applause). I felt bound so to protect them by giving honest and industrious tenants on my property, who are willing to improve, a permanent interest in their holdings, so that they may not be liable to meet such injustice as I myself had to encounter.

James' remarks show that, despite common myth, many landlords were genuinely concerned for their tenants' well-being. He had a desire to improve his estate and tried vigorously to do so during his short period of ownership. He was prey to creditors and this made him sensitive to his tenants' fears for their security. For its part, the *Cork Examiner* said that Lord Kingston richly deserved the people's welcome. He had shown 'a disposition to deal kindly by them and to manifest, in his treatment of them, a recognition as well of the duties as of the rights of property'.[23]

For all his promise and good intentions, however, James soon felt helpless in the face of a ruinous crisis in his extended family. This had its roots in the cadet branch of the King family at Rockingham where Robert, son of the first Viscount Lorton, was the cause of disaster. At an early age, Robert experienced serious financial difficulties. In 1829, he married Anne Gore-Booth of Lissadell. Neither the Kings nor the Gore-Booths approved of the marriage, but they were helpless to prevent it. Within ten years, Robert was suffering from *delirium tremens* and a partial stroke.

Feeling alienated, Anne engaged in a series of extra-marital affairs, some of which were public knowledge. In 1839, her involvement with a man at Enfield in County Kildare was so blatant that Robert could have sued for divorce, but he did nothing. A year later, the couple moved to Frankfurt where, by 1846, they were befriended by the French Viscomte Satge St Jean and his English wife. Soon, Anne and the Viscomte were much more than friendly. She gave him money and had a ring engraved 'Anne & Ernest, 23 November 1846'. The Viscomtesse found evidence that her husband and Anne were sleeping together and, in due course, she left him. In 1847, Robert, Anne and the Viscomte took a house in Boulevard Waterloo in Brussels.[24]

Among the staff was Julie Imhoff, who joined Viscount Lorton's family from Aix la Chapelle to look after the invalid Robert. During the next 18 months Robert was back in England, where his wife visited him to discuss financial matters. He then returned to Frankfurt and Anne to Brussels, where she gave birth to a second son; her first son, Robert Edward, would play a major role in the future of Mitchelstown. The new baby was baptised Henry Ernest Newcomen King, with Viscomte, Ernest, signing the birth certificate as 'oncle'. Proof later emerged that the Viscomte and Anne had been sharing the same bed during their stay in Brussels. Robert and all the Rockingham Kings took the view that the baby had been fathered by the Viscomte who, after an attempt to engineer a large loan from Robert, removed himself to France.[25]

In 1850, Robert sued for divorce. The case was heard in London, with all the attendant publicity. The counter-claim for divorce by Anne's lawyers alleged adultery between Robert and Julie Imhoff in the Ship Hotel at Dover in the autumn of 1848, and later in Frankfurt. At this time, Robert was very ill from alcohol and drug abuse. He was particularly ill at Dover, while travelling back to London and with only one room available, Julie had slept in a chair there for three nights. Hotel staff testified that nothing untoward had happened and that Julie was present only as his nurse. There is no record of what may, or may not, have happened at Frankfurt. It is certain, however, that in London years later, Julie lived with Robert when he was both Lord Lorton and sixth Earl of Kingston. During the court proceedings in London in 1850, the judge found ample evidence of Anne's adultery and admissible evidence of Robert's involvement with Julie Imhoff. As the law then stood, both parties were dismissed from the case and divorce was refused.

This outcome prevented the Kings from taking a paternity case on lines familiar under modern law. Robert Edward, the elder son, was removed from his parents by his grandfather, Lord Lorton. Anne and the new baby took up residence with her brother at Rockingham. From London, where he remained, Robert instructed his agent to put Rockingham under siege. With little food and no fuel, Anne and her entourage were forced to go back to the Gore-Booths at Lissadell. The elder son, Robert Edward, who was in line

End of the Line

to become seventh Earl of Kingston, grew up believing that his younger brother was illegitimate. Robert Edward was short of money and in poor health. Although he had one daughter, he felt that he would have no more children and might even die before his father.[26]

In 1867, Robert Edward found a way of solving some of his problems. As the eventual heir to Mitchelstown under the 1823 entail, he proposed to James, the fifth earl, that the entail at Mitchelstown should be cut. He would then allow all to be placed in James' name, upon payment of £120,000 from the Mitchelstown estate to provide for his wife and daughter. James told his cousin that he strongly concurred with his desire to 'prevent the spurious illegitimate offspring of any adulterer from acquiring the lawful inheritance of the Kings and the Fentons'. Robert the elder, now Viscount Lorton, lived in London and seemed to have been unaware of the arrangements between his eldest son and cousin. Neither did his younger son, Harman King-Harman, know anything about it. Under the entail, Harman would inherit Mitchelstown, if Henry Ernest was to be cut out, while James retained his life interest in the property. After some hesitation, James signed the Mitchelstown Disentailing Deed on 11 August, at Claridges Hotel in London. One of the witnesses was William Claridge, the one-time cook at Mitchelstown.

It was understandable that James and his cousin, Robert Edward, should want to exclude the illegitimate Henry Ernest from the King properties; but the decision by Robert Edward to disclaim on behalf of his own Lorton branch all future interest in Mitchelstown seems now – as it did then to his uncle Harman – extraordinary. Why James handed over Mitchelstown to his wife is equally baffling as such a move would put the estates out of King family control after almost 200 years.

The second indenture signed by James confirmed charges on the estate totalling £104,000, including the endowment of £25,000 to Kingston College. Subject to those charges, and the life interests of Viscount Lorton and his son, Robert Edward, the entire Mitchelstown estate was at James' disposal. Under this agreement, James' wife, Anna, Countess of Kingston, could reside at Mitchelstown Castle during the life interests of Lorton and Robert Edward. Anna received an additional £1,000 annually, in addition to the £1,200 a year provided by Big George for whoever James might marry. The third earl had also provided £15,000 for James' children. Such enormous provisions were often the ruin of Irish estates when the owner found most of his income going to beneficiaries of wills. It was agreed that, after the deaths of James and Viscount Lorton, £120,000 would be raised for Robert Edward, but not while he still enjoyed a life interest. This guaranteed him an income from the estate during his lifetime and, on his death, more than enough would be available for his wife and daughter.[27]

In the spring of 1868, the disestablishment of the Church of Ireland was being advocated by Gladstone's Liberal government. True to his class and creed, James opposed the bill when it came before Parliament the following year. He took a keen interest in the debates on the issue. After one of them – an early morning session on 19 June 1869 – he could not get a cab and had to walk in heavy rain to his hotel, Claridges. He caught a chill that 'produced organic symptoms which afterwards came against him'. Over the next two weeks, he was attended by three doctors who were unwisely confident of their patient's recovery. Of these events, the countess said that

> The doctors several times assured me, and I confidently believed, and so did my said husband ... that his illness was merely temporary, and that it was not at all likely to shorten his life. He apparently recovered completely, and I believed him to be as well as ever.

Over the next few weeks, James indeed seemed to have recovered and, on 13 July, the couple went to the wedding of his cousin, Colonel King. They then visited relatives, including Lady Louisa de Spaen, in Tunbridge Wells on 21 July; his nephew, Philip Cooke, at Oweston Hall, Doncaster, on 17 August, and Bryan Cooke, another nephew, four days later. On the last day of the month, the Kingstons returned to Mitchelstown Castle where the earl was in 'fairly good health'. Days later, and perhaps because of the rigorous voyage home, James caught another cold while staying at the Imperial Hotel in Cork. This brought a return of the previous symptoms. The best efforts of a Dr Tanner failed to save the life of the fifth Earl of Kingston and he passed away on 8 September 1869.[28]

He was succeeded by Viscount Lorton, who enjoyed the earldom for only six weeks, dying on 16 October. The sixth earl was succeeded by Robert Edward, who chose not to exercise his right to exchange the rents from the Mitchelstown Estate for the £120,000 specified in the agreement. But his tenure was also brief and he passed away within two years, in June 1871. Before his death, however, action was taken to keep Rockingham out of Henry Ernest's hands. While he became the eighth earl, Rockingham passed to Harman King-Harman and Mitchelstown became Anna's property.

James was the last of his line. With him died the family's United Kingdom peerage and the senior branch of the Kings. His only surviving sister, Lady Helena Cooke, could not inherit the family titles, which had to pass to the cousins in Rockingham. Like his father and brother, James was laid to rest in the vault at Kingston College. He was the last Kingston to be buried in Mitchelstown.

Anna inherited Mitchelstown Castle and the estate. But her late husband and his Rockingham cousins must have found it hard to rest in peace, as the nightmare they had tried so hard to avoid was now to become a reality: Henry Ernest Newcomen King was eighth Earl of Kingston. However, their plan to stop him acquiring the two properties succeeded. In 1872, he took the wives of the fifth and seventh earls, as well as others, to court in an attempt to gain possession of the Kingston and Lorton estates. The expensive legal proceedings only confirmed what had already been done, so that the eighth earl and his heirs gained nothing financially from either Mitchelstown or Rockingham. Henry Ernest offered Anna £100,000 for her interest in the Kingston Estate, but she refused.

The eighth earl managed, however, to ensure that his heirs would have Kingston blood, even if his own ancestry was in doubt. He married Florence Margaret Christine Tenison, of Kilronan Castle, County Roscommon, on 23 January 1872 – just four months before he initiated proceedings against Anna, Dowager Countess of Kingston. Florence was a great-granddaughter of the first Earl of Kingston, whose daughter, Frances, had married a Tenison. She was also the heiress of her father's estate and soon after her marriage to Henry Ernest they changed their surname to King-Tenison. On her father's death in 1883, Florence and Henry became the owners of Kilronan Castle, just twelve miles from Rockingham.[29]

8

Mountain of Misery

High on the Galtee mountains a remarkable saga began to unfold in the mid-1870s. It brought international attention to former Kingston tenants who had been subjected to exorbitant rent increases under a new landlord. Though removed from the ownership crisis facing the Mitchelstown estate, the Galtee affair gave a very important insight into the fate of many former Kingston tenants under new masters. The story of the Galtee tenants brought to light the harsh injustices of the Irish land system, especially as it applied to the occupiers of the 20,800-acre estate. Furthermore, it highlighted the negative results of land speculation.

The rugged seclusion of the Galtees might have continued to hide its human misfortune but for two related events: the execution of a land agent's would-be assassin and a consequent libel action, and the publication of a brilliant series of newspaper articles on the tenants' plight, later issued as a booklet entitled *Christmas on the Galtees*.[1]

After the Irish Land Company purchased the Galtee property from the Kingstons in 1852, it attempted to make some improvements there, but things generally remained as they had been for almost a century. A small number of tenants were evicted in the name of progress. In some cases rents were increased slightly while, in a few others, 'really and truly nominal rents applied' so that it was hardly worth collecting them. For the most part, relations between the tenants and the company's agent, E.B. Brogden, were as good as might be expected.[2]

In 1873, the Land Company sold the Galtees to Nathaniel Buckley, a Manchester MP and cotton millionaire who had been one of the company's principal directors. He intended to extract the maximum income possible from his new investment. He hired as land agent Patten Smith Bridge. On Buckley's instructions, the new agent hired, in turn, Joseph Walker to examine the holdings with a view to increasing rents, while adopting the 'live-and-let-live principle'. Walker had experience in valuing other estates, including Portarlington. In June 1873, he moved into the home of an English tenant on the Galtees and immediately set about his task. During that summer he walked each of the 517 holdings. When not working he sometimes dined with Bridge at Galtee Castle, but both denied that they discussed details of the valuation during this period.[3]

'The Walker', as he was called on the Galtees, was nearly always accompanied by the pleading tenant, and often by estate bailiffs, when a holding was being surveyed. He completed his valuation on 15 October and submitted his report to Bridge in January 1874. The increases recommended seemed reasonable enough, given that it had been decades since rents were last raised. The rental of the property was £4,160, and Walker proposed to increase it by 25 per cent to £5,477. By law, the county cess (tax) of five per cent was allowed against their rentals. The cess on rents less than £4 would be paid in full by the landlord. This would give Buckley a total increase of £1,046. Notices informing tenants of the increases caused consternation throughout the estate. In a few cases in Barnahown rents were reduced, but on over 100 holdings they were doubled or increased by anything up to five-fold.[4]

Bridge argued that many of the rents had not been increased since the end of the 1700s. In the years since, the tenants had greatly improved their holdings, though they had achieved this with back-breaking effort in the most extreme conditions. For all of that, Bridge believed that his master, Buckley, was now entitled to reap some of the benefits of their labours. The tenants bitterly opposed the increases. One tenant, John Ryan, had 37 acres at £30-5s-9d under a lease dating from 1798. Walker's valuation increased the rental to £44-5s, but Ryan refused to pay. Bridge offered him £200 if he would give up his lease. When that offer was also refused, an eviction order was issued. On the morning of 22 March 1875, Ryan was told by Bridge that the sheriff would evict him next day. Late that afternoon Bridge and his sister went for a walk on the avenue at Galtee Castle. Bridge described how

> We went around, and as we were coming home about 100 yards from the avenue gate I was shot in the back. I felt the wound and heard the report. I turned around and saw John Ryan with a double-barrelled gun in his hand. He fired two shots this way – slap, slap. He had the gun still pointing at me. I then shook my stick at him, and said, 'I see you, you villain'. He ran away, and I passed on.

Bridge was slightly wounded in the shoulder with one ball and in the spine with another. A third shot missed and struck a tree. As police from Mitchelstown and Cahir swarmed the district Bridge went about his business as usual next morning. With a party of bailiffs and police, he evicted Ryan's family but failed to find his attacker. From then on, two armed constables accompanied Bridge wherever he went.[5] For his pains he received £200 compensation at Limerick Assizes. A special cess was levied against the already hard-pressed ratepayers of the district to meet Bridge's award and his policemen's pay.

When the half-yearly rents fell due in 1876, Bridge went to the estate office in Mitchelstown. It was 31 March, a market Thursday, when thousands of country folk went to town. At about 5.30pm he set out for Galtee Castle, accompanied by Constable Nugent and Sub-Constable Jones; his driver John Hyland, and his steward, Patrick O'Loughlen. Two miles out of Mitchelstown – at Geragh, near Kilbehenny – an ambush party fired at the sidecar. Hyland was shot through the heart and fell dead. The policemen took cover and returned fire. Bridge grabbed the reins and sped off, leaving his guards to fight it out, but he did not escape unscathed: he had a pellet in his cheekbone under the left eye and another passed through his throat. Constable Nugent received several wounds; O'Loughlen was slightly injured and Sub-Constable Jones escaped unharmed. Despite his injuries, Constable Nugent chased some of the assailants. One pointed a heavy cavalry pistol at him but was over-powered and handcuffed. This was Tom Crowe, a 60-year-old uncle of the fugitive Ryan. Led by Resident Magistrate Richard Eaton, among others, the police searched the district, but it was easy to hide a man who had friends on the Galtees.[6]

This second attempt to murder Bridge caused a sensation at home and an outburst of anti-Irish racism in sections of the imperial press. The *Standard* represented the assailants as drunken savages. The attack, it sneered, was a case of 'infamously bad shooting'. The Nationalist MP, Joseph Biggar, said he disapproved of the shooting of landlords 'because the driver, a perfectly innocent person, was sometimes shot by accident'.[7]

A new name with a patriotic resonance now entered the Galtee drama – he was John Sarsfield Casey, a shopkeeper's son from Baldwin Street in Mitchelstown. In 1865, at the age of nineteen, Casey was convicted of Fenian membership and served three years of his five-year sentence in the penal colonies of Australia. His conviction came after he had been identified as the author of letters published in newspapers, under the pseudonym of the *Galtee Boy*, by which he became popularly known.

After his return in February 1870, Casey resumed writing letters to the newspapers giving detailed accounts of his experiences in Western Australia. To some extent, he hoped that by attracting public attention to the treatment of Fenian prisoners, their situation might be improved. After his dreadful experiences, the *Galtee Boy* was especially sensitive to the hardships endured by Buckley's tenants. His response was to write two letters for publication, the first of which appeared in the *Cork Examiner* on 13 April 1876, and the second in the *Freeman's Journal* five days later.[8] It was 'a sad day' when the lands in the Limerick portion of the Kingston Estate went to new owners, he said. The Kingstons had been 'excellent landlords', who charged rents 'which would excite a smile' compared to those demanded by some of the new owners. 'For though some of the purchasers are to this day excellent landlords,' he said, 'many more swept the poor tenants off their properties, and where hundreds of happy homes once stood nought but sheep walks and pasture lands meet the eye.'

There was precious little chance that Bridge or Walker – or, for that matter, Buckley – would ever experience the type of gratitude shown by the tenants to the Kingston agent, Massey, who was presented with an illuminated address and an expensive service of plate when the Galtee property was sold in 1852. Massey, in response, said that he had had 'many a sleepless night' worrying about having to preside over the sale of the estate and what might become of its tenants. The performance of such painful duty was, said the agent,

> rendered less disagreeable by the patience, order and excellent conduct of the tenantry – conduct which, for the twenty years I am engaged in the management of landed property, I have never seen equalled elsewhere, and which, under their privations, I consider to be miraculous.

On some of the poorest land, Bridge increased rents by up to 500 per cent. A mud cabin, a small patch of potatoes and a few sticks of furniture represented the entire possessions of many tenants. As proof of the injustice being inflicted on the tenants Casey listed the old and new rentals for 39 holdings. At least 53 were issued with eviction orders. Referring to Bridge, Casey remarked that 'he will stand another shot or eject the 53 families'.[9] Bridge's solicitor and his uncle immediately published rebuttals of Casey's letters for publication in the press.[10] These caused further controversy, which grew to fever pitch when Tom Crowe was hanged in Cork Jail on 25 August 1876, for his part in the murder of the driver Hyland.

Bridge now felt he had little option but to sue Casey for criminal libel. If guilt was proven then the punishment would almost certainly include a prison sentence. According to the land agent, Casey had made libellous claims in his letters to the press. He alleged that these had incited tenants to resist payment of rent and to make another attempt on his life.[11] Bridge's attitude was not improved by an avalanche of death threats in letters written anonymously, and beyond the reproach of the law. One of his correspondents, claiming to be from Skibbereen, concluded:

> I suppose you will send this letter to your attorney, to the devil with him, and the police too. I care as much for the police as I care

for a straw, and I hate the thought of you as God hates the thought of a renegade.[12]

The libel action opened before Lord Chief Justice May in the Court of the Queen's Bench in Dublin on 24 November 1877. Its political implications attracted enormous public interest. Up to 100 tenants were summoned to give evidence on Casey's behalf. For almost all of them, it was their first time leaving the Galtees for more than a day. Dublin must have seemed a very frightening place to the tenants – many still speaking only their native Irish tongue.[13] Indeed, Dublin was as strange to them as they were to Dubliners. 'Shawn Shaughnessy's body-coat was the wonder of Sackville-street,' said one observer.[14]

Casey was defended by the celebrated Nationalist MP and barrister, Isaac Butt, who had only recently lost the leadership of the Irish Home Rule Party to Charles Stewart Parnell.[15] Butt had also defended the teenage Fenian at his trial in Cork eleven years previously. The *Galtee Boy*'s friends, including the Catholic Archbishop of Cashel, Dr Thomas Croke, subscribed to the 'Casey Defence Fund'. The Archbishop declared that he wanted the full facts of the Mitchelstown case brought 'fully and fairly before the public'. In a letter to *The Irishman* on 30 June 1877, he called for public support for the defence fund.

Numerous witnesses were called during the eight days of the case. The defence emphasised the fact that neither Buckley nor Brogden (Bridge's predecessor as land agent) had been called to testify. The evidence of the twenty tenants who entered the witness box still makes startling reading. Many were debt-ridden, while some were forced to work elsewhere in an effort to meet the rents.[16]

Denis Murphy – a tall, gaunt man from Skeheenarinky – had to pawn his coat to pay the increased rent on his 10.75

acres. It had been doubled from £3-7s-6d to £6-15s. Like many of his neighbours, Murphy's wife had gone into service as a maid:

> I have my wife, and I had nine children. There are three of my children in America ... And there is not a man, my lord, in the world that is able to describe mountain land like a man who toils in it, neither a Walker nor a Bridge (laughter), and it is a scrupulous thing, my lord, that any gentleman, of decent appearance, should see hungry and naked creatures [with great energy], because, my lord, I am as healthy as any man in the courthouse, and my visage can show I am starving from the want of food.[17]

His neighbour, Patrick Burke, farmed sixteen acres near Galtee Castle. He worked hard, but had been unable to pay the old rent of £4-17s-6d, and had no idea where he could find the new rent of £8. His debts came to at least £60.

> Even the little coat he had put upon his back he had not paid for, and the little trousers he had was not his own – only a neighbouring man, seeing he had not another coat, lent it to him for good. He got only one frieze coat for fifteen years past, and he has to pawn it, and got 4s for it. When he and his family had the hamper of potatoes used, they would have stirabout, and perhaps now and then a bit of bread when they would be going to the mountains to sell turf.[18]

Patrick Kearney remembered the Galtees since childhood as bleak mountainy land made of nothing but heath, stone and bog:

> My brothers had to fly away when the times were bad, and I was the only one that stood on the ground, playing with that miserable place and getting hunger and starvation ... The potatoes were so bad this year that they were hardly worth digging. I got a pain in my heart, the same as if you stuck a knife in me, and I was thinking myself it was the croghauns of praties gave it to me ... I don't

get as much milk as would colour a sup of tea. I make no firkin of butter at all, but little knobs they send into market. Goats in other places are as good as the cows we have.[19]

At the end of the trial, the judge advised the jury to find the defendant guilty on all eight counts. Casey, he declared, liked seeing his name in the newspapers. He had maliciously written about the estate's affairs which were private matters not open to public comment or criticism. However, the jury took a different view and chose to look at the morality of Casey's statements, rather than the legal technicalities of criminal libel law. After an hour and a half they returned a verdict of not guilty on two counts and declared a failure to agree on the remainder. A great cheer greeted the verdict, which was tantamount to an acquittal. Casey received a hero's welcome home to Mitchelstown and, in Cork city, there was a victory celebration in his honour.[20]

The case attracted the attention of a young Mallow journalist named William O'Brien, who was working for the *Freeman's Journal*. He now decided to inspect the Buckley estate, arriving at the Galtees during Christmas 1877. Accompanied by Rev Dr Patrick Delaney of Ballyporeen, whose parish stretched to the top of the mountain, O'Brien wanted to see if the tenants' conditions were as bad as the public had been led to believe. Was it really, he asked, 'a gigantic conspiracy against truth, or the cry of honest industry driven to despair?' His series for the *Freeman's Journal*, published in five parts, was called 'Christmas on the Galtees' – probably the first and most outstanding piece of investigative journalism in nineteenth-century Ireland. Travelling through the most difficult terrain, O'Brien found conditions to be worse than he had imagined.[21]

On Christmas eve, he and the priest climbed one of the paths leading up the mountain at Skeheenarinky, where they found the home of Michael Dwyer. A pot of potatoes boiled in the fire – the only food for a family of ten children. O'Brien squeezed several potatoes to a pulp. 'These are not like any other potatoes I ever saw, except those picked out as refuse for the pigs in more favoured spots,' he said. 'I have not yet seen in Skeheenarinky a single potato as large as an orange.'[22]

Arriving at Patrick Burke's cabin, they were told by his wife that the rent on his sixteen acres had been raised from £4-18s-7d to £8. His home was typical of many on the mountain:

> The five members of the family sleep in two beds in the bedroom, whose poverty she shrank from exposing, but stated that she had put a sop of straw under their feet to keep the floor dry ... the den in which three people are huddled together in the adjoining cowhouse is an outrage upon civilization. I had to stoop on entering its crazy door, and as soon as I could make out anything in the gloom I discovered that I stood up to my ankles in a fetid pool of rainwater mixed with the droppings of cattle. Propped up on wattles in a corner of this stifling den was a filthy bag of straw, littered with some foul rags and tattered coverlids; and here I was gravely, but with manifest shame, assured that a man with his wife and daughter sleep nightly, while the cow lies down in the sodden manure beside them.[23]

O'Brien went to Mitchelstown workhouse on Christmas Day. 'The prospects I had seen of the festive season at Skeheenarinky excited a curiosity to learn how much worse off an idle pauper could be than a farmer who has spent all his days creating soil upon the breast of a mountain,' he said. To his surprise, the journalist found that the inmates of the workhouse were much better off than the farmers of the Galtees. They had breakfast of bread and coffee. Their dinners consisted of one pound of prime boiled beef and vegetables, with as much hot soup as they could eat. They were well clothed and each had a mattress of clean straw, with two pairs of woollen blankets, a pair of sheets, a warm rug and a pillow:

> I saw the old people attack their trenchers, and right heartily demolish their contents. They were cleanly and warmly clad and shod. I saw parties of infirm men and women lolling before bright fires in their day rooms, or basking in the sun in the exercise yards. I passed through the pure white dormitories, with floors scrupulously scrubbed and windows half opened to admit the bracing air from the hills.

The children looked healthy. They were clothed, fed and educated, and most days were allowed into the fields. Bedridden old people were allowed a diet of porter or wine, beefsteak or arrowroot, on doctor's orders. 'It was not very splendid as a prospect in life,' he said, ' but there were no dripping walls, no scanty clothes, no clamorous creditors, no hungry stomachs.'

None of the Galtee homes had any form of Christmas decoration. In the less stricken mountain cabins, there was bread, tea and pork for Christmas dinner, but for most it was Indian meal:

> As I drove [back to Mitchelstown] past the base of the hill after nightfall, when no cheerful twinkle lighted the cabin windows, and when a snowstorm breaking over the Galtees overspread it like a shroud, there appeared to be few spots in Christendom that had less business with a happy Christmas. [24]

During his ten days on the estate, O'Brien visited 226 holdings and spoke with the occupants of 30 others. 'My head almost swims with the tales of misery, poverty, squalor, and despair poured into my ears from 50 different sources,' he reported on Saint Stephen's Day. On their travels after Christmas, O'Brien and Delaney passed the farm of John

Hyland, the land agent's ill-fated driver, whose widow was awarded £700 compensation. At Widow Roche's cabin, they were told that her husband was sick for more than eighteen months before he died of rheumatic pains and dropsy. He was advised by the dispensary doctor to go to the workhouse hospital; but he refused at first, and by the time he did go, it was too late:

> The family sleep in two straw beds in a suffocating little apartment, some seven feet by ten, and the rain pours through the thatch within a few inches of the head of the bed in which a withered old man, Mrs Roche's father-in-law, lay for three months this year with swellings and pains in his bones.[25]

The most pitiful sight in Barnahown – on the hills south of Ballyporeen village – was John Creagh's cabin where his wife and six children huddled around the chimney corner. Things were not improved when he opened the door leading into a filthy receptacle of stable manure, where the donkey slept:

> A tall, gaunt, worn old man, palsied with rheumatic pains, and with lingering consumption stamped on every line of his wan face, staggering out of his miserable bed of straw to greet us feebly ... when I saw one of the rafters over his bed smashed and propped, I could not but think that if the rafters had mercifully given way and silenced all beneath, there had been small share of happiness the less in the world.[26]

In the townland of Knocknagalty, James Murphy lived on a farm nominally rated as 95 acres. Like many of his neighbours, he was facing eviction because he could not pay the rent, which had been increased from £4-7s-4d to £10-10s. 'My father lived here before me, for 80 years,' he said. 'I was not twelve years old when I remember rooting that unfortunate rock and, from that day to this, sorra the day's comfort we

Left to right: Margaret, William and Elizabeth King, children of James, 4th Baron Kingston, c. 1730.

Caroline, Lady Kingsborough, (later Countess of Kingston), 1775/'76.

'Big' George, 3rd Earl of Kingston, builder of Mitchelstown Castle.

Mitchelstown Castle, the last summer, 1922.

The hall, Mitchelstown Castle.

The gallery, Mitchelstown Castle.

A drawing room, Mitchelstown Castle.

Margaret ('Mrs Mason'),
Countess of Mount Cashell, c. 1810.

Henry Ernest, 8th Earl of Kingston,
who died in 1896.

William Downes Webber, 1885.

Anna, Dowager Countess
of Kingston, 1885.

Rockingham, County Roscommon.

Mitchelstown Castle, south wing and entrance front.

Kingston College, c. 1889.

New Market Square after the 'Mitchelstown Massacre' in 1887. Place where Michael Lonergan was shot is marked by white x.

South wing, Mitchelstown Castle after the fire, August 1922.

Galtee Castle in the Galtee mountains.

Tennis party at Mitchelstown, 1907.

Wentworth Alexander King-Harman, who died in 1949.

Colonel A.L. King-Harman in 1997 holding the 'loving cup' presented by Queen Caroline to Admiral James King in 1814.

ever had here.' O'Brien described how Murphy dug portions of the semi-reclaimed heathland, and after almost breaking his spade, brought up six inches of black soil, with a substratum of yellow mud and clay. His little cow, although looking hardy, was visibly bony and cramped from the cold of the wind-swept mountain.[27]

In Carrigeen, O'Brien clambered up a rocky watercourse into the heart of the hills:

> On one of the coldest and windiest summits of this wild region stands the hut of Shawn Shaughnessy – the foulest and dingiest human habitation I have yet set foot in. The whole construction is about nine feet square, and beside it the tottering walls of a roofless outhouse. Right in front of the door of the dwelling-house is built a wall to keep out the wind. It has the effect also of completely keeping out the light, save what struggles in through the broken window or the broken roof.

A spinning wheel and an almost empty dresser were all the furniture he could see in the darkness. A 'poor straw bed covered with ragged bedclothes' filled an alcove. Shaughnessy's wife was almost blind from working with her spinning wheel in the smoky darkness. Her husband was

> a huge, broad-shouldered, great-chested old man, straight as a ram-rod, with the purest type of Celtic face, half simple, half roguish, in primitive costume of caubeen, frieze coat, and knee breeches; and speaking a wonderful jumble of Irish and English. Shawn's rent was raised from £7-4s-6d to £11-19s-11d. He went three times to Mr Bridge with the increased rent, which he sold one of his two cows to make up, and was twice refused. Mr Bridge, however, afterwards accepted it.

One of Shaughnessy's sons had gone to New Zealand with only 21 shillings in his pocket. He was there only two months when he sent home £9 to his parents. 'He always told us never to give up the old place while there was a roof over it,' said his mother, whose tenacious hold on the land was typical of most of her neighbours.[28]

Christmas on the Galtees was published as a booklet by the Tenants' Defence Association, which circulated it to great effect in the propaganda battles against landlordism. In the preface, O'Brien wrote:

> I approached the estate, prepared to find that there had been more clamour than was just over the misery of the tenantry; I left it in despair of ever being able adequately to put before the eyes of the public, for their pity and indignation, the shameful scenes which passed under my own eyes, in a time of peace, and in the name of law.[29]

The landlord Buckley had to endure the embarrassment of being condemned by many of his parliamentary colleagues in the House of Commons, where the Galtee affair was hotly debated. His agent Bridge, still under police protection, remained at Galtee Castle for more than a year afterwards. Finally, it all proved too much for him, and his departure, in 1879, was greeted with delight by the tenants and reported in the *Freeman's Journal* on 24 March:

> He was unaccompanied by a single individual, save an unusually strong force of police armed for the most part with double barrelled breech-loading rifles. Though the ex-agent most ungraciously determined to depart in secret, the tenantry (among whom the news spread like wildfire) were determined to give him an ovation of such a nature as would indelibly fix in his memory the remembrance of Skeheenarinky.

An immense number of people, old and young, lined the roads. One reporter described how

> Poor widows in rags knelt, invoked the maledictions of Heaven,

whilst emaciated men, who looked as if they never ate a good meal, shouted themselves hoarse, danced for joy, and in their excitement set on fire all the furze bushes in the vicinity.

The tenants celebrated into the night, and lit tar barrels and bonfires on the roadsides. At Mitchelstown, the squares and streets were also lit and the brass band played national airs. There too events of an even more startling nature would soon unfold in the relations between Lady Kingston and her tenants.[30]

9

THE QUEEN'S CATTLE DRIVERS

Rack-renting on the Galtee estate made the neighbouring Kingston regime seem benign. There, in contrast, rents were remarkably low and the Mitchelstown estate was one of the few where many tenants already enjoyed fair rent, free sale and fixity of tenure. However, the landlord reserved the right to refuse 'free sale' to any prospective buyer who might be regarded as unacceptable. Furthermore, the 'three Fs' were granted largely by custom on the Kingston property rather than as part of a legal contract. Still, it was here that the anti-landlord forces chose to make a stand in the so-called Land War of the 1880s. The struggle in Mitchelstown was based on tenant unity organised – and where necessary, enforced – by strong local leaders. They employed a much feared new weapon known as 'The Boycott'. In their struggle the Mitchelstown tenants sparked off a dramatic series of events that would make their town the focus of international attention once again in 1887.[1]

The precarious financial position of the Dowager Countess of Kingston was obvious to the land agitators in the early phase of the 'war' on the estate. The rental from her 24,421 acres was almost £18,000 a year. From that, nearly £9,500 had to be deducted for interest payments to the Representative Church Body, with another £1,400 in Tithe Rent charges. After a small sum of about £500 per annum was also deducted from the principal, there were barely £6,000 a year left over to meet Lady Kingston's numerous other expenses.[2]

A key figure in the events at Mitchelstown during the 50 years after 1869 was William Downes Webber – or Willie Webber, as he was usually called. He was the eldest son of Rev Thomas Charles Webber of Leekfield, County Sligo. Willie's uncle, Charles Tankerville Webber, married Adelaide Charlotte, Big George's second daughter.[3] An arts graduate of Trinity College, Dublin, Willie was a modestly wealthy landowner who held 3,810 acres in counties Sligo, Kildare, Laois and Leitrim. These lands were valued in 1880 at a rental of £1,699.[4]

Webber assumed a central role in the affairs of the Mitchelstown estate after the fifth earl's death. Captain Richard Farrer continued as estate agent, living in the west wing of the castle. Farrer also farmed the demesne, which he rented from the dowager countess for £1,100 a year. According to Webber, Anna's Kingston in-laws 'cordially accepted her position under the will'. While that may have been true to a point, some were dissatisfied that ownership of the estate had passed out of the King family. They also resented Webber's influence in matters relating to the management of the property.

Anna consolidated all charges on the estate by raising a mortgage of £236,000 from the Representative Church Body. Of this sum, £106,000 was to pay off the original family charges. These included the endowment of Kingston College and payments to relatives of the fifth earl. Also, £120,000 was due to the heirs of the seventh earl, Robert Edward. Debts for the building of the demesne wall in the late 1700s remained unpaid, and were now Anna's responsibility. The remaining £10,000 was needed to pay off miscellaneous costs connected with the statutory declaration of title taken out on the property in the Landed Estates Court. This operation included the mapping of the entire estate, which was not completed until the end of 1875 when the Church Body issued its loan to the countess.[5]

In 1879, the total profit on the Kingston estate amounted to £7,108, or 38.4 per cent of the income. Robert Edward's death placed an additional charge of £6,000 a year on the estate, reducing the profit to £1,108. In 1875, the income of the estate totalled £18,553. Fixed costs amounted to £5,573, in addition to the interest on the mortgage. Assuming that the interest was paid on time, Anna had an income from the estate of £2,360. If she failed to pay the interest on time, her profit would be eliminated.[6]

It was during these transactions that Webber established himself as general factotum of the property and, on 29 July 1873, as Anna's second husband. He said that

> Several of her family were old friends of mine including her eldest brother, Richard Brinkley. I had met her occasionally both as Miss Brinkley and as Lady Kingston. In 1872 we became engaged and, after a year, the marriage took place at Kellavil in the Queen's County [County Sligo], then belonging to my mother.

The newly-weds, who were in their thirties and only a year apart in age, lived on the continent. Captain Farrer ran the estate in their absence. In 1877, as Anna and Willie returned to live at the castle, Farrer was declared bankrupt. Webber said:

> We were obliged reluctantly to take up the Agency from him. This involved us in a considerable loss. We had also to purchase from him all the farming stock of the Demesne amounting to £5,000 – to which I was able to contribute over £2,000 from my own resources.[7]

To save further expense, Webber undertook the collection of rents, with the assistance of 'the experienced office clerk Mr J. Mahony'. However, Mahony was dismissed because he 'repeatedly gave way to habits of drink'. But times were good and rents were paid promptly. After settling in Mitchelstown, Webber undertook several 'desirable improvements' for which he obtained loans of £3,000 from the Board of Works. He re-roofed the extensive castle farm buildings. Several labourers' houses were built inside and outside the demesne. A row of four houses was built in Robert Street. The main fish pond below the castle – 'which had become highly offensive through deposits of town sewerage' – was drained. 'Thus I got rid of a dangerous nuisance,' he said. He also drained a large area of wetland in the lawn around the castle.

> An early improvement affected by me was the erection of the front gate and piers of the Demesne. The gateway designed by Payne had never been built by Ld K, so the old and dilapidated piers and gate remained, which I replaced with a design more suitable to the castle.

A year after Captain Farrer departed, Webber hired Henry Cholmondeley – 'a young man who had studied and embarked on farming in his own account.' He was a nephew of Big George's grandson, Philip Cooke, and a grandson of Lord Delamere. This illustrates the marked difference between typical Irish land agents and their English counterparts.[8] Land agents in Ireland were generally of a much higher social status and were often university graduates. In England, agents tended to be sons of loyal family retainers and stewards. In Ireland, as can be seen from the Farrer and Cholmondeley appointments, and similar appointments on other estates, the agent was often the younger son of a gentleman or clergyman.[9]

However, it would take much more than Cholmondeley's farming expertise to offset the adverse effects of a combination of bad weather, poor harvests, and falling prices that broke an extended period of economic progress. The first of three successive bad years for farming occurred in 1877. Liver fluke wiped out large numbers of sheep and mutton prices fell by fourteen per cent. Cattle prices also dropped, as the country was plunged into economic crisis.

While many tenants found it hard to meet the rent, Webber was pleased with the general response. 'In many cases I voluntarily gave reductions and attended daily at the Estate Office and visited the farms for the purpose of ascertaining where they were required,' he said. Some of the reductions were permanent and, in all, he had reduced the income from the estate by £700 a year. While the tenants told Webber they were happy with the reductions, they had begun already to work towards ending the status quo in land ownership.[10] Aware of the financial difficulties of the dowager countess and her husband, political agitators and local tenant leaders combined to exploit this weakness as a means of bankrupting the estate and securing tenant ownership of the land.

There was little sign of discontent until the end of 1879. When the September gale (the half-yearly rent payment) fell due in December, the rents were paid without any great fuss. The *Cork Examiner* said that 'most emphatic assurances' had been given that 'an almost unlimited time will be granted to deserving tenants' who had met with particular hardships or difficulties in raising money to pay their landlord. This was a reasonable response from Lady Kingston but far short of what would satisfy her tenants.[11]

In 1880, however, there was a marked improvement in the financial affairs of the estate. Rents had been paid promptly since 1875, and the countess was able to avail of an even lower rate on her mortgage. However, the prospects for the tenants were not so good. The bad years had absorbed their savings, and many were in debt to shopkeepers and banks.[12] 'There is a great feeling of discontent,' said Richard Eaton, the resident magistrate, who predicted conflict on the estate. 'In this district the relations between landlord and tenant are greatly strained and might easily develop into a grave social disorganisation.'[13]

The Kingston tenantry were following, with keen interest, the progress of land agitation in the West of Ireland. There the demand was 'Griffith's Valuation, and no more' – a cry that drew considerable support from the Mitchelstown tenants. On 21 October 1880 – a most significant date in local history – the Land League formed a branch in Mitchelstown. It set about organising the tenants into a powerful and disciplined force for a final confrontation with their ancient rulers. The branch was supported by the parish priest, Rev Dean Denis O'Mahony, who feared a violent struggle and urged members to engage in peaceful agitation.[14]

Magistrate Eaton's reports throughout the 1880s show how the authorities reacted to the crisis. He said that 'a great change had occurred in this district' since the formation of the Land League. The result was a general refusal to pay rents. There was, he said:

> A state of feeling among the peasantry of an alarming character, and which daily gets worse. There is certainly a growing impression that as regards enforcing payment of rents, or any contract respecting land, the law is quite powerless. This state of things is intensified every day it is prolonged, and as far as I can see, any attempt to enforce payment of rent generally will be impossible without the employment of force on a large scale, and not, I fear,

without bloodshed. No pretence is put forward of an inability to pay on the part of the tenants, but they state generally that they dare not pay anything or under any terms except those sanctioned by the Land League.[15]

When 20,000 people attended a rally in Mitchelstown on 5 December they were further roused by the words of Michael Davitt. Of this event, it has been stated that

> It was hardly a coincidence that the first major land meeting should take place on the very day that the Kingston rents were due to be paid or that Michael Davitt, the founder and most revolutionary member of the Land League, chose to address the assembly.

The 'three Fs' were no longer enough, said Davitt. 'Fixity of tenure, fair rents, and free sale fixes Irish landlordism in the country forever,' he declared. The tenants had to go further than seeking basic land rights and lower rents – their aim had to be to smash landlordism and erase it from the landscape forever.

Grievances that had been forgotten during prosperous years were rekindled by the Land League leaders, who spoke of rents being increased by £2,000 in the eleven years after 1855 when the hated Patten Smith Bridge was land agent. They disputed Webber's claims that rents on the estate were moderate.[16] In contrast to his own assertion that they had been reduced by £700, the tenants accused him of raising them at every opportunity. He was also censured for interfering with their right of free sale.[17]

Things could hardly have been worse for Lady Kingston when 1,600 tenants paraded through the streets and up to the door of the castle. It was less than a fortnight after the Land League rally, and they had come to pay the September gale, at the level of Griffith's Valuation. Anna and her husband dismissed it all as people blowing off steam. If she held out, the agitation would blow over – or so she thought. When the tenants' offer was refused, they went instead to pay their debts to the local shopkeepers. Victory celebrations that evening featured torch-lit processions and a band playing national airs of defiance all in stark contrast to those of greeting for the countess when she had returned to Mitchelstown as the bride of the fifth earl twelve years earlier.[18]

By March 1881, most rents remained unpaid since the previous gale. Fr Timothy O'Connell told a League meeting that the Kingstons had always treated their tenants fairly. Urging 'give and take' on all sides, he said he could 'hardly believe that Mr Webber will act upon the policy of "No Surrender." A little sacrifice timely made may save himself and his tenantry unspeakable trouble,' he said. Much to the distress of Lady Kingston, the success of the struggle on the estate of Henry L. Young, who had bought Kingston lands at Curraghavoe, near Mitchelstown, in the 1850s, greatly encouraged the Land League. But Webber held out and resorted to issuing processes against large numbers of the tenants. In the opinion of one authority, the entire agitation would probably have ended that April if Lady Kingston had granted 'even a trifling abatement' at the time.[19]

Growing hostility in the neighbourhood worried Magistrate Eaton. The rent strike spread to neighbouring estates and a boycott of Lady Kingston and her employees was enforced. Eaton believed that nothing less than 'the actual suppression of the Land League in the country will restore law and order'.[20] In May, the authorities put on a show of strength in Mitchelstown where there was a ceremonial march of 150 soldiers of the 25th Regiment, a troop of the 3rd Dragoon Guards from Fermoy, men from the King's Own Borderers and a contingent of police. The first mass evictions on the Kingston estate occurred on 27 May 1881, a date that marked a decisive turning point in relations between Lady Kingston and her tenantry.

At 9am, 150 police, troops, cavalry and bailiffs gathered in New Square before setting off to carry out the first five evictions. In response, the tenants were summoned by the peeling of the Catholic church bell which, it was claimed, could be heard eighteen miles away in Cahir. The first to be evicted was John Donahue from his 25 acres at Pollardstown. A large and excited crowd threw stones and shouted abuse at the bailiffs. Donahue's front door was burst in and five chairs were removed to the yard. The next eviction was at Tom Casey's 27-acre farm in nearby Kilshanny, where the authorities were greeted with a fusillade of rotten eggs and buckets of dirty water. At both farms, however, the tenants paid the rents due and the bailiffs went off about their business.

Hostility from the crowd was so intense that Magistrate Eaton felt compelled to read the Riot Act, ordering the people to disperse or suffer the consequences. Only the intervention of Fr O'Connell and the *Galtee Boy* – now Coroner John Sarsfield Casey and an officer of the Mitchelstown Land League – prevented the situation from getting worse.

On their way to Thomas Donovan's and John Hanrahan's farms in Coolnanave, the Riot Act was again proclaimed. Now 5,000-strong and led by several bands, the crowd again turned on the military, this time at the junction of Clonmel Road with Lower Cork Street. Eaton warned that he would order his men to open fire unless the mob dispersed. Within minutes, the police made a charge with fixed bayonets and several people were wounded. Fr O'Connell placed himself in front of the soldiers' muskets, shouting; 'For Heaven's sake, don't fire!' A stone knocked a Private Smith senseless and a bailiff and a lance-corporal were also injured. The swords of the 3rd Dragoon Guards flashed in the sunshine as they carried out orders to break up the crowd.

That night, the atmosphere in Mitchelstown was extremely tense. Infuriated police made a bayonet charge through the streets while the cavalry rode down the townspeople, scattering them in all directions. Had it not been for Fr O'Connell and other Land League leaders who persuaded the magistrate to withdraw his forces, the confrontation could have resulted in fatalities.

The only fatality in this opening episode of the Land War was a Dragoon's horse killed at Hanrahan's farm. The following morning, its severed head was stuck on a tall pole at the Upper Cork Street junction with Brigown road. In its mouth was placed a note declaring, 'Webber, here's your rent'. Nearby, a large crowd cheered for 'an English head on an Irish stick'.[21] Magistrate Eaton demanded that the authorities increase the permanent local police force to a minimum of twenty 'effective men', but he believed that a much larger military force would be essential before further evictions could be attempted.[22]

Webber was as determined as ever to get payment of all rents due, but he was soon forced to compromise. In return for full payment of rents, the tenants could take their claims to court. If, within two years, their rents were deemed to be too high, they would be credited the amount that had been over-paid. This offer did little to ease the tension.[23] A large armed force of 700 troops and 300 police, under General Thomas Steele, was camped in the demesne for the rest of the year. The force consisted of half a battalion of infantry, two troops of cavalry from the dragoons and hussars, as well as a detachment of the Army Hospital Corps and the Army Service Corps.

'The journey [to Mitchelstown] in full marching order was very trying,' said one of Steele's soldiers. The only time the military were allowed come in sight of Mitchelstown Castle was when marching to or from venues where rent was to be collected. Orders were issued that no man was to go within viewing distance of the castle windows. There may have been mayhem in the streets and countryside but not a trace of it was to cause any upset to the ladies in the castle. The soldier recalled:

> On reaching camp, we pitched our small bell tents, to hold about eight men each, and a few larger ones for other purposes ... The weather was far from fine under the canvass ... In spite of oil, our rifles and bayonets were rusty every morning ... The rations were far better than those served to us in barracks, which helped us bear our lot more cheerfully, and to endure more easily our fatigues.[24]

On 30 June, two days after their arrival, the military accompanied the bailiffs on another round of evictions. Earlier in the day, the Land League had decided not to intervene and the evictions were carried out with success. Webber regarded the League's behaviour as blackmail and agreed only to consider individual cases of complaint. The Dublin office of the Land League sent Fr O'Connell a cheque for £129-19s-2d to cover the legal costs of the 200 tenants who had writs issued against them. With such solid backing, the tenants prepared for a more concerted struggle.[25]

The next round of evictions, beginning on 10 August, lasted ten days. Invariably, the tenants under threat paid rents and costs, and were reinstated. An inspirational figure throughout the campaign was Charles Stewart Parnell's sister, Anna, who was often accompanied by PP O'Neill, secretary of the Cork Land League. Ms Parnell frequently dashed over streams and across fields to beat the bailiffs to the eviction scene. The authorities went to extraordinary lengths in trying to apprehend her. Steele's soldier said that

> Her conveyance, containing one or two ladies, could be seen usually in front of the column ... One day a member of the Royal Irish Constabulary made an attempt to capture this lady; but she ran up a mountain side and got clear away from her pursuer.[26]

The tenants were not without imagination when it came to resistance. Bushes and tree trunks were used to block the windows and doors of cabins. In one case, when bailiffs broke open a door, they were showered with hot paraffin oil. In another house they found people dancing to the concertina while, at a third, 'a party was engaged in singing and dancing'. At the eviction on Glavin's farm in Corracunna, the tenant ingeniously caused a large bailiff to be badly burned when he was duped into trying to remove a hot anvil from the kitchen floor.[27] While stones rained on the bailiffs and soldiers at the scene of virtually every eviction, there were very few serious casualties. 'It was not pleasant to listen to the yells that greeted us on the road from knots of villagers,' said the soldier. After one eviction,

> We earned from the people of Mitchelstown, the title of 'The Queen's Cattle-drivers,' for that was our social status after safely escorting a number of bullocks from a farm, unto the park of the Kingstons. These had been taken in lieu of rent.[28]

On 9 September, Dublin Castle outlawed any assembly of people in Mitchelstown for the purpose of obstructing the sheriff in the execution of his duty. Any gathering could be dispersed by force. This order was timed to coincide with the final round of evictions planned for mid-September. The already powerful detachment of military was reinforced three days later when upwards of 700 men, including engineers, pipers and hussars, and 120 police from six counties, were drafted into town. In response, the tenants took to song and verse, most of it humorous, to vent their grievances and boost morale:

> Nancy Brinkley wants her rent and she
> Can't get it in
> Without the aid of Orangemen.
> Kelly, he goes by,
> And the people well do cry
> 'Here comes Webber's pimp and spy.'
> May long live our noble Queen,
> (I mean Miss Parnell),
> For the evictions did prepare
> For to watch the tenants care,
> And likewise brave P.P. O'Neill,
> 'No Surrender.'[29]

Willie Webber, whom the tenants nicknamed 'the gooseberry picker', blamed the Land League for the state of affairs on the property. 'Since the introduction of the baneful League, the peace, progress and goodwill which previously existed has been swept away,' he said, 'and every condition which a well wisher of the district could desire has been entirely reversed.' At the end of four months, the army had helped to collect rents from the 200 farms whose tenants had initially refused to pay. Nonetheless, the episode was a great victory for the Land League which proved that, given unity of purpose, the tenants were a force to be reckoned with.

January and February of 1882 passed without incident. Several tenants had already opted to take their cases to the land courts. In the first ten rulings, given in March, there were reductions varying from 30.1 per cent to zero. This was enough to destroy the unity of the tenants' struggle. Within a few weeks about 80 had paid, but there lingered what Sub-Inspector Carter called 'intense feelings of hostility'.

After much persuasion, Fr Burdon persuaded Lady Kingston to grant a general reduction of 2.5 per cent in rents. In cases where the rents were 25 per cent above Griffith's Valuation, an abatement of five per cent was offered and accepted. By the end of May, the first phase of the Land War in Mitchelstown was over, but the battle lines had been drawn and the sense of anger and injustice had eased only temporarily.[30]

Over the next two years, all was relatively quiet on the estate. For the second time in ten years, the dowager countess offered to sell their holdings to the tenants for 20 years rental. They could buy her out under the provisions of the recent Land Acts. Negotiations were still under way when Michael Davitt, at a public meeting, scuppered her efforts to sell by urging the tenants to hold out for a better deal.

In the autumn of 1886, Webber set out on a world trip that included a visit to Australia. He wrote in his journal that

> Before starting on 1 Nov., both Mr Frend [the land agent] and our local solicitor, Mr Standish O'Grady – who was a clever man & knew well the disposition of the Tenants – assured me that prospects were favourable. But in the month after my departure, when the September rents were called for, The Tenants, under the secret advice of the then 'National League', again refused payment without an all round reduction of 20 per cent.[31]

This strike lasted only a few weeks, but it formed the basis for the final struggle at national level for control of the land. Prophetically, Fr O'Connell told them that

> If they did not get the reduction they must fight, and within the lines of the Constitution. If there was to be a fight on the Kingston estate it would be a fight of great magnitude. It would be a fight on which the eyes of Ireland were directed and in its issue the Irish people would take keen interest.[32]

10

'REMEMBER MITCHELSTOWN!'

The second phase of the Mitchelstown Land War, which began at the end of 1886, was important in the context of the national campaign to smash landlordism. The unity achieved among the Kingston tenantry was unique and their campaign inspired the tenants of other estates to challenge their landlords.

The Land War also brought together town and country folk in Mitchelstown. Local shopkeepers and publicans such as Maurice O'Sullivan, supported by the *Galtee Boy*, played a pivotal role in the second phase of the campaign. Their businesses had suffered whenever farming went through difficult times. Many traders were the sons of farmers and some of those who were not had ambitions in the local political arena. It was natural also that their sympathies could be mobilised against a powerful and seemingly unreasonable landlord. The tenant campaign was given a morale boost when many businesses boycotted Lady Kingston and her associates. The Mitchelstown shopkeepers and publicans were also comparatively well educated and became valuable advisers to their customers who were the foot soldiers in the struggle.

However, fourteen evictions in April 1886, and 'a considerable number' of others in September, attracted little public attention. Webber gave evidence to the Cowper

Commission, which was convened to review the recent Land Acts. He acknowledged that it had been 'an exceptional year and, having regard to the fall in prices, there must be pressure on the tenants'.[1] Consequently, he offered an abatement of ten per cent on rents due in December. This was rejected by the National League, which had replaced the Land League in 1882 as the constituency organisation of Charles Stewart Parnell's Irish Parliamentary Party. The league's leaders sought to capitalise on the local tenants' anger, which had been simmering since 1881. At a public meeting on 7 December, John Mandeville, chairman of the Mitchelstown Board of Guardians, said he considered the offer to be 'practically useless', and the original demand for a twenty per cent reduction still stood.[2]

Mandeville played an heroic role in the struggle now about to sweep the estate. Unlike the tenants for whom he fought, he was an independent farmer who owned about 200 acres at Clonkilla, adjacent to the Kingston demesne wall. A nephew of the Fenian chief, Colonel John O'Mahony, he was the youngest of six brothers. As chairman of the Board of Guardians, Mandeville was keenly aware of the hardships endured by the ordinary people of the town and countryside.[3]

In December, the National League met the Kingston agent, Henry Frend, who told them that the Church Body had refused to reduce interest charges on the mortgage. Consequently, without jeopardising Lady Kingston's position, there could be no rent reduction. The tenants' response on 11 December was to institute the Plan of Campaign and Mandeville was chosen to be its director. The Plan, as everyone called it, was the most effective strategy ever devised for non-violent confrontation in Ireland. If the landlord, as happened in Lady Kingston's case, refused to reduce the rents by the amount demanded, the tenants were to pay none. The rents were then collected by the Plan leaders and banked in the name of trustees who could use the money to help evicted tenants.[4]

At the end of December 1886, the Kingston rents were collected by the league, under the direction of John O'Connor, MP. Shortly before daybreak on St Stephen's Day, the Mallow MP, William O'Brien, arrived in Mitchelstown. Plans were immediately put into effect to assemble the tenants under cover of darkness at various locations. Ten years previously, O'Brien had championed the cause of the Galtee tenants as a reporter with *The Freeman's Journal*. Now, as a politician, he gave inspirational leadership to the Kingston tenants. The collection of the 'Campaign Rents' he described in heroic terms in *Evening Memories*. He wrote:

> The arrangements worked with the clockwork precision of a conspiracy where practically the entire community were conspirators. We found the tenants almost to a man awaiting us in the different rendezvous. We held our meetings with none to bear evidence of our work except the friendly reporters ... and far into the night ... in half-a-dozen mountain cabins we sat at the receipt of the 'Campaign Rents' until the collections over more than half the vast estate were safe in our wallets and by some fairy machinery transported beyond the Queen's writ.[5]

A series of public meetings took place in December and January until another gale of rents was collected by the Campaigners in February. Emotional rhetoric from their spokesmen was designed both to threaten and coax the tenants to remain loyal to the cause. In the Plan of Campaign they were battling for their homes, families and liberty; that was the message from John O'Connor, MP, when he spoke to them on 30 December. On 2 January, Arthur O'Connor, MP, declared: 'We have been struggling and this is our last and final struggle. The landlords are on their last ditch; they are at their last rallying post, and we are giving them our parting volley, and we will entirely and forever rout them.'[6]

If the campaign meant war against landlordism, then it was going to be a 'holy war' backed by the Catholic Church. The Bishop of Cloyne, Dr James McCarthy, expressed his sympathy with the Mitchelstown tenants. Considering what happened, he said, 'no other alternative was offered to the tenantry but to defend themselves'. John O'Connor told a public meeting in mid-January: 'You are at war for your homes and children. Then steel your hearts and go to war in the name of God and with the blessing of the church.'[7]

A fresh round of evictions was threatened. In response, the tenants began disposing of their cattle to prevent them from being seized by the bailiffs. Over 1,000 horses were used to clear holdings on 18 January. At a huge fair on the following day, some 1,000 cattle were sold for over £9,000. 'You have made the square of Mitchelstown historic,' declared Thomas O'Connor MP. The tenants, he said, had

> shaken the buttresses of Mitchelstown Castle, struck a blow against the fell system that has robbed you, fought a fight not alone for yourselves, the tenants of the Kingston estate, but also for the tenants throughout the length and breadth of your long suffering motherland.[8]

Six shopkeepers who held farms from Lady Kingston opted to have their shop premises sold at giveaway prices rather than pay rent on their farms. The purchaser was the much-reviled solicitor Standish O'Grady, acting for Lady Kingston. By this means, Joanna Hyland lost her dwelling houses and shop for £42; Maurice O'Sullivan, who played a leading role in the Campaign, had his three houses in Upper Cork Street auctioned for £3; Thomas Delarue's four houses were sold for £5; John Hanrahan of Coolnanave, a victim in the earlier phase of the Land War, lost 21 acres for £3; and Julia Crotty's licensed premises and dwelling passed to O'Grady for the princely sum of £1.[9]

Webber was convinced that the tenants would have paid up happily if they had not been, as he saw it, coerced by the National League, while agent Frend claimed that 'the majority of tenants are anxious to pay their rents and avoid incurring further legal expense'. Even the authorities seemed unaware of the tenants' true mood. Magistrate Eaton believed that the deployment of a military force and vigorous government action would end the crisis. He was supported by County Inspector Brownrigg, who stated:

> Danger may be averted if the people were convinced by some forceful action that the government would protect Lady Kingston in enforcing her legal rights. The temporary occupation of the military barracks by a company of soldiers would have a most salutary effect.[10]

As spring arrived, thousands from neighbouring estates went to Mitchelstown to help the Kingston tenants sow crops. On 18 January, over 1,000 farmers and labourers gathered at Ballygiblin for the first plantings, which went on for five days.[11] Simultaneously, tenants were being warned, just in case they should waiver, that the Plan organisers were keeping 'a detailed list of those who are with us and against us, and when the day of reckoning comes ... each person shall be treated according to his desserts.'[12]

Anyone seen to be, or suspected of, supporting Webber and Lady Kingston was boycotted. At least 144 people (possibly as many as 290) were ostracised by their neighbours. Boycott notices scornfully defamed their enemies:

> Down with Anna Kingston, the usurper; Frend, the tyrant; Jim Neill, Power, the Exterminator; Judas Iscariot O'Grady, who out

Herod's Herod in his baseness and villainy ... His Cook and Mistress Maria; Johnny Coughlan, the renegade, his Dairyman and Workmen; the 'Cuckold' and the English Bastard Davis; and the shopkeepers ...[13]

Another notice, posted in Mitchelstown in February, told tenants to

> Boycott that disgrace of her sex – Anna Kingston, the grass widow, the hard-hearted ... Frend, the agent, the pig-headed representative of the Church Body, who dismissed the labourers ... Bullóg [a type of fungus] 'Maria' O'Grady, solicitor, who betrayed every client who had the misfortune to be associated with him ... Benson, the insolent whelp, whose insolence and extortion all of you have experienced.
>
> Strike at the outposts of the Castle; you know who they are. Boycott Jim Neill, the hangman, and family; Neddy Kelly, the ex-farmer; Dicky Fitzgibbon, clerk of the Union, the only land-grabber in the district, and his brood of upstarts; Gombeen man Couche and his apostate wife, the only associates of Benson and all bailiffs on the estate. Shun them. Let others, too, take warning and beware of their fate, or their turn will surely come.[14]

Despite the threats, some loyalists came to the aid of Lady Kingston and her boycotted supporters. The Property Defence Association, founded by the landlords in 1880, opened a special store in Mitchelstown to supply provisions for the boycott victims. George Pellew, a travel writer, said that 'everything was kept there, from pork to pepper, soda to stockings, and young ladies ran in and out with a most amusing air of proprietorship'.[15] O'Grady, a Catholic, told Pellew that his legal practice had been badly affected by the boycott.

> The Leaguers announced that they wouldn't let me, my clerk, servants, or their children go to the parish church, and the priests, through Father Sexton, requested me not to go for the sake of

peace. Two old clients of mine, one a shopkeeper and the other a seedsman, have been punished by fine and boycotting for employing me. They threatened to boycott O'Brien, a magistrate, for employing me, and he, for business reasons, purchased his peace with them.[16]

As in the earlier phase of the Land War, neighbouring landlords quickly succumbed to the League's demands. Nathaniel Buckley's Galtee tenants won a reduction of between fifteen and 25 per cent. A Cork landlord granted an all-round reduction to his Mitchelstown tenants of 42.5 per cent. Occupiers of the Robertson estate, near Glanworth, got a 50 per cent reduction in May. By the beginning of June, Lady Kingston's prospects were grim.[17] Pellew felt sorry for her:

> Yet there is something touching in the thought of that gentle, sad-voiced lady in that noble castle, for the last time perhaps, watching the peacocks strutting on the gravel, or for the last time strolling in through the vast conservatories. In the village the people speak with curious hatred of the Kingstons ... They repeat dreadful traditions of impossible cruelties in the eighteenth century, and refer vaguely to a curse that the estate shall never pass from father to son for more than two generations.[18]

Her predicament was not eased by her husband who was out of the country, and out of touch, during the early phase of the campaign. Webber wrote:

> Lady Kingston with much courage kept on living quietly at the Castle, supported by Mr Frend. Miss Minnie Fairholme was staying with her as a guest. The news of all these proceedings did not reach me in Australia, nor did I receive any reports until letters written in January and Feb'ry overtook me at San Francisco at the end of May 1887, with others of later date.

In July, Webber maintained that he was angry at the way the

dispute had been handled in his absence and he immediately reviewed the tenants' demands.[19] Meanwhile, the defence of farmsteads and tenants' homes was maintained. The most famous was Maurice O'Sullivan's shop in Upper Cork Street, which took on a bizarre appearance just two doors away from the RIC barracks. Inside it was 'a garrison of strapping men' who were prepared for any move to evict them.[20] Known as 'Sullivan's Castle', it was the Campaign headquarters. The *Cork Examiner* reported:

> An enormous pile of heavy logs fill up the interior, and whitethorn boughs bar the entrances by way of the windows overhead. A strip of calico across the front wall of the house bears the words 'Plan of Campaign: No Surrender. Evictors come on'!!![21]

Mass evictions were planned for August, but some minor clearances resulted in a weakening of tenant resolve. Not for the first time, William O'Brien, MP, hurried to Mitchelstown to rally the tenants. At a National League meeting in New Market Square, he declared

> If they carry out these evictions they will not be upholding the law ... you will be justified before God and man in resisting this outrage, and defending your homes against these assassins ... I ask you to be as alive and vigilant night and day as the corps of bailiffs up in the Castle. I ask you and every man for miles around here to set the estate in a blaze about these people's ears, and to make it a dear, a sorrowful and an expensive job for them if they carry out these evictions.[22]

John Mandeville, addressing another meeting two days later, told the tenants

> evictions will take place if they see that there is a way for evictions to be carried on, and the only way to prevent them is for you to be prepared to defend your houses whenever these people get it into their heads.[23]

The speeches had two significant results. First, they forced the authorities to postpone the impending evictions; secondly, the tone and wording of their remarks had violated the new Crimes Act. The government was determined to make an example of the two men and they were summoned to appear at Mitchelstown Petty Sessions on 9 September. As the day drew near, more police and military were drafted into the district. O'Brien and Mandeville were the first to be tried under the Crimes Act, a newsworthy event made all the more appealing by the celebrity of O'Brien in particular.[24] The *Cork Examiner* reported:

> Mitchelstown tonight seems in a state of perfect siege. In the streets long cordons of police march and parade with military show. The opening of the trial of William O'Brien and John Mandeville here tomorrow will probably be marked by a scene which if not unparalleled will certainly be historic.[25]

It was not known generally that the two defendants had no intention of turning up to oblige their prosecutors. From the early hours, large numbers poured into the town to support their leaders and protest against the Crimes Act. Several brass bands, numerous farmers on horseback, and thousands on foot, came from parishes and villages throughout Cork and the neighbouring counties.

However, the police and military prevented the crowd from entering the town while the court was in session. As the defendants did not appear, evidence was heard in their absence by two magistrates, Eaton and Captain Stokes. It took four hours to dispose of the evidence against the defendants, for whom arrest warrants were issued.[26]

After the court had risen, John Cullinane marshalled the people into New Market Square. John Dillon, MP, led a group of English and Irish parliamentarians, including

Henry Labouchere, T.P. Gill, Thomas Ellis, E.L. Brunner and P. O'Hea into the town. The march was led by the Mayor of Cork and the Mayor of Clonmel, as well as scores of clergy followed by contingents from National League branches in seven counties. A large wagonette for the speakers was drawn up at the top of the square, near the post office; another, for reporters, was placed at right-angles to it. Frederick J. Higginbottom of the Press Association in London wrote

> the League branches continued marching in one after another, at first composed of a few townspeople, gradually swelled and extended down the square, until the throng of countrymen became a densely packed mass for forty yards in front of the speakers' wagonette, so dense, indeed, that when at last the carriages containing the popular members and their English friends reached the square it was with the utmost difficulty that a passage could be cleared for them on the left wing of the assembly.

Higginbottom added that the scene, viewed from the top of the square, was 'most remarkable' as an estimated 8,000 people pressed in below him.

> On one side were grouped all the green banners of the League branches and the Gaelic Athletic Association teams; at the rear was a line of 'Land League Cavalry' – farmers on horseback; while to the right the cars, carts and other vehicles used by some of the visitors were grouped, filled with eager spectators. The windows of all the houses on the three sides of the square to the front, right and left of the speakers, were crowded with animated faces.

Not a policeman was to be seen, and Higginbottom felt that everybody was good humoured, orderly, and easily controlled by the marshals, Cullinane and Condon.[27] But Dillon sensed danger. He urged Labouchere to cut this as short as possible; they will send the police and military into town. They will attempt something, and something may occur if we go on long. I suggest that we say a few words and ask the people to disperse.[28]

Rev Dr McCarthy – the senior curate of the parish and a classical scholar – was elected to the chair. As Dillon rose to speak, there was a commotion on the fringes of the crowd. Head Constable O'Doherty, accompanied by sixteen policemen, tried to escort a government note taker, Sergeant Conderan, to the speakers' wagonette. Their purpose was indicated by Conderan who 'held up a red-backed notebook for an instant'. To get him in place, the police in single file passed through about 50 horsemen positioned around the edges of the crowd. They then formed into pairs as they tried to press on. After the police had made about six yards, Thomas Condon, MP, who was on the wagonette, stood up and shouted: 'Close up your ranks; they are far enough. Stand firm!'

The police intentions were misunderstood by the crowd. With the probable exception of Condon, whose remarks exacerbated an already tense situation, the speakers had little objection to the notetaker. Finding their way blocked, Head Constable O'Doherty responded by drawing his sword and his men produced their batons. Higginbottom noted the crowd's response when, as he later wrote, 'Sticks were raised in that peculiar manner which by Tipperary men is always employed as a sort of warning to an adversary'. The crowd turned and tried to push back the police. Condon leapt from the wagonette and forced his way to the disturbance in a bid to allay the commotion.

The horsemen drew up in a line, with flanks touching, between the crowd and the police. As Dillon began to speak a reserve of 30 policemen arrived under the command of

District Inspector Irwin.[29] As soon as O'Doherty saw them, he and his men made a fresh attempt to get through. Irwin said:

> I saw the men strike the horses on the hind quarters with their batons in order to make them move. Some confusion then arose. The horses commenced to plunge. One horse reared up, its rider was very nearly falling out of the saddle ... They [the horses] got in amongst my men and disarranged the ranks. The horsemen raised something like ashplants and struck at the police. The police used their batons and the muzzles of their rifles. A free fight commenced between the people and the police.

The hand-to-hand fighting was described by the *Freeman's Journal* as a 'series of Homeric battles'.[30] The police were hopelessly outnumbered and, amid great confusion, the order to retreat was given after about five minutes. Under a barrage of stones they fled in disarray to their barracks in Upper Cork Street. By the time Irwin and Constable O'Sullivan got to the barracks door, their entry was blocked by colleagues trying desperately to get in.

Amid scenes of mayhem, County Inspector Brownrigg issued orders: 'Men, load your rifles and come upstairs. I'll fire out of the windows.' After they had taken up their positions he instructed them not to shoot without orders. By now, the last two policemen, Sergeant Kirwan and Constable Leahy, were making their way back to barracks. Already injured and forced to crawl, Leahy was being harried by the crowd. Panic stricken and in fear for his life, Kirwan turned and fired a rifle-round into the air. 'I never considered my life more in danger,' he said.[31]

Dillon, meanwhile, had left the wagonette with Coroner Casey and an ex-priest named Cush. They headed for the barracks after Dillon had organised some priests standing at the corner of the square to stop the people from following.

'There was not a single policeman in the street,' he claimed later. 'There was not twenty men within 60 yards of the barrack door.' Inside, Brownrigg was 'like a lunatic, tearing up and down the room in an excited state.' Dillon told him to keep his men in the barracks so that the organisers would have a chance to clear the streets:

> I impressed on him that what we wanted was to avoid bloodshed. 'No, Sir; No, Sir', he said, 'I will do nothing of the sort. My men must form in the streets at once.' I caught hold of him and said, 'for God's sake give us a chance before you send the men out on the streets.' 'No,' said he, 'I won't have any dictation from you', or something of that sort.

County Inspector Brownrigg almost immediately became involved in a scuffle with Coroner Casey at the doorway. This was still going on when, in the confusion, police at the upstairs windows fired fourteen shots without orders. Michael Lonergan, a farmer from Galbally, who was standing in the square, was killed instantly; John Casey, a seventeen-year-old from Mitchelstown, and John Shinnick, from Fermoy, an army pensioner who had fought in the Crimea, were fatally wounded while standing on the street between the barracks and the square.

District Inspector Irwin took control of the police and, under his command, two further shots were fired. He gave 'positive and precise directions to fire at no man except a man they actually saw throwing stones at the barrack'. In this case, at least, Irwin's order seems to have had the desired effect as only four small panes of glass were broken in the barracks' windows during the entire conflict.

However, only yards away in the square, things were far from under control. Fifty police, under Captain Seagrave, RM, arrived from a temporary military barracks in King Square and laid into the people with their batons. Seagrave went to Fitzgerald's Hotel to read the Riot Act only to find that he had forgotten to bring it with him. 'The square was like a powder magazine, and one stone would have caused the police to fire,' said Dillon. At the top of the square, the police chased the speakers from the wagonette into Fr Morrisson's house. Inside, John Mandeville's brother, Ambrose, was struck on the forehead by a sword-bayonet. Others in the hallway were beaten with batons.[32]

'The police were under no visible command,' observed the PA correspondent, Higginbottom. Dillon and Labouchere, who by then had arrived at the priest's house, were told by Captain Seagrave: 'You should not have held the meeting in the square; I have a right to disperse it, and I have sent for the military.' Some control of the situation was taken following the arrival of a young army officer who ordered the police to return to barracks. Seagrave came back with a contingent of Leinster Fusiliers who took up firing positions at the bottom of the square. However, Dillon and others were already disbanding the crowd, most of whom were now on their way out of town. Shortly after the skirmish was over, 'the boys of the town, at a safe distance, kicked the trodden and battered helmets that lay on the square, like footballs'. The number of civilians injured was put at between 80 and 100. The police claimed they had 54 casualties, but only a dozen or so showed any signs of injury.[33]

The episode made dramatic news and the most effective report was telegraphed worldwide by Frederick Higginbottom, who was the only English journalist at the scene. As soon as he had arrived in Mitchelstown that morning, Higginbottom went to the post office in New Square to check its telegraph system. A Wheatstone system, one of the most modern machines then available, had just been installed. While the other reporters went to the hotel after the riot to discuss and agree the details of what they had witnessed, Higginbottom headed for the post office. It took him five hours to send out his story, and the others had to wait until he had finished with the telegraph machine. He recalled, 'The fact that I had the field to myself had the effect of reducing this, the most noteworthy piece of special reporting in my whole career, to the category of merely matter-of-course performance.'

During the night, 91,000 words were telegraphed from Mitchelstown:

> Under this condition of extreme pressure the story of Mitchelstown was given to the world, for it not only went to the chief daily newspapers of three countries as it left my pencil, but, through Reuter's Agency and the Associated Press, was flashed to the United States and at one length or another to every country in the world.[34]

In the House of Commons the following day, Arthur J. Balfour, Chief Secretary for Ireland, said that the attack on the police was 'utterly unprovoked and of the most violent and brutal character'. In his view, those who shot at the people were doing nothing more than defending themselves from a mob with murderous intent. Balfour's hard line greatly consoled the authorities and their supporters in Ireland, but for the mass of people the tragedy was more truthfully described as the 'Mitchelstown Massacre'. The opposition Liberal leader, William Gladstone, exploited it to full effect when, on the day after the shootings in the House of Commons, he cried 'Remember Mitchelstown!' to rebuke the Tory regime, and in particular the Chief Secretary who, because of the Mitchelstown fiasco, became known to Irish nationalists as 'Bloody Balfour'.[35] William O'Brien declared that before Gladstone's watchword of 'Remember

Mitchelstown', 'the walls of Dublin Castle and the walls of Mitchelstown Castle will go down and crumble in the dust'.[36]

Apart from Higginbottom and his press colleagues there was another very interested professional observer in Mitchelstown that day. He was Edward Carson, QC, the prosecutor of the case against O'Brien and Mandeville who later became famous as the Ulster Unionist leader. He witnessed the riot and said later that it was the events in Mitchelstown that made him decide how nationalists ought to be dealt with in violent situations from then on. Carson was one of those impressed by Balfour's political handling of the 'Mitchelstown Massacre':

> It was Mitchelstown that made us certain that we had a man at last. The affair was badly muddled. But Balfour never admitted anything. He simply backed his own people. After that there wasn't an official in Ireland who didn't worship the ground he walked on.[37]

Balfour became convinced that responsibility for the police actions in Mitchelstown stemmed from the 'helplessness of the ordinary Irish official in the face of an emergency'. The events of 9 September caused him to rewrite the instructions for members of the RIC present at proclaimed meetings. In future, if bayonet charging police failed to subdue a mob then a detachment of soldiers armed with rifles was to open fire. Depending on the circumstances, bayonets could also be used. It was this firm response, and his unwavering public defence of the police, which earned him staunch support from every British official in Ireland.[38]

Demands for a public inquiry were rejected. A sworn confidential inquiry was held into 'the handling of the men by their officers', but not into the event as a whole. 'There was a lamentable failure on the part of the officers in charge to appreciate the gravity of the situation,' said the Lord Lieutenant. Captain Seagrave, who was in overall command of Mitchelstown, was guilty of 'negligence and want of energy, judgment and foresight'. County Inspector Brownrigg and Captain Seagrave were severely reprimanded, but the only officer to be penalised was District Inspector Irwin, who was forcibly retired from the RIC. In October, a coroner's inquiry in Mitchelstown returned a verdict of 'wilful murder' against Brownrigg and five of his men. But that ruling was overturned in early 1888 by the Court of the Queen's Bench 'on the grounds of the irregularity of the proceedings and the misconduct of the coroner'.

During the latter months of 1887, the imprisonment of Mandeville and O'Brien in Tullamore kept the Kingston estate in the public eye. At their trial in Mitchelstown, it was discovered that there were two conflicting versions of Head Constable O'Sullivan's notes of their 9 and 11 August speeches. Apparently, O'Sullivan had been instructed by his superiors not to use his original account. There was a furious argument concerning the police notes between Tim Harrington, for the National League, and Edward Carson. Harrington threw his papers in the air and stormed out of the courthouse, thereby highlighting the duplicity of the Irish executive. Nonetheless, Mandeville received a two-month sentence and O'Brien three months. The Mitchelstown board of guardians denounced the trial as 'a screaming farce'. The Recorder of Cork, at a hearing in Midleton, refused an appeal and confirmed the sentences.[39]

In Tullamore prison Mandeville and O'Brien caused further embarrassment for the authorities by demanding political status and refusing to be treated as common criminals. Mandeville had a conscientious objection to wearing prison clothing, associating with common criminals and cleaning out his cell. Both men sought 'political prisoner' status, but this was sternly resisted by the government which secretly instructed the governor of Tullamore to take strong action against his two Crimes Act prisoners.[40]

Mandeville was held in the punishment cell, where his plank bed was fixed against the wall opposite a badly-fitted cell door that opened onto the freezing winter air. Both were put on bread and water for 24 hours, causing them to suffer a serious bout of diarrhoea. Fearing political consequences, the authorities decided to treat O'Brien, one of the country's most prominent nationalists, comparatively well. The prison doctor, James Ridley, sent the MP to the infirmary. While there his clothes were removed from the bedside when he was asleep. As he still refused to wear prison uniform, he was left with only the blankets for cover.

On 10 November, Mandeville was visited by Dr Moorhead from Tullamore who expressed concern about his condition. Mandeville complained of a sore throat and the doctor observed that his breathing was 'embarrassed'. Dr Ridley, on the other hand, declared the prisoner fit to undergo further punishment and, consequently, he was sentenced to another three days on bread and water. Over the next few weeks, Mandeville was repeatedly placed in the punishment cell and subjected to a bread and water diet. He endured severe diarrhoea and believed that he was being 'savagely ill-treated' by the prison authorities, and especially by their physician, Dr Ridley.

On numerous occasions Dr Moorhead called on the authorities to hospitalise Mandeville. When this met with no response, he leaked accounts of Mandeville's condition to the press and helped fuel a political storm over the affair. With O'Brien 'on the blanket' in the prison infirmary and

Mandeville's health deteriorating by the day, Dr Ridley found himself caught between the wishes of his superiors, who wanted to inflict further punishment on Mandeville, and his own desire to send him to the infirmary. On 19 November, to the relief of Dr Ridley and the Chief Secretary Balfour, 'friendly warders' smuggled a suit of Blarney tweed into O'Brien.[41]

Three days later, the governor was ordered to have Mandeville's clothes removed. That evening, in direct contravention of prison regulations, the governor, chief warden and four warders forcibly stripped Mandeville in a scene that reminded one of the warders of 'the Jews stripping Our Lord'. Mandeville was left with a prison uniform, which he still refused to wear, opting instead to cover himself with the quilt and sheet from his bed. Even these were removed a few hours later and the bitter cold left him with no choice but to wear the prison clothes. The Mayor of Cork, in a public letter, described the incident as 'barbarous' and the board of guardians in Mitchelstown described it as 'the latest display of Balfour's brutality in forcing the clothes off our patriotic chairman'.[42]

Moorhead's demand that Mandeville be allowed outside to exercise, and that he should receive proper food, was ignored. He stated that the treatment of his patient was 'calculated to undermine the constitution of the strongest man'. But then, to the surprise and delight of the nationalists, the government gave in and allowed Crimes Act prisoners to exercise separately. That capitulation virtually conferred the status of political prisoners on them. However, this 'great triumph', as Mary Mandeville's wife Mary described it, was short-lived. On 8 December, her husband was again sentenced to dietary punishment for 48 hours and this was repeated within a week of his release.[43]

'Remember Mitchelstown!'

On Christmas eve, 1887, Mandeville was unexpectedly released from Tullamore. The welcoming parade for the tenants' hero was as memorable as any held in former times for the Earls of Kingston. The entire route from Knocklong railway station to Mitchelstown was lit up by bonfires along the mountainside. One reporter described the scene:

> The procession was headed by a regiment of mounted men some hundreds strong, with their steeds gaily caparisoned; then came a long line of cars, with tar-barrels blazing in the rear ... On approaching Mitchelstown, the procession was met by the whole population, which turned out en masse. Every house in the town ... was brilliantly illuminated. Arches were suspended across the streets and the town decorated with great taste and artistic merit.[44]

Everyone who knew Mandeville before his incarceration was horrified afterwards by his appearance. Some of his hair had turned white; he suffered from rheumatism, his hands trembled and his sight was affected. He even complained that his overcoat and boots were too heavy. He was, said William O'Brien, 'a different man ... unhealthy looking, bluish, extremely nervous ... frequently trembling ... when I saw him in Tullamore after his release he appeared to a large extent a broken man.'[45]

The Land War was still being waged on the Kingston estate when Mandeville was released from prison on Christmas eve. The Mitchelstown branch of the National League had been suppressed since the previous that September, but its leaders continued to meet in secret and enlist new members, many from England and America. Boycotting continued, but in a less concerted fashion, and Lady Kingston's shop closed. The Plan of Campaign waned when the spotlight moved from Mitchelstown at the end of November. Under the new Land Act, leaseholders could avail of the land courts and this paved the way for a negotiated settlement.

In October, 540 tenants applied to have their 'fair rents' adjudicated by the Land Commission. Webber immediately asked the Lord Lieutenant to expedite matters and treat the estate as a special case. This, he hoped, would create an opening for talks with the National League as Lady Kingston could not afford the continuation of the rent strike. The impartiality of the Rents Commission was questioned by the tenants who felt that its members would strongly favour the dowager countess. Their request to alter its composition was dismissed but their appeals went ahead. The first decisions, affecting 111 leaseholders and nine yearly tenants, gave an average rent reduction of 20.1 per cent, but individual reductions varied from zero to 48.6 per cent.

This was a heavy blow to the countess. As the average 20.1 per cent reduction was almost exactly what the tenants had originally demanded, it was obvious that the commission had hoped to avoid further agitation and end the embarrassment for the government.[46] But the tenants scented outright victory and were in no mood to compromise. They resolved 'to make no settlement ... until all tenants legally evicted, or otherwise injured by their landlord, be reinstated in their former position'.

On New Year's Day, 1888, Thomas Condon, MP, declared that 'they had arrived at a great crisis in the history of the Kingston tenants'. A few days later, the Board of Guardians in Mitchelstown reiterated their support for the National League when they resolved that nothing less than a 25 per cent reduction would be acceptable. However, by the end of January 1888, cracks had developed in the Campaign's united front.[47] By that point, the Church Body had moved to secure its interest in the estate, when they placed it in the Court of Chancery with Willie Webber as receiver.

'Remember Mitchelstown!'

Meanwhile, there were private negotiations between him and the parish priest, Very Rev Dean Patrick O'Regan. On 9 February agreement was reached when a twenty per cent reduction was granted on all agricultural holdings up to 25 March 1887. All tenants evicted since 1 December 1886, were restored to their properties without liability for costs. Tenants were allowed the right of appeal under the terms of the Land Act passed the previous year. The National League agreed that tenants would pay a year's rent before 25 March 1888, and Webber agreed to be lenient in cases of hardship.[48]

The Land War in Mitchelstown was over. On 2 April, William O'Brien stood in New Market Square before a huge gathering of victorious tenants. He was ecstatic:

> The last time that you and I met on this historic spot there was a dark cloud hanging over the Mitchelstown estate. Your homes were in danger, the crowbar brigade was at your doors. Thank God, that cloud has gone, and the danger has gone, and the sheriff will darken your doors no more.[49]

As O'Brien addressed the jubilant tenants the saddest irony of all was that his close friend and colleague, John Mandeville, was about to become the ultimate victim of the campaign they had initiated. Mandeville's throat infection gradually worsened in the months following his release from prison. On 24 June – his 39th birthday – he told his brother, Frank, that he felt unwell, and a few days later he complained of a toothache, neuralgia and a sore throat. On 7 July, Dr Edward McCraith was called from Mitchelstown and, gravely concerned for his patient, summoned two more doctors, Patrick J. Cremin and William O'Neill.[50] They found that the patient was suffering from a 'diffuse cellular inflammation' of the pharynx and neck, and that his ailment was incurable. They applied leeches to his swollen throat, but all was in vain.[51] Mandeville's wife, Mary, described how, on Sunday, 8 July 1888, after weeks of terrible suffering,

> He held my hand in his & the Crucifix, for one second he looked startled, & then he raised himself slightly & smiled ... he pressed my hand faintly the last expression of his undying love, just laid back his head & was gone to God without a struggle.[52]

Nationalist Ireland was in mourning once again. Mandeville's remains were shouldered from Mitchelstown to the graveyard at Kilbehenny. The cortege was so long that the coffin had arrived in the graveyard as the last of the mourners were leaving Mitchelstown, four miles away. In his graveside oration a distraught William O'Brien insisted that 'the story of John Mandeville will have to be told and will have to come out'.[53]

Mandeville's death – which many regarded as martyrdom – sparked off another major controversy for the authorities. However, most of the Home Rule Party wanted nothing to do with William O'Brien's call for an inquest into his death. The party leader, Charles Stewart Parnell, had opposed the Plan of Campaign and now hindered rather than supported O'Brien. 'So anxious are they to get away that they are discouraging me right, left and centre from raising J. Mandeville's death,' said O'Brien. He was determined to vindicate the Nationalist view that the tragedy had been caused by his jailers. It was left to O'Brien to spearhead demands in the House of Commons for a full inquiry.[54] The highly publicised inquest opened on 17 July, with evidence from medical experts, prison officials, police, family and friends. The McDermott, acting for the next-of-kin, argued that Mandeville's disease existed in acute form since his release from prison. Three days later, when he was due to give evidence to the inquest, Dr Ridley committed suicide in a Fermoy hotel. This sensational news convinced nationalists that the doctor felt guilty and was unable to face the inquest.[55]

The verdict came as a blow to the authorities, who were assumed to have hand-picked the jurors in the hope of ensuring a result in their favour. The jury found, nonetheless, that Mandeville died of a

> diffused cellular inflammation of the throat ... brought about by the brutal and unjustifiable treatment he received in Tullamore Gaol. We enter our solemn protest against the system of Government in awarding similar treatment to Irish political prisoners as to common criminals, and the cruel method by which the rules are enforced.[56]

The coroner's inquest into Ridley's death dealt another serious blow to the government. It returned a verdict that he suffered 'temporary insanity produced by the apprehensions of disclosures at the Mitchelstown inquest', and concluded that 'he was compelled to act in his official capacity in contravention to his own humane and considerate views'.[57] Balfour considered taking legal action against an English newspaper, *The Star*, when it described Mandeville's death as murder. He accused opposition leaders of turning it into a 'sham tragedy' and refused to express regret. He told his uncle, Lord Salisbury, the Prime Minister, that 'the whole prison episode, though a storm in a teacup, is amusingly characteristic of Irish administration'.[58]

Almost twenty years later, on 9 September 1906, an 18-foot-high monument to John Mandeville – with honourable mention of the three victims of the Mitchelstown Massacre, John Casey, John Shinnick and Michael Lonergan – was erected in New Market Square at a cost of £1,050. It was unveiled by William O'Brien who addressed the last great gathering of the surviving members of the local branch of the

National League. Some 20,000 people heard him declare that, 'monuments of this sort are not mere monuments to individuals. They are monuments of undying principles. They are landmarks in the history of a race.'

Funds to pay for the Mandeville memorial were raised in Ireland and among exiles in America, Australia and England.[59] O'Brien's high political profile and his fragile health protected him from the worst excesses of the penal regime during his various periods in jail in the 1880s. He outlived his lesser-known Mitchelstown friend by 40 years. Despite his extraordinary work for the cause of Ireland and its tenant farmers, William O'Brien has not had a memorial erected to his memory in his native Mallow.

11

FEELING THE PINCH

For Anna, Dowager Countess of Kingston, the Land War was particularly damaging. During the agitation, she was unable to pay the mortgage to the Church Body. By the time of the settlement with the tenants, arrears of interest on the mortgage had soared to £15,000. Webber realised that it would be better tactically to resign as receiver of the estate in favour of Henry Frend. Following the rulings of the Land Commission, the income from rents was reduced to £14,500 a year. Webber said that 'the arrears of rents which have met this [the mortgage arrears] were in some cases lost; in most were only collectible after a long interval, or remained outstanding.'

Under the deed of receivership, Lady Kingston was granted use of the demesne and several evicted farms. She was also allowed an annual sum of £900, which was to include Tithe Rent charges and all taxes due on her lands. Webber complained: 'This practically gave us only about £300 a year in cash.' In 1897 the Church Body agreed to impose less onerous conditions on the mortgage repayments. They consented to an arrangement whereby, after the yearly interest had been met, the surplus was divided equally, half to the countess and half against the arrears. This left her with an additional £300 to £400 a year. Had it not been for Webber's personal income, or so he claimed, the

Countess of Kingston could not have afforded to live at the castle.[1] During the 1890s, Frend continued to manage the estate and, according to Webber, no further trouble arose. In the twelve years up to 1900, Lady Kingston had no surplus for her personal use. It was Webber's own income, which he estimated at between £600 and £1,200 a year, that helped to subsidise the running of the castle.[2]

In 1892, Tom Robinson – whom Webber described as 'very capable' – was appointed land steward of the demesne. With Robinson in charge, the profits from the demesne and farms improved significantly so that, by 1903, the income had stabilised. 'The returns became very satisfactory and more than covered the expenses of maintaining the demesne and garden,' said Webber, who was determined to keep the property in good order.[3]

Several acres of the estate were sold to the Fermoy and Mitchelstown Railway Company, which opened a line to Mitchelstown on 22 March 1891. One of its founders was the *Galtee Boy*. According to the *Cork Examiner,* the new line was 'wonderfully regarded as being an auspicious one for the future trade and interests of Mitchelstown'.[4] Webber also supported an attempt by local farmers to form a co-operative creamery. He knew Sir Horace Plunkett, the pioneer of the co-operative movement in Ireland, and they initiated efforts to found a co-op locally. In June 1895, R.A. Anderson, secretary of the Irish Agricultural Organisations Society, addressed a meeting of Mitchelstown farmers. Thomas Carroll, JP, owner of the creamery then serving the locality, offered to sell it to them 'on very fair terms'. While he had an obvious vested interest in their prosperity, it seems remarkable that Webber should still care enough about his tenants to want to encourage them to found a co-operative. But tenant distrust of the landlord had not eased since 1887 and that was one of the reasons why a co-op was not founded for another 24 years.[5]

A financial windfall came Lady Kingston's way with the sale to the War Department of 1,100 acres at Skeheen, Turbeg and Killickane in the Kilworth Hills.[6] The suitability of the rugged terrain for military purposes was recognised when the army held manoeuvres there in 1893. The generals believed that it was an ideal training ground for troops being sent on campaigns against the Boers and native tribes in Africa. The War Department bought a total of 14,000 acres, most of it from the estate of Florence, Countess of Mount Cashell. Dozens of tenants who were scraping a meagre living from their holdings on the barren mountain were bought out. The *Cork Examiner* declared that the opening of Kilworth firing range in May 1896 was 'an epoch in military affairs in Ireland ... Kilworth may be regarded as an important centre for training in the South of Ireland in the science of modern warfare'.[7] Webber, for personal reasons, was more ambivalent:

> While the Government was liberal in buying out the occupying Tenants they cut down the amount they offered to the owner so that an Arbitration Case had to be undertaken. Major General Webber, C.B., R.E., & Mr Usher Roberts acted as arbitrators. The award was higher than the terms we demanded, £2,000.[8]

Half of that sum was paid against the mortgage. A few years earlier Webber had renovated the courthouse, 'affording a fine room for Petty Sessions'. Some of the £1,000 from the Kilworth land sale was used to restore a corner house in King Square. The rest went towards work on the old hotel and other buildings which had fallen into disrepair.[9]

The town was in a very rundown condition by the beginning of the twentieth century. Since the Famine, the countryside was in decline, forcing more and more people to board the emigrant ships. Mitchelstown's population fell to 2,141 in 1901 – the lowest ever recorded. Only 2,041 people lived in the rural areas of the Catholic parish (Brigown and Marshalstown), or less than half the number before the Famine.[10]

After the 1880s, landlords generally were despised as a class with the result that they felt a growing sense of alienation. Under such circumstances, and having regard to the indebtedness of hundreds of estates, many wanted to give up the painful struggle and sell out. The Wyndham Land Act of 1903 was the death knell not just for the Mitchelstown estate but for thousands of other estates, large and small, all over the country.[11] The Act offered those who sold to their tenants a twelve per cent bonus in addition to the agreed price. The period for repayment of loans was extended to 68.5 years, on a low interest rate. However, the whole estate had to be sold, including the demesne parks, which could be bought back by the landlord on the same annuity terms as those applying to the tenants. Although opposed by Michael Davitt, John Dillon and other leading nationalists, the Act did more than anything else to bring about change of ownership. By the 1920s, over 326,000 holdings had been sold under that Act and another introduced in 1909.[12]

Webber was very critical of the Wyndham Act. It was, he said, 'not at all favourable for our future means of subsistence, & the necessary expenses of a large house & place'. Prior to the Act, the Church Body repeatedly refused Webber's requests to reduce the interest on the mortgage from four-and-a-quarter per cent to four per cent. This left the estate with heavy outgoings of over £10,000 a year to pay interest on the loan. Webber wrote:

Feeling the Pinch

> Under these circumstances there were strong reasons for us to lose no opportunity of making use of the Land Purchase Act. Therefore when in Jan'y 1904 an application came from the Tenants we were prepared to meet it by giving our consent to sell on reasonable terms. This application was conveyed to us through the Rev'd Canon Rice PP of Mitchelstown.[13]

By agreeing to the purchase, the tenant at once became the landowner. Payment of the annuities would be to the government until the loan was eventually paid off. 'They acted like deposits in a savings bank, & the value of his property w'd become enhanced year by year 'til it became entirely free of all payments,' said Webber. The transaction, in Webber's opinion, was 'practically a free gift of the Land to the occupier'. He set a price for the first-term tenants of five shillings in the pound; second-term tenants got a reduction of three shillings, and non-judicial tenants four shillings in the pound. 'By agreeing to this their holdings w'd become free from all payments in 68 years,' he said.

At a local meeting of William O'Brien's United Ireland League (formerly the National League), chaired by Canon William Rice, the price sought by the owner was described as exorbitant. Webber turned down a proposal from the canon – at a meeting in the castle on 3 February 1904 – that the land be sold at the general price of 20 years' rent. After further meetings of the league, the tenants decided to apply to the Land Commissioners to have their second-term rents fixed. They also hired Canon Rice's brother, a solicitor in Fermoy, to act on their behalf. Shortly afterwards, the canon withdrew from the negotiations and left the tenants to their own devices. In early March, Webber got Henry Frend to discuss the sale with a small number of tenants in their own homes. Frend was received by them most cordially & he found them nearly all anxious to become purchasers. The terms finally arrived at were that the 1st Terms should receive 6s; the 2nd Terms 3s; & the nonjudicial, some 5s and some 6s. In all cases the rent due up to 25 March 1904 to be written off.[14]

Agreeing to write off the rents due proved to be the clincher, although a number of tenants on the east side of the estate withheld agreement until July 1904. By writing off these rents, Lady Kingston received a bonus of £18,000 from the government. 'It appeared necessary to concede this; both in our own Interests & those of the Rep've Body,' said Webber. Agreements with about 600 tenants were signed in June 1904. The mapping of the estate had to be undertaken by a surveyor and the most minute detail of boundaries settled. In some cases, these were ill-defined or disputed and this further delayed the sales.[15]

Another problem was caused by six farms where there had been evictions. In order to remove objections, Webber agreed to sell these to the former occupants. Tom Robinson, whom Webber was anxious to reward for his dedication, applied to the commissioners for a portion of Kildrum. His claim was made on the basis that his mother had been evicted from land on the Bruen estate in Oakpark, County Carlow. Bruen promoted Robinson's case, with the result that the commissioners assigned him 120 acres, including farm buildings.[16]

'Having every confidence in him for honesty and fair dealing, I have found no disadvantage arising from his having an independent & permanent interest,' said Webber. However, Robinson was both land steward to an unpopular landlord and a Protestant. His purchase had 'raised a jealous feeling in a few of the neighbouring proprietors – not discouraged by the priests, but of little consequence', said

Webber.[17] Generally, however, relations between Protestants and Catholics in Mitchelstown were cordial at the end of the nineteenth century. For example, Canon Moore, the rector, had dedicated a booklet to his 'dear friend', Dean O'Regan, the parish priest.[18]

From 25 March 1904, the new landowners were liable for interest on their purchase money. This was fixed at four per cent on the calculation that it would be nearly sufficient to meet the interest due to the Church Body. These sums were paid without exception by the tenants when signing the sale agreement. All future payments, whether for this interest or for purchase instalments, would be collectable by the Land Commission.[19]

Webber believed that the countess would not lose in the transaction. However, the estate would be left with only 300 acres at Glennahulla and Garrane Close, in addition to the 1,240 acres of the demesne (less than one and a half per cent of the original Kingston holding). There was also a significant number of house rents in Mitchelstown. 'We believe that the result was the best attainable under all the circumstances,' he said.

Of most immediate importance to Lady Kingston was the fact that the money raised from the sale could be used to pay off the mortgage on the estate. The rest could be invested. From October 1904, the sales were completed at a snail's pace because of delays with the Land Commissioners. Webber recalled that 'no active step was taken on their part until July 1906 when their Inspector Mr Sydney Smith made his first visit to inspect the non-Judicial holdings of which there were a good many'.[20]

The inspector spent a fortnight examining the property before going off on holiday. After that, he spent several weeks going around the western portion of the estate. By 1907,

Webber was still uncertain whether the inspector's report had been filed with the commission office; he and the dowager countess felt very frustrated by the whole business. The countess had to continue paying four-and-a-quarter per cent on her mortgage, but her tenants were paying only four per cent. Consequently, the estate revenue fell short of the sum needed to service her mortgage. Webber complained that 'the expenses of the Agent, Clerks & other salaries cannot be dispensed with, representing a cost of another £500 a year'.[21]

Payment was finally made after four years of delays, and the countess also obtained the bonus. She received £300,000 for the 22,000 acres sold under the Act. Of that amount, £293,000 had to be deducted to pay the charges on the estate, leaving what Webber described as 'a doubtful margin' of £7,000 profit from the transaction. In August 1908, she was also paid the bonus of £36,000, allowed under the Act. After the sale, the estate was reduced to the town, the demesne and Mitchelstown Castle. In addition she was allowed the value of the six evicted farms, for which the reinstated tenants were to pay £5,000. Subsequently, the Commissioners reduced that amount by £600 pleading 'insufficient security, which is contrary to fact and absurd', said Webber. A further £3,800 was raised when the lands farmed by the estate were relet to tenants who then bought their new holdings.[22]

While the disposal of agricultural holdings delighted the majority of Kingston tenants, it left the urban tenants of Mitchelstown isolated. These shopkeepers and householders were slow to move and they were impotent in the face of the government's refusal to sell town and village properties on the same terms as those offered under the 1903 Land Act. The 400 town tenants in Mitchelstown formed a branch of the Town Tenants' League with the aim of launching a campaign to buy out their holdings. But it was already too late and the farmers showed little interest in coming to their aid. A public meeting in Mitchelstown in April 1906, called to address the issue, had only a 'fair attendance'. Those present heard little more than rhetoric from local politicians who deplored the 'base ingratitude' of the farmers who made no effort to have the town included in the sales.[23]

The estates at Rockingham and Newcastle, owned by other members of the King family, were sold on terms similar to the Mitchelstown property. However, Mitchelstown and Rockingham were more fortunate than Newcastle in that they both incorporated towns (Boyle in the case of Rockingham). Both estates retained a secure, if relatively small, source of revenue beyond the reach of the Land Acts. At the date of the sales in 1907, the town rents of Mitchelstown were still worth up to £600 a year. The profit from the Mitchelstown sales was invested in securities, which were first-charge mortgage bonds on preference shares in British and foreign companies. In his journal, Webber referred to these as the 'First Estate' owned by Anna, and the 'Separate Estate' owned by himself. 'The securities of each I keep in separate Deed Boxes labelled in this manner which I deposited in the strong room of the White Knights tower, which I believe is fire proof,' he said.

He invested £5,000 in Swedish Government Loans. An investment of £10,000 was made in the San Antonio Railway, and a further £5,700 in the Dalgetty Company. Other substantial investments were later made in the Scottish Power Company, Canadian Northern Railway Company and British Timber Corporation. Arrangements were also made to take an advance of £20,000 from the Estates Commissioners on the security of the demesne. This was to be repayable in instalments over 68 years. Of the advance, £1,000 were retained by the Commissioners to recover Tithe Rent charges which had been due on the demesne.[24]

A severe critic of some of these proceedings was Captain Robert Douglas King-Harman, great-grandson of the first Viscount Lorton. The captain disputed Webber's version of events concerning the financial affairs of the estate. The final sum received from the sale, according to King-Harman, came to £300,000, plus £36,000 in bonuses. 'It may be noted that the sum realised was the same as the value of the estate estimated at the time of the Disentailing Deed nearly forty years earlier, a rather remarkable instance of the stability of values and money in those days.'

King-Harman believed that 'a certain rough justice' was now at work regarding the estate debt. This was a convenient view, as the captain was a bitter critic of the details of the Disentailing Deed, which put additional debts of £120,000 on the estate in 1876. He wrote:

> The principal cause of all the financial difficulties was not so much the shrinkage in the rental as a millstone hung on the estate by the payment of the enormous sum of £120,000 involved in the Disentailing Deed. Had Anna's first husband James been able to look into the future, perhaps he would not have been quite so willing to fall in with the plans of his fellow-conspirator. As it turned out, in striking at the 'Lorton Branch,' he practically ruined Mitchelstown and left his wife with half a lifetime of monetary worries.

King-Harman said he could find no explanation of how the debt could have been as high as £293,000 in 1907. He was adamant that all charges were paid off by the £236,000 loan in 1875. The interest arrears, which had been £15,000 in 1887, were reduced to £12,000 a few years later. However, as we shall see, the disposal of Webber's personal estate may explain where some of the money went.[25]

While the sale left the dowager countess and her husband with a certain sense of loss, there was also a feeling of immense satisfaction, that for the first time in over 150 years, the estate was not in debt. 'Now that we are in so advanced age we are well content with the results of parting from almost the whole of the vast estate,' said Webber, '& the feeling that all its immense liabilities have been wiped out.' At long last they were now able to say that they 'owe no man anything'.[26]

Webber, meanwhile, strove to maximise the estate's income. He developed an enthusiastic interest in farming the lands still held by his wife and an important record of how he managed the demesne is to be found in his journal. When he took back management of the demesne in 1878, the land was let to Tom Richardson, a dairyman from Galbally, County Limerick. The rent paid per cow (including its calf) was between £14 and £15, depending on the quality of land and the class of cows kept. 'Now in 1907 the rents are much less, say £8 to £11, which is the result of the fall in the price of butter through foreign importation,' said Webber.[27]

Richardson 'proved himself during several years to be a most reliable and industrious man who carried out all he undertook most faithfully'. He and his family lived in the dairy house at the farmyard for several years. But the trade at the butter market in Mitchelstown fell drastically in the 20 years after 1887, largely because the butter was being taken up by private creameries. When he took over the demesne from Captain Farrer, Webber re-introduced the system of letting cows to dairymen who paid for each animal during the milking season, while feeding and caring for them in winter. In return, each dairyman was allowed a portion of land for potato growing.[28] In 1907, 863 acres of the demesne were under pasture, 361 planted with trees, and 8.5 in gardens.

Estate-style farming was extended to a few outlying holdings during Webber's time. In some instances, the tenants' interests were either bought out or, in one case, taken up through eviction when large arrears were unpaid.[29]

Of the land stewards employed by Webber – including Henry Cholmondeley and Thomas Doherty – Tom Robinson 'proved the most efficient of all'. Great value was placed on his ability and experience which, in turn, led to up-to-date farming methods. Webber stated:

> The general plan we now follow is to have from 60 to 80 statute acres under tillage in the most convenient fields, taking these by turns for a few years each, and then laying down to grass. By then we grow oats, Root crops and Ryegrass Hay, all for the feeding of the livestock during the winter. We keep some other fields for meadowing yearly, both in the Demesne and outside farms, in all from 150 to 200 acres.

After the sale of outlying holdings to the Land Commission, farming by the estate was much more curtailed than in years gone by. In 1909, tillage and meadowing were reduced to a portion of the Clyroe Field and the Pike Field, both in the demesne, and a meadow in Brigown. In 1910, Webber wrote that the sale of milk gave a steady return and any surplus was used to rear calves. 'For a long time past we have ceased to work a Dairy but have sold the whole milk both summer and winter to customers in the Town, & to the Creamery when there is a surplus,' he said.[30]

Farming was a serious business for Webber, who carried out many cattle breeding experiments. The main dairy breed was Shorthorn, which was kept by most Irish farmers until the 1950s. From these Webber bred various crosses with Pollard Angus and Hereford bulls. The calves from the Hereford crossbreeds proved to be 'large & thrifty & excellent outlyers'. He sold these animals, barely two years old, for £15 each. Heifers and bullocks were fattened or sold as stores, depending on the state of the market. Besides cattle, a breeding flock of sheep (Hampshire Downs and Oxfords) was also kept with good results.[31]

12

Vous-Avez Raisong!

Big George's family had grown up by the time his great house was completed in 1825. The fourth earl's homosexuality precluded marriage and children; the fifth earl's marriage to Anna was also childless, as was her second marriage to Willie Webber. This gave rise to a legend that the lack of male heirs was a curse on the White Knight and his descendants after his betrayal of the Sugán Earl of Desmond.

The dowager countess and Webber enjoyed the company of children, if only in a reserved Victorian manner. Visitors to the castle included Webber's nieces, nephews and cousins who enjoyed his generosity. The young guests fished on the Funcheon, went boating in the lake and played tennis and cricket. Lady Kingston's friends also came to stay; Minnie (Mary) Fairholme was her close companion and remained at the castle to the end of her life. Minnie was joint owner with her sisters of Comeragh House, County Waterford, but by 1900 she was in residence at Mitchelstown Castle as Webber's assistant.[1]

The German housekeeper, Madame Netta Hagerbaum, was there for more than 40 years up to the First World War. Servants were few compared to the number employed in Big George's day, as poorer circumstances forced Lady Kingston to make savings wherever possible and this involved reducing staff.[2] Still, there were at least twenty domestic servants in the castle; many were Scottish Presbyterians and Protestants whose Catholic descendants still live locally. In 1901, the butler was a 24-year-old German Lutheran named Herman Brachmann. Other retainers included a coachman, a nurse, two cooks, five gardeners, grooms, gamekeepers, foresters and farm workers. Of those living at the castle in 1901, only Lady Kingston and the kitchen maid were born in Ireland.[3] The custom of employing foreign domestics was normal in Irish country houses where it was felt that the native Irish did not have the skills required to carry out such work.

Even those gentry who had lost out after the Land War could manage to keep up appearances because food was cheap and wages were low.[4] However, after Frend's appointment as receiver in 1888, Webber and his wife had no choice but to reduce their household expenses:

> This we managed by not occupying four of the principal rooms, & using a small dining room & Kitchen & so reducing the number of servants & the number of guests, & living very quietly. As a result our household & personal expenditure which for 10 years before 1887 averaged £1,930, in the following 11 years was kept down to £675 a year and the years following 1899 has not exceeded an average of £890.[5]

For all of that, the image of an aristocracy living in their big houses and protected from the outside world by park walls still held at Mitchelstown. Anna and her husband no longer needed to use the demesne gate beside Saint George's Church when going to services. That had been put there in the turbulent days of the Land War so that they could travel safely to church rather than run the tenants' gauntlet as they rode through George Street. However, the days when all and sundry found a welcome at the castle were a fond memory. The demesne wall, and the screen of mature trees inside it, remained the physical evidence of the social and political barriers that stood between landlord and tenant.[6]

In the small Protestant community remaining around Mitchelstown, of which Lady Kingston was the most prominent figure, the threat of isolation was being felt more acutely than ever.

In appearance at least, the exclusive society into which the Ascendancy was born seemed secure, even if its wealth and influence had diminished in other ways. By the beginning of the twentieth century, the power of the Ascendancy was in rapid decline. Most of the great landlords had lost their properties. The Mount Cashell estates had been sold off under the Land Acts and Moorepark itself was sold to the War Department. Many properties in the general vicinity of the Kingston estate were also sold off – among them the estates of Lords Doneraile, Listowel (at Ballyhooly) and Lismore (at Shanbally Castle, near Clogheen).[7]

The establishment of county councils in 1899 introduced a level of democracy that curbed the influence of landlords over local government. As a Justice of the Peace, Webber had some judicial authority through the petty sessions. However, since the 1870s, the power to appoint police and raise militia rested with the resident magistrates. Politically, Webber was a staunch Conservative who opposed Home Rule and made donations to its opponents. In this he was typical of his class, most of whom dreaded the notion of Irish self-government.[8]

While Webber worried about the turn of events in the larger world, his wife devoted herself quietly to the re-establishment of her property. 'The part of the house which she occupied was maintained in the most perfect taste,' said her second cousin, Mrs Nora Robertson.[9] Elizabeth Bowen recalled how her grandfather, Robert Cole Bowen, and his friend, George Montgomery of Killee House, had a low opinion of the teas provided at the castle in Anna's time. Even fruit and raisins were now a rarity in the Kingston barnbracks, so much so that when a raisin was found it could become the subject of amusement. One such delicacy was discovered when the Duhallow Hunt came to tea after a day's sport. Mr Montgomery was favoured with a raisin and he held up the slice for all to admire. Bowen, in his best Cork French, caused consternation when he declared, 'Vous avez raisong!'[10]

Elizabeth Bowen's description of Mitchelstown as a place where frugality reigned was not supported by an even more famous literary guest, George Bernard Shaw, whose wealthy wife Charlotte was a close friend of Lady Kingston. The Shaws' visits to Mitchelstown at the turn of the century were occasions to be remembered and savoured, said Mrs Robertson.

In 1900, Anna was aged 67 and Webber a year younger. He was 'a picturesque old man', while she was 'dignified rather than dynamic'. Lady Kingston's relatives made up for her lack of dynamism. Mrs Robertson wrote that 'her brother, Captain Richard Brinkley, representing *The Times*, became the outstanding authority upon Japan – consecutively – married two Japanses ladies'.

Mrs Robertson remembered Anna's 'composed qualification' for the best Nanking porcelain. 'The white,' said Lady Kingston, 'must be the white of a young eye.' Mrs Robertson noted that Webber

> considered it immoral to sleep in any but woollen sheets ... After dinner, the butler would bring in a silver salver upon which rested a finely chased spirit lamp, some straw spills in a stand and a snuff-box of tobacco. A filigree-covered pipe, the size of an acorn, was slowly filled with fine golden tobacco. After lighting first the spill and then the pipe, Mr Webber reverently executed three puffs and the whole complicated outfit was gently removed from sight.

Nothing less than the King's Room was considered suitable

Vous-Avez Raisong!

for the Shaws, who loved doing the circuit of big houses. Mrs Robertson was amused at the thought of the playwright's 'carroty beard jutting out of the sheets beneath the crimson canopy' of the immense four poster bed. During these annual visits, the countess would spend the evening in conversation with Charlotte and some classical trios were performed in the ante-room as part of the ritual. Mrs Robertson said:

> An elderly cousin played on the violin. Mr Webber – with his feet fortified by immense Jaeger house-boots – [played] the 'cello, and any guest competent to do so (my husband took the role during our stay) played the piano. Bernard Shaw was never more welcome at any house than he was at Mitchelstown. Unflaggingly he would support his two enthusiastic elders at the piano, being far more appreciative of their musical ardour than critical of their defects in execution.

After one visit, Mrs Robertson suggested that the distraction of it all, and especially the immensity of the King's bedroom, may have accounted for the famous writer leaving his personal effects behind him. 'I arrived at the castle the day after the Shaw party had left to find the household disturbed,' she said. Apparently, a lengthy telegram has just been received from Shaw – 'the celebrated author had left pyjamas, camera, etc.' after him.[11]

Webber's love of good food and clothing is evident from the personal and household accounts book which he kept from 1895 to 1922. It certainly does not support Elizabeth Bowen's perception of frugality at the castle. Indeed, Webber and his wife were deeply conscious of their position as the owners of one of the greatest houses in Ireland. The book shows regular purchases of all forms of clothing from Jaeger and Company. Clothes were bought from Brown Thomas in Dublin and presents, sweets and groceries from Harrods of London. Irish tweed was purchased from Magee Brothers in

Donegal. Copious quantities of Bewley's coffee were bought, as were the finest cider, port, wine and champagne. Fruit included oranges and pears, while the menu also boasted duck, pheasant, salmon, trout and venison.

Electricity was installed in the castle by 1901, more than 50 years before it illuminated the lives of Webber's tenants' children in the rural parts of the old estate. However, most of the house was still lit by oil lamps and electrical fittings were confined to a few rooms. In 1919, when he was 85, Webber allowed himself the comfort of an electric quilt.[12] The town was lit electrically in 1913 by Russell's generator at Clonmel Road.[13]

Webber was a member of the country's most exclusive gentleman's club, the Kildare Street Club in Dublin, where he socialised with members of his class, including the co-operative pioneers, Sir Horace Plunkett and R.A. Anderson, whose endeavours he supported by annual subscription to the Irish Agricultural Organisation Society (IAOS). He was also a member of the Mitchelstown Board of Guardians. Webber was a great clubman; being also a member of the Irish Conservative Club, Cork County Club, Royal Society of Antiquaries of Ireland, the Royal Dublin Society, Cork Historical and Archaeological Society, Mitchelstown Lawn Tennis Club, Fermoy Polo Club, Duhallow Hunt and Mitchelstown Harriers. He was a founder of Mitchelstown Golf Club in 1908, which he provided with a small course in the north-west corner of the demesne.

Except for the First World War years, Webber was a traveller all his life, bringing back furniture, paintings and other items from trips all over the world. The countess rarely accompanied him to his more exotic destinations such as South America, China and Burma, preferring to join him on trips nearer home to Kerry, Dublin and London where they stayed in Claridges Hotel.[14]

Anna was unwell at the end of 1908, but appeared to have recovered by the middle of the following year. On New Year's Day, 1909, Webber fell from his horse while out hunting near Kilworth. He soon recovered and set off on a three-week cruise in the Baltic.

He remarked that before leaving on the cruise 'there seemed a prospect for us in our latter days of some tranquil enjoyment together. So the impending blow was entirely unforeseen by me'. On his return in the second week of September, he saw that Anna was not well. 'In a week her illness declared itself to my alarm & sorrow, but I could not realise how serious it was.' Over the next six weeks, Lady Kingston's health deteriorated again, though she appeared not to suffer any great pain from what was described as 'an attack of functional paralysis.' Throughout her illness she was attended by Dr Atkins of Cork and Dr Montgomery from Mallow, as well as two nurses. But their skill 'could not prevent the gradual advance of this disease in the brain that in the end became clouded. She passed away at quarter to 7pm without suffering at any time, like an infant falling to sleep.'[15]

Webber was inconsolable. Five months after her death he wrote in his journal:

> The smile on her beautiful features always gave me hope till gradually the end became apparent & the noblest of noble women passed away. I cannot add more now. My dear One left me on 29th October 1909. We were married for 36 years & 3 months of unbroken happiness ... In all these years our union was perfect & I cannot recall a conjugal dispute of any kind. So perfect was her temper & so just her judgment that there was nothing to quarrel about & I have the happiness of thinking that to the best of my ability my conduct was with the view to her happiness, & to help to carry out her wishes. In return I had the devotion of the most unselfish of women whose kindness to me was unceasing.[16]

Lady Kingston's funeral had none of the pomp and ceremony associated with previous Kingston obsequies. Many of her former tenants attended, as did their parish priest, Canon Rice, and their solicitor, W.J. Skinner. Among those past and present adversaries in attendance were a 'large number of sympathisers and friends'. The Ascendancy were well represented; among its number were Abel Buckley of Galtee Castle, Colonel Cooke-Collis from Castle Cooke in Araglin, the Hares of Convamore and the Bowens of Bowen's Court. Mitchelstown's rector, Canon Moore, officiated at the burial in the old graveyard beside the castle.[17] Webber wrote: 'At her own earnest wish we laid her to rest in the old church yard near the castle ... So my dear One rests not far from me where I hope to lie near her also.'[18] The remains were taken from the castle and down to the main gate. 'On reaching King Square a large crowd of people joined it. People were in attendance from all parts of the district,' reported the staunchly Unionist newspaper, the *Cork Constitution*.[19]

Three days after Anna's death, there was another unexpected bereavement in the family. Earlier in her illness, when she seemed to have recovered, Anna's older sister, Mrs Elizabeth Longfield, travelled from Dublin to be with her. However, Mrs Longfield, who was 82, suffered an attack of pneumonia, and died three days after the countess. Webber turned sadly to his journal once more: 'She rests beside her in the same plot of ground where now a plain cross of Norway Granite marks the consecrated spot.' In that dreadful October for the family, the Countess of Kingston's only other sister, Mrs Harriette Farrer, also died at her home in Dorset. Afterwards, Webber had part of the castle graveyard enclosed by a brickwork wall.[20]

Anna, Dowager Countess of Kingston, was one of the most remarkable figures in the history of the King family.

Vous-Avez Raisong!

Captain Robert Douglas King-Harman, of Rockingham, believed that she was weak-willed and easily influenced by her husband, but that was an opinion formed by his family's bitterness over her handling of events during the Land War and afterwards. Her standing among the tenantry was greatly diminished in the struggle of the 1880s, and it is in that context that she is best remembered.[21]

In her will, she left the castle and estate to her husband, and requested him, in turn, to pass them on to Lieutenant-Colonel Wentworth Alexander King-Harman, of Newcastle – though she did not stipulate this in writing. She regarded Alec, as he was called, as the rightful head of the family and rejected the legitimacy of the eighth earl. Her personal estate was valued at £74,263-15s-1d, of which £40,719 was in England. Bequests included £1,000 each to her brother, Captain Francis Brinkley, in Tokyo; her nephew, William Alexander, in Dublin; her great-nieces, Edith Kingston Webber and Adelaide Webber. Netta Hagerbaum received £200, with permission to reside in a house at King Square, and Minnie Fairholme got £600. What was left went to Alec King-Harman.[22] Ms Fairholme remained at the castle as companion to Webber, who was now almost 80. In January 1910, they tried to get away from all the recent tragedy by taking an Egyptian cruise together, in what was understood to be nothing more than a platonic relationship.[23]

Having obtained outright ownership of the Mitchelstown estate, Webber began to sell it piecemeal. The Kildorrery fair tolls were sold to Alexander McDonald in 1914 and, whenever the opportunity arose, Webber also sold properties in Mitchelstown.[24] He diminished the Kingston inheritance further than was necessary as he did not need the money. In 1911, he bought his first motor car for £433, and spent a further £4-4s on the chauffeur's licence. The vehicle was an open-back Laudelette No. 1 with a hood that could be pulled up in bad weather. Petrol was bought at O'Flaherty's bicycle shop in Baldwin Street, then the only suppliers of motor fuel in Mitchelstown. Much effort was put into training the driver, whose uniform was bought from Harrods. But he was not up to the task and, after crashing more than once, he was replaced by R.J. Ruane, who was paid £3-10s-2d a week for the safe carriage of his master in the years before the end of the First World War.

Politically, Webber and his class now faced the twin menace of German might in Europe and Home Rule in Ireland. Sir Edward Carson was leader of the anti-Home Rule movement. Webber supported the Unionist cause and, in that context, one of the most curious entries in his accounts was a donation of £5 to the Mitchelstown National Volunteers, made through a local engineer named Paddy Coughlan.[25] Perhaps he was making a small each-way bet should he find himself on the wrong side of history.

On the morning of 29 July 1914, two officers of the National Volunteers attended Sunday service at Mitchelstown's Protestant church. They were Colonel Maurice Moore and Captain Talbot Crosbie, both members of Ascendancy families.[26] Later that day, against the background of enormous tensions in Europe, several thousand Volunteers from Cork city and county paraded in the town. 'They composed a fine intelligent body of smartly drilled men and excited astonishment as well as admiration,' reported the *Cork Examiner*. Six bands from Mitchelstown and Fermoy led the various companies, which had been formed into the Galtee Regiment, past the reviewing stand where Colonel Moore, commander-in-chief of the Volunteers, and Captain Crosbie, took the salute.

Sir Roger Casement, a member of the provisional

Vous-Avez Raisong!

committee of the Volunteers and a friend of George Bernard Shaw, was to head the review but he had to cry off because of ill-health. His letter to the Volunteers, read out to the parade, invoked the spirit of 'Remember Mitchelstown'. He urged the Galtee Regiment to become

> the armed guards of Irish Freedom. You may be – you will be – called on to make many sacrifices yet for Ireland, but these are sacrifices every Irishman who loves his country would gladly make and that is to give up his life honourably, bravely and faithfully, even as the Fenians of old did ... for Ireland.[27]

One week later, the annual garden party at Mitchelstown Castle was held, as usual, on the first Sunday in August. Elizabeth Bowen's poignant account of that occasion was the swansong of the landed gentry in mid-Munster. Her cousin, Audrey Fiennes, came to stay at Bowen's Court, near Kildorrery. Both girls (Elizabeth was then fifteen) looked forward to the Mitchelstown party, which was one of the social highlights of the year. Years later, Bowen wrote:

> August 4th passed: in the course of it the rain stopped. August 5th was a white-grey, lean, gritty day, with the trees dark. The newspapers did not come. A wind rose, and, at about eleven o'clock that morning we drove down the avenue in the large pony trap – the only conveyance Bowen's Court now had: but for the pony the carriage-stables were empty – my cousin and I held on the hats we had elected to wear.

They planned to go by Rockmills and pick up a friend before lunching at her Aunt Sarah Bowen's house in King Square. However, Sarah remained at Bowen's Court, because she did not care much for castle parties since the death of her friend, Lady Kingston.

At Rockmills my father – whose manner, I do remember, had been growing graver with every minute – stopped the pony and went into the post office. There was a minute to wait, with the pony stamping, before I again saw him framed in the low dark door. He cleared his throat and said: 'England has declared war on Germany.' Getting back into the trap he added: 'I suppose it could not be helped.' All I could say was: 'Then can't we go to the garden party?'

After picking up their young friend, Silver Oliver, the party drove to Mitchelstown, with Henry Bowen enduring a barrage of questions from the girls. They hoped that, with a war going on, they might not have to return to school in England. The by-roads had dried in the wind and were glaring white, said Elizabeth, who added that the war had already given them an unreal look:

> That afternoon we walked up the Castle avenue, greeted by the gusty sound of a band. The hosts of the party [Willie Webber and Minnie Fairholme] ... were not young, and, owing to the extreme draughtiness everywhere, they received their guests indoors, at the far end of Big George's gallery. In virtue of this being a garden party, and of the fact that it was not actually raining, pressure was put on the guests to proceed outside – people only covertly made incursions into the chain of brocade saloons.

Wind swept round the castle terraces and blew grit into the ices. The band clung with difficulty to its exposed place. Elizabeth felt that had it not been for the stirring news of war, the party would have been rather flat:

> Almost everyone said they wondered if they really ought to have come, but they had come – rightly: this was a time to gather. This was an assemblage of Anglo-Irish people from all over north-east County Cork, from the counties of Limerick, Waterford, Tipperary. For miles round, each isolated big house had disgorged its talker, this first day of war. The tension of months, of years - outlying tension of Europe, inner tension of Ireland – broke in a spate of

words. Braced against the gale from the mountains, licking dust from their lips, these were the unmartialled loyalists of the South. Not a family had not put out, like Bowen's Court, its generations of military brothers – tablets in Protestant churches recorded deaths in remote battles; swords hung in halls. If the Anglo-Irish live on and for a myth, for that myth they constantly shed their blood. So, on this August day of grandeur and gravity, the Ascendancy rallied, renewed itself. The lack – it was marked – of one element at that party made us feel the immediate sternness of war: the officers from Kilworth, Fermoy and Buttevant had other things to do with the afternoon. They were already under orders, we heard.

She also heard voices among the guests saying, 'let us ask Mr Bowen'. Later she realised that the question was the likely impact of the war on the Home Rule campaign. Between 1914 and 1918, the unspeakable horrors of 'the war to end all wars' certainly hastened the end of many of the families represented at that great party. She concluded:

> It was an afternoon when the simplest person begins to anticipate memory – this Mitchelstown garden party, it was agreed, would remain in everyone's memory as historic. It was, also, a more final scene than we knew ... Many of those guests, those vehement talkers, would be scattered, houseless, sonless, or themselves dead. That war – or call it now that first phase of war – was to go far before it had done with us.[28]

13

History Gone to Blazes

In 1914 the sons of Ascendancy Ireland joined the fight for the Empire of which they were proud to be a part. In Mitchelstown, as in other Irish towns, many young men with no imperial ambitions also marched off to war. The horror of the conflict was felt almost immediately in the King family. Edward Stafford-King-Harman of Rockingham was killed in action in France in November 1914, only five months after he had married Olive Pakenham-Mahon. At home, meanwhile, other young men were preparing to exploit 'England's difficulty' by striking a blow for independence.[1]

In autumn 1914 the Mitchelstown Volunteers, by some ruse or other, secured 50 rifles and 5,000 rounds of ammunition from an English firm.[2] The importance of these weapons was noted by Ernest Blythe, organiser of the Irish Volunteers in Munster, on a visit to the Company in 1915. He observed that the rifles had given them a high level of confidence.

> Here as almost everywhere else possession of arms was vitally important in relation to the National attitude of both the Volunteers and the people around them. They could not have kept the Company as strong and enthusiastic as it was if it had not the rifles, which made even those who were among the flabbiest, nationally speaking, of their neighbours regard it as entitled to respect.[3]

In the years after 1914 the Mitchelstown Volunteers drilled and exercised in preparation for the rebellion at Easter 1916. The Galtee Battalion was assigned the task of destroying communications in the district. On Easter Sunday morning they received General Eoin McNeill's order, 'cancelling all Volunteer Parades for that day and until further notice'. The battalion commanders then organised a mock attack on Galbally village, in County Limerick, so that the men could let off steam, if little else.[4]

When the Easter Rising collapsed, Webber's class generally approved of the execution of its leaders. In his case, however, that attitude may not have extended to rebels such as Countess Markievicz, the former Constance Gore-Booth, at whose wedding Lady Kingston had been a guest. The rebel countess was sent to prison but was spared execution because of her sex.[5]

Webber's young cousin, Arthur D.M. Webber, stayed with him at this time. The young man took over the business affairs of the estate and was in line to inherit the unsold portions of Webber's own family properties in Sligo.[6] Taxes for the Great War effort were a burden. Webber's payments were £257-15s in 1916/17. Nonetheless, he continued to live in comparative luxury. Groceries and other supplies were shipped regularly from London. He spent heavily – far too heavily in Captain King-Harman's view – during the war years. From 1914 to 1918, he spent an average of £1,653 each year. This figure compares well with 1911, for example, when he spent £2,974-6s, which included the cost of a holiday in Egypt and Italy.

From the outset of the Great War he subscribed generously to causes such as the RSPCA's horse fund, the Salvation Army, Kensington Hospital War Supply Depot and the Friends of Armenia. Donations to charities were also substantial. His average contribution to local, national and wartime good causes was £350 a year between 1914 and 1918. He also maintained his memberships of the Kildare Street Club and the Royal Dublin Society. He joined the Royal Automobile Club in 1917. Like the rest of the new motoring class in Ireland, Webber was affected by petrol rationing after the Easter Rising but, unlike most of his fellow motorists, he was allowed to use his car during the war years. There were happy times, too, for some of his staff when Montgomery, the butler, married the Scottish cook.[7]

Victory in the Great War gave little comfort to the Ascendancy who were shocked by Sinn Féin's stunning success in the general election of December 1918. During the following year, the young guerillas in Sinn Féin's military arm, the Irish Republican Army, alias the Volunteers, took up arms against the British forces and, for the first time in decades, the doors of Mitchelstown Castle were locked at night.

Despite the menacing political climate, Webber remained committed to local economic progress. He played his part in the most important local development of the twentieth century – the formation of Mitchelstown Co-operative Agricultural Society Ltd. Demand for farm produce fell after the war but local merchants still charged wartime prices for grass seed, corn and fertilisers. In the spring of 1919, several Mitchelstown farmers who were dissatisfied with the situation decided to take matters into their own hands. Through Michael Casey, a shopkeeper and part-time farmer living at 29 Lower Cork Street, seed and fertiliser were bought in bulk by a number of young farmers. This venture convinced them that a united body would benefit the entire farming community.

By mid-May progress was made in the formation of a co-operative society under the auspices of the Irish Agricultural

Organisation Society (IAOS). The farmers decided to open a co-operative store rather than a creamery – a decision bitterly opposed by the shopkeepers who foresaw the consequences for themselves. The co-op was also opposed by some of the local Catholic clergy, who regarded it as something akin to communism.[8]

A problem for the organisers was the acquisition of a site. They approached Webber through the IAOS president, Sir Horace Plunkett. Paddy Courtney, the local IAOS organiser, reported that Webber was 'rather impressed by IAOS work, & appreciates this sort of thing'. He was willing to help but the site they most wanted met with local objections. Webber suggested that they opt for a location near the railway station and he offered to sell it to them at a very reasonable price. In a letter to Sir Horace, Webber reminded him that 'some years ago I suggested to the farmers around that such a co-operative should be started, but they failed to appreciate the matter at that time ... the possible sites here in my control are very few'.[9]

Jim Fant, IAOS technical adviser, reported that the site on offer was 'wholly unsuited' because it was 'too remote from the lower end of the town, where the principal roads converge'. Finally, a house at New Square was purchased from a doctor and the society formally came into being on 23 June 1919. The inaugural general meeting was held on 19 February 1920; the first chairman of the new society was Con O'Brien of Killickane. He remained in the chair of Mitchelstown Co-op for the next 40 years, during which time it grew to be the largest in the country. Some of that initial success could be attributed to Webber who, on 4 October 1919, invested £100 to become the co-op's largest shareholder. This was a badly needed financial boost for the fledgling business.

With the War of Independence at its height the new co-op could not have chosen a worse time to open its doors for business.[10] A reign of terror swept the country when the Black and Tans engaged in bloody reprisal for IRA actions. In the tit-for-tat warfare the big houses of the gentry became 'legitimate targets' for the IRA. Among the first to be destroyed in North Cork, in the summer of 1921, was Lord Listowel's stately Convamore House on the banks of the Blackwater at Ballyhooly.

> Of the houses destroyed in 1920 and 1921, the majority were burnt in retaliation for reprisals. The military were ambushed, a policeman was shot, a barrack was attacked, and as a reprisal a village was burnt. Then, as a counter-reprisal, the IRA burnt the neighbouring Big House, if its owner was thought to be pro-British. This was hardly fair, in that however pro-British the owner may have been, he or she would almost certainly have deplored the atrocities of the 'Tans' no less than the most ardent supporter of Sinn Féin would have done.

By whatever means, Webber managed to walk the tightrope between the local IRA and the military. In this way, he saved Mitchelstown Castle, at least for the time being. It was noted that 'the chances of a house being burnt on the whole bore little relation to the owner's popularity, still less to that of his or her forebears'.[11]

Political anxiety was no longer confined to the Ascendancy. It was just as dangerous now for Mitchelstown Co-op to have associations with the IRA. When this became clear to the management they decided to seek the resignation of any member who was active in the IRA. Consequently, Patrick ('Pa') Luddy, an IRA officer, was persuaded to abandon his co-operative role until the conflict ended.[12] When that happened – on Sunday, 11 July 1921 – the last 'official' attack on the British army is said to have taken place at

Mitchelstown. A small detachment of soldiers was ambushed when it left the barracks to get water from the public supply at the junction of Lower Cork Street with Clonmel Road. Both sides sustained casualties – none fatal – and the Republicans' bid to capture arms yielded only two rifles. As the truce was to come into effect a few hours later, the Mitchelstown engagement was regarded by some as a brilliant piece of opportunism and by others as a dastardly act of cowardice.[13]

Membership of the Volunteers increased enormously throughout County Cork in the aftermath of the Truce. In the Mitchelstown Company, in the spring of 1921, just 23 of its 36 members were considered 'reliable' and only five were on active service. By December 1921, the Company's membership stood at 75, but the new recruits were regarded with disdain by the older members who nicknamed them 'trucileers'.[14]

The Galtee Battalion, like the IRA in general, was starved of weapons and ammunition when the Truce was signed. Pa Luddy's inventory as battalion quartermaster showed the precise condition of its five companies from July 1921, to August 1922. These companies were Ballylough (A Coy.), Glanworth (B Coy.), Kildorrery (C Coy.), Ballygiblin (D Coy.) and Mitchelstown (E Coy). Between them they had barely 70 shotguns, one Mauser rifle, a few Lee Enfield rifles, revolvers and other firearms. They were also badly short of ammunition. In some cases, they had the wrong bullets for the guns held in the battalion area. However, funds raised through local levies were sufficient to support the families of men on the run, and this contributed to the battalion's effectiveness. Monies collected in 1921 totalled £3,224, with a surplus of £369 in January 1922.[15]

The Anglo-Irish Treaty, signed on 6 December 1921, was

greeted with grave misgiving by the Ascendancy who felt that they had been sold out by the government. Not for the first time, Webber grudgingly accepted the inevitable and lent his support to the new Irish government by contributing £40 to the Free State Election Fund in March 1922. However, the Treaty left loyalists with virtually none of the safeguards they had been promised the previous July by the Republican leaders. Webber must have hoped that by donating money to the election, he might be afforded some protection from the new government.[16]

In the civil war sparked off by the Treaty, the IRA commander-in-chief was General Liam Lynch, who was born in Anglesboro, County Limerick, in 1890. Lynch was among the first to join the Mitchelstown Volunteers in 1913. In the Civil War, most of the Mitchelstown Company opted for the anti-Treaty cause and, faced with little opposition, they took hold of the district. The loyalist and Protestant minority were left completely defenceless. They found themselves at the mercy of radical young militants who had old scores to settle and who despised everything the loyalists stood for.[17]

Amid great turmoil in the country, a party of armed men styling themselves 'The Republican Army' arrived at Mitchelstown Castle at 6.30pm on 29 June 1922. They were led by Pa Luddy, who held the rank of commandant. The Webbers – Willie, Arthur, Edith – some guests and the servants were ordered out immediately. Edith described the ultimatum as a 'notice to quit'. Her letters to cousin Alec King-Harman scarcely revealed the turmoil at Mitchelstown largely because she had to be very careful about what she put in writing. She said that 'a good many arrived in that evening & took possession of W.W. [west wing] saying they would go nowhere else, which of course they did twice in the big bedrooms as well'.

The family refused to go to the accommodation provided at the hotel because of the hour of the evening. The Republicans dug trenches and put up barbed wire, ruining the newly refurbished tennis courts in the process. 'All next day we put away things & did what we could,' Edith said. Luddy permitted the Webbers to remove only personal items such as sheets, plates, dishes and some silver. On the next day, they unwillingly accepted Luddy's 'eviction order'. Edith said that Mrs Franks, who lived at 'Gardenhurst' in King Square, was away, so Willie was put up there. 'I am sleeping at Sarah Bowen's who is away also,' she added. 'Arthur is with Mr Tomes [i.e. Rev Benjamin Tomes, Kingston College chaplain], we go over for all our meals to Gardenhurst: All the good people are huddled in the Square.'

The Republicans assured the Webbers that their occupation would last only a few days but Edith saw no sign of them leaving. 'I expect you can imagine what it looks like,' she wrote to cousin Alec. Members of the family went to the castle on several occasions to take things out. Edith said there was always a sentry at the gates and they had been given passes but were never asked for them.

'When I saw they had got hold of an album of mother's out of a locked cupboard and had been looking at it, I hated them touching her things,' she said. Even objects that Edith had hidden were taken out. 'But they open everything and ought to get some good hiding,' she declared. 'There is shouting or something at night; their flag is flying on a tower – One hears of things being taken, but only rumours,' she added. Webber's car was commandeered for Luddy's use. The old man was 'very well' but did not know the extent of what was happening in his home. On her return from the dentist in Cork, via Mallow railway station, Edith saw thousands of Republican troops. 'All the towny people are moving out to country places,' she said.[18]

Ten days before Edith wrote to Alec, the pro-Treaty parties won a resounding victory in the Free State election. During the weeks that followed, the castle garrison was on a 'war footing'. Furniture and other objects were used to bar entry to the mansion and sentries were placed at all entrances to the demesne. Republicans also occupied the old RIC barracks, workhouse and military barracks.[19]

The situation in Mitchelstown Castle was described in lurid detail on 19 July, in a letter written by the author, Edith Somerville, from her home at Drishane, near Castletownsend in west Cork. Her information had come from one of the Hares of Convamore who was with the Webbers when the Republicans arrived at the castle, but was now staying with the Somervilles. She also described how the family had refused to leave on the first night and how they spent that time taking up carpets and putting away valuable china, pictures and furniture into two rooms which they then locked.

Two days later, Miss Hare was allowed by Commandant Luddy to go to the castle and take out some of her personal possessions. She found that the locked rooms had been broken into and the contents taken out. Hobnailed boots had destroyed the parquet floor. The carpets had been relaid and were 'indescribably filthy with cigarette ends, mud and spit'. Edith Somerville wrote:

> Photograph frames were smashed and the bits of glass ... used as darts to throw at the valuable big Rembrandt that they had not been able to get down in time. Lavatories being considered useless institutions, the walls of the corridors were used instead. All the books in the library are being used as barricades for the windows, & as there are not enough, valuable old furniture is being used as well.

She said that the grounds of the castle were mined and trenched. Notices were placed everywhere to warn people that they were going about the demesne at their own risk.

> Streams of motor lorries and cars go to and fro from the castle all day & night, & so as to destroy the place even more thoroughly, they drive across the tennis courts to the house, though going along the drive is the easier way ... Imagine poor old Mr Webber's feelings! ... I should not think there would be much competition now as to who is to inherit the castle![20]

Admission to the castle was forbidden to the Webbers, except by written permission from Luddy. A visitor's permit was offered to the Kilbrides, then living next door to Gardenhurst. Mrs Kilbride, an O'Brien from Ballinwillin Lodge, was well known to the Republicans because her family were sympathisers in the War of Independence. Her husband was one of the few magistrates who resigned in protest following the burning of Cork city by the Black and Tans. While the Kilbrides chose not to avail of a permit, many others did so and in the process stole property from the castle.[21]

Arthur Webber was allowed to call to the castle regularly. His last visit was towards the end of July when he noted that the Republicans 'had the furniture stacked up against the windows as barricades'. However, there is reason to believe that, at this stage, looting from the castle was limited. Arthur alluded to this when he swore in evidence before a court in 1926 that furniture was 'all over the place', but he could not say that anything was missing.[22]

The Republicans took whatever they wanted not only from the castle but also from local farmers and townspeople. Bicycles, nails, petrol, animals and large amounts of food were commandeered. On 23 August, the *Cork Examiner* reported:

> The town rapidly realised that it had suddenly passed from its usual peaceful aspect into the very danger zone of strife. Soon the town was cut off by rail, telegraph, telephone and postal services, and supplies began to run short.[23]

When the military and police barracks and the workhouse were burned in early August, the Republican garrison at the castle was strengthened. After Clonmel, Tipperary and Limerick fell to the Free State Army, 'further considerable additions' were made to the Mitchelstown Republican contingent.[24] Michael Casey, son of one of the co-op's founders and a member of that force, contradicted newspaper claims that upwards of 2,000 republicans were in occupation of the castle in August 1922. The number, he believed, was not more than a few hundred. Edith Somerville stated that the castle had been taken by just 60 men. Casey was in the castle on the evening of 12 August when petrol was sprinkled around the building.[25] Earlier that day, the death in Dublin of Arthur Griffith, President of the Free State, sent shock waves around the country. The mood in Mitchelstown was worsening, and Edith Webber wrote again to Alec that day:

> One chances I will write a few lines but we are at present cut off from everywhere, Ballinderrik [Ballahaderig] bridge has just gone. The workhouse & Military Barracks burnt the night before & last night the Police Barracks. Also the first Bridge from this side going to the farm is blown up. I wonder now if one really ever fished there it seems such a long time ago. I think these people are pulling out but will take to the hills. Cousin Willie is wonderfully well and philosophic.

Loyalists now feared a concerted effort to drive them out of the country, Edith wondered:

> Do they really want to get everyone out of this Country as one cannot imagine the destruction of everything and everyone for

any good purpose? It rains every day, and very cold. I made various efforts to get into the house but was not let, nor allowed to have anything taken out.[26]

There was good reason now to bar the Webbers. On 12 August, and for some weeks before, scores of local people had been looting furniture, silver and anything else that could be hauled away.

The Grahams, who had a grocery in Upper Cork Street, moved their children to Richard Henry's home at the demesne farm. As her family was Protestant, Mrs Graham feared for her children if they remained in the town. There were rumours that the IRA intended to burn the town before their retreat from the advancing Free State Army. Anne Graham was eleven years old at the time. In her eighties, she vividly recalled how her family reacted to the Republican presence in Mitchelstown.

> On the afternoon [of Saturday 12 August, or possibly a day or two before] ... the Henrys called at our house with the pony and trap. As children we were taken out to the farm – leaving my mother and Reggie, that's my brother, and the staff at the shop.

She remembered 'a hushed excitement, a most awful feeling' about the town. It was as if everyone suspected that the end was near. 'I remember that night at the farm. In the dining room after tea we all knelt down and said prayers for the safety of the people of the town.'[27]

Just before midnight, Pa Luddy, the farmer's son and former co-op director from Coolyregan, issued the order to burn Mitchelstown Castle, the home of the co-op's largest shareholder. In making that fateful decision Luddy believed that he was avenging centuries of landlordism and English occupation, as well as erasing what little was left of the Kingston presence in Mitchelstown.[28] That was the

Republican's official line but the truth was not so easily confronted by Luddy's generation or, for that matter, their children. The castle had to be burnt to cover up the looting of priceless paintings, furniture and silver by the Republicans, their friends and supporters. They also claimed, pathetically, that by destroying the castle they were denying a base to their Free State enemies before whom they intended to retreat anyway.

By the end of the twentieth century a new generation, better educated and no longer enslaved by Republican ideology, regarded the action not so much as an attempt to rewrite history, but to eliminate it. By any civilised reckoning it was a monumental crime to destroy a building of such profound historical significance and, above all, to set alight the ancestral records of the ordinary people whose sweat and rents brought about its erection in the first place. In a social and architectural sense the town was diminished beyond recovery.

Everywhere people came out to see the inferno light up the sky on that wet and cold August night. Children were called from their beds to see the castle blazing and everyone sensed that, for good or ill, they were witnessing the turn of history. At close to midnight Arthur Webber was awakened by servants. He rushed to the main gates where a sentry stopped him from entering. He had no choice but to go back to bed and return early in the morning. Among the hundreds mesmerised by the conflagration was Daisy Flaherty, whose father ran the bicycle shop that also supplied petrol in Baldwin Street. Her young friend, Patrick Glavin, was one of several sitting on the demesne wall at Cahir Hill. He said, 'Getting back to Corracunna with the explanation of why I was late, my mother understood and quoted the old proverb, "The mills of God grind slowly, but exceeding small".'[29]

Some time between 2 and 3am, a Miss Needham, who had been evicted from the castle with the Webbers, returned to the main gates but they were locked. Except for the west wing, the building was now fully ablaze. In the next few hours, the Republicans pulled out, leaving behind a scene of devastation ripe for further looting. At 7am on Sunday, Arthur Webber finally made his way up the castle avenue. Flames and smoke billowed from the shell. He saw that 'the whole building was collapsed, except the basement, which was still burning. The whole place where the furniture was, was a mass of ruins'.[30]

No-one will ever know precisely who got what in the plunder of the castle but it is certain that the heaviest furnishings were consumed by the blaze. Not all the looters could be dismissed as rabble or members of the lower orders. A solicitor with an appreciation of the finer things in life was said to have removed paintings from the walls and arranged to have them taken away. Afterwards, many families in the town would have found it difficult to prove that none of their members was involved. There were many guilty consciences and the shame of it all brought a silence that endured for decades.'[31]

On the morning of the fire, Miss Needham saw people 'looting about the Castle, and putting stuff behind trees and bushes.' James O'Neill, a plasterer, saw 'a crowd of people, amongst them some women', removing furniture from the basement of the castle. Later, O'Neill witnessed people transporting these items towards the town.[32]

The shocking news was communicated to Alec King-Harman at Newcastle, County Longford. On Tuesday, 15 August, Edith Webber sent him a letter in which she said that the castle had been 'well paraffined and burnt'. She was cut off from everywhere with little sign of relief in sight. 'Worse than the burning was the way the place was looted & the behaviour of a good many of the people. One saw them taking out things & could do nothing.' She urged Alec to keep an eye on the Dublin shops for any silver or furniture that might come up for sale. She added that

> They would not let us take out things – I wrote you a letter the same day which I gave to a man who was riding to Cork so hope it turned up – There are such a lot of things I could say but can't – When one saw all the inside on various occasions and saw the West Wing basement over the Kitchens etc, the disgustedness & filth, only a fire can purify it all. The cellars are all intact but empty.[33]

On the day that Edith dispatched the dreadful news to Alec, the Free State Army marched into Mitchelstown from the Tipperary town direction. Their arrival was celebrated by several townspeople but was of no consolation to the Webbers. The *Cork Examiner*, on 18 August, reported some alarm at the fact that the force sent to secure the town was comparatively small. The commanding officer was undeterred when told by local people of the overwhelming strength of the irregulars in the castle. He had orders, he said, to occupy Mitchelstown and he would carry them out at all costs. He was greatly relieved to discover that Republican resistance was virtually non-existent. What he actually found was a town electrified by the events of recent days. The *Cork Examiner* reported:

> Where the Irregulars fled to nobody could guess. But the people did not go to any great pains to ascertain it, as what they desired had been bloodlessly achieved, and the National soldiers were loudly cheered as they marched through the town to the Christian Brothers' Schools, where they were accommodated.[34]

They were followed by further Free State troops who occupied buildings around the town, as well as the remnants of the castle where a tower was turned into a radio station. They also rounded up some Republican sympathisers. In the week after the castle blaze the troops came under sporadic fire, revealing some resistance. Shops closed when the funeral of a soldier killed at Kildorrery passed through the town in the Limerick direction. The *Cork Examiner* reported on 23 August that, 'a number of the general public took part in the procession, and lined the streets in sympathy. A contingent of National troops, also with arms reversed, took part.[35]

While the destruction of the castle was a terrible blow to old Webber, he was, nonetheless, 'splendid in the way he took it', according to Edith. 'Of course he is thinking over all he has lost, his cello and the collection of years.'[36] On 17 August, Webber sent news of the destruction to Alec:

> I write to tell you that the Castle has been burnt by the so called Republican forces who had been in occupation since the 29th June, on which date they took forcible possession ... It is impossible that it, the Castle, can ever be used again as a Family Residence, so the wish and proposal of my dear one in regard to yourself must be in abeyance. On me has fallen the consideration of what may best be arranged for the future and I trust I may be guided aright in many difficulties. Tell me freely what you feel in the matter. The whole thing is so dreadful ... in 5 hours they destroyed the ornaments & pride of the Country for this past century & all contained which they had not previously looted.[37]

Alec was taken aback by the suggestion that Webber was considering changing his will in favour of someone else. His reply, on 25 August, began with an expression of sympathy to the owner of the castle ruins:

> I am so sorry for you in the loss of so much that was dear to you from the association of many years: my Mother and sisters join in truest sympathy with you at this cruel blow. The looting must have been most disgusting and painful, and only shows the

hopeless state of degradation into which a large portion of the people seem to have sunk in these times.

Alec said that he would have considered it 'almost impossible to have burnt the whole of that magnificent building, and the most fiendish ingenuity must have been displayed to accomplish such an end.' Then came the shot across Webber's bows:

> I knew from Lady Kingston's lips, and from yours, what her wishes and your intentions were ... You will, I feel sure... realise that even in this terrible catastrophe I would not discuss the future, and the bearing which the past has on it, if you had not asked me to do it.

Webber was reminded in the letter that on many occasions Alec had discussed the future of Mitchelstown with Lady Kingston. There had never been any indication that it would be left to anyone other than himself should he survive Webber. Alec declared that

> It was fairly plain to me, that while I was very fortunate in being looked upon with affection by her, and though she was good enough to regard me as fairly competent and trustworthy, those were not the only reasons which influenced her in her choice of me as the ultimate successor to the old King property ... She told me plainly that though my Father was head of the King family ... I as a younger man would have a more reasonable chance of surviving her.

King-Harman had always looked forward to the day when the combined resources of Newcastle and Mitchelstown would be united in his name. This, he felt, would allow him to run Mitchelstown in a manner that would 'befit the head of a long established noble family'. He appealed to Webber not to give up 'the apparently hopeless struggle' of living in Mitchelstown.

> Though your life of late years has been largely centred in the Castle, there has always been the interests of the place generally, the farming, the gardens, the woods etc ... but personally, I hope that you will continue to live at Gardenhurst, or at any rate keep a pied a terre at Mitchelstown; will continue to supervise the management of the Demesne and what remains of the property; will put forward a claim for as large an amount of compensation as can be justly demanded; and will ensure under your will that I am to be the successor to that claim, as well as to what you leave me of the Mitchelstown Estate.

The intention to build a new residence was mentioned in later correspondence between them. 'Of course it could never replace the Castle, now so wickedly destroyed,' Alec admitted.[38] His views on the succession were reiterated when they met in Dublin in November. Alec then wrote another long letter to Webber:

> I do not question your legal right to do whatever you like with whatever Lady Kingston left you. But you will not be carrying out her wishes, and will be doing me a great moral wrong, if you leave away from me that which you got from her ... Now do you really think that if the Castle had been burnt in her lifetime, she would have changed her mind, passed me over, and left what remains to Arthur [Webber] or to anyone else?[39]

Alec's brother, Robert Douglas King-Harman, did not put a tooth in it. 'Old Webber wanted to leave all the King money he acquired by his wife's weakness and his own undue influence over her to members of the Webber family, particularly his cousin Arthur,' he said.[40] Alec's pressure had the desired effect on Webber, who promised finally to leave him Mitchelstown, but it took another year before he re-wrote his will. Webber conceded:

> I was glad to reach the conclusion which as far as I can will meet this your wish ... Meantime I also feel dreadfully the loss of the

home for myself which I so much loved and admired for almost 50 years of my life.[41]

Meanwhile, Webber had become despondent and disillusioned with Ireland and he realised also that he was unlikely to live much longer. Towards the end of 1922 he wrote several notes to close friends and relatives. On 1 December, he wrote to Minnie Fairholme to give her two items of jewellery and his watch and chain 'in memory for yourself'. Two months later, he sent Minnie a second note enclosing a diamond cross which had once belonged to Lady Kingston.[42]

The man who had so valiantly held the Ascendancy standard during the Land War was just a few months short of his ninetieth birthday when he died at his residence in Exmouth, in England, on 23 February 1924.[43] He was buried with Anna in the old graveyard beside the burnt-out shell of their beloved home. Webber had lived long enough to see the end of the Civil War, and the death in it of General Liam Lynch, the IRA commander-in-chief whose forces were responsible for the destruction of so many big houses. By April 1923, Lynch had realised that the Republican cause was lost. A meeting of IRA leaders was called in Cork to consider their desperate situation. On 10 April, the commander-in-chief was crossing the Knockmealdown mountains when he was shot by Free State troops. He was badly wounded and died a few hours later.[44]

14

DOOMED INHERITANCE

Mitchelstown Castle was the largest of the 200 or so big houses burned down in the Troubles between 1919 and 1923. To the Ascendancy of north Cork, it had represented the pinnacle of their influence and prestige. Its ruin shocked Nora Robertson who remarked that 'I shall not forget the dignity of its mutilated line, backed by the Galtee mountains, after its destruction in the Troubles. It was a sinister and melancholy silhouette to those of us, in my case from infancy, who had enjoyed its hospitality'.[1] Willie Webber's heirs believed that, without the castle, the Mitchelstown demesne ceased to serve the purpose for which it had been created and new options had to be considered for its future.

The loss of the great edifice was deplored not just by the Ascendancy but by nationalists with more refined sensibilities, such as John Dillon, despite his political campaign against its owners during the heady days of the Land War. When he visited Mitchelstown a couple of years after that struggle in the 1880s he outlined his vision of the future for properties of such magnificence. His travelling companion, Wilfred Scawen Blunt, commented: 'We passed along the park wall of the Mitchelstown estate, and he spoke with regret of the old Lord Kingstons, who must have been "princely fellows" in their day. Parks like these were an inheritance for the nation, and must be protected.'[2]

In the new Irish Free State preserving the parks of the scattered gentry was not high on the agenda. The priority for Webber's heirs now was to get as much compensation as possible from the new government. Previously, malicious damage claims had been met by increases in local rates. However, so much destruction had occurred in those years that local councils were unable to meet the enormous demands. The government promised that all claims would be paid promptly and in full, but when the total amount exceeded the money available the awards were reduced to such an extent that they bore no relation to the values of the properties destroyed. Payments were slow and the authorities insisted that the money be used for rebuilding. If the owners did not rebuild then the money was to be used to build houses elsewhere in the Free State.[3]

From the landlords' point of view, insult was added to injury in the 1923 Land Act which introduced compulsory purchase for tenanted land. The money for the purchases was paid to landowners in low-yielding bonds that could be redeemed only below par. This had further disastrous consequences for the Mitchelstown demesne and the Kingston finances.[4]

On 26 July 1923, Arthur Webber lodged a claim on his uncle's behalf for a total of £147,910-9s-5d compensation for Mitchelstown Castle. The claim was made under the new Damage to Property (Compensation) Act. It included £18,224 for silver, furniture, paintings and personal property.[5] Minnie Fairholme sought £300 for the loss of her Stradivarius violin, clothing and other items. Arthur's sister, Mrs Florence Ingouville-Williams, of Gosham, Hants, claimed £500 for silver, furniture and her personal effects.[6]

However, the State took little or no action to address the claims until pressure was exerted after Willie Webber's death. The main beneficiaries, Alec King-Harman and Arthur Webber, had to endure years of frustration while State officials compiled a large amount of documentation on the claims. Everything was queried. Old files held by the castle's insurance company were gone through in minute detail. Some officials were genuine in their efforts to compensate Alec fairly for the loss of his great inheritance; others approached the task with Republican zeal, tinged with meanness. Finally, it became apparent that full compensation would not be forthcoming because the State did not have the funds to meet the deluge of claims. Even if it had, there was no political willingness to accommodate the class it had been established to dispossess. For that reason, Alec was one of the great losers in the Irish revolution.[7]

Soon after the State investigation got underway, the valuation firm of Scanlan and Sons of Cork were asked to assess the market value of the castle prior to the blaze. They were also asked to advise on the feasibility of rebuilding it. On 21 June 1924, they reported:

> In estimating the value, the lands, gardens and grounds attached are excluded and that would probably render it almost unsalable or unlettable. The purposes, other than residential, which the Building might have suited, would be a Convent, College, Sanatorium, Hydro or possibly a Factory but the same difficulty would arise as to want of land.

They agreed that the castle was 'an outstanding specimen of architecture'. The valuers estimated that it would cost £75 a year in rates, £500 a year to maintain and £113 to insure. The rent to a landlord would be worth £500 a year. They estimated that, over a fifteen-year period, the cost of living in the castle would be £7,500. 'We are, however, of opinion that if the Castle as it stood prior to the burning, without any lands, was sold under normal conditions it might possibly realise

£10,000.' This was a damning blow to any hopes that Alec might have had for full compensation to rebuild. It was also an indication of depressed property values in the aftermath of political independence.[8]

Daniel Casey, the State Solicitor handling the claim, was told by the Minister of Finance to seek to have a rebuilding clause attached to any compensation payment ordered by the courts. Rebuilding Mitchelstown Castle was Alec's *raison d'etre* for two years after 1922 and he asked the Cork architect, W.H. Hill, to draw up plans for that purpose. He later proposed not to restore the original castle but to build a new residence in the demesne.[9]

At a meeting with the Minister of Finance, Alec was told that 'it would be absurd to build such a vast house in these days'. Under pressure from the Minister, he opted instead to build 17 houses in Dún Laoghaire and Clontarf, in Dublin. Consequently, the government agreed to pay him £27,500 for the castle on condition that all but £2,500 of it would be spent on building the Dublin houses. Alec was bitterly disappointed by the government's handling of his case. 'The methods of the Government are not much better than those of cardsharpers,' he said.[10]

Investigating the whereabouts of the castle treasures, especially the silver, took up a considerable amount of the investigators' time. Arthur and Alec were not helpful to the State investigation, probably because they believed that there was little difference between the Republicans who burned the castle and the government which had to compensate them under pressure from London.

One of the inspectors involved in the Mitchelstown case was John Butler. In June 1924, Webber's solicitor, Anthony Carroll of Fermoy, asked Butler to go to London to meet representatives of the insurers, Waring and Gillow, whose cover excluded damage caused by war. A visit to London would also have given Butler the opportunity to interview Minnie Fairholme, whose home in County Waterford had also been burned by the Republicans, who had 'an intimate knowledge of the contents of the Castle.'

Butler went to Mitchelstown immediately after his interview with Carroll. There he met with Arthur Webber, who told him that 'neither he nor Colonel King-Harman, the heir to the property, could be of any assistance to me [Butler] in my investigation'. Webber offered to send Butler to London at his own expense, but a year elapsed before the inspector was given permission from his superiors to go on the trip. On 10 June, Butler wrote

> I heard in Fermoy and Mitchelstown, in the course of conversation with different people, that there had been considerable looting from the Castle, and that the claimants either did not wish to go into the matter or were afraid to do so. I returned to Dublin and was instructed to make my valuation from the file, as I was unable to get any help from the Claimants in Ireland.

Butler expressed his frustration in reports to the Office of Public Works. He said he had 'great difficulty in dealing with this claim, as I have had no help whatever from the owners or their Agents to enable me to make my valuation. I have done all I could under the circumstances to be just to the State and the Claimants.' He examined the list of castle contents, based on Waring and Gillow's valuations, but found it almost impossible to select items that could be reduced in value. He stated:

> I went through the ruins of Mitchelstown Castle, and I formed the opinion that the contents must have been of the finest quality: as the Castle seemed to have been built regardless of expense. There was no salvage, but from my investigation I am perfectly sure

there was considerable looting. The fire did not seem to have reached the basement, yet none of the contents are to be seen, and all the fine mantelpieces seem to have been forcibly wrenched from the walls and carted away.

The inspector concluded that 'all the silver was looted before the Castle was set on fire'.[11] The treasure included candlesticks dating from 1746; a George IV fluted wine strainer; a George III circular squat teapot; five silver-lined horn cups; a tea urn on a stand weighing 126ozs and a 'richly chased tea tray' dating from 1881. Among the dozens of splendid pieces there was a stunning silver chandelier weighing 64lbs 4ozs.[12] Butler was mystified:

> The Civic Guard [Garda Siochána] ought to be able to trace a considerable quantity of the looted goods, some of which may have been taken to Dublin. I cannot understand why there was no salvage in the case of the silver, the silver could not have been burned away. I can only come to the conclusion that all the silver was looted before the Castle was set on fire.

However, Butler believed that £250 for the castle's rare book collection was 'a very fair allowance' but he estimated Willie Webber's personal wardrobe at only £40 if sold at auction.[13] Another report from Butler and C.H. Curnow, dated 18 August 1925, indicated the furniture values in newly independent Ireland:

> I feel confident that the Castle was furnished in early Victorian furniture, probably purchased at the time of the 1st London Exhibition in 1851. This furniture was undoubtedly very magnificent and very costly, but it has entirely gone out of fashion now and would be most difficult to dispose of.

The 'unfashionable' items included cabinets mounted in Ormolu, large sofas, cheval mirrors, wooden and brass beds in the Gothic style, large Victorian pier and mantelpiece mirrors. Many items had been made specially for the castle. The inspectors added that the contents 'would be entirely unsuitable for a modern house, or for a mansion furnished in period furniture'. The inspecting officers admitted in 1924 that if the furniture had to be replaced it would cost at least as much as, perhaps more than the amounts claimed. 'But there is no necessity for replacement now,' they remarked, before recommending £10,000, and not a penny more. The inspector concluded:

> I have no hesitation in stating that the Furniture and Effects of Mitchelstown Castle, although of the finest workmanship and in perfect condition, would not realise £12,000:0:0d because, as I said before, it is out of date, quite unsuitable for modern requirements, and unsought by Dealers or Collectors.

One of those who lost least in the fire was Willie Webber's sister, Mrs Ingouville-Williams, all of whose silver was recovered. Several items, valued at more than £100, were taken back from shops in the town. Arthur Webber, on the other hand, did not disclose that he had recovered some silver, although the inspectors heard that he had done so.[14]

Edward J. Kilbride, was a ten year-old living with his parents in King Square at the time of the fire. He recalled that, in the days afterwards 'several objects were thrown over our back gate possibly by way of restoring them to their owners – which we did'. He remembered 'a silver teapot & a broken epergne, as well as a muffin dish – very Victorian'.[15] The deputy secretary of the Office of Public Works advised the Department of Finance in December 1925 that some looted items had been recovered but the issue of compensation for the castle contents remained unresolved. When Butler travelled to London in 1925 he was told by Waring and Gillow that they valued the contents of the castle at £19,421-17s-5d.[16]

Of all the questions raised by the destruction of Mitchelstown Castle the most important remained unanswered 80 years later. This was the whereabouts of the magnificent collection of paintings – some of them priceless, even if their total value was put at a mere £1,364 then and the compensation at even less, £1,102. The collection included 'The Ladies Rawdon' by Thomas Gainsborough – easily the most valuable; 'Portrait of the Earl of Kingston' by Sir William Beechey (valued £157); Phillipe de Champaigne's 'Portrait of Henrietta Maria' (valued £52-10s); W.J. Leech's 'The Baily Lighthouse' (valued £33-12s); William Conrad's 'Royal Palace, Berlin' (valued £105). A tapestry by Mortlakes, entitled 'Release of Saint Peter', which hung in the entrance hall, was valued at £400 but the State allowed only £300 for it. Undoubtedly, many of these works were destroyed. Some of the smaller and more accessible ones were grabbed for souvenirs and the remainder – as has always been believed – taken away by a Republican lawyer for his personal pleasure and advantage.[17]

In 1957 a little light was shed on the route that took the paintings from Mitchelstown to their latest illicit owners in the shadier corners of the art world. A man from Kilfinane, in County Limerick, wrote to Sir Cecil Stafford-King-Harman, the owner of the Rockingham estate, to tell him of a sale of 41 paintings for £100,850 at Sothebys. The writer told Sir Cecil that, in the light of information given to him by one of the castle's Republican garrison in 1922, he believed that the works had come from Mitchelstown Castle. In the 1980s, the sale of a castle mantelpiece from a house in Mitchelstown realised a five figure sum at auction, also in London.[18]

The case for compensation for the contents came before

Cork Circuit Court in April 1926. Evidence was given that silver had been recovered from T.J. Hartigan, jeweller, who claimed that men had come into his shop at Lower Cork Street and offered it for sale. Hartigan refused to disclose names to Garda Sergeant J. Higgins. Although the jeweller bought some of the silver, worth about £10, he passed it on to Arthur Webber. Another Mitchelstown jeweller, Thomas L. Morrissey, swore that articles, including a silver salver, had also been offered to him but he had refused to buy them. Judge Kenny was critical of Webber's refusal to help gardaí to identify some furniture which they thought had come from the castle. The judge concluded that much of the furniture had been built specially for the castle. While he could not ascertain the amount of looting, he awarded £14,600 in compensation.

Finally, the court was told that Alec King-Harman had decided that it would be unprofitable to invest any of the previous award of £27,500 in Mitchelstown. Cork County Council objected to the money being used to build houses outside the county. The judge agreed that much of it should be spent locally to provide employment, but he could not make an order to that effect. Judge Kenny concluded that the burning of Mitchelstown Castle was an act of vandalism: 'there was no reason, from a military point of view, why they should have done so. There was no excuse, and no justification for the act which they perpetrated.'[19]

Alec was also awarded £650 for the destruction of Killaclug bridge, which he was compelled to rebuild, and he was also compensated for damage to Ballyarthur bridge. He believed that the compensation was inadequate in both cases.[20] For the wanton destruction of one of the most magnificent properties in these islands, the oldest and most distinguished of all Mitchelstown families was awarded

£42,100, less than one-third of their just demand.[21]

The end of the Mitchelstown Estate was now at hand. All that remained for King-Harman and Arthur Webber was to sort out the terms of Willie Webber's legacy. The extent of the property was defined in a document outlining its value at the time of the old man's death. Webber's will now robbed the Kings of the last small part of their once enormous inheritance. As we have seen, the dowager countess had wanted Alec to inherit everything after her second husband's death – but that was not to be. Under Webber's will, Alec was allowed the full £27,500 compensation for the castle but received only £4,000 of the £14,600 awarded for its contents. The remainder went to nephew Arthur, whose total inheritance amounted to £45,000 from Webber's estate.[22]

Old Webber's legacy to Alec was valued at £48,600. This consisted of what was left of the Kingston estate, including the castle ruins, the demesne and the town itself. He also inherited Kingston fishing rights on twelve miles of the Blackwater in the barony of Duhallow. Alec had to pay £200 yearly to Edith Webber and £400 to Willie's cousin, Captain Arthur Webber. Legacies totalling £525 were to be paid to five former employees. The generous bequest to the Webbers was condemned by Alec's brother, Captain Robert Douglas King-Harman. He acknowledged that the old man had met Lady Kingston's wishes as far as the Mitchelstown lands were concerned, but

> The value was small, consisting of about £600 a year from the town rents and the value of the demesne and the ruins of the castle. But the limit of £4,000 placed on Alec's share of the compensation for the contents of the castle is indefensible. The compensation was eventually agreed at £14,600, and the substantial sum of £10,600 which if the countess's wishes had been complied with should incontestably have gone to Alec, went instead to swell the residue of the estate going to the Webber family.

Doomed Inheritance

At least £25,000 of King money 'went into the pockets of the Webbers,' and the captain believed that this 'was a glaring example of breach of trust with the dead'. However,

> I do not think that in this unedifying affair Webber was consciously and deliberately dishonest. I should think it was rather a case of deceiving himself as to the rights and wrongs, and it must be remembered that for the forty odd years of his married life he had been somewhat vague, to put it mildly, as to the meaning of *meum* and *tuum* as between his wife and himself.[23]

Alec's speculative building of houses at Clontarf and Dún Laoghaire proved another costly venture. He reckoned that by the time the houses were sold he had been left with barely £20,000 of the original compensation sum. While he had received ten per cent in addition to the original £27,500, under amending legislation, this merely helped to reduce the losses made on the houses.

Alec now abandoned all hope of restoring the family fortunes in Mitchelstown. Although there was still a small estate there, including the demesne and houses in the town, he chose to live in the family's rather plain three-storey house at Newcastle. Meanwhile, he tried to maintain the demesne farm and take in the rents from the town properties.[24] Effectively, the last estate agent in Mitchelstown was W.B. Hickley, whom Alec appointed in May 1924, at a salary of £300 a year. He told Hickley in a letter dated 5 May 1924:

> The small amount of tenanted agricultural property is being sold under the 1923 Land Act. The town of Mitchelstown, at least that part which has not been recently sold, remains in hands: it is I think mostly let on ground leases; brings in well under £1,000 a year, and Arthur tells me that the rents are fairly easy to collect. I should like to continue to sell this as opportunity arises. Then there is the Demesne, which would require supervision, specially the Farming & Gardens.[25]

In 1925, Alec set about the demolition of Mitchelstown Castle. The abbot of the Cistercian monastery at Mount Melleray in County Waterford, Dom Marius O'Phelan, had decided to build a new abbey and he bought the great cut limestone blocks from Mitchelstown. Each work day for at least five years, two consignments were loaded into steam lorries and taken to the site.

As it was being laid out, Dom Marius died and his successor, Dom Celsus O'Connell, continued the monumental task. He opted for a more prominent site directly over the mortal remains of 180 of his fellow Cistercians. Big George's Gothic edifice gradually disappeared from the Mitchelstown skyline, only to reappear in a new – but altogether less impressive – form, 28 miles east in the Knockmealdown Mountains. The monks ended up with far more stones than they needed and these were eventually stacked in fields around the monastery.[26] But three of the most important carved stones went elsewhere. They were taken 200 miles to County Longford where they were placed against a gable at Newcastle. Over them was placed another with this inscription:

> These armorial bearings were brought from Mitchelstown Castle after it had been wantonly burnt on the 13th August 1922. They represent the arms of successive owners of Mitchelstown; Fitzgibbon the White Knight, Fenton and King, Earls of Kingston.

Alec sold off one town house after another until virtually nothing of the old estate was left.[27] Gardenhurst was bought by Eamon Roche, the general manager of Mitchelstown Co-op Creameries, which was founded in 1925. In 1940, the expanding co-op paid £450 for the Kingston Arms Hotel next door. The stable yards at the rear were converted into a factory where Mitchelstown's process cheese was manufactured.[28]

Some of the demesne lands were purchased compulsorily by the Land Commission 'for the relief of congestion,' as they put it. The final compulsory purchase took place on 20 January 1936, when 333 acres in the Ballyarthur area of the demesne were taken over and parcelled out among local farmers. The purchase price was £4,750, payable in four per cent Land Bonds.[29] In many cases, the Land Commission's disposal of the demesne was used to reward local freedom fighters of the War of Independence. One of them was Pa Luddy who proudly boasted of his role in burning the castle.[30] In the following 20 years, Alec was paid £3,038-8s in total for 209 properties in the town; he also sold a few in Kildorrery and raised a further £150 from the sale of fishing and hunting rights on the Blackwater. In 1944, the old military barracks were purchased by the Office of Public Works.

The market house and tolls of Mitchelstown went to the co-op for £800.[31] At first, the co-op planned to build an animal sales mart in New Market Square. Fortunately, this plan had to be scrapped when Cork County Council pointed out that ownership of the market rights did not include ownership of the square.[32]

Alec died on 5 July 1949 and was buried in Forgney graveyard, beside the gates of Newcastle. He left to his cousin, Anthony Lawrence King-Harman, the last fragments of 'The Mitchelstown Estate in the County of Cork inherited under the will of William Downes Webber, including all sporting and fishing rights which shall at the date of my death belong to me.'[33] Anthony fought in Africa in the Second World War, was promoted to the rank of colonel and mentioned in dispatches. Colonel King-Harman used the money inherited from Alec to buy out Arthur Webber's annuity on the estate – now, in essence, some houses in the town and a few minor rights to fishing, hunting, mining and the old Manor of Mitchelstown. The colonel's father, Captain R.D. King-Harman, took power of attorney to sell the remainder of the estate when his son was in America.[34]

The 103 town houses, which produced an income of a few hundred pounds a year, were sold off through the Mitchelstown solicitor, W.E. O'Brien, for about one year's rent. 'I remember my father saying that no way could we afford the annual repair bill for so many houses,' said Colonel King-Harman. The last great sale took place on 30 November 1964, when John D. Finn, a local butcher, bought 29 properties for just £300. Practically speaking, this represented the end of the Kingston inheritance at Mitchelstown.[35]

From 1925 onwards, the co-op creamery purchased several hundred acres of the demesne for farming and food enterprises. The society's first manager, Eamon Roche – a staunch Republican who was jailed with Eamon de Valera – built factories on the castle site, an achievement of great political symbolism to his old revolutionary colleagues in Mitchelstown and elsewhere. In the later decades of the twentieth century parts of the demesne wall were lowered beyond recognition for 'safety reasons' and breached at several points for the erection of bungalows. An earlier breach was made on the north-east side for extensions to the golf course which replaced a much earlier course donated by Willie Webber outside the wall at Ballinwillin. All the demesne's most attractive features fell to so-called industrial progress. The varied and magnificent species of trees were all cut down; the fish pond became the site of the town sewerage works and the boat lake an effluent lagoon. The Georgian stableyard was demolished by Mitchelstown Co-op in 1985. The Republicans had had their revenge.[36]

On a cold, wet January day in 1994, Colonel Anthony

King-Harman, the 76-year-old heir of the third Earl of Kingston, walked onto the site of his ancestral home in Mitchelstown for the first time. Though he had inherited the remnants of the great estate in 1949, he had never seen it because his family's memories had been too painful to contemplate. All that was left of the original mansion was an unsightly stump behind the co-op's enormous glass-plated milk powder mills. The factory towers gave the colonel an idea of the castle's enormity but conveyed no sense of its beauty. He fell silent for a few moments, before resuming in the soft voice of an English gentleman: 'My word, I never knew that even this stump had survived.' He looked north from the castle site over the old demesne to the Galtee Mountains shrouded in cloud. This was once Big George's country. Today most of it is owned by the descendants of his tenants.

The man whom history had robbed of his inheritance said that he had come back finally because of his interest in the family's origins. 'Mitchelstown passed out of the family in 1869 when the fifth earl died,' said Anthony. 'The tragic events which took place between the Land War and 1922 didn't really make me want to come back.' He emphasised that, during the Land War, it had been the Dowager Countess of Kingston and her second husband, Willie Webber, who owned the estate. It was they – and not the Kingstons – who were answerable to history. 'To a certain extent we have always felt that the way things were handled by Webber and his wife contributed to the burning of the castle by the IRA,' he said. Colonel King-Harman continued:

> The disasters here were inevitable. I think, at the time, there was great bitterness. My cousin, Alec, certainly felt it; my father did also. But these things one does get over, and you do forgive and forget ... It is wrong to carry hostility forward for more than a

generation or two at the most. My children, certainly, have absolutely no feelings about it. I think I feel far more about the way Webber handled the estate. He put it in the position where people wanted to burn down the castle.

When his father sold the last of the estate while he was in America in 1949, Anthony was out of touch and had an extremely limited knowledge of the family's remaining stake in Mitchelstown. 'I accepted my father's advice, which may have been a mistake,' he concluded. In the colonel's own interest it proved to be a very expensive error because the property that sold for £300 in 1949 was worth at least £4 million at the end of the twentieth century.

By the middle of that century the family's three other great properties had gone the way of Mitchelstown. Rockingham, like Mitchelstown, went up in flames in 1957. Its owner, Sir Cecil Stafford-King-Harman, was away on business at the time and many suspected that the blaze was 'political'. Soon afterwards, the burnt-out shell was demolished and the demesne was sold to the Land Commission by Sir Cecil, who died in 1987. Even its name was discarded when the property was fashioned into a public leisure amenity and re-styled Lough Key Forest Park.[37]

The Tenison mansion, Kilronan Castle near Boyle, was the seat of Henry Ernest Newcomen King, the eighth Earl of Kingston, who assumed by Royal Licence the surname of King-Tenison when he married Florence Francis Tenison. The estate was relinquished after the War of Independence when the ninth earl, Henry Edwyn, abandoned the house and sold the property to the Land Commission. Once a beautiful building, Kilronan Castle fell into ruin in the middle of the twentieth century.[38]

A few decades later Newcastle was another sad reflection of former glory. The house and lands were sold by

Robert Douglas King-Harman after his cousin Alec's death. Again it was the Land Commission that presided over the demise of this property: the picturesque avenues were closed off and planted with forestry. R.D. King-Harman was bitter and blunt about the fate of his class and his own property:

> In Ireland there is but one chance, that 'Holy Church' may be on the look-out for a bargain in the way of another nunnery or monastery. So it proved, and in the end Newcastle was sold to the Missionary Nuns of Killeshandra. Our Protestant ancestors would not have liked that, and nor did I. On 18th June 1951, I left Newcastle for ever, driving out by the Ballymahon gates on my way to England. I remember thinking that it was Waterloo Day. Not far short of four centuries had passed since Sir John King crossed to Ireland in the days of the First Elizabeth.[39]

Down south, meanwhile, the old Kingston hunting lodge, Galtee Castle, was pulled down in 1940 and – also like Mitchelstown Castle – the stone was carted off to build a church, at Glanworth. Moorepark, home of the Mount Cashells, who were doubly linked by marriage to the Kingstons in Big George's day, was purchased by the War Department and destroyed in an accidental fire in 1908. The shell of the big house became the property of Mitchelstown Co-op which, in the 1960s, demolished its ruins to make way for piggeries.[40]

But not all the Kingston houses were lost. A handful of others used as homes by the family can still be found around the country. These include Kingsborough in County Sligo, Araglin Cottage and Mounteagle Lodge both in the Mitchelstown area. In 1995, King House in Boyle, the first home of the family in Ireland, was saved from ruin and restored to its original splendour at a cost of £3 million by Roscommon County Council. The project was funded largely by the European Union. It became an important tourist attraction for the story of the family and their influence on the Roscommon region. If only the stones of Mitchelstown had been left where they were!

In 1999 the heir to the Mitchelstown estate, Anthony King-Harman, resided with his wife in an English manor house. Margaret Mount Cashell's descendants, the Cini family, lived in Italy. Other descendants of the King family resided in Canada, the United States, Britain and Australia. Some of the Webbers lived in County Donegal. A brass memorial to Willie was to be seen in the Church of Ireland church at Screen, County Sligo. Another memorial to him and his wife was in the chancel of Saint George's Church, Mitchelstown.[41]

Barclay Robert Edwin King-Tenison became the eleventh Earl of Kingston when his father, Robert Henry, died in 1948. He inherited four other family titles – Viscount Kingsborough, Viscount Lorton, Baron Kingston and Baron Erris of Boyle. As his peerage is Irish, he did not have the right to sit in the British House of Lords. In the 1960s he visited Mitchelstown where his enquiries about the destruction of his ancestral home were greeted with silence. He returned in 1996 when he attended a reception at which he was warmly welcomed to the town by the local heritage society.

He delighted those present when he presented an eighteen-inch-wide silver salver to the society. Crafted by Thomas Boulton of Dublin in 1717, the ornate tray bears the coat of arms of the first Earl of Kingston. He also presented the townspeople with other items of family memorabilia. Although he would not have owned the castle even if it were still standing, Barclay said it was his sense of family history that brought him to Mitchelstown. 'I am very touched by the welcome I received,' he said. 'One always gets a welcome in Ireland because it is a friendly country, but the welcome for me in Mitchelstown was astonishing.' Later, in the chapel of Kingston College, the earl read the Kingston family's brass memorial and sat in pews once reserved for his ancestors.[42] Beneath him, in the family vault, were the remains of three Earls of Kingston, one Viscount Kingsborough, one Baron Kingston, one countess and two baronesses.[43]

King Square at the castle entrance – where brilliantly uniformed army officers from Kilworth and Fermoy courted the young ladies of the castle – proved to be the Kingstons' most enduring legacy to Mitchelstown. It alone has survived virtually unchanged since its erection by James, the fourth baron, in the 1760s. But the family's greatest surviving monument is the town itself. One of Ireland's few planned towns from the late eighteenth century, it is commended for its fine layout and wide streets in many studies of urban design in Ireland. While there was considerable change to its fabric in the twentieth century, to the observant eye it retains an essential Georgian character that is rare among Irish towns. For that, at least, the Kings, Barons and Earls of Kingston, deserve Mitchelstown's gratitude.

APPENDIX A

Kingston lands offered for sale under the Landed Estates Court on 17 June 1851, in the parishes of Ballylanders and Kilbehenny, County Limerick (LECR vol. 13). Figures shown are for acres, roods and perches.

Ballyshonakin	453.0. 7
Ballyfrootamore and Ballyfrutacreagh	392.0. 6
Ballyfrootamore	56.3.13
Killeen	672.4. 9
Spittle	607.2.23
Ballylanders	747.4.23
Curraghturk	794.3.10
Ballyfaskin	440.2.18
Ballyduff	503.3. 9
Upper Cullane	637.4.15
Middle Cullane	491.3.37
Cullane South	747.2. 9
Fehawnasudry	411.0.12
Knockadea	380.0. 1
Ballybrien	519.1.25
Lisnalaniffe	365.2.32
Coolenemohague	517.3.10
Kilglass	670.4.18
Glenacurrane	422.2.17
Geragh	423.3. 7
Carhue or Carrow	501.3. 7
Scrowmore or Shrovemore	377.4.15
Knockrour	249.0.17
Castlequarter	254.3.26
Coolboy	250.2.14
Knocknascrow	1,571.2.22
Boher	208.0.14
Coolattin	198.2.38
Behinagh	230.1.27
Churchquarter	98.1.12
Ballinatona	309.1.12
Loughananna	457.2.21
Knockcomane	293.0.28

Knocknagalty	1,754.3.13
Carrigeen	602.3.22
Carrigeen Mountain	2,082.1. 1
Brackbaun	351.0.12

Total area = 20,985.0.33 acres. Total rental =   £8,281-8s-1d

Areas of the estate offered for sale under the Landed Estates Court on 1 July 1851 in the parish of Templetenny, County Tipperary (LECR vol. 16).

Cooleprevane	722.1.34
Currighleigh West	322.1. 3
Currighleigh East	422.2.31
Ballywilliam	457.2.31
Lyrefoune	1,652.0.20
Glenacunna	1,393.3.25
Barnahown	1,437.2.16
Gurtishall	1,177.2.14
Kiltankin	1,187.3.18
Doolis	228.1. 2
Knocknagopple	186.1.10
Cooladerry	434.1.32
Kilnamona	146.0.32
Dangan	562.3.24
Drumroe	141.2.35
Newcastle	162.1. 5
Ballyporeen	148.0.15
Moher	98.3.39
Carrigvisteal	380.0.13
Lisfuncheon, Rossclevin & Farranclery	722.0.11
Skeheenarinky	3,023.4.28
Coolegarranroe	3,492.2.22

Total area = 18,181.2.28. Total rental =   £5,768-1s-4d.

Appendix A

Areas of the estate offered for sale under the Landed Estates Court on 1 July 1851 in the parish of Leitrim and Macroney, County Cork (LECR vol. 18).

Bellerough	905.2.21
Lyrebarry	648.2.28
Gortnaskehy	935.0.31
Macroney Upper	739.1.10
Macroney Lower	677.4. 1
Kylebarry	144.1.23

Total area = 3,951.2.32. Total rental =   £1,402-2s-6d.

Areas of the estate offered for sale under the Landed Estates Court on 20 February 1855, in the Baronies of Coshlea, Condons and Clangibbon, Fermoy and Duhallow (LECR vol. 12).

Labbamolagga West	323.2.39
Labbamolagga Middle	443.1. 9
Labbamolagga East	409.0.28
Derrylahan	333.1.26
Tooreagh & Gortnaminna	123.0.31
Shraherla	381.2.17
Knockanevin	257.1. 6
Baunnanooneeny	250.1. 5
Derrynanool & Curraghgorm	462.2. 0
Knockanevin	183.3. 3
Curraghgorm & Derrynanool	254.0.13
Knockanevin & Curraghgorm	155.2.31
Marshalstown	372.4.25
Marshalstown & Glenahulla	178.2. 6
Glenahulla & Ballydeloughy	136.2.28
Glenahulla & Marshalstown	194.1.13
Cloghleafin & Glenahulla	184.3.19
Cloghleafin	509.0.37
Ballydeloughy	656.0. 1
Kilclooney	77.3.30
Graigue	561.0.10
Boleynanoultagh	589.2.30
Ballyvisteen	388.1.31

Gortnacurrig	321.3.39
Quit Rent	1,195.2.28
Springvale, Kilmaculla & Glasvaunta	396.0. 5
Oldcastletown	450.2. 3
Cullenagh	364.2.21
Ballysurdane	381.3.30
Kildorrery	109.0.23
Scairt	439.3. 5
Glenatlucky	454.2.25
Killickane	821.1.39
Skeheen Upper	1,207.0.32
Glenduff & Curraghavoe	1,197.0.38

Total area = 26,743.2.30. Total rental = £7,190-3s-3d.

In the Barony of Duhallow a total of 9,117a-1r-24p were offered for sale at the same auction. The townlands were,

Drumcummerbeg	Gougane	Kilcaskin South
Gurteenbeha	Curraghrour	Coolroebeg
Coolnahane	Gortmore	Roskeen
Clonmeen	Coolroemore	Kilrarrahan
Cloonteens	Glenaneathagh	Duinch
Inchadaly		

Areas of the estate offered for sale under the Landed Estates Court on 20 February 1855, in the Baronies of Coshlea, Condons and Clangibbon, Fermoy and Duhallow (LECR vol. 12).

Ballydeloughy	196.1.26
Graigue	561.0.10
Quit Rent Mountain	1,195.2.18
Springvale, Kilmaculla & Glasvaunta	396.0. 5
Cullenagh	364.2.21
Glenatlucky	454.2.25
Killickane	821.1.39
Skeheen Upper	1,207.0.39
Curraghavoe	876.2. 0
Glenduff & Curraghavoe	1,197.0.38

Total area = 7,270.3.24. Total rental = £1,862-1s-3d.

APPENDIX B

The townland areas named under the Declaration of Title, dated 13 December 1875, by which Anna Dowager Countess of Kingston established her ownership of the Mitchelstown Estate. Figures shown are for acres, roods and perches.

Barony of Fermoy, County Cork
Ballyhooly South   39.1.36

Barony of Condons and Clangibbon, County Cork
Flemingstown   544.3.11
Kilphelan   0.0. 8
Boleynanoultagh   589.2.30
Oldcastletown   863.3. 9
Kildorrery   109.2. 8
Scairt   510.1.31

Barony of Coshlea, County Limerick
Tooreleagan   250.2.32

Barony of Condons and Clangibbon
Gortnaminna   189.3.28
Tooreagh   251.2.30
Shraherla   381.2.17
Kilclooney   777.2.21
Baunnanooneeny   250.1. 5
Curraghgorm   721.1.30
Ballysurdane   381.3.30
Knockanevin   536.0.34
Derrynanool   458.1.17
Marshalstown   474.2.26
Cloghleafin   681.0.21
Cloghleafin Commons   11.2. 4
Glennahulla   615.0. 8
Ballydeloughy   459.3.35
Ballydeloughy Commons   25.3.28
Coolyregan   543.2.27

Corracunna	374.0.18
Garryleagh	185.1.27
Carrigane	798.3.30
Furrow	425.1.10
Gurtyeennaboul	223.1.16
Curraghmore	523.3.17
Parknakilla	151.1.35
Knocknamuck	259.1.11
Ardglare	239.1. 3
Kildrum	410.2.39
Ballygiblin	191.2.27
Pollardstown	487.2. 6
Ballynabrock	347.0.30
Skeheen	478.1. 3
Skeheen Upper	1,207.0.32
Labbamolagga West	343.2.39
Labbamolagga Middle	443.1. 1
Labbamolagga East	409.0.28
Derrylahan	333.1.26
Gortroe	482.3. 5
Booladurragha	98.1.36
Gorteenatarriff	417.3.27
Killaclug East	189.3. 5
Ballyarthur	848.1.27
Boolakelly	144.1.26
Gortnasna	117.0.37
Clyroe	63.0.35
Killaclug West	201.2. 8
Ballykearney	225.1.31
Mitchelstown	1,233.1.34
Garrane	487.1.26
Coolnanave	403.1.15
Ballinwillin	138.3.32
Kilshanny	365.2.35
Cloonlough	327.0.25
Stagpark	205.3.32
Carriganleigh	69.2.39
Ballinamona	370.3. 4
Brigown	661.0.36

APPENDIX C

Titles held by the King family

Baron Kingston
Created 4 September 1660.
Granted to Sir John King, son of Sir Robert King of Boyle Abbey.
Extinct on the death without surviving male issue of James King, 4th Baron on 28 December 1761.

Baron Kingsborough (I)
Created 13 June 1748.
Granted to Sir Robert King, 4th Baronet.
Extinct on his death, unmarried, on 22 May 1755.

Baron Kingston of Rockingham (I)
Created 13 July 1764.

Viscount Kingsborough (I)
Created 15 November 1766.

Earl of Kingston (I)
Created 25 August 1768.

These three titles were granted to Sir Edward King, 5th Baronet, son of Sir Henry, 3rd Baronet and brother of Sir Robert King, Baron Kingsborough.

Baron Erris (I)
Created 29 December 1800.

Viscount Lorton (I)
Created 28 May 1806.

Both of these titles were granted to Robert Edward King, second son of the 1st Earl.

Baron Kingston of Mitchelstown (UK)
Created 17 July 1821.
Granted to George King, 3rd Earl of Kingston.
Extinct on the death without issue of James, 5th Earl of Kingston on 8 September 1869.

A baronetcy of Ireland was conferred on Robert King, brother of the first Baron Kingston on 27 September 1682.

Sir Barclay Robert Edwin King-Tenison, 11th Earl of Kingston is 11th Viscount Kingsborough, 7th Viscount Lorton, 11th Baron Kingston, 7th Baron Erris and 15th Baronet.

ENDNOTES

CC: *Cork Constitution*
CE: *Cork Examiner*
CSORP: Chief Secretary's Office Registered Papers
FJ: *Freeman's Journal*
KHP: King Harman Papers
LECR: *Landed Estates Court Rentals*
NAI: National Archives of Ireland
NLI: National Library of Ireland

1. Edward C McAleer, *The sensitive plant, a life of Lady Mount Cashell*, (University of North Carolina Press, 1958), pp 11-2, 14.
2. Kenneth Nicholls and Paul MacCotter (eds), *The pipe roll of Cloyne*, (Cloyne, 1996), pp 239-40.
3. E Rynne (ed), Gerard A Lee, 'The White Knights and their kinsmen,' *North Munster studies*, (Limerick, 1967), pp 260-1.
4. JS Brewer and William Bullen, *Calendar of Carew manuscripts, 1578-1588*, (London, 1868), p. 347.
5. *Historical and archaeological association of Ireland journal*, ser. 3, vol I, pt 2, (Dublin, 1869); James Graves, 'Unpublished Geraldine documents,' p. 610.
6. E Rynne, *North Munster studies*, p. 260; *JCHAS*, P Raymond, 'The Condons of Cloghleigh, Barony of Condons and Clongibbons,' vol II, (Cork, 1896), p. 483.
7. Bill Power, *Mitchelstown through seven centuries*, (Fermoy, 1987), p. 13.
8. JS Brewer and W Bullen, *Calendar*, p. 347.
9. EC McAleer, *Sensitive plant*, pp 13-4.
10. Ibid, p. 15.
11. CJF MacCarthy in correspondence with author, 1988, enclosing a copy of 'King James I, patent for the creation of the manor of Mitchelstown, AD 1618; also forfeited lands to Sir William Fenton and his wife Dame Margaret.' AF O'Brien, *The impact of the Anglo-Normans on Munster*, (The Barryscourt Trust, 1997), p. 57. By this grant of free

warren, park and chase, the Fentons had the right to keep and breed rabbits, and to keep and hunt deer. Both activities were valuable sources of income.

12. EC McAleer, *Sensitive plant*, pp 15-6.
13. TCD Ms 826, fol 298, transcribed by Virginia Teehan, archivist, UCC.
14. *JCHAS*, 'A Cromwellian made Cork baronet'; vol XXI, (Cork, 1915), p. 101.
15. *Burke's peerage and baronetage* (London, 1975), p. 1,500.
16. Robert Douglas King-Harman, *The Kings, Earls of Kingston, an account of the family and their estates in Ireland between the reigns of the two Queens Elizabeth*, (Cambridge, 1959), pp 9-13.
17. Ibid, pp 15-8.
18. Charles Chenevix Trench, *Grace's card, Irish Catholic landlords, 1690-1800*, (Cork and Dublin, 1997), pp 113-4.
19. Courtenay Moore, *The ecclesiastical antiquities of Brigown, with a sketch of the life of Saint Findchua* (Dublin, 1891) p.11.
20. John Heron Lepper and Philip Crossle, *The history of the grand lodge of Ireland*, vol. I, (Dublin, 1925), p. 148. *Burke's peerage and baronetage*, (London, 1975), pp 1,500.
21. Ibid, vol II, pp 262-3, 285.
22. B Power, *Mitchelstown*, p.26.
23. *Mitchelstown charity, minute book*, pp 3, 13. Author's collection.
24. *JCHAS*; Courtenay Moore, 'Some account of Kingston College, Mitchelstown, County Cork,' vol IV, (Cork, 1898), p. 108.
25. *Mitchelstown charity, minute book*, pp 18-23.
26. *JCHAS*; Courtenay Moore, 'Some account of Kingston College,v Mitchelstown, County Cork, Vol IV (Cork, 1898), p. 108
27. *Mitchelstown charity, minute book*, p. 9.
28. Ibid, pp 10-1.
29. EC McAleer, *Sensitive plant*, pp 17-8.

CHAPTER TWO
1. RD King-Harman, *The Kings*, pp 36-9.
2. Edward, 1st Earl of Kingston letter to Colonel Richard Fitzgerald, December 1789. KHP.
3. EC McAleer, *Sensitive plant*, p. 18.
4. RD King-Harman, *The Kings*, p. 59.

Endnotes

5. *Burke's peerage and baronetage*, p. 1,502.
6. RD King-Harman, *The Kings*, pp 63-9.
7. Robert, Viscount Kingsborough, letter to his father, the Earl of Kingston, November 1771. KHP.
8. RD King-Harman, *The Kings*, pp 63-9
9. M Betham-Edwards, (ed), *The autobiography of Arthur Young*, (New York, 1967), pp 76-7.
10. Constantia Maxwell (ed), *A tour in Ireland in 1777... by Arthur Young*, (Cambridge University Press, 1925), pp 157-8.
11. Ibid, pp 163-4.
12. Ibid, pp 158-61.
13. EC McAleer, *Sensitive plant*, p. 20.
14. *Mallow field club journal*, Seamus Crowley, 'The Hartland nursery family in Mallow and Cork,' No 3, (Mallow, 1985), pp 131-2.
15. C Maxwell, *A tour in Ireland by A. Young*, p. 160.
16. Ibid, pp 161-2.
17. M. Betham-Edwards, *The autobiography of A. Young*, pp 78-9.
18. C Maxwell, *Young's tour*, p. 161.
19. EC McAleer, *Sensitive plant*, p. 31.
20. Thomas MacNevin, *The history of the volunteers of 1782*, (Dublin, 1882), pp 104, 161, 226.
21. EC McAleer, *Sensitive Plant*, pp 31-2.
22. T MacNevin, *History of the volunteers*, pp 104, 161.
23. Patrick C Power, *History of south Tipperary*, (Cork, 1989), p. 101.
24. T MacNevin, *History of the volunteers*, p. 161.
25. B Power, *Mitchelstown*, p. 31.
26. RF Foster, *Modern Ireland*, 1600-1972, (London, 1989), pp 193-4, 204.
27. Robert Day and WA Coppinger (eds), Charles Smith, *The ancient and present state of the county and city of Cork*, vol I, (Cork, 1893), p. 318.
28. NLI, Ms 3275, Lib A, fol 751; Lib F, fol 225. William Downes Webber, *Some records and recollections of events relating to Mitchelstown Castle, and to its founder, George 3rd Earl of Kingston, and to his family and successors*, unpublished ms, written c. 1908-1911, pp 5-6. KHP.
29. NLI, Ms 3275, fol 594.
30. WD Webber, *Some account*, pp 6-7
31 B Power, *Mitchelstown*, pp 28, 31.
32. Mrs Ellen (Nellie) Quinlan, Thomas Street, Mitchelstown note to author, c. 1987.
33. NLI, Ms 3275, Lib A, fol 783.

34. William Coppinger, *The Rt. Rev. Dr Coppinger's letter to the Rt. Hon. and hon'ble Dublin Society with additional documents and explanatory remarks as seem called for by the Rev. Horatio Townsend's observations upon this letter and with a supplement to his appendix,* (Cork, 1811), pp 13-4

35. NLI, Ms 3275, Lib A, fol 783. B Power, *Mitchelstown,* p. 31.

36. NLI, Ms 3275. Keith Lamb and Patrick Bowe, *A history of gardening in Ireland,* (Dublin, 1995), pp 40, 47.

37. WD Webber, *Some account,* pp 7-8, 8a.

38. B Power, *Mitchelstown,* p. 104.

39. Ordnance Survey of Ireland (1st edition, 1841), sheet nos 10 and 19.

40. B Power, *The development and destruction of Mitchelstown demesne, 1776-1949,* (Certificate in local and regional studies, dissertation, University College, Cork, 1995), pp 5-6. NLI, Ms 3275, Lib A, fol 751.

41. Horatio Townsend, *A Statistical Survey of the county and city of Cork.*

42. NLI, Ms 3275, Lib A, fols 751, 771 and 783.

43. RF Foster, *Modern Ireland,* pp 171, 172n. Peter Jupp, *British and Irish elections, 1784-1831,* (Newton Abbot, 1973), p. 158.

44. James Kelly, *'That damn'd thing called honour,' duelling in Ireland, 1570-1860,* (Cork, 1995), pp 144-6.

CHAPTER THREE

1. RD King-Harman, *The Kings,* pp 59-61.

2. Edward, 1st Earl of Kingston, letter to his son, Robert, Viscount Kingsborough, 23 February 1773. KHP.

3. Robert, Viscount Kingsborough, letter to his father, 1st Earl of Kingston, 29 January 1773. KHP.

4. RD King-Harman, *The Kings,* p. 59.

5. EC McAleer, *Sensitive plant,* pp 35-6.

6. Ralph M Wardle (ed), *Collected letters of Mary Wollstonecraft,* (London, 1979), p. 140.

7. Ibid, pp 120, 123.

8. Ibid, p. 140.

9. Ibid, p. 120.

10. Ibid, p. 122-4.

11. Ibid, p. 132.

12. Ibid, pp 126-7.

13. Ibid, p. 131.

14. Ibid, pp 124, 128.

15. Ibid, pp 126, 133
16. Claire Tomalin, *The life and death of Mary Wollstonecraft*, (Middlesex, 1985), p. 78.
17. RM Wardle, *Collected letters*, pp 135, 155.
18. C Tomalin, *The life and death*, pp 78-81.
19. RM Wardle, *Collected letters*, p. 140.
20. Ibid, p. 147.
21. Ibid, p. 156.
22. Ibid, p. 140.
23. EC McAleer, *Sensitive plant*, pp 52-3.
24. B Power, *Mitchelstown*, p. 41.
25. PC Power, *History of south Tipperary*, p. 106.
26. EC McAleer, *Sensitive plant*, p. 64.
27. Frances Calvert, (Mrs Warrene Blake, ed), *An Irish beauty of the Regency, compiled from 'mes souvenirs' – the unpublished journals of Mrs Calvert, 1789-1882*, (Lane, 1911), p. 36. RD King-Harman, *The Kings*, p. 79.
28. EC McAleer, *Sensitive plant*, p. 63. We have no idea what became of these illegitimate offspring.
29. *Walker's Hibernian Magazine*, April 1790.
30. EC McAleer, *Sensitive plant*, p. 63.
31. F Calvert, *An Irish beauty*, p. 11.
32. Owen D Madden, *Revelations of Ireland in the past generations* (Dublin, 1848), p. 86.
33. EC McAleer, *Sensitive plant*, pp 69-70.
34. OD Madden, *Revelations*, p. 85.
35. Ibid, pp 88-93.
36. Ibid, pp 97, 99. RD King-Harman, *The Kings*, p. 76. William Lecky, *A history of the 18th century*, vol VIII (London, 1898), pp 39-40.
37. Sir Jonah Barrington, *Personal sketches and recollections of his own times*, (Glasgow, 1876), p. 195.
38. OD Madden, *Revelations*, pp 101-4.
39. J Barrington, *Personal sketches*, p. 200.
40. EC McAleer, *Sensitive plant*, p. 75. OD Madden, *Revelations*, p. 105.
41. Will of Caroline King, Dowager Countess of Kingston, proved 22 February 1823. Somerset House, London.
42. EC McAleer, *Sensitive plant*, pp 4-8.
43. TU Sadlier, *An Irish peer*, p. 71.
44. EC McAleer, *Sensitive plant*, pp 100-1.
45. TU Sadlier, *An Irish peer*, pp180-1.

46. Ibid, p. 182.
47. Ibid, pp 185-6.
48. EC McAleer, *Sensitive plant*, pp 115, 118-9, 123. NLI, Ms 3275, fol 709. For biographies of Nerina and Laurette see Mary Shelley's, *Maurice, or the fisher's cot*, edited by Claire Tomalin, (London, 1998).
49. EC McAleer, *Sensitive plant*, pp 148-9, 169, 182, 189, 215.

CHAPTER FOUR
1. Thomas Pakenham, *The year of liberty, the history of the great Irish rebellion of 1798*, (London, 1992), pp 90-1.
2. EC McAleer, *Sensitive plant*, pp 61, 80, 85.
3. Francis Plowden, *An historical view of the state of Ireland, from the invasion of that country, under Henry II to its union with Great Britain*, vol IV, (London, 1801), p. 152.
4. Ibid, p. 252-3. JM Barry, *Pitchcap and triangle, the Cork militia in the Wexford rising*, (Cork, 1998), pp 176, 186.
5. T Pakenham, *Year of liberty*, pp 191, 247.
6. Ibid, pp 251-4, 259.
7. Ibid, pp 256.
8. Ibid, pp 266-7, 272.
9. EC McAleer, *Sensitive plant*, p. 89.
10. PC Power, *History of south Tipperary*, p. 106.
11. RD King-Harman, *The Kings*, pp 77-8, 81.
12. EC McAleer, *Sensitive plant*, pp 90-2.
13. British Library, Ms 40,355/90, Sir Robert Peel to the Earl of Kingston; Ms 40,355/91, Earl of Kingston to Sir Robert Peel.
14. *Burke's peerage and baronetage*, pp 1,500, 1,502. George's elevation to the Peerage of the United Kingdom coincided with the coronation of George IV on 19 July and his subsequent state visit to Ireland during the following month in which, it seems, the seeds were sewn for the building of a new mansion at Mitchelstown.
15. RD King-Harman, *The Kings*, p. 75.
16. NLI, Ms 3275, fol 709.
17. EC McAleer, *Sensitive plant*, p. 27.
18 NLI, Ms 19,077, *Timber and garden accounts book* of Caroline, Dowager Countess of Kingston.
19. EC McAleer, *Sensitive Plant*, p. 26.
20. Indenture between Caroline, Dowager Countess of Kingston, and

Endnotes

John Power, farmer, Glenatlucky, Mitchelstown, 4 April 1818. Author's collection.
21. Horatio Townsend, *Statistical survey*, pp 486-8.
22. EC McAleer, *Sensitive plant*, pp 16, 27. JCHAS, Courtenay Moore, 'An interesting literary fact connected with the early history of the Kingston family,' vol XXX, (Cork, 1909), pp 41-2.
23. William Maziere Brady, *Clerical and parochial records of Cork, Cloyne and Ross*, vol II, (Dublin, 1863), p. 70.
24. H Townsend, *Statistical survey*, pp 486-7.
25. WM Brady, *Parochial records*, p. 70.
26. H Townsend, *Statistical survey*, pp 488-90.
27. Coppinger to the Dublin Society, pp 11-2.
28. Cloyne Diocesan Archive, 1809/35, Handbill issued by the Dowager Countess of Kingston, 13 November 1809.
29. Coppinger to the Dublin Society, p. 11-5.
30. *Cahir Heritage Newsletter*, No. 37, 1 September 1989, (Cahir, 1989), p. 3. This cottage was restored in the 1980s and is now the property of the Irish State.
31. RD King-Harman, *The Kings*, pp 93-4, 101-2, 111.
32. Ibid, pp 113-4.
33. Ibid, pp 116-21. The loving cup presented by Queen Caroline is still owned by the King family.
34. Ibid, pp 121-4.
35. Puckler-Muskau, (Herman Ludwig Heinrich, Furst von), *Tour in England, Ireland, and France, in... 1828-1829... by a German prince*, vol II, (Effingham Wilson, 1832), p. 23.
36. RD King-Harman, *The Kings*, p. 126.
37. NLI, Ms 3275, Lib F, folios 223, 233, 238.
38. RD King-Harman, *The Kings*, p. 81. King-Harman says that she died in Mitchelstown. This is incorrect. Her tomb is in Putney Churchyard, beside Putney Bridge, London.

CHAPTER FIVE
1. Aubrey de Vere, *Recollections of Aubrey de Vere*, (New York and London, 1897), p. 53.
2. *The Irish Builder*, 1 January 1878. James Pain stated in his will, dated 11 January 1863, that he was still owed £1,096-19s-3d for work on Mitchelstown Castle. It remained unpaid up to his death in 1877. Pain

left a model of Mitchelstown Castle to his niece.
3. WD Webber, *Some records*, pp 11-2.
4. 'ATH', *Encumbered estates of Ireland, 1850*, (London, 1850), pp 44, 48.
5. Ibid, p. 47.
6. Valuation Office Housebooks, Brigown parish, no. 5.0316, pp 31-2; and Housebook no. 5.0319, pp 77-8. NAI. Ian Chilvers and Harold Osborne (eds), *The Oxford dictionary of art*, (Oxford University Press, 1997), p. 53.
7. 'ATH', *Encumbered estates*, p. 47.
8. Housebooks. no. 5.0316, pp 31-2 and no. 5.0319, pp 77-8. NAI.
9. WD Webber, *Some records*, p. 12.
10. Nora Robertson, *Crowned harp, memories of the last years of the Crown in Ireland*, (Dublin, 1960), p. 90.
11. 'ATH', *Encumbered estates*, p. 48.
12. CJF MacCarthy, in correspondence with the author, 1989.
13. Prince Puckler-Muskau, *Tour*, pp 21-2.
14. Ibid, pp 28-9.
15. Lady Chatterton, *Rambles in the south of Ireland during the year 1838*, vol II, (London, 1839), p. 2.
16. Ibid, p. 3. 'ATH', *Encumbered estates*, p. 48.
17. WD Webber, *Some records*, pp 13-4, 14a.
18. Lady Chatterton, *Rambles*, p. 3.
19. *Landed estates court rental* [hereinafter cited as LECR], vol 16, July 185.1. NLI.
20. Lady Chatterton, *Rambles*, pp 3-6, 9.
21. A de Vere, *Recollections*, pp 53-4.
22. House of Commons, *Report from the select committee on Manor courts, Ireland*, (London, 1838), pp 131-2.
23. House of Commons, *First report from the select committee on the state of Ireland*, vol VII (London 1825), pp 396-7.
24. Indenture between George, Earl of Kingston and James Mahony, Robert Street, Mitchelstown, 25 March 1829. Author's collection.
25. Ms 37301,279 and 213, Earl of Kingston to the Marquess Wellesley, September 1823. British Library.
26. *Mallow Field Club journal*, Cal Hyland, 'The Franks, murder for love or revenge?' no. 4, (Mallow, 1986) pp 141-3. NAI, CSORP, 2345/32, 2347/49.
27. Ms 37301,279 and 213, Earl of Kingston to the Marquess Wellesley. British Library.

Endnotes

28. *Mallow Field Club journal*, C. Hyland, 'The Franks,' pp 141-3.
29. *Minutes of evidence taken before the select committee of the House of Lords ... into the state of Ireland* (London, 1825), pp 435-6.
30. Donald Mackay, *Flight from famine, the coming of the Irish to Canada* (Toronto and London, 1990), pp 53, 56-61.
31. CSORP/1824, 9182, letter from the Earl of Kingston to the Chief Secretary, 19 July 1824. NAI.
32. WM Brady, *Parochial records*, vol I, pp 71, 347-8.
33. *The Avondhu*, B Power, 'Mitchelstown's parish church', 29 January 1998.
34. CSORP/1824, 1,982; CSORP/1829, 324; CSORP/1824, 10,934; CSORP/1824, 9,182; CSORP/1822, 4,088. NAI.
35. WD Webber, *Some records*, p. 83.
36. Ian d'Alton, *Protestant society and politics in Cork, 1812-1844*, (Cork, 1980), pp 124-6. John Hyde was an ancestor of Douglas Hyde, the first President of Ireland, 1938-1945.
37. BM Walker, *Parliamentary election results in Ireland, 1801-1922*, (Dublin, 1878), p. 36.
38. I d'Alton, *Protestant society*, pp 124-6.
39. A de Vere, *Recollections*, pp 54-5.
40. Ibid, pp 55-7.
41. BM Walter, *Parliamentary election results*, p. 40.
42. CC, 27 July 1833.
43. RD King-Harman, *The Kings*, pp 84-5.
44. Henry D Inglis, *Ireland in 1834, a journey throughout Ireland during the spring, summer and autumn of 1834*, (Whittaker, 1834), p. 142.
45. Ibid, pp 143-5.
46. Ibid, pp 146-8.
47. CC, 7 November 1839. In 1995, I examined the contents of the vault when, with the permission of the family, it was opened for a short period. Big George's coffin was in a remarkably good state of preservation, as was the coronet which has rested on it since 1839. The vault contained a total of nine lead-lined caskets.

CHAPTER SIX
1. Peter Somerville-Large, *Irish eccentrics*, (London, 1975), pp 204-7.
2. WD Webber, *Notes on events connected with Mitchelstown Castle, compiled in 1905 by WD Webber*, unpublished manuscript in Webber

Collection, pp 15, 15a.
3. RD King-Harman, *The Kings*, pp 84-5.
4. P Somerville-Large, *Irish eccentrics*, pp 205-208.
5. RD King-Harman, *The Kings*, pp 84-5.
6. Alexis de Tocqueville, *Journey to England and Ireland*, (London, 1857), pp 158-9. These cottages were probably located at Mulberry Lane.
7. John Kegan, *A young Irishman's diary*, (Cambridgeshire, 1928), p. 35.
8. 'ATH', *Encumbered estates*, pp 44-5.
9. HD Inglis, *Ireland in 1834*, p. 141.
10. 'ATH', *Encumbered estates*, pp 47-8.
11. WD Webber, *Some records*, p. 22. Mounteagle was owned in 1999 by Mr and Mrs Robin Smith.
12. *Report of the eight days' trial in the Court of the Queen's Bench on a criminal information against John Sarsfield Casey, at the prosecution of Patten Smith Bridge; from November 27th to December 5th, 1877*, (Dublin, 1877), p. 12. Hereafter cited as *Bridge vs Casey*.
13. RD King-Harman, *The Kings*, pp 50-1.
14. Bill Power, *From the Danes to Dairygold*, (Mitchelstown, 1996), p. 63.
15. Ibid, pp 58-9.
16. *Parliamentary gazetteer of Ireland*, pp 773-4.
17. CC, 20 September 1845.
18. James S Donnelly, Jr, *The land and the people of nineteenth century Cork*, (London and Boston, 1975), pp 108, 113.
19. B Power, *From the Danes*, p. 59.
20. Edward Garner, *To die by inches, the famine in north east Cork*, (Fermoy, 1986), pp 30, 34.
21. Ibid, pp 34, 47-8.
22. Ibid, p. 51.
23. CE, 1 October 1846.
24. E Garner, *To die by inches*, pp 56-7. RD King-Harman, *The Kings*, p. 86.
25. E Garner, *To die by inches*, pp 67-8.
26. CSORP/1847, 8,877; CSORP/1847, 10,145; CSORP/1847, 10,279, Rev Henry Disney to Sir Randolph Routh. NAI.
27. E Garner, *To die by inches*, p. 71.
28. Relief Commission papers, county Cork II/2 15,676, letter from Rev. Henry Disney to Sir Randolph Routh, 26 March 1847. NAI.
29. E Garner, *To die by inches*, p. 77.
30. Ext. will prerogative 21.3.1848, vol 13, p. 141, will of Helena,

Endnotes

Dowager Countess of Kingston, 17 September 1846, NAI.
31. E Garner, *To die by inches*, p. 116.
32. Ibid, pp 64, 100-02, 113.
33. Outrage reports, 1847, Cork, correspondence and reports, 15 March, 28 April, 6 March 24 May, 21 June and 25 October 1847, written by Neal Browne, RM, Mitchelstown. NAI.
34. *The Times*, 31 March, 1 April 1848.
35. 'ATH', *Encumbered estates*, pp 45-6.

CHAPTER SEVEN
1. J Kegan, *A diary*, p. 36.
2. CE June 1856. For a full account of Sadleir's activities see James O'Shea, *Prince of swindlers, John Sadleir, MP, 1813-1856* (Dublin, 1999).
3. FJ, 13 October and 11 December 1856; *Limerick Reporter*, 8 July 1856.
4. LECR, June 185.1, vol 14, lot 91.
5. Mary Cecilia Lyons, *Illustrated incumbered estates Ireland, 1850-1905, County Clare*, 1993, p. 17. Araglin Cottage was owned in 1999 by Mr and Mrs Joseph Lomasney.
6. LECR, July 185.1, vol 16; February 185.5, vol 51.
7. CE, 13 December 1856; FJ 13 October, 1856.
8. LECR, July 185.1, vol 16, lot 87. Among the townlands sold at these auctions was that of Doolis, near Ballyporeen, part of which had been rented by the O'Regan's, whose descendant was Ronald Reagan, 40th President of the United States, 1981-1989.
9. WD Webber, *Some research*, pp 21a, 22a.
10. Lawrence M Geary, *The land war on the Kingston estate, 1879-1888*, (unpublished MA thesis, University College, Cork, 1979), pp 16-7, 20.
11. B Power, *Mitchelstown*, p. 67.
12. WD Webber, *Some records*, p. 24. *The Gentleman's Magazine*, 11 January 1867, pp 380-1.
13. *Illustrated London News*, 15 September 1860. James' name and the family crest is inscribed on the ruined church in Ballylanders.
14. WD Webber, *Some records*, pp 26, 26a.
15. Ibid, pp 24a, 26-27; WM Brady, *Parochial records*, p. 72.
16. *The O'Mahony Journal*, Brendan O'Cathaoir, 'John O'Mahony, moulder of the Irish-American dimension,' vol 3, (Dublin, 1973), pp 3-4.
17. *The Capuchin Annual*, Brendan O'Cathaoir, 'John O'Mahony, 1815-1877,' (1977), pp 185-6.

18. DJ Hickey and JE Doherty, *Dictionary*, p. 105.
19. WD Webber, *Some records*, p. 27. RD King-Harman, *The Kings*, p. 89.
20. CSORP/1867, 7,602, James, Earl of Kingston to JB Kennedy, solicitor, 61 Mountjoy Square West, Dublin. NAI.
21. WD Webber, *Some records*, pp 27, 27a.
22. LM Geary, *The land war*, pp 16-7.
23. CE, 23 July 1868.
24. RD King-Harman, *The Kings*, pp 127-30.
25. Ibid, pp 133-8.
26. Ibid, pp 141, 143-5, 152-3.
27. Ibid, pp 157-65.
28. *The answer of Anna, Countess of Kingston, filed 5 August 1872, record no. 1773, in proceedings between Henry Ernest Newcomen, Earl of Kingston (plaintiff) and Anna Countess of Kingston, Augusta Countess of Kingston, and others (defendants)*. KHP. [Hereafter cited as *8th Earl of Kingston vs Anna Countess of Kingston*].
29. RD King-Harman, *The Kings*, pp 164-5, 187, 194-5.

CHAPTER EIGHT
1. Michael Crotty, *John Sarsfield Casey and the Galtee case*, (unpublished BA research project, St Patrick's College, Maynooth, 1990), p. 1.
2. *Bridge vs Casey*, p. 12.
3. Ibid, pp 31-4.
4. Ibid, pp 20-1.
5. Ibid, pp 26, 28.
6. CE, 1 April 1876.
7. Michael Davitt, *The fall of feudalism in Ireland*, (London and New York, 1904), p. 141.
8. Bill Power, *Mitchelstown*, pp 69, 72.
9. FJ, 13 April 1876, 27 April 1876.
10. *Bridge vs Casey*, p. 46.
11. M Crotty, *The Galtee case*, pp 8-9, 13.
12. *Report of the arguments in the Court of the Queen's Bench on shewing cause against the conditional order for a criminal information against John Sarsfield Casey at the prosecution of Patten Smith Bridge*, (Dublin, 1877), p. 29.
13. WD Webber, *Some account*, p. 22a. M Crotty, *The Galtee case*, pp 13-5.
14. William O'Brien, *Christmas on the Galtees: an inquiry into the condition*

Endnotes

of the tenantry of Mr Nathaniel Buckley, (Dublin, 1878), p. 19.
15. M Crotty, *The Galtee case*, pp 13-4.
16. Ibid, pp 34-5.
17. *Bridge vs Casey*, pp 52-4.
18. Ibid, p. 54.
19. Ibid, p. 56.
20. Ibid, pp 91, 96-8.
21. W O'Brien, *Christmas on the Galtees*, pp 1-2.
22. Ibid, pp 7-8.
23. Ibid, p. 9.
24. Ibid, pp 19-21.
25. Ibid, pp 21-3.
26. Ibid, pp 34-5.
27. Ibid, pp 23-4.
28. Ibid, pp 27-8.
29. Ibid, p. 3.
30. FJ, 24 March 1879.

CHAPTER NINE
1. LM Geary, *The land war*, pp 18-9.
2. WD Webber, *Some records,* pp 32-3.
3. *Burke's landed gentry of Ireland*, (London, 1904), p. 641.
4. John Bateman, *The great landowners of Great Britain and Ireland*, (Leicester, 1971), p. 253.
5. WD Webber, *Some records*, pp 32-3, 33a.
6. LM Geary, *The land war*, p. 12.
7. WD Webber, *Some records*, pp 33-4.
8. Ibid, p. 34a.
9. JS Donnelly, *The land and the people*, pp 253-4.
10. WD Webber, *Some records*, p. 36.
11. CE, 25 November 1879.
12. LM Geary, *The land war*, p. 25.
13. CSORP/1880, 34,686. NAI.
14. LM Geary, *The land war*, p. 27.
15. CSORP/1880, 29,093. NAI.
16. LM Geary, *The land war*, pp 28-9.
17. WD Webber, *Some records*, pp 36-7.
18. CE, 18 December 1880.

19. LM Geary, *The land war*, pp 32-4.
20. CSORP/1881, 16,900. NAI.
21. CE, 28 May 1881.
22. CSORP/1881, 17,645. NAI.
23. CE, 1 July 1881.
24. 'An English soldier', *Memories of Ireland*, pp 22-5. Author's collection.
25. LM Geary, *The land war*, pp 39-40.
26. 'An English soldier', *Memories*, p. 25.
27. LM Geary, *The land war*, p. 43. CE, *North Cork News* supplement, 6 January, 1995.
28. 'An English Soldier,' *Memories*, p. 27.
29. LM Geary, *The land war*, p. 42.
30. Ibid, pp 45-8.
31. WD Webber, *Some records*, p. 40.
32. LM Geary, *The land war*, p. 53.

CHAPTER TEN
1. LM Geary, *The land war*, pp 57-9.
2. CE, 9 December 1886.
3. James F Maher, *Chief of the Comeraghs, a John O'Mahony anthology*, (Mullinahone, 1957), p. 126.
4. LM Geary, *The land war*, p. 60.
5. William O'Brien, *Evening memories, being a continuation of recollections by the same author*, (Dublin and London, 1920), pp 201-2.
6. CE, 4 January 1887.
7. Ibid, 14 January 1887.
8. LM Geary, *The land war*, pp 64-5, 67.
9. CE, 26 February 1887.
10. LM Geary, *The land war*, pp 65-6.
11. CE, 19 January 1887.
12. LM Geary, *The land war*, p. 67.
13. Ibid, p. 73.
14. CSORP/1887, 2,589, Land League papers, pp 5-6. NAI.
15. George Pellew, *In castle and cabin, or talks in Ireland in 1887*, (New York and London, 1888), p. 92.
16. Ibid, p. 42.
17. LM Geary, *The land war*, pp 73-4.

Endnotes

18. G Pellew, *In castle*, p. 94.
19. WD Webber, *Some records*, pp 41-2.
20. W O'Brien, *Evening memories*, p. 280.
21. CE, 17 August 1887.
22. Ibid, 10 August 1887.
23. CC 12 August 1887.
24. LM Geary, *The land war*, pp 72-3.
25. CE, 9 September 1887.
26. Frederick J Higginbottom, *The vivid life, a journalist's career*, (London, 1934), pp 88-90. CE, 10 September 1887.
27. FJ Higginbottom, *Vivid life*, pp 91-2.
28. FSL Lyons, *John Dillon, a biography*, (London, 1968), p. 88.
29. FJ Higginbottom, *Vivid life*, pp 93-6.
30. FJ, 10 September and 28 September 1887.
31. LM Geary, *The land war*, p. 83.
32. Ibid, pp 84-5.
33. FJ Higginbottom, *Vivid life*, pp 101, 102-3.
34. Ibid, pp 106-8.
35. LP Curtis, *Coercion and conciliation in Ireland, 1880-1892, a study in conservative unionism*, (Princeton and London, 1963), pp 197-8. 'Remember Mitchelstown' is quoted in James Joyce's *Ulysses*. Eamon de Valera, then aged five years, said that hearing neighbours talking about the riot and shootings in Mitchelstown was his earliest political memory.
36. G Pellew, *In castle*, p. 95.
37. LM Geary, *The land war*, p. 89.
38. LP Curtis, *Coercion and conciliation*, p. 197.
39. LM Geary, *The land war*, pp 92-3. FJ Higginbottom, *Vivid life*, pp 111-2.
40. *Mandeville inquest, copy of typescript of shorthand writers' notes of proceedings*, (London, 1888), pp 7-8.
41. *Irish historical studies*, LM Geary, 'John Mandeville and the Irish Crimes Act of 1887,' vol XXV, no. 100, (November, 1987), pp 362-5.
42. Ibid, p. 366.
43. *Mandeville inquest*, pp 15, 78-80.
44. FJ, 27 December 1887.
45. *Mandeville inquest*, pp 3-4, 99.
46. LM Geary, *The land war*, pp 97-8.
47. CE, 3 January and 17 January 1888.

48. LM Geary, *The land war*, pp 99-100.
49. CE, 3 April 1888.
50. JF Maher, *Chief of the Comeraghs*, p. 136. *Mandeville inquest*, p. 6.
51. *Mandeville inquest*, p. 110.
52. Mary Mandeville, *A narrative of my husband's treatment at Tullamore, as stated by him to me on his return, written between 24 and 31 November 1888*. William O'Brien papers, University College, Cork.
53. *United Ireland*, 21 July 1888.
54. Sally Warwick-Haller, *William O'Brien and the Irish land war*, (Dublin 1990) pp 108-9.
55. *Irish historical studies*, 'John Mandeville,' p. 371.
56. *Mandeville inquest*, p. 116.
57. LP Curtis, *Coercion and conciliation*, p. 224.
58. Ibid, pp 225-6.
59. CE, 10 September 1906.

CHAPTER ELEVEN

1. WD Webber, *Some records*, pp 43-4.
2. Ibid, pp 44a, 62a.
3. Ibid, pp 45a, 6b.
4. CE, 24 March 1891.
5. *Cork Weekly Herald*, 15 June 1895.
6. WD Webber, *Some records*, p. 41a.
7. CE, 24 March 1891. LG Pine, *The new extinct Peerage 1884-1971*, (London 1972), p. 200. Florence was the last Lady Mount Cashell. On the death of her husband, the 5th earl, in 1898, the title passed to his cousin, Edward George Moore, on whose death in 1915 the title became extinct.
8. WD Webber, *Some records*, p. 41a.
9. Ibid, pp 41a, 42a. Blackrock Castle, near Cork, was also designed by the Pain brothers, who originally drew the plans as the entrance gateway for Mitchelstown Castle.
10 *Census of Ireland*, 1911, province of Munster, county and city of Cork, (London, 1912), table vii, pp 129-31.
11. M Bence-Jones, *Twilight of the ascendancy*, pp 92-3.
12. DJ Hickey and JE Doherty, *Dictionary*, pp 288-9.
13. WD Webber, *Some records*, pp 46-7.
14. Ibid, pp 47-8, 47a.

Endnotes

15. Ibid, pp 49, 48a.
16. Ibid, pp 51a, 1b.
17. Ibid, un-numbered page adjoining 46a.
18. C Moore, *Ecclesiastical antiquities of Brigown*, p. 2.
19. WD Webber, *Some records*, p. 49a.
20. Ibid, pp 50, 48a, 1b.
21. Ibid, pp 50-2.
22. Ibid, p. 51a.
23. CE, 10 April 1906. The farmers' treatment of Mitchelstown's shopkeepers in 1906 and the founding of Mitchelstown Co-op in 1919, were the genesis of tensions between the two groups which persisted up to the end of the twentieth century.
24. WD Webber, *Some records*, pp 59-61, 61a.
25. RD King-Harman, *The Kings*, pp 244-6.
26. WD Webber, *Notes*, pp 22-3.
27. WD Webber, *Some records*, p. 4b.
28. Ibid, pp 4a, 3b-4b.
29. Ibid, pp 5, 5a.
30. Ibid, pp 6b-7b.
31. Ibid, pp 6b-7b.

CHAPTER TWELVE

1. *Census of Ireland, 1901*, (Cork); ref. no. 298/24/1, townland of Mitchelstown, form A. NAI. G Pellew, *In castle*, p. 94.
2. *8th Earl of Kingston vs Anna Countess of Kingston*. WD Webber, *Some records*, p. 46a.
3. *Census of Ireland, 1901*, (Cork); ref. no. 298/24/1, form A. Seán and Síle Murphy, Mahon Bridge, County Waterford, in conversation with the author, October 1999.
4. M Bence-Jones, *Twilight*, p. 59.
5. WD Webber, *Some records*, p. 46a.
6. Margaret (Peggy) Quinlan, Main Street, Kilworth, County Cork, in conversation with the author, September 1987.
7. M Bence-Jones, *Twilight*, pp 126-7.
8. WD Webber & A Kingston, *Household and personal accounts, 1895-1922*, entries for June and January, 1910. Author's collection. [Hereafter cited as *Household accounts*].
9. N Robertson, *Crowned harp*, p. 89. Janet Dunbar, *Mrs GBS, a portrait*,

(New York and Evanston, 1963), pp 17, 106.
10. Elizabeth Bowen, *Bowen's Court, & seven winters,* (London, 1984), pp 348-9.
11. N Robertson, *Crowned harp,* pp 90-1.
12. *Household accounts,* for examples see entries for 1896, 1898, 1900, 1902.
13. Church of Ireland, *Preachers' book 1909-1939,* parish of Brigown, entry of 19 January 1913, Diocese of Cloyne, entry of 19 January 1913 (The Rectory, Fermoy).
14. *Household accounts,* for examples see 1899, 1900, 1908 and 1912.
15. WD Webber, *Some records,* pp 53, 56-8.
16. Ibid, pp 52, 54, 58.
17. CC, 4 November 1907.
18. WD Webber, *Some records,* p. 58.
19. CC, 4 November 1907.
20. WD Webber, *Some records,* pp 58-9. Most of this graveyard was obliterated by Mitchelstown Co-op during the 1940s, '50s and '60s.
21. RD King-Harman, *The Kings,* pp 247-8.
22. Ibid, p. 309. CC, 3 May 1910.
23. E Bowen, *Bowen's court,* p 435. *Household accounts,* entry of January 1910.
24. Kingston papers, miscellaneous documents. O'Briens, Solicitors, Mitchelstown.
25. *Household accounts,* see entries of June 1910 and January 1912.
26. Church of Ireland, *Preachers book 1909-1939,* entry of 29 July 1914.
27. CE, 30 July 1914.
28. E Bowen, *Bowen's Court,* pp 434-6.

CHAPTER THIRTEEN
1. M Bence-Jones, *Twilight,* pp 159, 165.
2. *The Kerry News,* 12 March 1937.
3. Ernest Blythe, 'Kerry better than Cork in 1915,' *An tOglach,* Christmas 1962, pp 3-4.
4. *The Kerry News,* 12 March 1937.
5. M Bence-Jones, *Twilight,* pp 177-9.
6. RD King-Harman, *The Kings,* p. 248.
7. Ibid, p. 263. *Household accounts,* for the years 1914-1918. M Bence-Jones, *Twilight,* p. 179. *Census of Ireland,* 1911, ref. no. 301/24/1, DED Mitchelstown rural.

Endnotes

8. DJ Murphy in conversation with author, December 1986.
9. ICOS file no. 1088/694A/1 WD Webber to RA Anderson, 16 July 1919. NAI.
10. Ibid, file no. 1088/694A/1, Jim Fant to RA Anderson, 16 July 1919. DJ Murphy in conversation with author, December 1986.
11. M Bence-Jones, *Twilight*, pp 195-6.
12. DJ Murphy in conversation with author, December 1986 and March 1995.
13. *The Kerry News*, 12 March 1937.
14. Peter Hart, *The IRA and its enemies, violence and community in Cork, 1916-23*, (Oxford 1998), p. 228.
15. Photostat copy of IRA *Quarter-Master's book* recorded by Patrick (Pa) Luddy, for IRA companies at Ballylough, Glanworth, Kildorrery, Ballygiblin and Mitchelstown, from July 1921 to February 1922. Author's collection. The original manuscript is now believed to be in the United States.
16. M Bence-Jones, *Twilight*, p. 214. *Household accounts*, April 1922.
17. B Power, *Danes to Dairygold*, p. 133. *The Kerry News*, 12 March 1937.
18. Edith Webber in correspondence with WA King-Harman, 26 July 1922. KHP.
19. CE, 29 April 1926.
20. Letter from Edith Somerville, 19 July 1922. Somerville Papers, Drishane, Castletownsend, County Cork.
21. Rev. Fr Edward J Kilbride in conversation with the author, May 1990. Correspondence from Fr Kilbride to the author, 14 January 1990.
22. CE, 29 April 1926.
23. Ibid, 23 August 1922. Michael Casey in conversation with the author, December 1989.
24. Ibid, 18 August 1922.
25. M Casey in conversation with the author. Edith Somerville letter, 19 July 1922.
26. Edith Webber in correspondence with WA King-Harman, 12 August 1922. KHP.
27. Anne Doyle, nee Graham, in conversation with the author, January 1990.
28. DJ Murphy in conversation with the author, March 1995.
29. Patrick Glavin, in correspondence with the author, 19 October 1987. Author's collection.
30. CE, 29 April 1926.

31. Information provided to the author by a member of the castle garrison who wishes to remain anonymous.
32. CE, 29 April 1926.
33. Edith Webber, in correspondence with WA King-Harman, 15 August 1922. KHP.
34. CE, 18 August 1922.
35. Ibid, 23 August 1922. Tom Feeney in conversation with the author, 1982.
36. WD Webber to WA King-Harman, 15 August 1922. KHP.
37. Ibid, 17 August 1922. KHP.
38. WA King-Harman to WD Webber, 25 August 1922. KHP.
39. Ibid, 9 November 1922. KHP.
40. RD King-Harman, *The Kings*, p. 261.
41. WD Webber to WA King-Harman, 8 December 1922. KHP.
42. WD Webber to Mary Fairholme, 1 December 1922. Another dated 1910, and another on 1 February 1923 from WD Webber to Mary Fairholme, Salthill, Monkstown, County Dublin. Author's collection.
43. *Burke's Irish family records*, (London, 1976), pp 1,193-4.
44. DJ Hickey and JE Doherty, *Dictionary*, pp 321-2.

CHAPTER FOURTEEN
1. N Robertson, *Crowned harp*, p. 88.
2. Wilfred Scawen Blunt, *The land war in Ireland*, (London, 1912), p 329.
3. RD King-Harman, *The Kings*, pp 264-6.
4. M Bence-Jones, *Twilight*, p. 237.
5. Board of Works, specimen files relating to claims under Damage to Property (Compensation) Act, 1923, Mitchelstown Castle, County Cork, file no. 2D-62-73, claim dated 26 July 1923, signed by Arthur DM Webber. [Hereafter cited as Compensation claim]. NAI.
6. Ibid, document dated 24 April 1926.
7. RD King-Harman, *The Kings*, pp 265-7.
8. Compensation claim, document dated 21 June 1923. NAI.
9. Ibid, Daniel Casey, State solicitor, to Secretary, Office of Public Works, 6 May 1924. Daniel Casey to OPW 18 June 1923. Letter from Ministry of Finance to Sir Philip Hanson, OPW, 14 Samhain [November] 1924. NAI.
10. RD King-Harman, *The Kings*, pp 265-6.
11. Compensation claim, J Butler, inspector, OPW, report of 10 June

Endnotes

1924. NAI.
12. Ibid, list of contents of Mitchelstown Castle prior to the fire of 12 August 1922. NAI.
13. Ibid, J Butler report, 10 June 1924. NAI.
14. Ibid JC Butler and CH Curnow, report of 18 August 1925. NAI.
15. Fr EJ Kilbride, letter to author, 14 January 1990.
16. Compensation claim, T Cassedy, deputy secretary, Commissioners of Public Works, to the secretary, Department of Finance, 2 December 1925. NAI.
17. Ibid, list of paintings and contents of castle, including estimates of their value. Additional information provided to the author by a member of the castle garrison who wishes to remain anonymous.
18. Correspondence from DF O'Shaughnessy, The Rectory, Kilfinane, County Limerick, to Sir Cecil Stafford-King-Harman, Bart, 3 December 1957. Attached to it are press cuttings, one of unknown origin dated 21 November 1957, and another from *The Sunday Times* of 10 November 1957. KHP.
19. CE, 29 April 1926. Additional information provided to the author by an anonymous informant.
20. File relating to compensation for damage to bridges in Mitchelstown Demesne, including letters from the Department of Finance to WA King-Harman, dated 17 February 1927, 30 April 1928, 9 January 1929, 17 August 1929 and 3 January 1930. Author's collection.
21. Compensation claim; total cost of damage to the castle and loss of contents was calculated from various documents within file no 2D-62-73. NAI.
22. RD King-Harman, *The Kings*, pp 265-6.
23. Ibid, pp 262-3.
24. Ibid, pp 265-6.
25. WA King Harman to WB Hickley, May 1922, Kingston Papers; WE O'Brien & Co, Solicitors.
26. Rev. Fr Colman Foley, conversation with the author, May 1993.
27. RD King-Harman, *The Kings*, p. 250. These armorial bearings were brought back to Mitchelstown in 1996 by the author and are now owned by Cork County Council. They have not, as yet, been placed on permanent display and are at present stored in the author's garden.
28. Documents relating to the sale of the King-Harman estates, 1923-1964. Author's collection. DJ Murphy in conversation with the author. It may be recalled that the Kingston Arms Hotel cost £1,200 to build in

the 1780s.
29. *Iris Oifigiúil*, 31 January 1936.
30. DJ Murphy and M Casey in conversations with the author.
31. Schedule of sales titled 'Estate of Lt. Colonel WA King-Harman, sales to 30 September 1943.' KHP. Colonel AL King-Harman, in conversation with the author, 13 January 1994. Sale document of 6 January 1940, of the Kingston Arms Hotel to Mitchelstown Co-operative Agricultural Society Ltd. Kingston Papers; O'Brien & Co, solicitors.
32. DJ Murphy in conversation with the author.
33. RD King-Harman, *The Kings*, p. 276.
34. Colonel AL King-Harman, in conversation with the author, 13 January 1994. CE, *North Cork News* supplement, 28 January 1994.
35. Indenture between Colonel AL King-Harman of Great Gransden, Sandy, Bedfordshire, (vendor), and John D Finn, 58 Lower Cork Street, Mitchelstown (purchaser), for the sale of 29 properties in Mitchelstown. KHP. Colonel AL King-Harman, in conversation with the author, 13 January 1994.
36. M Casey and DJ Murphy in conversations with the author. *Irish Geography*, D Vida Henning, 'The demesne at Mitchelstown, County Cork,' *Irish Geography*, vol I, (Amsterdam, 1970), pp 99-101.
37. Colonel AL King-Harman, in conversation with the author, 13 January 1994. CE, *North Cork News* supplement, 28 January 1994. A tall concrete observation tower built on the site of Rockingham is one of the ugliest buildings in Ireland.
38. Barclay, 11th Earl of Kingston, in conversation with the author, August 1996. Mark Bence-Jones, *Burke's guide to country houses*, vol I, Ireland (London, 1978), p. 176.
39. RD King-Harman, *The Kings*, pp 277-8.
40. CE, *North Cork News* supplement, B Power, 'A Swiss fairytale on the Galtees,' 20 November 1992. Mark Bence-Jones, *Country houses*, p. 211. DJ Murphy in conversation with the author. The piggeries were designed by Eamon Roche's son, Kevin, who became one of America's most famous architects.
41. AL King-Harman in conversation with the author, and correspondence of various dates. Webber memorial was seen in the church at Screen, County Sligo, in July 1994.
42. Barclay, 11th Earl of Kingston in conversation with the author.
43. Brass memorial in Kingston College chapel. See also endnote number 47 of chapter five.

BIBLIOGRAPHY

MANUSCRIPT MATERIAL
BRITISH LIBRARY
Ms 40,355/90, Sir Robert Peel to the Earl of Kingston.
Ms 40,355/91, Earl of Kingston to Sir Robert Peel.
Ms 37,301, 279 and 213, Earl of Kingston to the Marquess Wellesley.

CHURCH OF IRELAND, FERMOY
Preachers' Book 1891-1900, parish of Brigown, diocese of Cloyne.
Preachers' Book 1909-1939, parish of Brigown, diocese of Cloyne.

CLOYNE DIOCESAN ARCHIVE, Cobh, County Cork
1809/35, Handbill issued by Caroline, Dowager Countess of Kingston, 13 November 1809.

KING-HARMAN PAPERS, now in the Public Records Office, Northern Ireland
Edward, 1st Earl of Kingston, letter to Colonel Richard Fitzgerald, December 1789.
Robert Viscount Kingsborough, letter to his father, the Earl of Kingston, November 1771.
William Downes Webber, *Some records and recollections of events relating to Mitchelstown Castle, and to its founder, George 3rd Earl of Kingston, and to his family and successors.*
Edward, 1st Earl of Kingston, letter to his son Robert, Viscount Kingsborough, 23 February 1773.
Robert, Viscount Kingsborough, letter to his father, 1st Earl of Kingston, 29 January 1773.
The answer of Anna, Countess of Kingston, filed 5 August 1872, record no. 1773, in proceedings between Henry Earnest Newcomen, Earl of Kingston (plaintiff) and Anna Countess of Kingston, Augusta Countess of Kingston, and others (defendants).
Edith Webber, three letters to Wentworth Alexander King-Harman, 26 July, 12 and 15 August 1922.

William Downes Webber letter to WA King Harman, 15 August 1922.
WA King-Harman letter to WD Webber, 25 August 1922.
WA King-Harman letter to WD Webber, 9 November 1922.
WD Webber letter to WA King-Harman, 8 December 1922.
DF O'Shaughnessy, The Rectory, Kilfinane, County Limerick, letter to Sir Cecil Stafford-King-Harman, Bart, 3 December 1957, enclosing newspaper cuttings.
Schedule of sales titled 'Estate of Lt. Col. WA King-Harman, sales to 30 September 1943.'
Intenture between Colonel Anthony Lawrence King-Harman of Great Gransden, Sandy, Bedfordshire, (vendor), and John D Finn, 58 Lower Cork Street, Mitchelstown, (purchaser), for the sale of 29 properties in Mitchelstown.

NATIONAL ARCHIVES OF IRELAND
Valuation Office Housebooks, Brigown parish, Barony of Condons and Clongibbon, County Cork, no. 5.0316 and 5.0319.
Chief Secretary's Office, Registered Papers 1822, 1824, 1829, 1847, 1867, 1880, 1881, 1887.
Land League Papers for the years 1886-1888.
Relief Commission papers, county Cork II/2 15,676, letter from Rev. Henry Disney to Sir Randolph Routh, 26 March 1847
Ext Will Prerogative 21.3.1848, vol 13, will of Helena, Dowager Countess of Kingston, 17 September 1846.
Outrage reports, 1847, Cork, correspondence and reports written by Neale Browne, RM, Mitchelstown.
Census of Ireland, 1901, Cork, ref no. 298/24/1.
Census of Ireland, 1911, ref. no 301/24/1, DED Mitchelstown rural.
Irish Co-operatives Organisation Society, (ICOS) file no 1088/694A/1.
Board of Works, specimen files relating to claims under Damage to Property (Compensation) Act, 1923, Mitchelstown Castle, County Cork. File no. 2D-62-73, claim dated 26 July 1923, signed by Arthur DM Webber.

NATIONAL LIBRARY OF IRELAND
Ms 3275, Kingston vs Kingston.
Ms 19,077, *Timber and garden accounts book of Caroline, Dowager Countess of Kingston.*
Landed Estate Court Rentals, June 185.1, vol 14; July 185.1, vol 16;

Bibliography

February 185.1, vol 16; February 185.5, vol 51.

O'BRIEN & CO, SOLICITORS, Bank Place, Mitchelstown
Kingston Papers, miscellaneous documents.
Sale document of 6 January 1940 of the Kingston Arms Hotel to Mitchelstown Co-operative Agricultural Society Ltd.

AUTHOR'S COLLECTION
'An English soldier,' *Memories of Ireland*, place and date of publication unknown. Photocopied book pages sent to author by Niall Brunicardi, MA, Fermoy, County Cork.
Mitchelstown Charity, Minute Book. Proceedings, orders and resolutions of His Grace the most Reverend Lord ArchBishop of Cashel and the Right Reverend Lords Bishops of Cloyne, Waterford and Limerick, Trustees, nominated and appointed in and by the last will and Testament of the Right Honourable James Lord Baron Kingston, deceased.
Bill Power, 'The development and destruction of Mitchelstown demesne, 1776-1949,' (Certificate in Local and Regional Studies, dissertation, University College, Cork, 1995).
Indenture between Caroline, Dowager Countess of Kingston, and John Power, farmer, Glenatlucky, Mitchelstown, 4 April 1818.
CJF MacCarthy correspondence, 1988, enclosing a copy of 'King James I, patent for the creation of the manor of Mitchelstown, AD, 1618.'
Patrick Glavin, correspondence with the author, 19 October 1987.
Indenture between George, Earl of Kingston and James Mahony, Robert Street, Mitchelstown, 25 March 1829.
WD Webber & A Kingston, *household and personal accounts book*, 1895-1922.
Photostat copy of IRA Quarter-Master's book recorded by PJ (Pa) Luddy, for IRA companies at Ballylough, Glanworth, Kildorrery, Ballygiblin and Mitchelstown, from July 1921 to February 1922. Location of the original is unknown, but it may be in the United States.
Rev. Fr Edward J Kilbride, SJ, Limerick, correspondence, 14 January 1990.
Colonel Anthony Lawrence King-Harman, correspondence with the author 1987-1999.
Patrick A Glavin, United States, correspondence 19 October 1987.
WD Webber to Mary Fairholme, 1 December 1922.

WD Webber to Mary Fairholme, 1910.
WD Webber to Mary Fairholme, Salthill, Monkstown, County Dublin, 1 February 1923.
File relating to compensation for damage to bridges in Mitchelstown Demesne. Originally part of King-Harman Papers.
Documents relating to the sale of the King-Harman estates, 1923-1964.
Mrs Ellen (Nellie) Quinlan, Thomas Street, Mitchelstown, note to author, c. 1987.

WEBBER COLLECTION, County Donegal
William Downes Webber, *Notes on events connected with Mitchelstown, compiled in 1905 by WD Webber;* manuscript notebook consisting of 23 pages and notes, all in the handwriting of Mary Fairholme.

SOMERSET HOUSE, LONDON
Will of Caroline King, Dowager Countess of Kingston, proved 22 February 1823.

TRINITY COLLEGE, DUBLIN
Ms 826, fol 298.

UNIVERSITY COLLEGE, CORK
William O'Brien papers.

PARLIAMENTARY PAPERS
First report from the select committee on the state of Ireland, vol VIII, House of Commons, 1825.
Minutes of evidence taken before the select committee of the House of Lords... into the state of Ireland, House of Lords, 1825.
Report from the select committee on Manor Courts, Ireland, House of Commons, 1838.
Report from the select committee on the state of Ireland, vol III, House of Commons, 1825.
Return of the number of barracks in the United Kingdom, House of Commons, 1847.

SOMERVILLE PAPERS, Drishane, Co. Cork.
Letter from Edith Somerville, 19 July 1922.

Bibliography

PRINTED MATERIAL

'ATH', *Encumbered estates of Ireland, 1850*, London, 1850.

Barry, JM, *Pitchcap and triangle, the Cork militia in the Wexford rising*, Cork, 1998.

Barrington, Sir Jonah, *Personal sketches and recollections of his own times*, Glasgow, 1876.

Bateman, John, *The great landowners of Great Britain and Ireland*, Leicester, 1971.

Bence-Jones, Mark, *Burke's guide to country houses*, vol I, Ireland, London, 1978.

Bence-Jones, Mark, *Life in an Irish country house*, London, 1996.

Bence-Jones, Mark, *Twilight of the ascendancy*, London, 1993.

Blackstock, Allan, *An Ascendancy army, the Irish yeomanry, 1796-1834*, Dublin, 1998.

Blunt, Wilfred Scawen, *The land war in Ireland*, London, 1912.

Bowen, Elizabeth, *Bowen's Court and seven winters*, London, 1984.

Brady, William Maziere, *Clerical and parochial records of Cork, Cloyne and Ross*, Dublin, 1864.

Brewer, JS, and William Bullen, *Calendar of Carew manuscripts, 1578-1588*, London, 1868.

Burke's Irish family records, London, 1976.

Burke's Landed gentry of Ireland, London, 1904.

Burke's Peerage and Baronetage, London, 1975.

Calvert, Hon Mrs Frances, *An Irish beauty of the Regency, compiled from 'mes souvenirs' - the unpublished journals of Mrs Calvert, 1789-1882*, ed. Mrs Warrene Blake, Lane, 1911.

Chatterton, Lady, *Rambles in the South of Ireland during the year 1838*, London, 1839.

Chilvers, Ian, and Harold Osborne, *The Oxford dictionary of art*, Oxford University Press, 1997.

Connolly, SJ (ed), *The Oxford companion to Irish history*, Oxford, 1998.

Coombes, James, *A bishop of penal times*, Cork, 1981.

Coppinger, the Rt. Rev. Dr William; *The Rt. Rev. Dr Coppinger's letter to the Rt Hon and Hon'ble Dublin Society with additional documents and explanatory remarks as seem called for by the Rev. Horatio Townsend's observations upon this letter and with a supplement to his appendix*, Cork, 1811.

Crotty, Michael, *John Sarsfield Casey and the Galtee case*, (BA research project, St. Patrick's College, Maynooth. Unpublished, 1990).

Curtis, LP, *Coercion and conciliation in Ireland, 1880-1892; a study in con-*

servative unionism, Princeton and London, 1963.

d'Alton, Ian, *Protestant society and politics in Cork, 1812-1844,* Cork, 1980.

Davitt, Michael, *The fall of feudalism in Ireland,* London and New York, 1904.

de Tocqueville, Alexis, *Journey to England and Ireland,* London, 1857.

de Vere, Aubrey, *Recollections of Aubrey de Vere,* New York and London, 1897.

Diamond, Colum Michael, *The children of the settlers,* Oshawa, 1985.

Donnolly, James S, Jr, *The land and the people of nineteenth century Cork,* London and Boston, 1975.

Dunbar, Janet, *Mrs GBS, a portrait,* New York and Evanston, 1963.

Durant, David N, *A historical dictionary, life in the country house,* London, 1996.

Foster, RF, *Modern Ireland,* 1600-1972, London, 1989.

Gahan, Daniel, *The people's rising, Wexford 1798,* Dublin, 1995.

Garner, Edward, *To die by inches, the famine in north east Cork,* Fermoy, 1986.

Geary, Laurence M, *The land war on the Kingston estate, 1879-1888,* MA thesis, University College, Cork, 1979. Unpublished.

Hart, Peter, *The IRA and its enemies, violence and community in Cork, 1916-1923,* Oxford, 1998.

Hey, David (ed), *The Oxford companion to local and family history,* Oxford and New York, 1996.

Hickey, DJ, and JE Doherty, *A dictionary of Irish history, 1800-1980,* Dublin, 1987.

Higginbottom, Frederick J, *The vivid life, a journalist's career,* London, 1934.

Inglis, Rev. Henry David, *Ireland in 1834, a journey throughout Ireland during the spring, summer and autumn of 1834,* Whittaker, 1834.

Jupp, Peter, *British and Irish elections, 1784-1831,* Newton Abbot, 1973.

Kegan, John, *A young Irishman's diary,* Cambridgeshire, 1928.

Kelly, James, *'That damn'd thing called honour,' Duelling in Ireland 1570-1860,* Cork, 1995.

Kinealy, Christine, *This great calamity, the Irish famine 1845-'52,* Dublin, 1994.

King-Harman, Anthony Lawrence, *The Kings of King House,* Bedford, 1996.

King-Harman, Robert Douglas, *The Kings, Earls of Kingston, an account of the family and their estates in Ireland between the reigns of the two Queens*

Bibliography

Elizabeth, Cambridge, 1959.

Lamb, Keith, and Patrick Bowe, *A history of gardening in Ireland*, Dublin, 1995.

Lecky, William, *A history of the eighteenth century*, vol VIII, London, 1890.

Lepper, John Heron, and Philip Crossle, *The history of the grand lodge of Ireland*, vol I, Dublin, 1925.

Lewis, Samuel, *A topographical dictionary of Ireland*, London, 1837.

Luddy, Rev. Ailbe J, *The story of Mount Melleray*, Dublin, 1946.

Lyons, Mary Cecelia, *Illustrated incumbered estates Ireland, 1850-1905*, Whitegate, 1993.

Lyons, FSL, *John Dillon, a biography*, London, 1968.

Mackay, Donald, *Flight from famine, the coming of the Irish to Canada*, Toronto and London, 1990.

MacNevin, Thomas, *The history of the volunteers of 1782*, Dublin, 1882.

McAleer, Edward C, *The sensitive plant, a life of Lady Mount Cashell*, University of North Carolina Press, 1958.

Madden, Owen D, *Revelations of Ireland in the past generations*, Dublin, 1848.

Maher, James F, *Chief of the Comeraghs, a John O'Mahony anthology*, Mullinahone, 1957.

Malius, E, and the Knight of Glin, *Lost demesnes, Irish landscape gardening 1660-1845*, London, 1976.

Mandeville inquest, copy of typescript of shorthand writers' notes of proceedings, London, 1888.

McDowell, RB, *Crisis and decline, the fate of the southern unionists*, Dublin, 1997.

Moore, Rev. Canon Courtenay, *A side light on Irish clerical life in the 17th century*, Dublin 1891.

Moore, Rev. Canon Courtenay, *The ecclesiastical antiquities of Brigown, with a sketch of the life of Saint Findchua*, Dublin, 1891.

Nicholls, Kenneth, and Paul MacCotter (eds), *The pipe roll of Cloyne*, Cloyne, 1996.

Nolan, William (ed), *The shaping of Ireland, the geographical perspective*, Cork and Dublin, 1986.

O'Brien, AF, *The impact of the Anglo-Normans on Munster*, The Barryscourt Trust, 1997.

O'Brien, William, *Christmas on the Galtees; an inquiry into the condition of the tenantry of Mr Nathaniel Buckley*, Dublin, 1878.

O'Brien, William, *Evening memories, being a continuation of Recollections by the same author*, Dublin and London, 1920.
O'Connor, John, *The workhouses of Ireland, the fate of Ireland's poor*, Dublin, 1995.
O'Donoghue, Florence, *No other law*, Dublin, 1986.
O'Flanagan, Patrick, and Cornelius G Buttimer, *Cork history and society, interdisciplinary essays on the history of an Irish county*, Dublin, 1993
O'Laoghaire, *An tAthair Peadar, My own story*, Dublin, 1973.
Ordnance Survey of Ireland, first edition, Dublin, 1841.
O'Shea, James, *Prince of Swindlers, John Sadleir, MP, 1813-1856*, Dublin, 1999.
Packenham, Thomas, *The year of liberty, the history of the great Irish rebellion of 1798*, London, 1992.
Parliamentary gazetteer of Ireland, Dublin and London, 1845.
Pellew, George, *In castle and cabin, or talks in Ireland in 1887*, New York and London, 1888.
Pick, Fred L, and G Norman Knight, *The pocket history of Freemasonry*, London, 1992.
Pine, LG, *The new extinct Peerage, 1884-1971*, London, 1972.
Plowden, Francis P, *An historical view of the state of Ireland, from the invasion of that country, under Henry II to its union with Great Britain*, London, 1801.
Power, Bill, *From the Danes to Dairygold, a history of Mitchelstown*, Mitchelstown, 1996.
Power, Bill, *Mitchelstown through seven centuries*, Fermoy, 1987.
Power, Patrick C, *History of south Tipperary*, Cork, 1989.
Puckler-Muskau, Prince, (Herman Ludwig Heinrich, Furst Von), *Tour in England, Ireland, and France, in... 1828-1829, by a German prince*, Effingham Wilson, 1832.
Report of the arguments in the Court of Queen's Bench on shewing cause against the conditional order for a criminal information against John Sarsfield Casey at the prosecution of Patten Smith Bridge, Dublin, 1877.
Report of the eight days' trial in the Court of Queen's Bench on a criminal information against John Sarsfield Casey, at the prosecution of Patten Smith Bridge, from November 27th to December 5th, 1877, Dublin, 1877.
Robertson, Nora, *Crowned harp, memories of the last years of the Crown in Ireland*, Dublin, 1960.
Rynne, E (ed), *North Munster studies*, Limerick, 1967.
Sadlier, Thomas U (ed), *An Irish peer on the Continent 1801-1803,*

Bibliography

London, 1920.

Shelley, Mary, *Maurice, or the fisher's cot*, (Claire Tomalin ed), London, 1998.

Smith, Charles, *The ancient and present state of the county and city of Cork*, vol I, eds. Robert Day and WA Coppinger, Cork, 1893.

Sommerville-Large, Peter, *The Irish country house, a social history*, London, 1995.

Somerville-Large, Peter, *Irish eccentrics*, London, 1975.

Tomalin, Claire, *The life and death of Mary Wollstonecraft*, Middlesex, 1985.

Townsend, Rev. Horatio, *A general and statistical survey of the county and city of Cork*, vol I, Cork, 1815.

Trench, Charles Chenevix, *Grace's card, Irish Catholic landlords 1690-1800*, Cork and Dublin, 1997.

Walker, Brian M (ed), *Parliamentary election results in Ireland 1801-1922*, Dublin, 1978.

Wardle, Ralph M (ed), *Collected letters of Mary Wollstonecraft*, London, 1979.

Warwick-Haller, Sally, *William O'Brien and the Irish land war*, Dublin, 1990.

Wollstonecraft, Mary, V*indication of the rights of woman*, Penguin Books, 1988.

Young, Arthur, *A tour of Ireland in the years 1776, 1777 and 1778*, ed. Constantia Maxwell, Cambridge, 1925.

Young, Arthur, *The autobiography of Arthur Young*, ed. M Betham-Edwards, New York, 1967.

NEWSPAPERS
The Avondhu
The Cork Constitution (CC)
The Cork Examiner (CE)
The Corkman
Cork Weekly Herald
The Freemans Journal (FJ)
The Illustrated London News
The Kerry News
The Limerick Reporter
The Times
Walker's Hibernian Magazine

JOURNALS AND PERIODICALS
An tÓglaigh
Cahir Heritage Newsletter
The Capuchin Annual
The Gentleman's Magazine
Hansard
Historical and Archaeological Association of Ireland Journal
The Irish Builder
Irish Geography
Irish Historical Studies
Iris Oifigiúil
Journal of the Cork Historical and Archaeological Society (JCHAS)
The Limerick Reporter
Mallow Field Club Journal
The O'Mahony Journal

INTERVIEWS AND CORRESPONDENCE
The following persons corresponded with, or were interviewed by, the author.

Anonymous member of Mitchelstown IRA, circa 1918-1924, interviewed at intervals during the 1980s.
Bence-Jones, Mark; historian and writer; interviewed November 1993.
Casey, Michael; (born 1902), member of the Mitchelstown company of the IRA and participant in the occupation of the castle in 1922; interviewed, December 1989.
Doyle, Anne, nee Graham; (born 1911), parents owned a business at Upper Cork Street, Mitchelstown, during 1919-'22 period. Her family were friends of Richard Henry, who was WD Webber's estate agent in 1922; interviewed, 5 January 1990.
Feeney, Tom; member of the IRA, circa 1918-'21, and subsequently a private in the Irish Free State Army, 1922-'40s; interviewed at intervals 1978-'82.
Foley, Rev Fr Colman, O.Cist; a member of the Cistercian community at Mount Melleray Abbey, County Waterford, who witnessed the building of the new abbey with Mitchelstown Castle stone; interviewed May 1993.
Kilbride, Rev. Fr Edward, SJ; son of retired resident magistrate who resided in King Square, Mitchelstown, during 1922; interviewed May 1990.

Bibliography

King-Harman, Colonel Anthony Lawrence; heir to the Mitchelstown estate, interviewed January 1994.

Kingston, Barclay Robert Edwyn King-Tenison, 11th Earl of; interviewed, August 1996.

MacCarthy, CJF; historian, correspondence, 1980-1998.

Murphy, Denis J; (born 1910), of Ballyhooly, County Cork, former chairman, Mitchelstown Co-operative Agricultural Society Ltd; interviewed December 1986 and March 1995.

Quinlan, Margaret (Peggy); of Main Street, Kilworth, County Cork, local historian with considerable knowledge of Mitchelstown, in conversation September 1987.

INDEX

A
A Vindication of the Rights of Woman, 38
Act of Union, 44, 58, 59
Advice to Young Mothers on the Physical Education of Children, 50
Anderson R.A., 190, 206
Anglo-Irish Treaty, 219
Antiquities of Mexico, 95
Arabian Knights, 96
Araglin, 4, 100, 116
Araglin Cottage, 116, 249
Ardskeagh, 2

B
Baily, Francis, 117
Balfour, Arthur J., 178, 179, 182
Ballylanders, 2, 20
Ballyporeen, 20, 116, 146
Bandon, Earl of, 87
Bantry, Lord, 86
Barry, Stephen, 102
Beechey, Sir William, 74, 240
Biggar, Joseph, 138
Black and Tans, 218
Blackwater river, 73, 116
Blunt, William Scawen, 233
Blythe, Ernest, 214
Board of Works, 153
Bonaparte, Josephine, 47
Bonaparte, Napoleon, 47
Borghese, Princess, 48
Botanologia Universalis Hibernica, 7
Bourke, 82
Bourke, Lieutenant, 55
Bourke, Redmond, 2, 3
Bowen, Elizabeth, 203, 204, 211
Bowen, Henry, 212
Bowen, Lt-Col. Henry Cole, 19
Bowen, Robert Cole, 203, 208, 213
Bowen, Sarah, 211, 221
Bowen's Court, 211, 213
Boyce, Robert, 89
Boyle, Co. Roscommon, 5, 6
Boyle, Viscount, 43
Brachmann, Herman, 202
Bridge, Patten Smith, 114, 136-138, 148, 156
Brigown, 6, 62, 81, 101, 102, 192, 200
Brinkley, Capt. Francis, 209
Brinkley, Capt. Richard, 204
Brinkley, Richard, 152
Brogden E.B., 136
Brown, Capability, 24
Brown, Neal, 110
Brownrigg, Inspector, 168, 175, 176, 180
Brunner, E.L., 173
Buckley, Abel, 208
Buckley, Nathaniel, 136, 139, 148, 170
Burdon Fr, 162
Burke, Patrick, 142, 144
Bushe, Charles Kendal, 8
Bushe, Rev Thomas, 8, 9, 19
Bute, Marquess of, 15
Butler, Dr James, Archbishop of Cashel, 66
Butler, John, 236–238, 239
Butt, Isaac, 141
Byron, Lord, 49

C
Cahir, Emily, Lady, 67, 68
Calvert, Hon. Mrs Frances, 40
Cantwell, John McNamara, 115, 116

Carew, Sir George, 2
Caroline, Queen, 70, 74
Carroll, Anthony, 236
Carroll, Thomas, 190
Carson, Sir Edward, 179, 180, 210
Casement, Sir Roger, 210, 211
Casey, Coroner John Sarsfield, 175, 176 (see *Galtee Boy*)
Casey, Daniel, 236
Casey, John, 187
Casey, Michael, 216, 224
Casey, Tom, 158
Cashel, Archbishop of, 7
Catholic Emancipation, 76
Caulfeild, Bishop, 56
Charles Emanuel IV, 48
Charlotte, Queen, 56
Chatterton, Lady, 76-79
Cholmondeley, Henry, 153, 154, 200
Christmas on the Galtees, 135, 148
Church Body, 189, 192, 195
ClanGibbon, 1, 2
Clare, Earl of, 44–46
Clarence, Duke of, 70
Claridge, William, 77, 131
Cleaver, Caroline, 70
Cleaver, Most Rev Euseby, Archbishop of Dublin, 70
Clogheen, Co. Tipperary, 52
Clonmel, Mayor of, 173
Cloyne, Bishop of, 7, 9
Comeragh House, Co. Waterford, 201
Conderan, Sgt., 174
Condon, Thomas, 174, 184
Conrad, William, 96, 240
Convamore House, 218
Cooke-Collis, Capt. William, 103
Cooke-Collis, Col., 208
Cooke, Philip Davies, 111
Coppinger, Dr William, Bishop of Cloyne, 23, 66, 67

Cork Constitution, 89, 92–94, 208
Cork Examiner, 106, 139, 154, 171, 172, 190, 191, 210, 223, 224, 229, 228
Cork, Earl of, 3
Cork, Mayor of, 173, 182
Coughlan, Paddy, 210
Courtney, Paddy, 217
Cowper Commission, 165
Creagh, John, 146
Crime Act, 181
Croke, Dr Thomas, Archbishop of Cashel, 141
Croker, James Dillon, 103
Cronin brothers, 82
Crosby, Miss, 17
Crowe, Tom, 138, 140
Cull, George, 110
Cullinane, John, 172
Cullinane, Patrick, 110
Curran, John Philpot, 45
Curran, Sarah, 45

D
d'Aiguillon, Duc, 12
Danby, 12, 13
Davitt, Michael, 156, 163, 192
de Champaigne, Philip, 240
de Ricci, General John Robert, 71
de Ricci, Herman Robert, 71
de Tocqueville, Alexis, 97
de Valera, Eamon, 246
Delaney, Rev Dr Patrick, 143, 145
Desmond, James, Earl of, 21, 201
Devonshire, Duke of, 86
Dillon, John, 172–177, 192, 233
Disney, Thomas, 60, 61, 85
Disney, William, 60
Disney, Rev Henry, 107
Dixon, Capt. Thomas, 54, 55
Doherty, Thomas, 200
Donahue, John, 158
Doneraile Rangers Light

Index

Dragoons, 19
Doneraile, Lord, 203
Donovan, Thomas, 158
Dublin Castle, 51, 179
Dungannon Convention, 19
Dwyer, Richard, 144

E
Easter Rising, 216
Eaton, Richard, 138, 155, 168, 172
Elizabeth I, 1, 3, 5
Ellis, Thomas, 173
Emmett, Robert, 46
Encumbered Estates Act, 117
Evening Memories, 166
Eyre, Thomas J., 114, 115

F
Fairholme, Minnie (Mary), 201, 209, 212, 232, 234, 237
Fant, Jim, 217
Farrer, Capt. Richard, 151, 152, 199
Farrer, Harriet, 208
Fenton, Catherine, 5
Fenton, Sir Geoffrey, 3
Fenton, Sir Maurice, 5
Fenton, Sir William, 3, 4, 5
Fermoy and Mitchelstown Railway Company, 190
Fermoy, 101, 104, 106, 109, 157
Fiennes, Audrey, 211
Finn, John, D, 246
FitzDavids de St Michel, 1
Fitzgerald, Col. Henry, 41–43
Fitzgerald, Col. Richard of Mount Ophaly, 9
Fitzgerald, Edward, Lord, 52
Fitzgerald, Margaret, 9
Fitzgerald, Mrs, 30, 36, 37
Fitzgibbon, 1
Fitzgibbon, Edmund Fitzjohn, 1–3

Fitzgibbon, Margaret (Fenton), 3, 4
Flynn, Ellen and Margaret, 109
Fortiscue, Sir Charles, 44
Fox, Dr Charles Joseph, 89
Fox, Dr Francis Ker, 90
Frankenstein, 38
Franks, Henry Mansfield, 81
Franks, Margaret, 82
Franks, Thomas, 81–83
Frederick William IV, King of Prussia, 96
Free State Army, 228, 232
Freemasons, 6, 7
Frend, Henry, 163, 165, 168, 189, 193, 202

G
Gainsborough, Thomas, 240
Galtee Boy, 138, 139, 141, 158, 164, 190 (see *John Sarsfield Casey*)
Galtee Castle, 26, 78, 136–138 142, 148, 208, 249
Galtee Estate, 118, 139, 145, 148, 150, 166
Galtee mountains, 13, 26, 67, 135, 233, 247
Galtee Regiment, 211, 212 216, 219
George III, 15, 40, 59, 74
George IV, 59, 69, 75
Geraldine, House of, 1
Gill, T.P., 173
Gladstone, William, 178
Glavin, Patrick, 226
Godwin, George, 38
Gort, Lord, 72
Grace, Olive, 8
Graham family, 225
Grattan, Henry, 20
Graves, Dr Richard Hastings, 107
Great Famine, 69, 102–112

Griffith, Arthur, 224

H
Hagerbaum, Madame Netta, 201, 209
Hallenan, Eliner, 40
Hanrahan, John, 158
Hares of Convamore, 208, 222
Harrington, Tim, 180
Hartigan, T.J., 241
Hartland, Richard, 8, 15, 60
Hartney, John, 43
Henry, Cardinal Duke of York, 48
Hickley, W.B., 243
Higginbottom, Frederick J., 173, 174, 177–179
Hill, W.H., Architects, 236
Hogan, 82
Holmes, William, 111
Hyde, John, 86
Hyland, John, 138, 146

I
Imlay, George, 38
Inglis, Rev Henry, 90–92, 99
Ingouville-Williams, Florence, 234, 239
IRA, 216, 218, 219, 220, 232, 247
Irish Agricultural Organisation Society (IAOS), 190, 207, 217
Irish Civil War, 220–232
Irish Home Rule, 141, 186, 204, 210, 213, 240
Irish Land Company, 117, 118, 135, 136
Irwin, District Inspector, 175, 176, 180

J
James II, 6
James, Earl of Desmond, 2, 201
Johnstone, Miss, 39

Jones, Sub-Constable, 138

K
Kearney, 81
Kegan, James, 111, 113
Kegan, John, 98
Kenny, Judge, 241
Keogh, Capt., 55, 56
K'Eogh, Rev Dr John, 7
Kilbehenny, 2, 186
Kildorrery, 109
Kiely, Fr John, 80
Kilbride, Fr Edward J., 239
Kilmallock, 1
Kilmurry, Co. Kilkenny, 9
Kilquane, 2
Kilronan Castle, 248
Kilworth Volunteers, 19
Kilworth, 42, 43, 46, 103–105, 109, 191, 207, 251
King House, Boyle, 10, 249
King, Lady Adelaide T. Webber, 39, 93, 151
King, Archbishop of Dublin, 6
King, Caroline (Morrison), 29, 61
King, Edward, 1st Earl of Kingston, 10, 11, 26, 43, 249
King, Edward, 65
King, Edward, Viscount Kingsborough, 39, 90, 93
King, General Sir Henry, 61, 69, 70, 92
King, George, 3rd Earl of Kingston, 11, 26, 29, 39, 53–61, 68, 72–94
King, Helena Caroline, 39
King, Henry, 86
King, Isabella, 7
King, James, 4th Baron Kingston, 6–9
King, James, 5th Earl of Kingston, 39, 93

Index

King, Lady Jane Diana de Ricci, 29, 61, 71
King, John, (Secretary to the Elector of Wurttemberg), 29, 61, 70
King, John, 1st Baron Kingston, 5
King, John, 3rd Baron Kingston 5, 6
King, John, 5
King, Lady Louisa Eleanor de Spaen, 29
King, Margaret, 11
King, Margaret (see *Margaret Moore, Countess of Mount Cashell*)
King, Lady Mary Elizabeth Morrison, 29, 40–42, 46
King, Rear-Admiral James William, 29, 61, 70
King, Richard Fitzgerald, 29, 61, 70
King, Robert Edward, 1st Viscount Lorton, 29, 41–43, 57, 60, 61, 68, 69, 86
King, Robert Edward, 2nd Viscount Lorton, 7th Earl of Kingston, 151, 152
King, Robert Henry, 4th Earl of Kingston, 39, 86, 93, 95, 98–118
King, Robert, 2nd Baron Kingston, 5
King, Robert, 2nd Earl of Kingston, 9–46, 51, 67
King, Sir John, 1, 5
King, Sir Robert, 5
King, Thomas, 29
King-Harman Lt-Col. Wentworth Alexander, 209, 215, 220, 221, 227, 229–231, 235–237, 241–243
King-Harman, Capt. Robert Douglas, 198, 209, 242, 243, 246, 248, 249
King-Harman, Col. Anthony, 245–248, 250
Kingsborough, Caroline, Lady, (see *Caroline, Countess of Kingston*)
Kingsborough House, Co. Westmeath, 249
Kingston College, 7, 8, 15, 18, 57, 151, 251
Kingston, Anna, Dowager Countess of, 150, 151, 156–158, 164–169 183, 184, 189–209, 247
Kingston, Caroline, Countess of, 9–11, 17, 28–40, 61–72
Kingston, Helena, Countess of, 39, 56, 108,
King-Tenison, Barclay Robert Edwin, 11th Earl of Kingston, 250, 251
King-Tenison, Henry Edwyn, 9th Earl of Kingston, 248
King-Tenison, Henry Ernest, 8th Earl of Kingston, 248
Kirwan, Sgt., 175

L
Labouchere, Henry, 173, 177
Lake, Lieutenant-General, 56, 57
Land Acts, 163, 165, 185, 192, 193, 196, 203, 234, 243
Land Commission, 184, 189, 195, 197, 200, 245, 248, 249
Land Improvement Act, 118, 162
Land League (see *National League*), 155–160, 162, 165, 175, 193
Land Wars, 118, 150, 159–170, 183, 185, 189, 202, 209, 232, 233, 247
Landed Estates Court, 116
Leahy, Constable, 175

Leech W.J., 240
Limerick, Bishop of, 7
Limerick, Lord, 87
Listowel, Earl of, 86, 204, 218
Lonergan, Michael, 176, 187
Longfield family, 86
Longfield, Elizabeth, 208
Lorton (see *King*)
Lough Cutra Castle, 72
Louis XVI, 12
Louis XVIII, 70
Luddy, Patrick, 'Pa', 218–222, 225, 245
Lycidas, 65
Lynch, General Liam, 220, 232

M
Mahony, J., 153
Mahony, James, 81
Mallow, 2, 25, 103, 143, 188, 207, 221
Mandeville, Ambrose, 177
Mandeville, John, 165, 171, 172, 177, 179, 180–183, 185–187
Mandeville, Mary, 182, 186
Manor Mill, 63
Markievicz, Countess, 215
Marshalstown, 84, 100, 104, 192
Mary, A Fiction, 38
Mason, Mrs, (see *Margaret Moore, Countess of Mount Cashell*)
Massey Dawson, James Hewitt, 87, 88
Massey, John, 100, 102, 108
McCarthy, Rev Dr James, Bishop of Cloyne, 167
McCarthy, Rev Dr, 174
McDonald, Alexander, 209
McNeill, General Eoin, 215
Meares, George, 46
Milton, John, 65
Mitchelstown Board of Guardians, 106, 108, 165, 184, 206
Mitchelstown Castle, 2, 30, 42, 90, 99,108, 112, 124, 133, 152, 159, 160, 167, 179, 196, 211, 216, 218, 233–237, 239–244, 249
  Building of, 72–79
  Destruction of, 220–228
Mitchelstown Caves, 78
Mitchelstown Cooperative Agricultural Society Ltd, 216, 244
Mitchelstown Independent Light Dragoons, 19
Mitchelstown library, 9
'Mitchelstown Massacre',172–179
Mitchelstown poor relief committee 103, 107
Mitchelstown Volunteers, 219, 220
Mitchelstown workhouse, 109, 124, 144
Mitchelstown, King Square, 8, 22, 23, 25, 42, 121, 127, 176, 191, 208, 209, 211, 221, 239, 251
Montgomery, Arthur, 89
Montgomery, George, 203, 204
Moore, Rev Canon Courtenay, 195, 208
Moore, Col. Maurice, 210
Moore, General Sir John, 52
Moore, Margaret, Countess of Mount Cashell, 29, 32, 33, 37, 46–51, 250
Moore, Stephen, 2nd Earl of Mount Cashell, 46–49, 58
Moorhead, Dr, 181, 182
Moreland, John, 116
Morris, Albert, 27
Morrison Fr, 177
Morrison, John, 8
Morrison, Lady Caroline, 61

Index

Morrison, Sir Richard, 8
Morrissey Thomas L., 241
Mortlakes, 241
Mount Cashell estate, 21, 38, 103, 105, 203, 249
Mount Cashell, Florence, Countess of, 191
Mount Cashell, Stephen, 2nd Earl of, 19
Mount Cashell, Stephen, 3rd Earl of, 93
Mount Melleray, Co. Waterford, 244
Mountain Lodge, 67
Mounteagle Lodge, 100, 249
Munster, Lord President of, 2
Murphy, 82
Murphy, Denis, 141
Murphy, Ellen, 108
Murphy, James, 146
Myers, Mary, 81

N
Nash, John, 68, 72
National League (see *Land League*), 163, 165, 168, 171, 173, 180–185, 188, 193
National Volunteers, 210
Needham, Miss, 227
Netterville, Lord, 43
Newcastle, Co. Longford, 230, 243–245, 248
Newcastle, Co. Tipperary, 4, 49, 197, 209
North Cork Militia, 39, 52–57
Nugent, Constable, 138
Nugent, Fr John, 65

O
Ó Dálaigh, Aonghus Mór, 3
O'Brien, Con, 217
O'Brien, Rev Dean Morgan, 107
O'Brien, Edward, 100
O'Brien, James, 26
O'Brien, W.E., 247
O'Brien, William, 143–145, 147, 166, 171, 172, 178–183, 185–188
O'Cahan, Margaret (Peggy), 5
O'Connell, Daniel, 76, 82,
O'Connell, Fr. Timothy, 157–160, 163
O'Connor, John, 166, 167
O'Connor, Thomas, 167
O'Doherty, Constable, 174, 175
Ogle, George, 34–36, 54, 67
Ogle, Mrs George, 54
O'Hea, P., 173
O'Keefe, 82
Oldcastletown, 2, 3
Oliver, Silver, 212
O'Loughlen, Patrick, 138
O'Mahony, Col. John, 165
O'Mahony, Rev Dean Denis, 155
O'Meara, E., 107
O'Neill, P.P., 160
O'Neill, Dr Eugene, 88, 89, 117
O'Neill, Dr John, 102, 104, 107, 108
O'Neill, James, 228
O'Regan, Rev Dean Patrick, 185, 195
O'Sullivan, Head Constable, 180
O'Sullivan, Maurice, 164, 171

P
Pain, George Richard, 72, 84
Pain, James 72, 84
Pakenham-Mahon, Olive, 214
Parnell, Anna, 160
Parnell, Charles Stewart, 141, 165, 186
Peel, Sir Robert, 59
Pellew, George, 169, 170
Pius VII, Pope, 48
Plowden, Francis, 53

Plunkett, Sir Horace, 190, 206, 218
Ponsonby family, 86
Poor law unions, 101
Power, John, 62, 63
Prescott, W.H., 96
Pritchard, Dr, 90
Property Defence Association, 169
Prussia, King of, 70
Puckler-Muskau, Herman Ludwig Heinrich, Furst Von, 70, 75

Q
Quayle, Rev Dr Francis, 5

R
Rambles in the South of Ireland, 76
Rents Commission, 184
Representative Church Body, 151
Rice, Rev Canon William, 193
Rice, Richard, 105
Richardson, Tom, 199
Ridley, Dr James, 181, 182, 186, 187
Riot Act, 158
Robertson, Hon. Mrs Nora, 75, 203–205, 233
Robinson, Peter, 83, 84
Robinson, Tom, 190, 200
Roche, Eamon, 244, 246
Roche, James, 2
Roche, Viscount, 2
Rockingham Estate, 5, 10, 57, 68, 197
Rockmills, 212
Roper, William, 71
Routh, Sir Randolph, 107
Ruane, R.J., 210
Russell, John, Lord, 106
Russia, Emperor of, 70
Ryan, John, 137, 138

S
Sadleir, John, 114–117
Santry, Lord, 43
Scott, Sir Walter, 75
Scully, Vincent, 114, 115
Seagrave, Capt., 176, 177, 180
Shanbally Castle, Co. Tipperary, 24, 203
Shannon, Earl of, 26 24, 27, 86
Shaughnessy, Shawn, 147
Shaw, Charlotte, 204, 205
Shaw, George Bernard, 204, 205, 211
Shelley, Mary, 38, 49
Shelley, Percy Bysshe, 38, 49, 50
Sherlock, Jonathan Wigmore, 111, 112
Shinnick, John, 187
Slieve Grot, 3
Smith, Rev Charles 21
Smith, Sydney, 195
Smith, Wyndham, 118
Somerville, Edith, 222, 224
St Fanahan's Catholic chapel, 23, 84
St George's Church, 22, 84, 250
Stafford-King-Harman, Edward, 214
Stafford-King-Harman, Sir Cecil, 240, 248
Standish O'Grady, Lt-Col., 88, 163, 167–169
Statistical Survey, 65, 66
Steele, General Thomas, 159
Stokes, Capt., 172
Stories of Old Daniel, 50
Sugán, Earl of, (Earl of Straw), 21, 51, 201

T
Talbot Crosbie, Col., 210
Tandy, Napper, 45
Tenison, Florence Francis, 248

Index

The Freeman's Journal, 139, 143, 166, 175
The Irishman, 141
The Parliamentary Gazeteer of Ireland, 102
The Sensitive Plant, 50
The Standard, 138
The Times, 111, 204
Thornhill, Major James Badham, 16–19
Thornhill, Mrs, 17
Tickell, Mr, 11
Tighe, George William, 49
Tighe, Laurette, 49
Tighe, Nerina, 49
Tipperary Freeholders, 19
Tomes, Rev Benjamin, 221
Tone, Wolfe, 45
Tour of Ireland, 13
Townsend, Rev Horatio, 25, 64–66
Townsend, Richard, 27
Tuchet James, Earl of Castlehaven, 4
Tullamore Prison, 180, 181

U
United Ireland League (see *National League*), 193
United Irishmen, 45, 51–55

V
Victor Emanuel I, 48

W
Walker, Joseph, 136
Walsingham, Sir Henry, 2
Waterford, Bishop of, 7
Webb, John, 24
Webber Adelaide, 210
Webber Arthur D.M., 215, 220, 223, 226, 231, 234–237, 241, 242, 245
Webber, Capt. Arthur, 242
Webber, Charles Tankerville, 93, 151
Webber, Edith Kingston, 209, 220, 221, 222, 227, 229, 242
Webber, Rev Thomas Charles, 151
Webber, William 'Willie' Downes, 77, 118, 151–163, 168–171, 184, 189–209, 213, 215–217, 220, 229–233, 238, 247
Wellesley, Marquess, 82
White Knight, John Oge, 1
White Knight, Maurice Oge, 3
White Knights Castle, 20
White Knights Tower, 72
White Knights, 1, 59, 74, 201
Whiteboys, 81, 82
William III, 6
William IV, 70
Wilmot, Katherine, 47, 48
Windsor Castle, 56, 72
Wollstonecraft, Mary, 28–38, 46, 49, 50, 61
Woodward, Rev Richard, 82
Wurttemberg, Duchess of, 70
Wyatt, 72

Y
Youghal, 3, 73
Young, Arthur, 13–18, 27, 33
Young, Henry L., 157

OTHER TITLES FROM THIS PRESS

Bowen's Court
Elizabeth Bowen

Now back in print, this is the history of an Anglo-Irish family that arrived in north Cork as settlers in 1649. It is a classic history of the rise and fall of an Anglo-Irish family by one of this century's most highly regarded novelists and short-story writers. Throughout the book, Elizabeth's attachment to Bowen's Court, to tradition and to correct social behaviour are constant themes.

'encompasses the history of Ireland told dispassionately' – Magill

1 898256 44 6 PB £8.99   1998

The Pleasing Hours
The Grand Tour of James Caulfeild, First Earl of Charlemont (1728-1799)
Cynthia O'Connor

The 1st Earl of Charlemont is best remembered today for having built the architectural masterpiece, the Casino at Marino, and Charlemont House, both in Dublin. He embarked on a Grand Tour from 1746 to 1754. In 1749 he sailed to Constantinople, Egypt, Asia Minor, the Greek islands and Greece. This voyage is historic in the annals of archaeology as he discovered the site of the lost city of Halicarnassus, the friezes from the Mausoleum of Bodrum and the description fizzles with excitement. He was founder of the Royal Irish Academy and became its first president in 1785.

'comprehensive, detailed and lucid ... a treasure'
– The Examiner

1 898256 66 7 HB £20.00   1999